LOOKING FOR DEI

DAVID A. WILLSON

F
c

T
o

Y

SEEKER
PRESS

Library of Congress Control Number: 2018902445

Edited by Susanne Lakin
Map by Jackson Cunningham
Cover art by Diana Buidoso

For more information visit: www.davidawillson.com

Thank you to my wife, Suzanne, for always thinking this book would be great, and for losing so many days to the effort.

Thanks to my early reviewers, who invested so much time into correcting my foibles.

And thank you to God, wherever you are, for making billions of beautiful stories, each filled with their own magic.

For Laura,
who always manages to shine through the pain.

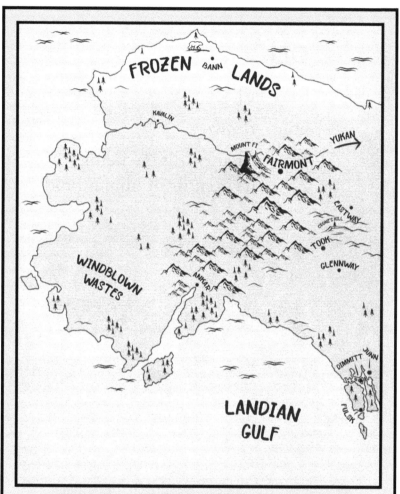

THE GREAT LAND

DEI

[day-ee]

noun, *Breshi.*

1. a deity – divine being
2. the creator of humankind

CATACLYSMOS

And the phyili was put asunder; separated, but not destroyed. Each defied the other, bringing conflict, pain, and death to many. In the end, only one remained.

Cataclysmos 18:10

PROLOGUE

Southside Orphanage
Fairmont – Capital of the Great Land
652PB (Post-Breshi)

The toddler blew at the dandelion bloom until its seeds broke free and floated away on a breeze that gusted past the man watching her from the bushes. His breath hitched as his burdens were lifted and briefly forgotten.

It had taken ten years to locate her. A life of study, prayer, and service to Dei in a monastery had not prepared him for so many years on the run, hiding under false names while he searched for the one he feared he might never find. His grizzled, greying goatee and unkempt hair might have labeled him a beggar or a desperate criminal, but the hope in his eyes told a different story.

Oblivious to the nearby threat, the girl dropped the crumpled dandelion stem and stumbled clumsily near a pile of stones. No more than two years old, she waddled across the overgrown orphanage courtyard, her cloth diaper askew. She plucked more flowers, her red hair dancing as she hopped after the seeds. She seemed to favor the world as her playmate, ignoring the twenty other children in the courtyard. She bumped into a small boy, fell down, and hopped back up with a baby-tooth grin before trotting off.

When she fell, a glimpse of her back jolted the man to his task. It was the blemish that beckoned him here—an ugly red scar stretching from upper back to waist, announcing her identity as the prophetic treasure he had sought for so long. The weight of the manuscript in his backpack grounded his thoughts, and he glanced around the area. There were no fences, plenty of bushes for cover, and a single matron leisurely surveying the yard. The woman sat on the aging building's back steps, watching the little ones as they ran about. She wore a dress and would be unable to chase him. How long would it take for her to alert the authorities?

As he surveyed the grounds to plan his escape, the girl waggled her hand at a passing butterfly and giggled as it flew away. Fortune favored his plans when she ran to a group of dandelions just a few feet from his hiding place. Squatting, she grabbed several stems, preparing to blow and release the seeds.

The man looked over to the matron, who had turned away to manage a quarrel between two other children. Knowing this might be his only chance, he burst forward and scooped the babe up in one arm, then raced back through the bushes behind the orphanage. He ran as fast as he could, unable to avoid jostling the child in his arms. She began to cry at the shock of her abduction, still gripping the dandelion stems in one tiny fist.

Back at the orphanage, the matron in the dress looked toward the back of the yard. The only evidence of a disturbance was a cloud of dandelion seeds that drifted upon the air, scattering in the light breeze. She turned to the many children she cared for, oblivious to the crime that had just been perpetrated under her watch.

PART ONE

The announcement ceremony is the catalyst that discovers the gifted and sets our armies apart; a fundamental difference between victory and defeat. Without it or the powers it unveils, the Great Land would not be great at all.

Governor Maximus Arametto, Junn, 551 PB

1

FRIENDS

Village of Dimmitt
Southeastern Corner of the Great Land
665PB

"Slow down," Mykel said, clearly winded. "I can barely keep up!"

Mykel's plea made Nara realize how fast she had been running, but she didn't want to stop. Perhaps she was propelled by the anticipation of tomorrow's ceremony, but although the climb often exhausted her, it was no challenge today. She wasn't even breathing hard.

Upon reaching the top, they turned to look down upon the village. They stood far above Dimmitt, past the altitude where trees gave way to bushes and grasses. It had been months since they last ascended the mountain, but they had never run so fast. The fervor of the exertion served as a welcome break from the preparations for tomorrow's big event.

Mykel came up beside her, out of breath, and together they looked out over their village. She dared a glance at him, not wanting him to know her thoughts. He was dark-skinned, and she was pale.

Tall and strong, his physique was muscular for a sixteen-year-old, and she imagined if someone saw them side-by-side, they would think them complete opposites. Next to him, she felt small, and weak. Even though she was barely a year younger, he seemed far older, almost like an adult.

A drizzle spread coolness across her warm skin, and an eagle passed slowly, sustained by rising air currents.

"It's beautiful from here," Mykel said, still catching his breath as he looked upon the coastline, the boats, and the busy dock below.

"Yes," Nara responded. "But so tiny." She turned to view the main coast of the Great Land to the north. It made this tiny island look even smaller and she wondered what big world lay beyond her modest village.

He turned to her. *You're beautiful,* his eyes seemed to say. She returned his admiring gaze and smiled briefly, then looked back to the village below.

Nara didn't fit in with the other girls, and she wondered what Mykel saw in her. She didn't look like the other girls either, with bright-red hair that others often commented on. Few in Dimmitt wore nice clothing, but Nara's was among the rattiest of those her age. It bothered her, but at least it covered the scar on her back. The scar she could never see.

She didn't fault her adoptive father for the lack of money; few in Dimmitt had any wealth. Bylo was old and his work as a laborer brought few coins although he did the best that he could.

But there were the headaches. If ever she felt set apart, broken, it was never more poignant than when she was in bed for hours, unable to move. She had always wondered why she had been afflicted with the pains. Why nobody else suffered them as she did. Was Dei really that angry with her?

But she felt no pain yet today, and that she could climb the mountain was a blessing. She sent a prayer of gratitude heavenward even if He didn't care to hear it.

At their first meeting, because she was so small, Mykel mistook her to be much younger than he, but they soon became great friends.

They shared so much in common: their love of the wild, of animals, and of the sea. Over the years, after completing their school, church, or family duties, they would race across the island—up the hills or the mountain, picking berries or fishing. Sometimes they would spy on other villagers or build a raft and paddle around a cove. They had become inseparable.

"What's the smile for?" Mykel asked.

"I've never seen the village so busy," she answered. "It seems so alive. Has it really been that long since the last ceremony?"

"Three years," he said.

The residents of Dimmitt appeared as tiny ants, and just as busy. They were setting up tables in the field outside the church and Nara worried that her absence might soon be noticed. She had been assigned cooking and cleaning duties today, but Mykel's challenge to race up the mountain just couldn't be passed up.

"Bitty, are you worried?" Mykel asked. "About the ceremony, I mean."

She smiled. It was an apt nickname; she was indeed small. He only used it in private, though, and never meant it to be an insult.

"Not really."

Every few years the announcement ceremony was supposed to bring great hope to the community—for magic and for wealth. Sadly, Dimmitt had not announced a gifted youth in many years. Yet, villagers held out hope that one would come soon. She had heard many folks speaking this way in recent weeks, about how it had been so long since a gifted had been announced that it must happen this time, right? Perhaps their optimism was a blessing, hardy hearts that dwelled on the positive despite all evidence to the contrary. Or perhaps their hope was a survival strategy produced by spirits that couldn't bear to consider another three years of hunger. Another three years of abandonment by their god.

Children who recently entered adolescence would submit to the ceremony, and if gifted children were identified, it could be transformative for the village. Not only would they earn money in royal service or private employment, but the magic was a gift from Dei. A divine blessing. A reminder that they were loved.

A child announced as a flamer could produce magical fire. A cutter could cleave flesh or even armor. A bear had magical strength. Announced as a knitter, a child would attend the Royal Academy of Medicine, where she would develop and refine her healing skills. A watcher might become a great hunter, with vision that would detect animals from far away and could help feed others in the village. If announced as a harvester, she would collect magic for others to use. That magic would come from living things such as plants or, sadly, from sacrificed animals. Each of these gifted youths would earn his or her fortune in the military or serving the crown, sending earnings home to battle the poverty that threatened to overwhelm them all.

Nara thought of the children of her village. It amazed her how resilient the little ones were, and she longed to bring good things to them. She had heard stories of the rich folks in big cities who ate every day and whose children always had shoes. If they could see the children in Dimmitt, if they could know how precious they were, they would help, wouldn't they? Maybe they just didn't know what it was like to be hungry and cold.

The thoughts fed a guilt within her that had been growing for years. Tomorrow's announcement might be very different for her. Although she had never endured an announcement ceremony, she had manifested gifts long ago, and not just one talent. She had several. Would the ceremony reveal her magic to all? Reveal that she had been hoarding it rather than using it to help feed her neighbors? Would they understand that it wasn't her fault, that she had been forced to keep it secret from them? Would they care? Would Mykel care? Would he judge her for her sins and abandon their friendship because of it?

She wondered how it would feel to have the sharp blade pierce her skin. "I've heard it doesn't hurt much," she lied, rubbing her right palm.

"I've heard that too."

A thin-bladed dagger called a ceppit was the instrument used by the priest to reveal a youth's magic potential. The priest would intone a prayer and use the ceppit to impale each child's palm. The ceppit acted as a catalyst to awaken dormant talent in the child.

With a non-gifted child there would be pain, no power would manifest, and they would be bandaged and forgotten. Poverty would pave their future as they assumed a mundane role among the villagers, a lifestyle of subsistence and struggle, as their parents had done.

Some children had a different destiny entirely. Eons had passed since the last cursed child was identified in Dimmitt, but several years ago one had been announced in the village of Fulsk. A prosperous town, Fulsk sat on an island to the south. Fillion was a tall, affable boy, so they said. Nara knew someone who used to go fishing with him. But Fillion was dead.

Nara hadn't been present, but she had heard about it from others. The ceremony started as they all did, with screaming, crying, and the blood of children dripping onto the stage. Then it was Fillion's turn.

As the story went, when the dagger pierced the boy's palm, everything changed. Fillion fell to his knees, his face went white, mouth open in horror, and a stifled squeal left his throat. Blood oozed from multiple fissures on his head, neck, and arms. By the time the priest pulled the dagger from his palm, it was over.

The boy's death reminded folks of the gamble all children took when they participated in the announcement ceremony. Not that they had a choice; participation was compulsory and must be completed between the ages of fifteen and eighteen. It was an act of service mandated by the crown, and according to the church, by Dei.

"If you are announced with a gift, what will you do?" Nara asked.

"I don't know, but I won't stay here."

"I would miss you."

"No you wouldn't, because you'd come with me!"

Nara smiled at him. "Of course I would." But she wasn't so sure. Bylo was here, the only family she had ever known. She would also miss the mountain and the lagoon, the dogs that played in the streets and the smell of fish on the docks. As poor and simple as it was, Dimmitt was her home.

"We should head back," Nara said. Dimmitt's priest would return late tonight, and little time remained to finish preparations before tomorrow's feast.

"I'll race you again!" challenged Mykel.

It took far less time to get to the bottom of the mountain than it had to climb up, but it was not without difficulty. Sweat dotted Nara's brow, and her hair became even messier than it had been atop the windy peak.

As they entered the periphery of the village, Mykel waved goodbye and headed home. Nara waved back, glancing over her shoulder to watch as her friend disappeared over a hill. She walked slowly, not because of her fatigue but rather to calm her anxious heart.

For tomorrow may reveal the secret she had been keeping for years.

2

MYKEL

As Mykel walked home, he thought about the girl who had captured his heart. Most of all, he pondered her smile. When Nara smiled, it would often be followed by a giggle, which would then erupt into a laugh. The world brightened, flowers bloomed, heaven opened wide, and Mykel's soul would dance.

Suspecting she saw him only as a friend, he had never summoned the courage to voice any other expectation. So valuable was their friendship that he didn't have the courage to test it. After all, he couldn't blame her for not being interested in him. He was ugly. Sure, he had a strong and lean body and stood taller than most of the other boys. And he excelled at the more physical endeavors, like working on fishing boats, cutting wood, and hunting. Mykel had a reputation for being one of the hardest-working youths in the village, albeit one of the more irreverent ones.

But his face.

The cleft palate from his birth had been repaired years ago by a knitter visiting the town, but the evidence of it remained. The knitter had worked for the church, correcting health problems in villages that were far from the wealth of the capital, Fairmont. If there was one thing Dimmitt had an abundance of, it was poor folk.

But the scar remained on Mykel's upper lip, and every time he gazed at himself in a clear pool of water, he was reminded that he was broken at birth. Twisted. Different. Nara saw it every day, the ever-present mark of Mykel's inferiority when compared to the others—the boys with normal faces.

Mykel once asked if the scar bothered her, and she had cocked her head, looking at him like he was just so crazy. "What are you talking about?" she said. "Mine is way bigger."

But that was just Nara being Nara, the nice girl. His scar was on his face, obvious for all to see, not hidden under clothes.

As he reached the cottage that he and his little brother called home, he saw Sammy beaming with pride and working at the outdoor cut table.

"Two today, Mykel!" Sammy grinned, brown eyes sparkling behind his long black bangs. "I'm almost done skinning them too!"

Sammy's new traps had apparently worked, ensnaring not one but two young coneys in their jaws, and the prizes now came apart under the boy's sharp blade. What a bounty! Thanks to Dei, they would be eating well tonight.

"Wow, Sammy. Great job."

Mykel came closer to inspect his brother's work, particularly the fat one Sammy was working on presently. Only ten years old, and he already brought home more food than Pop. "Did you use the round trigger I showed you?" Mykel asked.

"No, the notched. Couldn't get the round to work."

"You'll figure it out."

"Caught this one with a deadfall." Sammy held up the smallest rabbit with its legs achingly askew. Not many grown men in Dimmitt boasted such trapping skills, and even fewer boys did. Mykel looked at the tightly closed cottage door, and his enthusiasm faded.

"Pop home?"

Sammy nodded but said nothing.

Jimm Aragos had good days, and he had bad days. As a young man, their father had apparently been happy, strong, and full of life.

A member of the Shem tribe, he came from a moderately prosperous and proud people, masters of the southeast lands. Pop had taught Mykel to fish and hunt from an early age. But when Mykel's mom had died birthing Sammy, Pop's drinking turned him to anger— anger that sought an outlet.

Mykel carefully cracked the door and crept into the cabin, hoping Pop was still asleep. A loud, bitter cough alerted him to the contrary.

"Bring me anything to eat?" Pop asked.

"Um, Sammy trapped two coneys," Mykel said.

"Well, why are you standing there? Cook 'em, boy."

"Yes, sir."

Mykel started a fire in the small iron stove, then placed a wide-bottomed pot on top. Behind the thick cloud of smoke coming from his pipe, Pop sat in a chair in the corner. "Announcement tomorrow?" Pop asked.

"Yes."

"You gonna ditch? Cowards always ditch."

The insults were so common, they no longer stung.

Mykel shrugged. "I'm going. I have to. I'll be eighteen before the next one."

"No point to it," Pop said. "Dimmitt is cursed. No gifted here. That idiot priest is wasting his time and yours."

After pulling the last few potatoes from the root basket by the stove, Mykel quickly chopped them, then threw the pieces into the pot with a spoonful of lard. What he would have given for a bit of salt, but the few traveling merchants who passed through Dimmitt always wanted more coins than could be spared.

Sammy finally came in with the coneys, which were clean and ready for the stove. Mykel peeled the raw meat off the bones, cut it into small strips then tossed it in with the potatoes. Pop released another puff of his pipe, and Mykel tried not to choke on the smoke.

"Don't cry like a baby when they do it. Aragos men are tough. Hunters and builders, all of us."

Mykel was tired of the rant. "Built anything lately?"

Silent looks passed between Sammy and Mykel.

Pop gritted his teeth. "You got a smart mouth, you ungrateful rat," he growled, then took a deep puff and glared at Mykel.

He would never have tested Pop when younger, but the man wouldn't dare hit him now. It had been more than a year since they last tangled. When that battle ended, however, Pop was the one left bleeding.

"And what should I feel grateful for?"

"Grateful I didn't drown you at birth, you ugly wretch." Pop moved to the small table. "Your momma was a beauty. I do not understand how she spawned the likes of you."

Some folks told Mykel that before his momma died, Pop had been a gem of a man. Mykel wished he could remember, but that was more than a decade ago, and he recalled nothing. And nothing of his mother. Her absence produced an emptiness that could have been filled by the affection of a loving father, but there was no such person in sight.

Mykel served the coney and potatoes into a bowl for Pop, who always ate first. If there was anything left, the boys would share it.

Pop's pipe filled the small cabin as he ate, and the brothers moved outside to sit on the porch, hoping to satisfy their hunger soon.

"Beautiful coneys, Sammy. Thank you."

Sammy smiled.

"Going tomorrow?" Mykel asked.

"To the ceremony? Sure."

"Will be good to have you there."

"Is Pop going?" Sammy asked.

"Dunno."

"I think you're gonna be a bear," Sammy growled and made clawing motions with his hands. "Uproot a tree with a single pull."

"I hope so."

"Nara scared? Girls always scared."

"Yeah."

"I like her, Mykel."

"Me too." Mykel smiled at his little brother, and something caught his eye. He reached up to brush back Sammy's hair, but the boy pulled back, his smile vanishing.

"Sammy, let me see."

Mykel reached again, and Sammy did not pull back this time. Pushing the hair aside, Mykel spied a new bruise, fresh and purple on the side of his head near the temple.

"He shouldn't hit you there. Could knock you out."

"He did," Sammy said, his voice pained.

Fury swelled inside Mykel, but he said nothing. He had become accustomed to being Pop's target, but the angry man had clearly moved on to easier prey. They sat a few moments more, without words. What would happen to Sammy if Mykel was announced with a gift? Could he take Sammy away from this horrible home? A long shot, yet a gift would allow escape from this dismal place and this dismal man. He thought of what was more likely to happen. No gift would come, and they would be stuck here. How much longer could Mykel share a house with Pop? Families were expected to stay together in Dimmitt. Take care of each other. But Pop seldom worked, and without their own efforts, they would starve. It would not be a promising life for either of them, and the thought of it brought nothing but despair. Mykel moved to dispel the cloud that hung over the moment.

"I saw Lina Tibbins yesterday. She asked about you," Mykel said. "I think she has a crush."

"Naw, she don't." Sammy scratched his chin in a gesture of sudden discomfort. He often did that when he became nervous.

"I think she does. You sweet on her too, right?"

Sammy smiled but wouldn't look his brother in the eye.

"Thought so."

"I'm out," Sammy said, getting up and walking toward the cleaning table. By this time tomorrow, he'd likely have taken the coney hides to the tanner for a few iron pennies. Most of it would go to Pop, but he might keep some for himself.

"Don't miss tomorrow." Mykel's voice rose. "Lots of food there . . . and Lina!"

Sammy turned to flash a smile back at his brother and picked up his pace. After a moment, Mykel worked up the courage to go back inside. An inspection of the cooking pot revealed that nothing remained of the coney meat, but there were a few pieces of potato he would share with Sammy. He avoided any further conversation with Pop, who rested on his bed. Without a gift, Mykel wondered how he might find a way to support Nara and Sammy, far from here.

Then he daydreamed of magic and love and an escape from Dimmitt.

3

DISCOVERY

B ylo sat at his workbench in the cottage, armed with ink and
stylus. The runes were baffling him again. No matter how
many times he tried the water rune, he failed to get it just right.
What would happen when he mastered it?

It had now been more than thirteen years since he found Nara
and carried her to Dimmitt, a town with no gifted and no wealth—a
perfect place to hide her.

These years had been full of hard work, but also fervent study,
searching for the power in the runes of scripture. The designs had
power, and Nara was part of all that, but he didn't know exactly
how. He was determined to find out, but there was nobody he could
ask, and his only guide was an old book. A book about magic. A
book he kept very close.

He reminisced about the night he had first experimented with the
magic runes—long after leaving the monastery but before finding
Nara and coming to Dimmitt. While posing as a scribe in the
Ministry of War in Fairmont, the capital of the Great Land, he had
occasion to sup with a harvester. Harvesters took the life force from
living things and transferred it into receptacles, often called cepps,
for storage. That magic could then be used by gifted folks to power

their talents. This harvester casually mentioned imbuing a very odd cepp recently, one fashioned of bone with a liquid inside that was made from berries. Bylo recalled the inks he used in his illustration work at the monastery. Inks made of berries.

He had wondered if ink could be imbued apart from a cepp. If so, would imbued ink used to scribe a rune then impart power to the object so marked? The prophetic power of the runes was significant, and Bylo had spent much of his adult life copying the runes and illustrations in the margins of holy manuscripts. His passion for the runes had powered a curiosity in his mind about what might happen if he inscribed one with imbued ink. The notion had grown, tickling him, pestering him. There in Fairmont, frustrated with his failures to find Nara, he had chosen to conduct an experiment. He walked to a harvester's shop in Scrap Hollow, one of the less reputable areas of Fairmont, carrying with him a small pot of ink made from boiled shee-berries. If something could be gained from imbuing ink, he didn't want to attract attention from more influential harvesters.

The man had given little protest when Bylo made the strange request. Either he didn't think it would work, or didn't care, and simply retrieved a dove from a cage behind the counter. After breaking its neck, he held the dying bird in his hand, transferring the energy into Bylo's ink simply by putting a finger in the well. Bylo recalled how the bird had shriveled as it was harvested, shrinking, its eyes draining and turning black. A macabre process, yet the man performed it very quickly as if he had practiced it a thousand times.

Bylo had taken the ink in a stoppered vial back to the inn where he slept. Late that night, he left and walked to a nearby alleyway. Some lamplight from the porch of a nearby inn provided enough illumination for his efforts, and he pulled the ink, a small inscriber, and a flat stone from his pocket.

On the stone in the dim lamplight, he had painstakingly etched a perfect earth rune. Upon completion, he blew the stone dust away and dabbed ink into the design, careful not to let the ink run. His anticipation grew as he gently blew it dry.

The stone sat there on the dirt alleyway, motionless. Very carefully, he picked up the stone. Or that's what he tried to do, but when he clasped his fingers around it, it fell immediately to the ground. So heavy! Bylo had frozen with fear, but after several heartbeats reached again for the rock. Gingerly, he used two hands to lift it, his mind reeling at the implications. The rock's weight had been magnified ten times.

"Crazy fool. What have I done?" he said in fearful self-deprecation. He imagined the consequences of someone stumbling upon such a stone, enchanted as it was. Using another, much larger rock, he hammered upon his new creation, shattering it and dispelling the rune's magic.

That discovery, almost twenty years ago now, had sent Bylo to a renewed study of the one ancient manuscript he possessed. Research had revealed the meanings of some runes, but his training in illustration had taught him how to beautify a manuscript, not perfectly replicate it. Because of this, his peers had associated runes with decoration, not with meaning. The artistic license employed by him and his fellow illustrators had stripped these designs of their power.

He had since learned that when a rune was painted on the top of the skin, it imparted a marginal effect but dissipated in minutes. Perhaps living beings rejected the magic quickly, or the ink found no purchase on the top of skin and simply evaporated away. Helpful in healing, a rune of health would quickly stop bleeding and repair small wounds when placed near the injury but did little more than that.

Tattoos were his latest experiment. He had recently tattooed himself with a rune of strength on his thigh using an ink made of powdered bone, bean oil, and violet petals. At first, he suspected the magic might disfigure him, breaking bone or tearing flesh, but nothing happened, the skin bleeding from the needle as with any tattoo. Moments later, however, he felt a vigor in his body he hadn't felt since his youth and he cut a wagonload of wood with his axe in only an hour. This was several times the strength and endurance he would normally possess doing such a task, and the results had pleased him. Its power faded in less than a day, however, leaving nothing but an inert pattern.

Knowing there to be ancient manuscripts that preserved the designs in their original forms, Bylo wondered who else might have discovered the effects of these runes. How many such manuscripts still existed? His own book contained the scriptures of Cataclysmos, and from it he had found less than twenty runes, of which he divined the meaning of only a few: strength, health, god, human, air, and earth. Still others he had guessed at: speed, silence, fire, and water. But Bylo suspected there were other ancient manuscripts, perhaps dozens, held by the church around the realm. Still more must reside in the libraries of wealthy nobles. Secrets undiscovered? The magic of the gifted was known, but why not this? Had the secrets been learned long ago, only to disappear into the histories? Could this magic be used to feed and clothe the poor? To bring healing to those who suffered?

As he practiced his designs in the cabin on the outskirts of Dimmitt, dwelling on the potential in powerful secrets, a more practical concern interrupted his musings. His inkwell had gone dry.

"Nara!" he called.

Silence. Where had she gone? Then he remembered she was with Mykel today. Again. One rarely found them apart for long. She had told Bylo at breakfast that she was leaving for the day and gave some instructions about dinner or laundry or something he had since forgotten about.

The early manifestation of Nara's gift had been a boon for Bylo's work. Whenever he needed imbued ink, he had no need of a harvester because Nara took care of him.

Her gifts first appeared when she was only six years old, long before any announcement would occur. Bylo would see her flare anger or get excited about something, and her eyes would flash a glow, barely perceptible unless he was close. The flash would be orange or red, deep within her pupil and just for an instant. The first time he saw it he was petrified, but then dismissed it as a fearful imagining. When he saw it a second time, he had a long talk with her about how to keep her temper in check. He admonished her to quell any passionate emotions, concerned that they would ignite whatever power she held within.

One day, when Nara was eight or nine years old, Bylo had saved a few coins from selling wood and fish. He prepared to travel, hire a harvester, and imbue some ink for his research. He planned on leaving Nara with old Miss Nettle, the spinster who lived a short walk away, but the girl would have none of it. She insisted on going with him. During a heated discussion, she insisted on remaining by his side and offered to imbue the ink for him. Bylo laughed, but she was nonplussed by his ridicule as if it would be no effort at all. When challenged on the matter, she imbued a deep-yellow ink he had fashioned from sulphur and dried pig tendon.

The subsequent fatigue she experienced stood out in his memory. She had spent several hours in bed, so exhausted that Bylo had worried about her, but the ink worked better than any Bylo had ever paid for. Far better. Was she a harvester, then, his little Nara? And with power that manifested without an announcement ceremony?

She seemed to understand much for a little girl, even the nature of his runes. Oh, she never studied them, nor did she practice calligraphy or anything like that. He wouldn't even let her read the manuscript. But she would watch his work and guide him when he formed a rune incorrectly. She possessed an intuition about them, and while she didn't know what they did or what they meant, she could see when they weren't quite right.

Ever perceptive in other areas as well, she would give Bylo what he needed: hot tea, a blanket, or a late dinner, before he realized he needed it. This applied to other folks as well; she always knew which girl was sweet on whom and who would be with child. She knew who might be having a bad day and in need of a visit, a comforting word, and perhaps some salmon pie.

Nara's knowledge of plants and animals amazed Bylo as much as her intuition regarding people. She knew where the best berries grew, which farmer's potatoes would be the biggest when harvest came and under which log the coneys kept their babies in the springtime. And all with such a tender heart, unless she felt pain. Then things changed. Once, a boy threw a rock at her, hitting her in the nose. She completely lost her temper, jumping on the miscreant, fists a-swinging. When it was all over, his nose bled worse than hers.

But oh, did Bylo love that passionate little girl. He had never planned on being a parent, and even now didn't truly consider himself one. It was why he never let her call him Papa. But serving as her caregiver was rewarding work, even when she was paralyzed with pain from the headaches. No source could be found for the ailment despite inquiries of traveling physicians, and Bylo's own efforts to treat the pain always failed. He hoped she didn't suffer the pains today.

He stepped out the door of their humble cottage to sit on the porch. Watching the sun dip low on the horizon, he wondered when his treasure would return home.

4

CONFESSION

Nara ambled up the hill, one of the village dogs trotting alongside her with a stick in his mouth. She stopped to wrestle the stick away from the pup, then tossed it back down the path, happily waiting for her little friend to retrieve the toy and catch back up to her. As she approached the cottage, she saw Bylo standing on the porch.

"Bylo!" she yelled, then dismissed the pup and picked up her pace. "I'm so sorry, I've been gone all day."

"It's okay, little one. I figured you'd be out making a raft or climbing trees with Mykel."

"Actually, we raced up the mountain. Took all morning!"

The look on Bylo's face made it clear that her disheveled hair and dirt-covered legs were bearing witness to her claim.

"Weren't you supposed to help out at the church kitchen for tomorrow?"

"I did," she said.

"The ladies let you cook in that pristine little kitchen, looking like that?"

"Actually, they had me emptying trash, doing dishes, and setting up chairs for the reception afterward. Heidi Trinck and Fannie Taylor helped in the kitchen."

Whether community settings or school-related functions, Nara often got stuck with the grunt work, but she didn't care for the company of the other girls, anyway. Something about their prim and prissy ways didn't feel honest, as they gossiped about boys or other girls, never saying what they were really thinking. As much as she tried, she couldn't fit in. A certain kind of discretion was required to blend with the other kids, a skill in subtlety that Nara couldn't get quite right. Saying the wrong thing, or saying too much, she would often embarrass herself. A desire to share her own heart or to connect intimately with someone often had the opposite effect, pushing them away. Was there something wrong with her, at some basic level? Even Mykel knew when to stop talking and when to give people their privacy. And he knew when not to trust people—a skill Nara had never mastered.

"A shame," said Bylo. "You're the best young cook in the whole village. Your mashed potatoes are divine!"

She entered the front room of the cottage. "Are you out of ink again?"

"How did you guess?"

The cottage was mostly dark, lit by a single lantern. Still, the inkwell on his little writing desk was obviously empty. She turned to him, raising her eyebrows in disbelief, then reached for a new well from the cupboard. Bylo was a simpleton sometimes. Amazing that a wise man, so educated and traveled, could be such a silly goose when it came to obvious things. She looked about, seeing an empty sink and no dishes on the counter.

"Did you eat?"

"Um, I think so," he said.

"Been working all day again, I see."

The papers on his desk were stacked high, multiple iterations of carefully inked runes on pages, evidence that he had been practicing for hours.

"Did you get any new ones to work?" she asked.

Bylo merely grunted, betraying a lack of success in his efforts as he busied himself with preparing dinner. Nara grabbed the ink in her left hand, then dipped her right index finger into the well. Closing her eyes, she reached inward with her awareness, tapping the presence that she had felt for so long, that glowing energy inside her. She poured some into the liquid as if exhaling a long, slow breath.

It amazed her to think that nobody else felt their own energy like she did, tapping it to do wondrous things. The first few times she had imbued ink, she gave too much and exhausted herself. With practice, she learned that ink required very little energy to be useful for Bylo's work.

And such things he did with it! Rocks became heavy, and he could make paper fly around the room by itself, which fascinated her when she was younger as she chased it about. The fun always came with admonishments from Bylo to keep it secret. She never told.

In school, which was taught by Father Taylor at the church, she learned about the announcement ceremony they would be forced to participate in when they were older. How special children might be discovered in the ceremony and would do things or see things normal people could not. Such children would be heroes and bring great honor to their families, the village, the church, and to the Great Land. It sounded like such a good thing, and yet Bylo still wanted her to keep her talents hidden. He had never fully explained what he was afraid of.

More questions arose in her mind. Why did a gift manifest before her announcement ceremony? And why didn't her gift match the types Father Taylor mentioned? He spoke of some who could harvest power, filling cepps that other gifted folk would use. Some children displayed extreme strength or speed. Others could shoot fire out of their hands, but he made it clear only one gift was given to each. Two gifts were something only for legends. Yet Nara possessed even more.

She could imbue ink with energy, like a harvester, and had been doing this for several years to help with Bylo's work. But she didn't move energy from trees or plants into the ink; she just put her finger into it, so she wasn't a harvester, was she? Father Taylor never mentioned anything about ink.

When she was younger, she discovered animals could talk, and she learned to talk back to them. Oh, they didn't talk like people—not at all. It was more like they *felt* at you—all emotions, not really words. She knew when they were happy and when they were hurting, feeling the pain of their injuries as if it was her very own. Sometimes she could even feel the pain of people if they were close. And for as long as she could remember, she could see things, even when she closed her eyes—the energy people gave off, their spirit. Animals and plants glowed too, but not as much as people, and it bothered her that she was the only one who seemed to detect the auras.

The unanswered questions turned to concerns about what would happen at the announcement ceremony tomorrow. The village could finally learn how different she was, and if so, why wasn't Bylo concerned about her participation? He had always coached her to hide her talents from the villagers and she had complied, becoming quite adept at the secrecy. Even Mykel didn't know. But tomorrow the unveiling would occur, and Bylo had not mentioned it at all.

"Bylo?" she asked.

"Yes?" He was chopping carrots and potatoes for dinner.

"What will happen tomorrow at the announcement?"

Silence filled the room for several moments as she sat down at their only table and started to fidget with a wooden cup.

"I don't know," he finally said.

"Everyone will find out, won't they?"

"I don't think so."

"Why not?"

Another silence. This time he didn't fill it with a response.

"Bylo?"

"Yes, Nara?"

"How am I different?"

Another silence.

"Bylo!" she insisted. "Tell me!"

He sighed, put down the knife, washed his hands in a basin of water, and came to sit next to her at the table.

"I don't know, Nara."

Bylo knew everything. How did he not know this?

"What do you mean, you don't know?"

"I've never met anyone like you." He reached for her hand and held it gingerly in his. "In truth, I don't think anyone has."

Nara nodded slowly but pulled her hand away, looking into his old eyes and concentrating on his words. Important words.

"Some children, rarely, have two gifts," he continued.

"The blessed, yes. Father Taylor told us. Minister Vorick is blessed, right?"

"Yes, the minister is blessed. But, Nara, you aren't gifted. And you aren't blessed. I truly don't know what you are."

"Don't know what I am? I'm a person, Bylo!"

"Of course you are. But you are also something more."

Or something less, she thought. She remembered the stories in church about Kai's sinister servants.

"Am I a demon?"

"Certainly not!" He rose to his feet and headed back to the kitchen.

But she wasn't so sure. Perhaps she was indeed a demon.

"Bylo?"

Silence again.

"Bylo!" she shouted, standing suddenly and knocking over her chair.

Bylo turned. "I don't have anything to tell you, Nara. I don't know!"

She picked up her chair and settled back into her seat, shoulders drooping in disappointment and defeat. He didn't know.

"Why would I not be announced tomorrow? I will surely be, right?"

"Not necessarily," he said as he scooped the vegetables into two small bowls.

"Why not?"

Bylo seemed to ponder his answer a moment. "No gifts will be found."

"Why not?"

"Gifts are rare, Nara."

An insufficient answer and he was clearly avoiding the truth. And her gaze.

"Bylo!"

He turned to face her. "Okay, okay. Taylor will announce no gifts because he can't."

She screwed her face up at him, perplexed. "What does that mean?"

He brought both bowls to the table and offered Nara a spoon. As usual, she was hungry and ate quickly to quell the pangs. He took a seat next to her.

"Nara, no gifted have been announced in Dimmitt for many years. Don't you find that odd?"

She did find that odd. One of the nearby villages announced a child five years ago, and another had announced one a few years before that. Dimmitt was suffering a long, dry spell as far as gifts were concerned.

"Why haven't we?"

"Nara, someone has to imbue the ceppit, and we have no harvester here. Nor do we have the money to fill it—it costs much more than it does to imbue ink."

It took a moment for her to absorb his words. Of course, the ceppit! The dagger used to pierce the hand of each child during the ceremony was a receptacle of power. The power stored therein was a catalyst that awakened the latent magic of the child. If it was empty, there would be no announcement.

"Wow, how long have you known the ceppit was empty?"

"I've always known."

A long pause ensued as she contemplated what this meant.

"Nara, I was in Fairmont, long ago, before I found you. Once I located you, I needed to keep you safe. There are records in the grand archive of the Ministry of War and Justice, records of announcements from throughout the Great Land. Records that might provide clues on where I could hide you."

Nara hadn't ever heard that Bylo visited Fairmont, and it was odd how he mentioned the Ministry of War. The words ministry and war seemed ill-suited partners. War was anything but a ministry. Despite the questions that tried to work their way out of her mouth, she let him continue.

"Having learned through my research how expensive it was to hire a harvester, I concluded that in the poorer parts of the Great Land there would be villages that couldn't afford to hire one."

"But they still hold announcement ceremonies," she said.

"Exactly. It's a legal decree."

"And why is that?"

"The queen needs gifted for her armies, Nara. There are many gifts, and almost all have some value in war."

Goosebumps rose on her forearms, and she grabbed a blanket off her cot, then wrapped it around herself as Bylo continued.

"I figured any village so poor that it could not afford to imbue the ceppit would bear a significant record of empty ceremonies."

"You chose Dimmitt to hide me?"

He nodded.

"We can fix it," she said after a moment.

"Fix what, my dear?"

She looked up at him.

"The village. Dimmitt can't have a proper announcement. There could be gifts all over the village, and those gifts are Dei's blessing. Our town has been robbed, but we can fix it."

"No! Absolutely not!"

He let go of her and stood to his feet suddenly, his face growing red. "I forbid it."

His reckless movement caused a cup of water to fall over and drench the table, then drip onto the floor. His eyes widened, and she couldn't tell if it was from rage or from the shock of his own anger taking control of him. The gentle monk forbade nothing, and he had never shown such anger, causing her to tremble partly in surprise and partly in fear. He gritted his teeth, clenched his fists, then walked over to take a seat at his desk.

"I should never have told you," he said, leaning his elbow on the desk for support and hanging his head. "I'm a fool."

Now she knew why he never explained—his reluctance was clear. Oh, how he must have been proud to hide her here, and how he must now be angry with himself for leaking the secret that would unravel it all. She might cure Dimmitt's poverty by bringing overdue gifts to this little town, but she would do so at the risk of revealing her own talents. It would be worth it.

Despite Bylo's discomfort, she resolved that the needs of the village were of greater priority. "You've always told me to hide my talents. Nobody has trained me. I don't even know what I can do. Maybe I could have helped, these past years. Brought money to Dimmitt. Fed my friends. But you said to be quiet, so I was. I won't be quiet anymore, Bylo. I won't."

He didn't say a word.

"We may not be able to help everyone tomorrow," she said. "But if we break the news to the village, we can announce everyone for the last decade or more. Think of it!"

Nara's heart warmed at the thought of bringing relief to her impoverished friends and neighbors.

Bylo turned to her with a pained expression, anguish clearly building as he considered the consequences of her stated intentions. "If they announce you with an imbued ceppit, Nara, who knows what will happen? I've never heard of anyone like you, not even in stories. You could die, or they might find out you're not like anyone else. You're not just a gifted. Who knows what people would..." he said, his voice cracking. "And I might..." he choked on the words, "... might lose you."

From across the room, she saw the agony on his face, his usually bright eyes now tired, melting her heart. She wanted to go to him, but her mind raced as she weighed her love for this man against the welfare of hundreds. She came to her decision quickly.

Bylo put his head on the desk, knocking over a small tray holding quills and a stylus. He made no move to gather them and was motionless for a time.

"I love you too, Bylo," she said, knowing his turmoil. "And I won't do it."

He lifted his head, apparent relief chasing the anxiety away from his aging face. "Really?"

"I swear it," she said, but had no such intention. She didn't lie often, but this was different. People were suffering, and she had a way to help. She needed to help.

Nara got up, put the blanket back on her bed, and went over to Bylo, squeezing his shoulder and smiling. As she walked toward the kitchen, she thought she heard a sigh of relief. After tidying up the kitchen, she headed toward her cot. "I'm off to bed. Long day."

"Good night. And... thank you, dear. I'm sorry."

She spent a moment brushing her hair so she wouldn't wake with it in knots, then slipped under her blankets, turning away from him as she did so.

Bylo snuffed out the lantern and headed to bed himself. As he closed his eyes in the darkness, head on his pillow, an uncomfortable doubt crept into his thoughts. It couldn't be that easy. Nara had given up fast, and that wasn't like her.

For years, he had feared a knock at the door that would take her away to strangers who would use his child as a weapon. He thought of the stories of gifted in battle, how innocent women and children often fell under the destruction wrought by the magic. Nara would not be able to endure it, he was convinced of this; she would sooner take her own life than preside over such havoc.

He thought of the day he carried her away from the orphanage. If tomorrow didn't go well, would they be required to run again? With frustration, he prayed to the god who never answered.

Dei, if you allow evil here, I'll carry her away again. I swear it. As many times as it takes.

A flapping of wings called his attention to the tree outside his cracked window. A short time later, an owl hooted softly. Bylo glanced at the moon that seemed to fill the clear, dark sky. From time to time he turned, looking across the room to make sure Nara was still sleeping on her cot. Eventually, fatigue overcame his suspicions, and slumber captured him.

5

DEFIANCE

Nara lay on her cot pretending to sleep, her thoughts lingering on Bylo's secrecy. Anger welled up at what seemed like a betrayal—not just of her, but of the entire village. The ceppit needed power, and she would fill it tonight.

Bylo didn't fall asleep quickly, but once he had, she made her move. The rain pit-pattered on the roof, giving her ample noise cover to steal away. Her exit out the front door was soft but still disturbed a white owl in the nearby tree. Ruffling its feathers, the bird turned its head to face her disapprovingly.

Darkness reigned, and none of the village folk were out, but she moved with caution to avoid waking any dogs that might announce her skulking. The walk to the church took longer than it should have, or maybe it just seemed that way. What she intended could not be undone, and the risk weighed heavily upon her. This was a bold move and she knew it, but felt compelled to continue. It might be the first act of her life that would make a difference. A *real* difference. A way to help.

Was that the only reason, or was there more? Did she want to imbue the ceppit to help other people, or was this also a way to feel some power of her own? A way to defy her destiny as the girl who must remain quiet, who could not be noticed. The girl who kept secrets.

Being announced in front of the whole village would end those secrets. Nara would be a gifted, and people would take notice of her. She would be seen as valuable. Important. Yes, she wanted that, too.

Upon arrival at the church, she found a window near the back door. She slid it open, pulled herself up over the sill, and landed inside on her bum. Holding her breath, she listened and waited, hoping Father Taylor was slumbering in his room down the hallway.

After a few moments of silence, she rose to her feet, tiptoed to Taylor's study, and tested the door handle. Unlocked. After turning the knob, the door fell open a few inches, but the agonizing creak that came was enough to wake the dead. Fear of discovery paralyzed her, and she heard the priest grumble something in irritation from his room, bed squeaking as he shifted in his slumber. A moment later, the silence resumed. Proceeding into the room, she squeezed through the open doorway and moved quietly to the sacristy behind his desk. Just a fancy footlocker, the chest sat on the floor beneath Taylor's threadbare, stained ceremonial robes that hung on a wall peg above. It bore a padlock.

Curse it! What now?

Kneeling down, Nara inspected the lock in the near darkness, but her only allies were a few stray moonbeams sneaking in through his study window.

Old, rusty, and rarely used, the lock failed to disengage after a hearty tug. Then, as she did when imbuing ink, she closed her eyes and reached down into her energy, grabbing hold. Swirling patterns danced about her vision as she wrapped the power around herself and descended. The internal workings of the device became clear to her—the tumbler, the cylinder. All it would take was a little push. . . click!

Opened. With a thought!

Victory swelled inside her, and she wished to share it with someone—to tell Bylo or Mykel. As quickly as it came, the pride abandoned her. There was nobody she could tell.

Focusing again on her task, she removed the open lock and lifted the lid on the chest. Inside, she found two shiny goblets, several metal plates, and an engraved wooden box. Opening the box revealed a prize: the bladed bone-handled ceppit, unwitting focus of the evening's controversy. She moved her hand to reach out, then stopped, compelled to consider more deeply.

The potential implications of her actions tonight brought a concern. Burgling the church, breaking into the chest, grabbing a strange weapon so she could enchant it with magic that would reveal her talents to the village. Was she a criminal or just a fool?

Thoughts of warning came to mind. Might she hurt someone she knew? Sure, the discovery of a cursed was rare, but if things went wrong, could she justify her actions?

Ultimately, she decided that she had come this far and couldn't stop now. The problems of this poor town, this home that she loved, could be cured with a few good announcements. That the ceppit hadn't been imbued for so long was the true crime, one she could not allow to continue.

With new resolve, she grasped it by the handle, inspecting the blade in the faint moonlight. This was the closest she had been to the valuable relic that was sometimes seen in church ceremonies. It now seemed plainer than she remembered. A chunk of bone formed the grip, and metal wire had been pounded into grooves, forming a design that reminded her of Bylo's drawings and the patterns she sometimes saw in her mind when using her talents. The blade itself was only a couple of inches long, though the handle was twice that. An odd-looking thing, for sure, and clearly no use for hunting, cooking, or whittling. Crafted for one purpose only. Magic.

Although heavy, she sensed its emptiness. An odd feeling, reminiscent of holding an empty bowl or perhaps a cup before filling it with water. But not just empty. Hungry. New doubts crept into her as she held the implement that carried so much meaning. It did not seem like a talisman that brought reward, nor a mechanism for inviting joy or celebration. It was dark and deadly and might bring destruction. She should put it back in the box and run from this place as if her life depended on it.

"What am I doing?" she whispered, then thought of the village folks and bit her lip to stop any further protest.

She summoned courage, dismissing her fears. There was no choice. Squatting behind the desk, she gripped the knife with both hands. Closing her eyes and reaching deep within, she drew upon that reserve of something inside—of energy, of spirit. She poured it into the blade.

At first, it seemed like exhaling, but at the end of her breath, she ran out of air. The ceppit did not care for her discomfort and kept pulling, with increasing insistence. Sucking harder, the relic leeched Nara's strength like a parasite. It had become a monster that had taken a bite of her, enjoyed the taste, and resolved to consume her entirely. Weakness spread through her legs and they failed, dropping her to the floor. She tumbled onto one side, still gripping the knife firmly with both hands in panic and confusion. She willed her fingers to release the handle of the blade, but they disobeyed.

As she despaired at her foolishness, she bit down on her tongue. The physical pain, surprise, and taste of blood directed her attention from the dagger. The shock of it loosened her grip, and she dropped the knife to the floor, where it stuck in the wood, blade first, with an audible thud.

Horrifying! Is that what harvesters experienced when they imbued something? Her essence was being robbed. Her soul. No amount of money would be worth that job.

Footsteps shuffled down the short hallway outside the office. Father Taylor! When she fell over and dropped the knife, she must have made an awful racket.

With no time to spare, she managed to quickly and quietly place the blade inside the chest and close the lid. She noticed that it was lighter now that it was imbued, an odd side effect she had not expected. She replaced the padlock and retreated from the sacristy.

The priest opened the door while she sat under the desk and brought her legs to her chest as tightly as they would go.

Don't breathe.

The light from his candle danced around the room, blinking in and out, reflecting off the padlock she had forgotten to latch.

Don't see it. Please don't see it.

She heard the priest take a step inside, but then he paused. Nara hoped he was convincing himself that he had imagined things. When he closed the door and shuffled back to his room, she sighed in relief.

After a long wait, it seemed safe to move again. She snapped the rusty padlock shut, then closed the study door and snuck back down the hallway. At the back of the church, she lifted the window, slipped over the sill, dropped to the grass below, then ran home for all she was worth.

On her way back to the cottage, she wondered about the ceppit. What a horrible thing it was! Yet, she had overcome it. As she approached her home, she thought upon the consequences of her actions tonight. Would tomorrow bring victory, or tragedy? She snuck into the cottage and set a damp head on her pillow. Only then did she realize her fatigue. Not just tired but exhausted as never before. She prayed before falling asleep.

Oh, Dei, if you're there, please help us in this. Please don't let it be a mistake.

6

MEMORIES

Bylo woke early, last night's conversation with Nara lingering in his thoughts. He glanced at her cot. She slept, but he was not fooled into thinking that her slumber was a precursor to inaction. The girl was clever but naive, although that was largely Bylo's fault. He had never told her the truth about who she really was and how much she mattered.

He thought back to the day it all had become clear to him, more than twenty years ago. He remembered the fear. And the soldiers. It was the last day he ever saw his friend.

Veniti Monastery
West of Fairmont
642 P.B.

Bylo had been sleeping in his cot when Phelan woke him with excited chattering.

"They have it wrong," Phelan said. "They misunderstand!" His unkempt white hair, deeply wrinkled skin, and body odor gave witness to both his age and recent lack of hygiene.

"I was trying to sleep," Bylo said as he struggled to rise. "What are you talking about?" he asked, eager for the reason he had been so rudely awakened.

"The runes have meaning, Bylo. Phyili. The twins." Phelan spoke quickly, his eyes sparkling with enthusiasm. "There is no longer any doubt."

Bylo scratched his own head, further mussing his tousled, greying hair. The sounds of boots in the hallway outside the room announced another patrol of soldiers. The queen's men had swarmed the monastery in recent days, with no explanation given by the abbot.

"Say something!" Phelan pleaded.

Bylo took a moment to focus on the frantic words, rubbing his eyes. "Hold on a minute," he said, climbing out of his cot. "The twins have power?"

"The twins aren't the twin peaks; they are actual human twins! Phyili is used in several places, and in the scriptures of First Light, it refers to the gods Dei and Kai as brothers."

Bylo nodded, following along.

"As you know, the runes in the margin modify the meaning of the nouns in the scripture text. In most of the scriptures, when we see the word phyili, we see the god rune in the margin, making it clear that the writer refers to the twin gods. But in Cataclysmos, where we read of the separation, we see another rune in the margin. It is not the god rune but instead the human one!"

"Phelan, the human rune in Cataclysmos is off. Higher in the margin. One would more likely associate it with a phrase above," Bylo said.

"That's what we always thought," Phelan said. "But if so, why no god rune near this passage, or even on this page, like all the others? If referring to a mountain, as many scholars guess, why no earth rune? Phyili is always accompanied by a god rune, but it is not here!"

"How do you account for it?"

"An error," said Phelan. "You should know. As a scribe, you've been trained to illustrate, like an artist. Embellishment, not replication."

"We couldn't anyway, Phelan. We aren't allowed access to the original manuscripts, so we couldn't be accurate if we wanted to."

"Exactly." A powerful pause built, and an impish grin crept across Phelan's face. "So, I stole one."

"You're crazy!" Bylo said. "From the abbot?" Concern for both his comrade's safety and sanity washed over him. "They'll whip you—if you're lucky!"

"Probably," Phelan said, but the grin remained on his face. "After the abbot left on his latest trip, I made an excuse to return a codex to his quarters. Brother Alen fell for the ruse and allowed me access.

"I searched the abbot's room. There, I found the oldest manuscript I have ever seen, tucked away in a sealed compartment under his bed. I had no key, so I used a log poker to force the compartment open."

Bylo was horrified. Lying to get into the abbot's room and then destroying his furniture? Not to mention the theft!

"I waited until after you fell asleep before I took my first glance." Phelan continued, leaning in and resting a hand on Bylo's shoulder in a gesture of affection. "If I couldn't confirm my suspicions, I wanted no witnesses to my crime. Not even you."

Bylo was having difficulty with the implications of his friend's offense. "Where is it now?"

The remnants of a prideful smile still on his face, Phelan reached behind to grab something that rested at the foot of the cot. A musty odor tickled Bylo's nose, and his heart skipped a beat at the sight of the treasure. Scratches in the leather and yellowed pages gave witness to both its authenticity and fragility.

Phelan spoke in a slow-moving, reverent tone. "This manuscript contains the book of Cataclysmos in the original Breshi script, but the second half of the book is translated to Landian. Every reference to phyili has the god rune in the margin, centered to the right."

"Except one?"

Their eyes locked for a moment, and Phelan turned to one of the final pages. "Yes, except one. The last one, right here, in chapter eighteen of the Landian section. The human rune rests in the margin, not the god rune. Perfectly centered. There can be no mistake."

The implications were earth-shattering.

"Our understanding of Cataclysmos is wrong," Phelan said. "Phyili doesn't mean the twin peaks—we should be looking for an actual human being!"

"A person will become two, Bylo. Somewhere, a woman will give birth to a special child. This child will somehow become separated, like Dei and Kai. Twins, perhaps."

"So how would a child be separated into two?" Bylo asked. "It would die. That doesn't make any sense."

"I don't understand it either, but if we don't find this person, or these twins, someone else will. No good will come from allowing them to fall into wicked hands. Remember the scripture. 'Conflict, pain, and death to many.' Bylo, this child may bring the end of all things. Or perhaps a new beginning."

"You are brilliant, my friend, but there are other scholars in this world. Perhaps employed by the queen and the archbishop. They may have come to the same conclusion. Maybe that is why the soldiers are here, seeking this manuscript and those like it."

"I know," Phelan said.

A hard knock on the closed door sent a shiver down Bylo's spine.

Phelan re-wrapped the text, setting it under the cot. Bylo reached the door, opening it to reveal a man standing outside. Captain insignias were visible on his epaulets as he imposed himself into the room.

"I'm here for Phelan."

A heartbeat later, Phelan stepped forward.

"Come with me," the soldier said, his fingers playing upon the pommel of his sword.

"I'll see you later," Phelan said, then turned to put a hand on Bylo's shoulder.

Barely a whisper in his ear, Bylo heard the last word Phelan would ever say to him.

"Run."

Then Phelan exited the room with the soldier.

Bylo stood still, contemplating the peril he now faced. His heart pounded against his rib cage, fear battling a rising sense of urgency. After a moment, the urgency won and he resolved to act. He snatched the book and dashed out of the room. If he could make it to the back of the building unseen, he might escape.

A well-timed scurry through several corridors brought him near the exit. As he walked down the final hallway, he heard the first of several bells ring from far within the structure, driving him to burst out of the monastery into the darkness beyond.

In the fields south of the building, he turned to deliver a final gaze at the place he had called home for nearly ten years. The place he thought he would always call home. An ache grew within his breast as he wondered what would become of his friend. Then he turned and ran. He had a special child to find but did not know where to look.

So much had happened in intervening years that the memories seemed like those of another man entirely. Bylo had decided to protect Nara before she was even born and until now had done a fine job. Things were changing, however, and today brought the opportunity for disaster. But the announcement ceremony wouldn't take place until evening, giving him an opportunity to make preparations of his own.

A breakfast of cold carrots started the morning, then he stepped out to the shed and gathered travel gear, a large backpack, several knapsacks, and salted preserves. With the door closed and a candle lit, he pulled out a quill, a needle, and a bottle of imbued ink. There was much to do, and little time.

7

OBSERVATIONS

The most popular drinking establishment in Dimmitt was the Draggin Tavern, and its barkeep was Amos Dak. Dak was a retired fisherman who spent his early days trying to make a living upon the waters of the Landian Gulf. By his own admission, he was a terrible captain, having smashed his boat many times upon rocks but somehow never sinking it, drowning a mate, or cracking his own skull.

While still a young man, Dak chose to avoid further calamity and sold his oft-broken vessel to chase a dream to sell beer. He was equally unskilled in business matters, however, and his brewing trade danced on the fringes of bankruptcy until fortune favored him by allowing a marriage to Gretchen Wipp. The town's oldest widow was the child of a man who built the Draggin fifty years ago. The old man had left it to Gretchen following an accident involving a bottle of whiskey and a broken handrail. Few had ever called Wipp a pretty woman, but she wielded a sharp wit, an even sharper tongue, and a mind for business. Long ago, she wooed Amos and his brewing skills into what some called a marriage and others properly recognized as a business partnership.

Last night's crowd had been rowdy, and more than the usual

portions of watery ale and fish stew had been served. Not only had the herring fishery closed, bringing captains and crews to the tavern, but the announcement ceremony scheduled for this evening would be the first in several years. Such events often became a rallying cry for outlying folk to storm the village with the meager coppers they had saved. More than a few would be eager to visit family and friends and spend their coins at the local businesses. Patrons had been in town for the better part of two days now, and no matter how poor they were, folks always managed to buy a good time.

With only a modest amount of grumbling and a fair amount of appreciation for his circumstances, Dak moved about the place, sweeping, mopping, wiping, washing, and organizing. So busy was he that for almost an hour he failed to notice the dark-haired stranger sitting in front of the hearth, warming herself by a fire that Amos had no part in starting.

He thought to approach her, but he had nothing to offer. The Draggin was not an inn, didn't serve breakfast, and what woman would want cod casserole or a shot of brandy this early in the morn? Dressed for traveling, she wore a thick, dark-green cloak. Medium-length, brown hair was tied back with a band and dropped into the hood of the cloak. As she warmed her feet and hands in front of the flames, Amos saw a wet pair of walking boots and a brown pack on the floor in front of the hearth.

He couldn't spy her face, but as he moved about the tavern, removing dishes from tables, he maneuvered well enough to catch her profile. Not young, but neither was she old. She was lean of face, with high cheekbones, dark eyebrows, and ears covered by wavy locks that escaped her hair band. She would know that he was there, probably even knew he was looking at her, but made no move to acknowledge him. He figured to leave well enough alone and continued about his duties.

After a time, the woman placed another log on the fire and turned her boots, probably to dry the backsides. She removed her cloak and Amos could see two small, thin swords strapped to her back. Each was sheathed in a plain leather scabbard, free of decoration, buckle, or etching. Not just a traveler but a soldier. A woman soldier. Who had ever heard of such a thing?

Her brown tunic was made of fine leather, also free of any sign or symbol. Her breeches were of thick cloth and also brown. When she stood, Amos could make out a small sheath hanging from her belt, the grip of a simple dagger protruding. Her sleeves were rolled up, revealing wiry forearms that exhibited a strength far greater than one usually saw among the fairer sex.

Amos had welcomed many interesting folks in his tavern, but a woman soldier, armed with blades a-plenty on an announcement day brought alarm.

"Can I 'elp ye, ma'am?" he called to her in his thick coastal accent.

No answer.

"I ca' muster up bread and chee', if ya like, a-hungry 'n' such," he tried again.

Without responding to his questions, the woman slid her feet into the boots, threw the cloak over an arm, the pack over her shoulder, and walked straight at Amos. He could see her face clearly as she approached—sharp, angled features and a visage bereft of emotion. Then, as if quickly bringing flame to a lantern, she smiled and her blue eyes brightened as she arrived at the counter.

The sudden change took Amos aback, and he stood motionless in front of a tub of soapy water, still holding a dishrag in one hand and a dirty clay mug in the other. She reached into a small pouch at her waist and dropped three copper bits onto the counter in front of him. As she did so, he saw two bone rings, one on the third finger of each hand.

"Thank you for use of the fire," she said. Her words were fine, well-annunciated, and deliberate, like the careful motions of a surgeon. She didn't come from around here. "Announcement tonight, no?"

"Yes, ma'am," he said. "Big party too."

"Thank you." Then her smile disappeared—gone as quickly as it had turned on. She swiveled gracefully, then walked out the front door.

"Well, I'll be..." the old man said, letting out a soft whistle as he exhaled. He shook his head incredulously, then went back to scrubbing the mugs.

The only lingering evidence that the stranger had been in the tavern that morning were copper coins on the counter, a warm crackling from the fireplace, and the lonely mumblings of an old drunk.

Gwyn Khoury had been camping in the hills above this little fishing town for the last few days. The cool fall air, accompanied by the occasional rainstorm, had taken their toll and she had become truly uncomfortable. Less than an hour in front of a fire, however, and life had returned to her bones. It was fascinating how the local residents didn't blink an eye at the constant fall of water, managing soggy clothes, mud, and damp air with aplomb, as if they knew nothing else.

Although no stranger to travel or bad weather, Gwyn preferred the cold and snow of the interior, not the constant precipitation of these coastal regions. Setting up a good shelter did not challenge her, but making a fire for warming or cooking, armed only with wet wood, was nigh on impossible. This was a dismal place to live.

As a watcher, Gwyn had long ago become accustomed to seeing a little more than other folks. As long as she had a cepp available, such as the rings on her hands, she wielded a special sight. She could detect sources of life, whether they be animal, plant, or people. It helped her to be the first to find moose on the game trail, to know which trees bore rot, and to spot where the human quarries hid when she was on a job. It also helped her to see the gifted—a talent of great appeal to rich men. A noble who had gifted in his employ was formidable, and watchers like Gwyn could note the bearers of magic from far away. Not only could she spy the wielders of magic, she could also see cepps when they were carried by others—a sure giveaway that the bearer was gifted.

Gwyn was a quick study, had mastered her ability soon after her own announcement ceremony at age fifteen, and was conscripted into the service of Baron Chak of Took. She welcomed the opportunity. No family protested her departure, and the folks who raised her harbored no concern for her welfare, having cared for her only in respect for Gwyn's dead mother. It was good to be free of that loveless home.

Baron Chak owned the land around her home village of Eastway. He was paranoid of rival nobles' efforts to undermine his political aspirations and had first drafted Gwyn into his household to ferret out any spies. Gwyn was effective, and more than a few of the baron's rivals had met a quick end due to her efforts.

She learned archery and woodcraft and loved to wander the lands around the barony watching wildlife. The wanderings helped her master an ability to sneak through the woods, testing her skills by following big game for miles without disturbing them. She hunted occasionally, as she loved the taste of fresh venison and coney, often leaving some of her kill with a poor family fallen on hard times. Such was the custom of the watchers—to provide for the bellies of the poor. But hunting was easy, of little challenge because of her gift, and it didn't take long for her to tire for the lack of sport.

Chak assigned her—more often as she got older—to pose as a lady at garish functions, where she would mix with the elite in her efforts to identify his enemies and gauge their strengths. At his direction, she practiced languages and fine culture. She developed false identities, learned how to waltz, and how to strike with a blade. As years passed and her skills were refined, she turned from a watcher to a weapon, from talented girl to surgical killer. She witnessed the fates of many who had chosen to defy powerful lords. No, not witnessed. She was not a member of the audience for such plays; she was an actor on the stage, lucky to be playing the part of villain—a fortunate role when compared to the victim. She had looked in the eyes of those victims as her blade cleft flesh, sinew, and scraped against bone. As hearts stopped and dreams died. She had seen it in their eyes—the fear, the confusion, the realization that it was over. Everything was over. They were done.

Gwyn would avoid that pitiable role. She would never be a victim.

Her eventual orders to report to Fairmont and serve the Ministry of War and Justice had been no surprise. Minister Vorick had heard of her successes over the years and paid Chak to release her. She still wondered how much it had cost him. The monies she received in soldier's wages were greater than those of common folk, but meager compared to the coins exchanged by powerful men. She had few complaints, however, as her belly never hungered, she never lacked adventure, and as long as she obeyed, she was safe. The missions she fulfilled for the minister were of the same sort as those given to her by Chak. At Vorick's direction several years later, Chak fell under one of Gwyn's own blades, having become a victim of the very weapon he had crafted. A painful irony.

This particular mission had a different flavor, though—one she had just begun to taste. She was looking for a girl, a hidden gifted, probably sequestered in one of the poorer villages of the Great Land. She had spent several years looking, casually wandering from village to village, camping on the outskirts of towns.

It was yesterday that she saw her target.

When engaging her sight, Gwyn could see life. But she could also see magic, whether produced by cepps or by the gifted. A fully charged cepp, even when hidden under clothing or behind a wall, was visible from a dozen yards away. Uncovered, it could be seen from fifty or a hundred yards away.

Gifted could be seen from slightly less distance unless they actively used their talent. In that case, they lit up like a torch. The minister, a blessed with two talents, was easily twice as bright as a gifted unless he took specific measures to suppress himself. She had met him on several occasions, far from his seat of power in Fairmont. He usually kept people like Gwyn away from his inner circle—away from respectable folks. When she did see him he would puff himself up, magnifying his brightness once he knew that she was watching. As if anyone needed to be reminded that the minister was a powerful man.

But yesterday Gwyn saw a light from miles away, shining from someone who climbed the mountain over Dimmitt. It was a beacon of incredible brightness that lingered for more than an hour. It only faded from her vision once the light reached the top. Such power! The light was many times brighter than any she had seen, dwarfing even that of the minister's. Racing through the woods, she had followed the light, spotting it when it descended the mountain again. The source was a teenage girl, her light bearing a myriad of colors— a scintillating nature, shifting slightly from hue to hue as if unstable. Or undecided. What sort of creature did she chase? Gwyn followed the girl to a cottage in the woods where she apparently lived with an old laborer.

Knowing now that it wouldn't be hard to find her, Gwyn decided to hang back and get word to Fairmont that the search was over. And such a find!

She left the tavern and visited the local post, scribing a short note to Fairmont. It would cost four silver drachmas for a private courier to carry it. As she handled the coins, she thought of how many she would receive for her efforts and wondered who else might pay for the information she now held. That light announced a gifted that wielded more power than Gwyn had ever seen, or even heard of, and information on the girl's location would be worth a king's ransom. Then she remembered who she considered betraying and dismissed the fanciful imaginings. Invoking Vorick's wrath would not be worth any price.

The young clerk behind the mail counter seemed surprised by the request for private post—and even more so when the silver coins dropped onto the counter. Dimmitt's postal service clearly didn't receive lavish requests, and Gwyn wondered if such a courier could even be found.

"Is this going to be a problem?" Gwyn asked.

"N-No," the girl stuttered. "I can get Abel to take it north. He's the best rider in town, and he'll be happy for the work. It's just been a long time since anyone has commissioned a private carrier, ma'am."

"Tell him to leave today."

"Yes, ma'am."

Gwyn pulled her hood over her head as she left the building.

It would take more than a week for the fastest courier to make the journey, and much of the payment would be spent on horses and food. It would take just as long for the minister to send someone in response. Two weeks. Gwyn would continue to camp in the woods, watching and awaiting their arrival.

Curiosity mixed with caution as she wondered about the potential of tonight's announcement ceremony. Would this child be announced, or had she been, already? Gwyn had never recognized a gifted unless they had first been announced by a ceppit in a proper ceremony. If so, why was no such child on record at the Ministry of War and Justice as living in Dimmitt? The child was surely a blessed, but wouldn't that have been known all over the Great Land? There were things Gwyn did not understand about this mission, but the merit in the minister's interest was now as apparent as a thunderstorm. This child had value.

Questions would have to wait, for she had a job to do. Gwyn would watch, she would wait, and she would do what she was told. A good soldier, she would be rewarded for her loyalty. Obedience was all that she had ever known.

8

PREPARATIONS

Mykel occupied himself by moving wood scraps from the mill to supply the bonfire for today's announcement, hoping to fuel the heat all day and much of the night. Nobody helped him, but neither did he need it, possessing a strong back, a powerful resolve, and a sturdy wheelbarrow borrowed from the docks. Nervous excitement for today's ceremony swelled deep inside his breast.

As he pushed the load of wood, his eyes wandered about, spying his neighbors as they made preparations. School held no classes, the town hall was sealed and dark, and community members were cooking food and planning games. A sanguine expectation, only mildly articulated in their conversations, seemed to fuel the plans they had begun several days ago. Perhaps this year would stand apart from previous announcements.

As he rounded the church building and headed to the mill to collect more wood, a little lady sprang into the empty wheelbarrow and sent it careening sideways. The muscles in his back and shoulders strained to keep it upright.

"Hey," he blurted out.

"Hey yourself," Nara responded, a rascally smirk on her face. "Give me a ride."

Mykel grimaced, unable to rouse an angry word, his surprise vanishing in the wake of her playful attentions. Launching forward, he drove the wheelbarrow and its stowaway up the slight hill toward the mill.

Nara turned forward, the breeze taking her hair. "Faster!" she cried to him, pushing herself to a standing position as he bounced and jostled her on the bumpy road, catching disapproving glances from people they passed. Slowing, they pulled up beside the mill.

The exertion produced a sweat, and Mykel's shoulders and legs were spent from the effort. Nara hopped down from the wheelbarrow and came around to him with a grin, then squeezed his right upper arm. "So strong!"

"Why did you stand up? You could have fallen."

"I knew you wouldn't drop me," she responded. "But you didn't slow down either. Maybe you were hoping to teach me a lesson for stealing a ride, eh?"

Working together, they filled the wheelbarrow, then pushed it to the field where they neatly stacked the logs next to the bonfire, then returned for another trip. Sometimes Nara would steal a ride back; other times she would walk alongside Mykel, talking about their hopes for the evening ceremony. Once she even pushed it back with him inside, albeit at a slow pace and with much complaining both during and afterward. The physical effort did much to quell the anxiety that ruled the day.

Inside the church, Father Taylor washed, shaved, and dressed for the ceremony that was now just hours away. He glanced out the window to see more folks making their way to the church field. A light rain continued, wetting the grass and causing rivulets of runoff to wander the paths and sometimes puddle, but the residents didn't seem to notice. The smells of watery soups and freshly-baked bread came in through the open window, accompanied by conversations and laughter as they continued their happy work.

Taylor turned back to the looking glass. Thinning hair and a bushy white beard seemed to stand out more than they had in recent years. A solemn expression came upon his wrinkled face as he recognized the effects of time, proceeding mercilessly despite healthy living and faithful service to his deity. Mostly faithful, anyway.

Despite the joy many felt during the morning's preparations, Taylor's mood remained solemn. The villagers were full of hope at the possibilities in today's announcement, creating a guilt over the deception he would continue to perpetrate on them.

He wished he could choose another path, but the price of hiring a harvester to imbue the ceppit was insurmountable for churches of small means. The harvesters always claimed that filling a ceppit took far more energy than any normal effort, and the prices were set accordingly. Some of Taylor's peers blamed a lack of announcements for the problem. There were few harvesters available, especially in more remote regions. The lack of competition had created a commensurate spike in prices.

Whatever the reasons, Taylor and other pastors often pressured the church to fund the imbuing of their ceppits—a recent inquiry had resulted in a quote of three gold crowns. Three crowns!

Taylor couldn't bear to lay this burden at the feet of the townspeople. Almost daily he received news of village folk having trouble finding food, unable to afford care at the clinic or sometimes even firewood to keep warm. Dimmitt could never have raised three crowns. He couldn't imagine what such a burden would even look like.

Many years ago, one of his predecessors dodged the issue entirely by simply not paying for the ceppit to be imbued, and Taylor had followed suit. The costly consequence, however, was that there hadn't been a successful announcement in Dimmitt for decades, and the village was empty of gifted folks.

Every few years, Taylor would deceive those in his care by telling them that enough funds had been saved to imbue the ceppit. A great sermon would convey feelings of loyalty to the Great Land and seek the divine approval of gifts from Dei. Then, he would pack for a long trip. With much fanfare, he would leave Dimmitt and encamp on the other side of the island for a few weeks, empty ceppit in hand. When he returned, looking disheveled and weary from travel, the children would squeal delighted alarms at his arrival, and many would come out and greet him. Hope would rise at the thought of a gifted announcement, and Taylor's ruse would weigh even heavier on his heart—yet another sin stacked upon his history of good intentions gone wrong.

He continued his preparations, eager to enjoy the food and song, running the sermon through his mind so he wouldn't forget anything. The scriptures he would speak tonight were not of glory or victory, as they often had been, but instead of hope and encouragement as if to assuage the villagers during a null announcement. Perhaps Dei would bless them somehow, if not in arcane gifts.

A bell rang from above, undoubtedly Simon Tinny pulling the rope that announced midday. Simon had bell duty this week and had been dependable. Often, the duty was not taken seriously by those assigned, but Simon was a faithful lad. The bell sounded once, then twice, then three times. Taylor longed to feel as righteous and honorable about performing his own duties as Simon felt about ringing that bell.

There were only a few more hours before supper and ceremony, with still much to do, and Taylor continued about his business with a renewed urgency.

9

ANNOUNCEMENT

N ara sat still in her assigned chair at the front of the throng, a prodigious headache pounding away at her. She was dressed in old breeches, worn shoes, and a green blouse that matched her eyes. The blouse remained bright despite its age—she only wore it on special occasions. Extra time to brush her hair and clean her dirty shoes had further polished her appearance.

"How bad is it?"

Mykel's words startled her as he appeared by her side. He was wearing mostly clean trousers and a dusty brown jacket that he had probably smuggled out of his father's closet. Nara smiled but winced as she did so, nevertheless comforted that he had noticed her struggle.

"I'm okay," she said.

"Liar," he said with a gentle smile, then put a hand on her shoulder. "Hang in there, Bitty. You can rest soon."

"I know," she said, reaching up to place her hand on his. She held it there for a moment.

The grassy field near the church looked very different with the many chairs set out, and the several hundred villagers wandering about. They shook hands in greeting near the tables where meager portions of food were waiting to be eaten after the ceremony. The aroma of the soup made Nara's belly gurgle, although it was hard to think about eating at a time like this. With so much at stake.

Father Taylor wore his formal robes, slightly less stained than his normal garb, trimmed with blue satin and only torn in a few places, suitably decorative for the special event. His silver hair was pulled back into a plait, and his salt-and-pepper beard was neatly trimmed. It was a wooden stage that he stood upon, with enough room for six or eight people to stand if they crammed together. Several boards on one side formed crude steps. Father Taylor took the stage and raised his arms. It took a few moments for folks to settle down, and another moment for conversations to stop, children to quiet, and seats to be taken.

"Let us pray," he said, bowing his head, arms still raised in a gesture of blessing.

"Holy Dei, bless us this day as we seek your favor upon our village, your comfort on our hearts, your grace in our lives. May gifts be upon our youth so that our town can find prosperity. Forgive us our failings and have mercy on us, sinners we are. In your name we pray, blessed Dei. Amen."

Father Taylor reached into a long pocket in his flowing robe and retrieved a piece of parchment, then gently unrolled it with a seemingly deliberate slowness as if to add drama to the moment. "The words of Dei."

"Blessed be Him," said the crowd.

"And in the third month of the seventeenth year, Jasep journeyed to the mont in search of the talisman spoken of by his fathers. He left his mother, who was called Meryim, his sister, who was called Nerum, and his wife, who was called Heidi."

The passage from the Book of Journeys was familiar to Nara and one of Taylor's favorites. She had always wondered what the talisman was, but even Father Taylor had never given a decent explanation, instead talking about the mysteries of scripture or something.

"Jasep arrived at the mont and searched for the talisman. Forty days and forty nights he searched, and the on the fortieth night he prayed.

> Lord, I have not found your great talisman, which you
>   sent me to find,
> I have failed at what you sent me to do.
> I am hungry, I am lonely, and I am cold.
> I have left my wife and family and am on a mountain
>   in the middle of winter.
> Have mercy on me and let me die."

A young mother sitting in one of the back rows jostled a baby in her arms as it fussed. A little boy near the front row squirmed on his father's lap as the man tried to keep him still. Father Taylor cleared his voice and continued.

"Then Jasep lay down under a tree, in the snow high on the slopes of the mont, and went into a deep sleep. In a dream, the Lord responded.

> My child, you are hungry, you are lonely, and you
>   are cold.
> You have left your wife and family and are on a
>   mountain in the middle of winter.
> I will have mercy on you, but I will not let you die,
> for your race is not yet run, your quest is not complete,
>   and you have not found my talisman.

After sleeping for seventeen hours, Jasep awoke, still hungry, still lonely, and still cold. He was still on the side of the mountain in the middle of winter and had not yet found the Lord's talisman. He left and journeyed home, and in the seventeenth month, he arrived. The words of our Lord."

The crowd responded, "The words of our Lord."

Father Taylor cleared his throat.

"Life can be terrible and seem absent of purpose," he said. "Each person possesses life, a gift from Dei, and is running his race, seeking his fortune, doing what he can to follow Dei's will. Someday, all die and receive the reward they have earned. Until then, we must climb our mountains, as Jasep did, to endure to the end, despite all hardship."

He concluded with a heartfelt prayer for patience and health for the village. A long, drawn-out "amen" ended the brief homily, and the townsfolk echoed in response. It was a more somber sermon than Nara could ever remember hearing, and she noticed hope fading from the crowd as the priest concluded. Father Taylor expected no gifts today. Nara hoped he would be wrong.

"Are you ready?" Mykel whispered, close to Nara's ear.

"Not at all," she said, giving him a fearful, sideways look. Mykel didn't know about her magic. He didn't know how she was different, but he might know soon. "How about you?"

"I'm fine. It will all be fine, you'll see."

She smiled a shallow, awkward smile for him, knowing that it did little to hide her fear.

Father Taylor waved a hand, inviting Elden Sack, Gilbert Bonny, Nara, Mykel, Heidi Trinck, and Finn Willy to climb the stage. They left their seats and approached the steps. Elden Sack walked in front but waited for the others to catch up before climbing the few stairs. They formed a line in order of their ages, with Finn at the back, then turned to face the priest and the crowd.

Father Taylor called for a couple of volunteers to help with the ceremony, and both Amos Dak and Bran Fedgewick came forward. Elden moved to stand next to Father Taylor. Taylor arranged Amos and Bran on either side of Elden, and the men grabbed the boy under the arms to steady him.

The priest lifted a hand and placed it on Elden's head. "This youth, whose destiny is now unknown, comes forth to answer the call of Dei. He submits himself for testing, to unveil his purpose. To reveal his soul."

Father Taylor walked to the table near the back of the stage and opened the engraved wooden box, which Nara recognized from the sacristy in the church office. He retrieved the ceremonial knife from within, and she saw a strange look on his face as he moved it from hand to hand. Had he noticed that it was lighter?

Her anxiety grew as she remembered how it felt when she had imbued the ceppit with her magic. How it had leeched her strength like it was hungry, as if alive. Would that happen again today?

Father Taylor shrugged his shoulders and walked back to the front of the stage near Elden. The ceppit rested on the top of his open palms.

"Behold the instrument of Dei, the ceppit that bears His power and through which He bestows gifts."

Father Taylor lowered his arms and moved to grip the ceppit in his right hand, blade pointed down. It was now that Elden should have extended his palm in offering to the priest, but Elden remained still, hands at his sides. Nara could sense the fear that paralyzed him.

In a quiet voice that only those on stage could hear, Father Taylor spoke. "Elden, you are fifteen years old. Your announcement is here. This will hurt, but you will recover. Be brave, lad."

Elden slowly lifted his right hand, palm facing upward, then closed his eyes. Father Taylor positioned the tip of the blade on the soft flesh between Elden's thumb and first finger. Elden's arm twitched, and he released a quiet whimper. Amos and Bran tightened their grip on him, surely in support for the pain the boy was about to endure. Out of the corner of her eye, Nara noticed Elden's sister position herself near the side of the stage, ready with a handful of bandages.

Anticipation in the crowd grew thick, and the townsfolk held their breath as if deep underwater, lungs bursting with discomfort until they could reach the surface and exhale the anxiety of the moment. Nobody stirred, no babies cried, and even dogs that wandered about sat and faced the stage in expectation.

In a loud voice, Father Taylor continued, "Holy Dei, reveal your will in this boy, Elden Sack!" He thrust the ceppit downward, impaling Elden's hand, and Nara felt a sympathy pain in her own palm as she grieved for the boy's plight and his fear. Elden screamed and tried to pull his hand away in reflex but was held firm. Tears escaped his eyes as blood streamed down the blade, dripping onto the stage below.

Please, Dei. Give Elden a gift.

Father Taylor held the blade in place for a full minute, perhaps watching for the early manifestation of a gift, and Nara looked with her sight as well, eager to see a change, holding her breath in anticipation. She saw nothing. Elden was in pain, but didn't appear to be experiencing the onset of any new power or awareness. Father Taylor looked deep into his eyes and whispered something Nara couldn't hear, then Elden shook his head in the negative. Father Taylor hastily pulled the blade straight up and out, then ushered Elden off the stage to be cared for by his kin. The crowd exhaled.

Nara was disappointed, almost having expected Elden to shoot fire out of his eyes, or for his image to shimmer and glow, or to throw big pot-bellied Amos twenty feet with newfound magical strength.

Father Taylor spoke words of encouragement. "I should remind you that the lack of an immediate manifestation does not mean there is no gift. I will work with the youths in the next few days. They will be tested, and we will know for sure by the end of the week. Some gifts won't show right away."

The words seemed like empty comfort, but folks in the crowd nodded in response, and one man put an arm around his wife's shoulder.

Father Taylor then gestured for Gilbert to step forward, who almost tripped on a loose board that he pushed back down with his foot. Nara thought of this quiet boy, how he was always in the back of the class, hiding under the big mop of shoulder-length, blonde hair that grew from his head. There would be no hiding for Gilbert today, and she wondered what he was feeling right now. Once he was in position, with Amos and Bran at his sides, she noticed that his breaths were short and shallow. She saw him glance back and forth several times between the blood on the stage and the ceppit in Father Taylor's hand.

"Holy Dei, reveal your will in this boy, Gilbert Bonny," said the priest, then impaled Gilbert's hand. Gilbert's knees buckled under him, and for a moment his weight seemed entirely borne by Amos and Bran. When he gathered himself again and stood, Nara heard Amos make a comment of encouragement, something about promising him a beer later. Gilbert turned and gave Amos a big grin through the tears, and the man snorted in apparent satisfaction. A minute passed, Taylor removed the ceppit to the crowd's dismay and directed Gilbert off the stage.

Nara rubbed at the discomfort in her palm, a lingering sympathy pain from Gilbert's injury. The time for her own test had now come, and she cringed at the thought of what might happen. Fear that she had made the wrong choice now chipped away at her confidence. When she sneaked into the church last night to imbue the ceppit, she had intended to bless others with her efforts. Those intentions had been focused on her neighbors and friends, and the gifts they might hold in their souls undiscovered. But now, she might pay the true price. Would her true nature now be revealed, no longer a secret shared with Bylo? Would she lose control of her magic, bring darkness like one of Kai's servants, casting a shroud over the stage, an evil spirit destined to deliver pain to all? Now that Father Taylor wielded a charged ceppit, her true nature might be revealed, and she would learn if she was the angel Bylo thought of her, or a monster that warranted destruction.

She stepped forward, offering her hand to the priest so that he could perform his duty. As Bran and Amos gripped her arms, her mind calmed. This was a necessary part of her story and not to be avoided. Still, she yearned for comfort from Bylo, and her eyes scanned the crowd for his face but could not find him. How could he not be here at this moment?

She turned to Mykel and gave a brave smile for him, then looked back to the crowd and closed her eyes, steeling her will against what was to come.

"Holy Dei, reveal your will in this girl, Nara Dall," said Taylor as he pushed the blade through Nara's palm.

Nara held her breath. The powerful pain came as metal pierced flesh, in one side of her hand and out the other. Her heart pounded with the anticipation as she waited for the horrible magic to follow. But other than the pain, there was nothing. Not like she expected. Not like Bylo had feared. Then, she began to notice the ceppit's energy. Through the pain, it was warm and familiar to her, its energy comforting. Even with her eyes closed, she could see the glow and feel its warmth leaking into her, returning to her spirit as if returning home.

"Open your eyes, girl."

Nara shook herself from the sudden calm that came over her, and Father Taylor looked at her straight on.

Quietly, he whispered, "Do you notice anything? Any change at all?"

"Um, nothing," she said, hoping to hide the truth of her magic. As the priest looked into her eyes, she wondered what training he'd had in the discovery of gifted. Was he sincerely looking for a change in her or merely performing a charade for the villagers? Could he see through her lie? Should she tell him? That she had magic, and that she could help? Or could gifts still come to the others on stage, gifts that would bring food to this town and allow her to keep her secret hidden? She *wanted* Father Taylor to see. She *wanted* him to know. Then it wouldn't be her fault at all, and Bylo's efforts would not have been unraveled by her, but instead by Dei's will, right?

Look deeper, Father Taylor. Can you see that I'm different? Can you tell?

But after a moment, he looked away, and she exhaled in both relief and disappointment. She scanned the crowd again for Bylo, but her attention was jolted when Taylor removed the blade and a fresh stab of pain lanced up her arm.

Far from the stage, Bylo watched. A pack and knapsacks rested on the grass near his feet, stuffed full of food, blankets, and travel gear for what he expected would be a necessary escape from Dimmitt. Now that Nara had been announced without incident, he exhaled a sigh, the tight ball of stress in his mind uncoiling. He should have trusted her.

A skiff was ready in a cove on the other side of the island, and he'd made plans to sail far away. The newly-inked strength tattoo on his left thigh throbbed, ready to power him for miles, even bearing heavy packs and his little girl on a shoulder. He now felt silly for the preparations, and as many of the crowd turned to him, expecting him to rush up and care for Nara's injury, he realized just how poor his judgment had been.

He reached inside one of the packs, grabbing an old shirt and chiding himself for having no suitable bandages. As he ran toward the stage to help Nara, Elden Sack's sister passed in front of him, grabbing Nara's injured hand and catching it up in a bandage. Bylo followed them both as they moved around the back of the stage to wash and dress the wound. Shame overcame him as several in the crowd snickered in his direction.

Mykel was relieved. Worry about the day melted away as he realized that his anxiety had been focused on Nara, not himself. Her announcement was safely past, no gift was apparent, and there was no danger of losing her. He took a cleansing breath and his heart rate slowed, shoulders relaxing.

The priest gestured for Mykel to step forward, and as he did so, Mykel noticed Nara pull away from the aid station, squeezing the bandage in her right hand to staunch the bleeding. She moved toward the side of the stage, eyes fixed on him.

As he offered his palm, Mykel looked briefly over at his friend and duplicated her small, brave smile. Would he be gifted today? Would he be able to take Nara and Sam away from this place, leaving Dimmitt behind? Even if he received no gift, they would leave Dimmitt. He'd take his brother and his friend, and they would find a place to live in peace. Away from Pop.

He looked out at the audience to find Sammy there, sitting next to Lina, his eyes full of expectation and hope, as if he agreed with Mykel's plan. Mykel smiled. They would soon be free.

Then the pain came.

The pain jarred Mykel—not for its intensity but for its nature. It was different from what he'd expected—a pulling sensation. It wasn't just a knife, it was a living thing, tugging at him.

It began to grow, the intensity increasing. It sucked at his essence, becoming a dark pit that drew him in, a leech that now clamped onto his whole arm. That drained him of life. A wave of cold rose to his shoulder, and panic struck him like a mule kick to the chest. What was happening? Something was wrong! He tried to pull away, but the wave moved higher, freezing him in place. He couldn't move at all. It flowed up to his torso, to his neck, and then to his head. The wave was not just cold, it was alive, it was famished, and it was angry.

His vision faded, his legs went rubbery, and he dropped to the stage. Then the fearful cold disappeared in an instant, replaced by physical pain of incredible power throughout his whole body, active and tortuous. Streaks of fire lanced across his skin as if he were being attacked with a hundred knives. He could feel his muscles tear and his bones weaken, preparing to shatter.

Mykel tried to scream, but his lungs held no air, already stolen by the demon that was this ceppit, the knife that now consumed him. His mind felt dizzy, then dark.

Like a candle blown by a gust from an open window, Mykel Aragos' spark winked out.

As sympathy pains racked her whole body, Nara sprinted for the stage on stumbling legs, the bandage on her hand coming loose and dropping onto the grass of the field as she launched herself toward her friend with reckless abandon. The world seemed to darken as the panic in her heart narrowed her vision, allowing her to see only Mykel. She launched herself upon him even as Bylo, Father Taylor, and the other villagers froze in place, recognition of the threat now apparent on their faces.

Mykel Aragos was cursed, and he was dying right in front of them.

Nara kneeled and hugged Mykel tightly, covering him in a protective embrace, willing his wounds to heal and his light to brighten, even as she pressed against his cold skin with her warm hands. He was fading quickly.

"Hang on, Mykel," she said. "I'm here."

Defiance surged inside her, and as she had done with the ceppit last night, she reached inside herself, drawing upon the reserve of energy within, and poured herself into Mykel.

At first, nothing happened. Then she noticed the flow begin, some warmth returning to his skin under her hands, and she realized it was working. Hope sprang up inside her as she poured more and more of herself into him, even as a weakness grew in her own legs. Then panic came over her as the warmth under her hands disappeared, Mykel's spirit fading with it. A dark fog engulfed her, obscuring her vision of the stage and the world around her. Looking only with her special sight, she saw her energy pouring into him like a river, flowing down his arm, and disappearing into the ceppit that still impaled his palm.

Of course! The ceppit was draining him, and through him, it was draining her too!

She willed her arm to move with what little strength remained and reached for the glowing ceppit, then extracted it from his limp, cold hand and tossed it as far away as she could. Then she reached inside herself again to pour more strength into Mykel, to rekindle his flame once again, but there wasn't enough of her. She had wasted too much. She was failing, and her friend was dying because of it.

Straining, her vision faded and her head pounded with each painful heartbeat, yet the only things she saw were her own light and his weak spark, flickering and fading out. Dizziness overcame her, and she lost the ability to think, focused only on this task, this effort to save him, even if it cost everything.

In mindless desperation, she reached out for help, looking through the fog to find thousands of little bits of light around her. The blades of grass. Energy. Life. She gathered them up, pouring all of them into Mykel. When those were gone, she looked again, and another light caught her eye. It wasn't bright, but it was close.

She reached out with her mind and tried to tap it but found it to be enclosed in something hard like glass that repelled her efforts to reach it. But this light carried a strength that might save them. With desperation and focus, she reached out and broke the hard covering, cracking it. The energy flared in her vision like a sun, unleashing a torrent of warmth and power and strength. She called, and it responded, pouring down through her arm, across her body, and into her fallen friend.

The light's power had immediate effect, and she saw Mykel's flame rekindle and grow stronger. As she pulled more of the strange, comforting energy, she fed it to him and Mykel shuddered beneath her hand. She kept some for herself, just enough to stay conscious, and poured all the rest into him. When she looked at the light source again, it was gone; the glass-like shell that once held it was blackened and dead. She tried to pull her mind out of the fog, but didn't have the energy.

She looked at Mykel's still form, wanting to talk to him, whisper words of encouragement or perhaps to scream for him to wake, but her tongue was heavy, her strength gone, and her vision fading. She collapsed upon him in an awkward position, and the last thing she saw was her right palm, absent its dressing, dripping blood onto the announcement stage.

A prayer escaped her lips, thanking Dei for sending the source of strength that had saved them both, then consciousness left her like the last ray of light at sundown.

10

AFTERMATH

Father Taylor tried to pick up the pieces of what had become a disaster. Sure, he'd received training on how to manage the grief and chaos following the announcement of a cursed, but he never expected to preside over one.

How could this have happened? The ceppit wasn't imbued, no more than a bone-handled knife. How could Mykel Aragos have been announced by it? Remembering back to the ceremony, he realized the blade had felt lighter, and he then realized what must have happened. It must have been imbued, and he had missed the signs. But by whom?

Amos Dak now lay dead upon the stage, his skin shriveled, blackened, and bloody as if he had been the unholy one rather than the Aragos boy. Perplexing.

As if that wasn't enough, Taylor now had to tangle with Gretchen Wipp. When Bylo Dall had scooped up the fallen kids and ran into the woods, Wipp had stepped forward, screaming that someone murdered her husband.

A throng of villagers had soon after rushed to her side.

"What?"

"Who?"

"How?"

Taylor saw Wipp looking about, wide-eyed and apparently dizzy in confusion with the sudden attention.

"Did you see?"

"A cursed, could you believe it?"

"Oh, honey, I—"

"Which way? I'll chase them down!"

Their fearful quips soon became jeers as their confusion turned to anger, directed at the villager they had chosen to blame.

Bylo Dall.

The betrayal spread through the mob faster than a well-fueled fire, and many townsfolk began to demand answers. And justice.

It was all too much for a tired priest to manage, so he had locked himself in his office and set his head upon the desk. Eyes closed, he shut out the sounds of angry townsfolk in the sanctuary who screamed at each other and took the Lord's name in vain.

Taylor replayed the scene in his mind, trying to make sense of the events that had unfolded too rapidly to understand. Mykel had fallen, writhing in agony. Then, Nara Dall had launched herself on the stage to embrace him. After a moment, the boy's condition had improved, color coming back to his face. Then, Amos Dak leaned down to offer help and Nara reached up and gripped Dak's arm, who then fell down like Mykel Aragos, his portly shape striking the wood planking of the stage with an audible thud. Amos' face went pale, mouth open in shock and pain, his skin shriveling up, blackening, and cracking. Taylor recalled the guttural scream that came from Dak just before he died. Horrible.

A few moments later, when Taylor descended the steps of the stage, he saw that much of the grass in the field below, once green, was now blackened and dead. Closer inspection revealed the grass to be brittle and shriveled as if burned by a great fire. Harvested.

Villagers now milled about the field in confusion. The window was ajar, and he heard talk of Kai's demons, others planning to alert the constable's office in Junn, and still others griping about the church. Several wanted to form a posse to apprehend Bylo Dall.

Still, some youths remained to be announced, and while Taylor didn't feel the strength to do so, it was expected that he would manage things somehow.

A deep breath filled his lungs as he opened the office door, resolving to calm the chaos with a comforting scripture. Perhaps something from the Book of Joy would help. He stepped out of his hiding place with a smile on his lips, but despair in his heart.

Bylo ran. His feet pounded the forest floor, avoiding the main paths, breaking twigs and leaving deep footprints as he flew from the village. The unconscious bodies of Nara and Mykel weighed him down, and he occasionally misplaced a foot and sank deeply into wet ground. After what seemed like an hour, he slowed and set the youths down in a grassy clearing, the fading sun providing barely enough light to check on them.

Although unconscious, they were still breathing. Both were pallid and weak, and a glance at Mykel confirmed Bylo's fears. The boy's skin was hard and dry, with cracks apparent all over his face, arms, and chest. The fissures oozed dark blood, and his breath was shallow and erratic. Being carried over the last few miles had surely not improved his condition.

Bylo thought to use a rag as a bandage but then had a better idea. He dropped his packs on the ground and opened a side pocket to retrieve ink and a stylus. He pulled up Mykel's sleeve, exposing an upper arm. Using spittle and a rag, he wiped away the blood and fluid from an area of skin. Carefully, Bylo drew a rune of health on the surface.

His eyes strained in the growing darkness, but the wounds near the rune stopped oozing and closed slightly. Not enough. As if to emphasize Bylo's failure, Mykel seemed to stop breathing altogether for a moment, then moved again, letting out a low raspy noise. His airway was closing.

Bylo turned the boy on his side, hoping it would help move air more easily. He checked Nara and was grateful to find her faring better, with steady breaths, although still unconscious. Bylo pulled a blanket out of his pack and laid it over her gently, then turned back to Mykel.

The sun was almost over the horizon and along with it would go his ability to see. Bylo considered his remaining options. If he stayed here and cared for them, avoiding the trauma associated with movement, villagers might find them and prevent their escape. The clumsy run through the woods had surely left signs that would be easy to follow.

As he had feared, Nara had imbued the ceppit. There could be no other explanation. The chaos of the ceremony and the fall of the innkeeper had likely ushered in the truth about Nara. Consequences would be paid. Add to this that Mykel was cursed, an altogether unforeseen event, and Bylo's anxiety was palpable. The boy's nature bore religious implications. Even if his condition improved, he would eventually be imprisoned and executed by the church. The cursed did not survive announcements, and that Mykel still lived was an affront to everything holy.

This was all Nara's fault, wasn't it? No, of course not. She wanted to help her neighbors, nothing more. Bylo should have expected her to imbue the ceppit, and he bore the true guilt for this catastrophe.

But there was little time for such thoughts. The strength rune he had inscribed into his own thigh earlier in the day was large, but its power was not infinite. The size of the tattoo was intended to extend the duration of the magic, but Bylo was sure that precious little remained. He needed the power to finish the trip across the island, but if he moved Mykel again, he would surely perish. The health rune on the surface of the boy's skin did little more than stop the bleeding on nearby eruptions before running dry, evaporating into the air. The tug of war in his mind between the urgency of moving Mykel and the need for him to rest gave birth to an idea that was both bold and stupid. A health tattoo?

He turned to Mykel and pulled his trousers down slightly over his hip, exposing an area with no open wounds. He wiped a portion of skin clean with a rag, then went into his pack to retrieve his tattoo needle. Experiments showed that while a rune painted on the skin gave minimal effect, a tattoo under the skin carried the magic for hours. A health tattoo would be the best hope for Mykel's medical condition and might help him survive the rest of the violent journey.

As he inked Mykel's skin, he squinted ever harder in the failing light, pausing periodically. Doubts emerged in his mind. Inscribing a magical tattoo onto an unconscious person without their permission was a bold plan that could not be undone. When he first attempted this on himself, the power faded later that day and left no lasting side effects. But he was in uncharted territory here, performing magic on a wounded, barely breathing young man.

He lifted the needle away from Mykel's skin. He had planned to finish the tattoo and carry the boy away, but if the tattoo failed to heal him, the rest of the journey would surely kill him. Maybe it would be better to leave him here and let the villagers do what they would? Mykel might live a while longer, or at least wouldn't die because of some madness Bylo had concocted.

But how would such an act be seen by Nara? Considering this, all doubt left his mind. Nara would not be able to bear the death of her childhood friend, and success was imperative. He would save this boy. It was all or nothing, and if he didn't finish soon, he would be inking a magical tattoo onto a dying, cursed boy in complete darkness. He hurried.

As he finished, the last of the ambient light departed, and he could no longer see to check if Mykel's wounds were healing. He fumbled about with his packs, replacing ink, stylus, needle, and blanket, then strapped it all onto his back. He gingerly hefted the youths onto his shoulders and walked through the darkness in what he hoped was the right direction. The inking of the tattoo had been hasty and misguided in the half-light and surely wouldn't work. Mykel would die on his shoulder, and there was nothing he could do about it.

He bit his lip in frustration at his poor planning. Dimmitt should have been a haven for him and Nara, but he had botched everything.

Where would they go, and what would they do? How might he explain Mykel's death to his dear girl? What excuses could he fashion, and would she ever forgive him?

Suppressing his self-loathing, he focused on the task before him. There were miles to go before they reached the cove. Darkness would make travel slow, and his strength would not last much longer.

A few rays of moonlight illuminated his way well enough to avoid running into trees, but twigs broke and branches bent as he carried the youths onward. A wild dog barked and a raven crowed, evidence that a trespasser was disturbing the forest in clumsy haste.

Unseen by Bylo as he labored, a newly inked rune of health under the skin of an unconscious young man began ever so slightly to glow.

FLIGHT

Gwyn had watched the announcement from behind a tree in the nearby woods, but had not been prepared for what transpired. Not only had a cursed boy been announced, but the girl had sucked the life out of a villager to save him. As a watcher, she had been privy to many secrets, but she'd never seen *that* before.

Now, an old man carried two youths on his shoulders, and even under the heavy burden, was able to run for miles. At first, she was convinced that he was a bear, possessing the magical gift of unfathomable strength. She found it difficult to keep up with his pace and eventually fell behind. When the sun finally set, she ran to the top of a hill and looked in the direction they had traveled, gratefully finding them with her vision: three glowing lights in a distant grassy clearing. One of the lights was shifting, clearly belonging to the girl.

She approached cautiously, picking her footfalls with care to avoid making noise. As she got closer, she saw the man attending to the boy in the dim light, perhaps dressing his wounds.

After a short time, he picked them both back up and moved again. She watched as they traveled several more miles, albeit at a much slower pace. Finally, the man stopped at the entrance to a small cove, barely discernible, even with her sight. They were now at least eight miles from the village. A cabin would have made for a much more suitable and comfortable resting place, and the oddity of his choice puzzled her until she saw what he had hidden there.

A boat. Small but sturdy, a thin sail hung loosely on its mast.

Curse Dei! The bear and his children would be on that boat in no time, and she would be unable to follow without a skiff of her own. She briefly toyed with the idea of contriving a chance meeting to petition a ride but realized the craziness of it. What man running across an island, assisted by strange magic and carrying two half-dead children on his shoulders, would welcome an encounter with a stranger, then dare to invite her along? Gwyn refocused her thoughts, as there were clearer solutions at hand.

She wasted no time, turning and sprinting for Dimmitt. She ran through the heavy woods, periodically falling in the dark onto sharp rocks or branches. Her legs ached from the exertion, and halfway back she was forced to detour around a group of villagers carrying torches and wandering the woods. Vigilantes who sought the fleeing outlaws? They seemed to lack direction, moved slowly, and would not find the man or his children tonight.

The village was dark and quiet upon her arrival. It would have been ideal to commission another post to Vorick, updating him on the announcement disaster and the girl's subsequent departure from town. Unfortunately, she had to make haste and could send no such note. Yet, the late hour favored her in another way; there would be nobody to stop her from getting what she needed.

She made for the dock and selected a small skiff. The dim light could not hide its age, sun-bleached wood and fraying mooring ropes, but it was equipped with two solid oars and a strong sail. She grabbed a snack from her pack to replenish her failing energy, then untied the boat and pushed off. A stray dog on the shore barked as she pointed the skiff northwesterly and rowed. As she left the small harbor, she scanned the cottages near the shoreline, but they remained dark with no evidence of a witness to her theft.

No wind assisted her, and she focused on the task ahead as she rowed. She was chasing a man so strong that he would easily outdistance her. Trying to reach him tonight would be a foolish ambition, so she must guess where he was headed. The north side of Dimmitt was devoid of homes, and the closest village would be Junn, across the sea. Junn was on the mainland and would provide options for further escape by road to the north, to the west toward Ankar, or by another boat to parts unknown. Yet the rough waters that typically accompanied a crossing to Junn could prove perilous. If a storm arose, a small craft would fail. How desperate must this man be to try such a dangerous trip in the dark?

There was no choice but to follow and hope for success. At least in Junn she could update the minister on her progress.

As if in response to her resolution, the loose sail began to dance, announcing a proper wind. She dropped the oars inside the boat, adjusted the sail, and turned in her seat to mind the tiller. As the skiff moved forward, she thanked the breeze and sat back to gaze at the distant horizon.

She would catch them soon.

Bylo placed the two youths on the rocky beach as gently as he could. He felt strength leeching away from his body, the last vestiges of magic dissipating from his rune. A growing fatigue commanded him to drop his packs, but he managed to carry them to the boat before resting. He placed Nara on a bedroll in the middle of the craft, grateful for her small size and commensurate lack of weight. Putting Mykel into the boat taxed him, however, and he strained his shoulder in the process. Weakness continued to overwhelm him and his body felt assaulted by the burdens he had carried. Sharp pains lanced from deep within his legs, and he was convinced that the rune had caused damage. Were bodies meant to bear this strain? Fortunately, honest labor had kept him healthy, and he might recover if he could rest.

He untied the skiff from the tree on the shore, coiling the rope and throwing it onto his seat near the stern. He tried to launch, but as if loading the gear and unconscious youths were not hard enough, the boat now carried so much cargo that he could not push it off the beach. Fortunately, the tide was heading in, and in less than an hour, the boat's weight would be suspended by new water.

He crawled inside to wait, then lay down between Nara and Mykel, his spirits lifted by their regular, easy respiration. There was no sign of a pursuit by villagers, they had almost escaped Dimmitt, and blessings could be found in that. He exhaled deeply, and while waiting for the tide to rise and release them from the shore, he took some rest.

A short time later, he was alerted by the morning sun dancing across his face as it lazily rose over the eastern horizon. He sat up to find the boat gently rocking among small waves, a light breeze brushing against his cheeks. They were floating away from shore, heading out of the cove. He fixed the sail and pointed the craft to the north. Junn was the closest town, and they would need supplies—he had not packed well enough for three people to travel far. After a time, he looked at Mykel and saw something he did not expect.

The wounds on Mykel's face were healed! Several thin pink scars could be seen on his cheeks and forehead, which had previously been marked by gaping wounds. Carefully, so as not to overturn the boat, Bylo checked Mykel's arms, legs, and impaled hand, holding his breath in anticipation. Although covered in dozens of tiny new scars, the skin was healthy and vibrant. The tattoo had worked far better than he could ever have hoped and in such a short time! Perhaps Nara needn't ever be told how close her friend had come to the grave.

Pride leaped up from deep within him as he took joy in the accomplishment. He often thought of the gifted and the great power they held in the world. As a young man, he had been overcome with envy when he had received no gift during his own announcement. As old ambitions flooded back in a wave of nostalgia, an odd smile tugged at his lips. He had magic after all, but of a very different sort.

Nara awoke to the gentle sound of waves lapping and the scent of sea spray. She was in a boat. Confused, she lifted her head slowly, her vision blurring for several moments before she managed to make out Bylo sitting at the tiller. A sail flapped noisily in the wind over her head.

"Bylo?"

Her voice was faint, but he somehow heard her. "Nara!" His face lit up with apparent relief, and he abandoned the tiller and went to her, causing the boat to shake in his urgency. He felt her forehead and checked the bandages on her hand. "You're okay?"

"I'm tired. Where are we?"

"Oh, thank Dei. I was so worried," he said, visibly relaxing. "We're almost to Junn." He moved back to take his seat at the tiller. "Go back to sleep."

With a slight nod, she pulled the blanket tighter and rolled to her side with eyes half-closed, only to discover Mykel at her left, deep asleep. A raw, guilty ache dawned in her gut, and without knowing why, Nara found herself shaking.

Timidly, she reached out to place a hand on his chest. He breathed and his skin was unwounded, but bore small marks that could barely be seen. Scars?

"He's fine, Nara. Really."

Memories of the announcement ceremony flooded back. The pain of the ceppit through her palm. Mykel had fallen, ghostly pale, with horror in his eyes. She ran to him—she remembered that part clearly. What had happened after that was a blur. Mykel's light had faded, nearly winking out. Her desperation and plea for help, that special energy coming so close. Had it been Dei?

"He's okay. Seriously. Please rest."

She wanted to. Her fatigue was deep, more profound than ever before. She felt thin, insubstantial, like threadbare cloth. Her head remained heavy, and she could barely lift her arms. Perhaps sleep would be a good idea. She reclined again on the bedroll.

"Bylo?" Although her body had stopped shaking, her voice remained unsteady.

"Yes, dear?"

"Do you believe in Dei?"

"You know I do," he said.

"I have always wondered. I mean, I know what Father Taylor says. But you don't really talk about Dei much."

"He is a mystery to us all."

"He saved us. On the stage. Mykel and I were dying, and I think He was there. I felt Him."

Bylo said nothing.

She lifted herself slightly, propping up on one elbow.

"Mykel's energy faded, so I poured into him, like with your ink. But I saw that the ceppit was stealing his energy. I got rid of the knife, but there was so little left of him, and I... I had no strength left." Her voice cracked as she continued talking. "It was horrible... but He came. Dei came to us. I felt a light come close, and I reached out and took His energy, and it filled us... and Mykel came back to me."

Bylo said nothing, although her words clearly demanded a response. What wasn't he telling her this time? His silence drew her to darker places, reminding her of their new status as fugitives, away from Dimmitt for the very first time. Away from home. When would they be able to return? Would they ever?

"Bylo?" Her voice was stronger this time.

"Yes, Nara."

"How old was I when you chose Dimmitt?"

"You were just a baby."

Bylo had told her long ago that he had adopted her and would have been a grand fool to pretend otherwise. For who would have believed her to be his relation with that nose of his?

She paused a second before summoning up the courage to blurt it out what now nagged at her. "How could you be sure I would be gifted?"

Silence.

"Bylo!" She sat up completely, fueled by frustration. These secrets had been undisturbed for far too long.

The old man's eyes filled with a quiet sadness. "Nara, it's complicated."

"No, Bylo, it's truth. Truth is easy. Give it to me. Please." Fully awake now, she implored him further. "I deserve to know who I am, and every single time I ask, you push me away."

Bylo closed his eyes and sighed deeply. A distant seabird squawked loudly before he finally spoke again. "I stole you, Nara. That's the truth—my truth and your truth."

Stole her? The anger subsided, replaced by confusion. "You mean you kidnapped me from my parents?"

"Oh no, not like that. You were in a church orphanage. I took you from the yard where you played. No papers, no names. Knowing what I did about you, I didn't want someone else to figure it out and find you."

"What did you know about me?"

Bylo adjusted the tiller and took in a deep breath. "Nara, at the monastery where I worked, I had a wise friend named Phelan. In his studies, he uncovered an error in scripture."

An error in scripture? Nara remained riveted as he began to speak the words she had longed to hear.

"Not an error in scripture, exactly. More like an error in our understanding of it. You see, when Breshi was first resurrected, the church began to translate the scripture texts. But they paid no attention to the runes in the margins. These runes give clues, Nara, and through study of them, Phelan found an error. Foretold by Dei, scholars in the church thought that the twin peaks of Fairmont would split, but Phelan discovered that actual human beings would separate, instead. Such a prophecy, if true, must surely involve magic. I was convinced that you would be gifted. Or more."

Bylo shifted in his seat, then fiddled with the sail and the tiller. Nara's brow twisted in confusion. "How can a human being separate, and what does that have anything to do with me?"

"Twins, Nara. Not the twin peaks near Fairmont that people talk about. Real human twins. Conjoined."

"But conjoined twins are an abomination," Nara said, repeating what she'd heard in church. She stopped talking, reaching to her back to touch her scar. "Am… am I…?"

"Yes," Bylo said.

A shiver ran from her head to her toes, freezing her in place. "Bylo, are you saying I have… a sister?"

He nodded quickly. "I think so, yes. I tried to find her."

"But the church didn't kill us."

"Maybe they didn't know," Bylo said.

The wonder of such a revelation about her origins seemed overwhelming. What exactly did this prophecy say, and could it really be about her? She was a conjoined twin that had been allowed to survive. A human being carved in half, or two that Dei wanted to remain joined? Or was it Kai that had created them?

Questions arose in the wake of this. Why had the physician defied the church to separate her and her sister? A kindness, or an experiment?

She often felt like half a person and now she knew why. Perhaps her headaches were part of this, as well as the emptiness that sometimes came. Knowledge that she was different. Broken. It was there now, but more poignant, deeper with the revelation Bylo brought. Deeper now that it had a reason.

Fatigue commanded her notice, and her eyes were heavy as she shifted her gaze to stare at the water. She focused on a log that floated nearby, bouncing in the waves, unable to do anything about the water and wind that pushed it to destinations unknown.

Bylo continued to explain. "If conjoined twins had survived, I knew that the evidence would be easy to find. Surgery would leave scars. Because of this, I traveled to the larger cities and eventually to Fairmont. A surgeon with supreme skill would be required to accomplish such a separation. It wasn't as hard as you might think once you start with the assumption that the scriptures predicted the separation of human twins. That was Phelan's theory. Where else but rich, populated, well-connected cities for skilled physicians?"

Nara nodded. His logic made sense, but hearing the mysteries of her childhood unraveled had unsettled her, and she didn't have words. She belonged to a tale from scripture? Like Jasep and the talisman, perhaps?

Bylo continued. "Such a special set of twins could be born to rich folks or poor folks, but a rich couple would destroy such a child right away. The embarrassment of a broken birth would be devastating to a family that dwelled among folks in high society. They would not allow the shame."

Nara's face flushed.

"I'm sorry, Nara. I'm not ashamed of you. I was talking about how rich folks think." The words were insufficient to suppress the truth that she had been unwanted. A scarred, broken baby.

"It's okay, Bylo. I get it."

After a pause, he swallowed and continued. "If such a surgery were to be successful, the children's recovery would be difficult, the care of them time-consuming, and a poor family would not have the resources to bear it."

A breeze swept across the boat, bringing a chill, and Nara huddled closer to Mykel as he slept.

"Such twins could not be delivered normally, and the physician would have to cut the woman to extract them. She would probably not have survived. The poor man who was your father would have been overwhelmed."

Her mother was likely dead. Her father was likely poor, overwhelmed with two broken babes. "He abandoned us, didn't he?"

"I would think so. In anticipation of this, I searched orphanages in Fairmont. Ten years of looking, of waiting, volunteering to help here and there, until I saw you."

Lifting her head again, she gazed upon his old, kind face.

"So small, but you played just as hard as the other kids. Maybe only two years old, but you ran like the wind and laughed just as loud."

"How did you know? I mean, how did you know it was me?"

"Your scar."

"Oh," she said.

"Little ones run around and play with no shirt on in the middle of the summer, my dear."

"Of course."

The scar. She couldn't see it herself and had always sought to hide it with her clothing. The mark was something she remained only subtlety aware of.

"Did the prophecy give a date?"

"No, it didn't."

"Then how did you know it would be in your lifetime, and had not happened long ago?"

"Great question, and one that I asked myself many times," Bylo said, then cleared his throat. "If it had happened long ago, then the histories would have shown a time when there was conflict and pain to many, as the scripture foretells. The only such time would have been the mysterious disappearance of the Breshi civilization. That was certainly a possibility that haunted me as I searched. The second option would have been that it wouldn't happen until after I was too old to search. Or after I was dead. It brought on thoughts that I would be looking until my last day, feeling like a fool the whole time. But I don't believe Dei does things without a reason. I had faith that Phelan's discovery was timely and purposeful, so I remained steadfast."

"You are an amazing man, Bylo."

Bylo smiled. "During those ten years of looking, I didn't feel so amazing."

"Are you sure I had a sister? Or would it be a brother?"

"Sister. I'm pretty sure conjoined twins are always identical. I searched and searched but never saw another child who looked like you. Knowing the two of you would be alike, I thought she would be simple to find."

"How long did you look?"

"Two more years."

So, there had been a sister. Conjoined at the back, near the spine. What would it be like, attached to another human being? And how skilled must that surgeon have been to perform such a delicate operation along so sensitive an area, with both children surviving? Or had they?

"She may not have survived the surgery," Bylo said as if reading her thoughts. "Or she could have died later. Lots of poor children die."

"Oh."

"I love you, little one. I'm sorry I never told you the full truth."

"I want to go home."

"We can't."

"Because they'll be looking for us?"

"Yes."

"Our friends and neighbors. I didn't help them at all, did I?"

Bylo said nothing.

She reached over and rested a hand on Mykel. He was warm and breathing steadily. She lay back and folded her hands on her chest. Bylo was right; they couldn't go home, and she knew what they ran from. Mykel was cursed, and she had shown magic without an announcement, bringing a cursed boy to life in defiance of everything holy.

So now they would run from the church, who could not let Mykel live. And from the authorities, who needed gifted for their armies. Soldiers and princes and monsters at the Ministry of War and Justice who would take her and make her kill on their behalf, as they did with all the others. But where would they go, and what would she learn in the days to come? Was her father still alive? Had he and her sister been looking for her? Should she look for them? Was her sister like her, with strange magic?

"I love you, Bylo."

"I love you too."

"Thank you for carrying us. For saving us."

"You're welcome."

But despite her gratitude, the thoughts on Nara's mind were not of seeking escape, or safety. If Bylo was to be believed, her magic was part of something bigger. Scripture. Prophecy. Or destiny. She could not hide forever, could she?

Too tired to wrestle with such troubles further, she closed her eyes and let the waves rock her away.

12

VORICK

Fairmont Castle
665PB

Nikolas Vorick, Minister of War and Justice, stood in the great hall of the castle waiting to answer a summons from the queen. While he waited, he gazed upon the paintings and tapestries that hung on the stone walls. He had always held a strange fascination for painting but had quickly decided that it was a useless skill. It brought little money, even less power, and required endless, tedious practice. When he had abandoned his own artistic efforts at a young age, it had been a salient point in his personal journey. He held no regrets.

Since then, he had accomplished much, having learned mathematics, history, and politics. When announced as a blessed at age sixteen, the world had become his oyster. He was both a cutter and a harvester, and no such combination of gifts had been documented in any of the histories. The church heralded his announcement as a sign that Dei was smiling upon the Great Land, and he was a rising star in Fairmont.

In the following years, he had found great fascination with the human body and employed his cutting talent in pursuit of knowledge in that area. It led him to study with the physicars, medical professionals at the university hospital, learning anatomy, dissecting corpses, and pondering the mechanisms of death.

He eventually found employment at the Ministry of Justice as an executioner, the first physicar to ever do so. He became a key player in removing the barbaric position of headsman from the ministry and instituting more humane executions. So skilled had Vorick become that he could place his hand on the back of a man's neck and visualize the subject's brain stem beneath his fingers. A single cut and they would expire, peacefully. It was less like taking a life and more akin to laying a child down to sleep.

But despite all his learning, he had always struggled with patience, having acquired a disdain for waiting. Today, he waited to meet with the queen. Fortunately, the art in the entrance of the throne room was magnificent and occupied his time. One piece in particular captured his attention: a canvas depicting the Oracle of Ankar, standing proudly on a plateau with the Humble Guardian at her side. An ornate tattoo decorated the Guardian's chest.

Vorick marveled at the painter's skill, depicting the ancient heroes in such fine detail, and his thoughts moved to the legends and of their adventures. She, the ancient builder of kingdoms, guiding and teaching kings and princes over the ages. With the tall, dark, bare-footed warrior at her side, she had brought peace to a chaotic world following the mysterious fall of the Breshi civilization. The Guardian's right arm rested around the Oracle in a gentle embrace, his muscular physique in stark contrast to the woman's tiny body. An odd match, the combatant and the counselor, yet one that was compelling to look upon.

The Oracle appeared small in this painting, although she was often described differently in the histories. Silver-haired and wise looking, it was difficult to imagine her as a leader of men. Her companion seemed to tell a different story. Shoulder-length black hair blew in the breeze, and the regal-looking man gripped a white staff in his left hand. Power and peace were portrayed in his stature, echoing throughout the popular tales of his victories. Vorick thought of the legends about the Guardian and his mighty men, the soldiers who gathered at his side for every battle.

He pondered about his own image when compared to this legendary warrior. Vorick's impeccably groomed jet-black goatee and neatly cropped hair portrayed a regal bearing, but his below-average height and thin, crooked frame dispelled the impression. Vorick was feared for his magic, not his manliness.

Vorick wondered about the choice of colors the artist had used to depict not only the lifelike skin tones but the swirling maelstrom of wind, rain, and lightning that encompassed the figures. They appeared peaceful together, despite the storm about them. He thought on his own efforts at such artistry, and how his immature works had fallen short of greatness such as this. If he had continued his pursuit of the craft, what might he have achieved? Memories from childhood rushed in, a time when painting had held a special place in his heart.

Outskirts of Fairmont
Estate of Weldon Vorick
630 PB

Nikolas was thrilled. He stayed after school to work on his painting, and after covering the mistakes today, it was perfect. Although frustrated that he had mixed the wrong color, some help from his art master had produced a new color, a dustier brown. Standing in his father's study, it was clear that the new color matched the old books on the shelves. Papa will love it.

Nikolas was nine years old. He possessed few friends and endured ridicule due to his curved spine and the unsteady gait it produced when he walked. Painting had become his refuge. He loved the time in the classroom each day after the other children left. It was time that he had used to pursue art and the peace it provided.

His master had noticed Nikolas' interest and stayed with him often, teaching about ink, brushes and tiny knives. Palettes, pots, and primary colors. He learned about stippling, flicking, and dabbing to produce different textures and about different work surfaces: paper, canvas, and leather. He cherished the smells of the pigments when mixed with oil and how his hands would bear stains well after his time in the studio had ended. Sometimes, after completing chores, he would sniff at his fingers to catch a hint of gum, resin, or solvent, one of his favorites. Solvents were used to clean up the mess after painting, and he associated the odor with cleanliness, something he cherished. The contrast between the mess of painting followed by the ritual order of the cleanup sparked a joy he experienced nowhere else.

Nikolas' latest work was by far his best. The master had taught much about lighting and shadows, helping him to paint his father's study complete with sunlight from the window. The illumination fell perfectly on one side of his father's profile, leaving the other side dark and mysterious. Papa would adore it.

Professor Weldon Vorick was an important man, an architect and engineer at the Grand University of Fairmont. "The Grand" held the distinction of being the greatest institution of learning in all the Great Land, and Papa maintained a respectable position as a chief engineering instructor. The queen hired Papa to design many royal projects, including some of the walls and fortifications around Fairmont. Nikolas had great pride in his father and bragged to his peers about the man's position. Papa frequently spoke at important functions, and Nikolas followed along, wearing fancy clothes. He would smile and clap when Mother instructed but would not speak until spoken to, and then only to say "yes, sir" or "no thank you, sir" and things like that.

Today was a special day. There was much to prepare, and Papa would come home late, as he always did, giving Nikolas plenty of time. With his master's permission, Nikolas borrowed an easel from the school. It was heavy, and several of his classmates laughed as he dragged it along the city streets under one arm, his painting tucked under the other.

The easel now stood in the middle of Papa's study, the painting sitting upon it, perfectly centered and held fast with two pieces of twine. Nikolas knew the study was off limits. It was Papa's private room, and even Mother wasn't allowed inside, but this one time would be okay. Papa always went into his study upon arriving home, and it was the perfect spot to put the surprise. When Papa saw the painting, how well he'd matched the colors and the beautiful light from the window, he would be proud and forgive the offense.

Nikolas completed his chores and put on nice clothes for the occasion. It took a long time for his father to arrive, and Nikolas slumbered in the entryway, waiting. Mother tried to encourage him to go to bed many times, but he resolved to wait, no matter how long it took.

When Papa finally came in through the door, Nikolas stood, yawning, then composed himself. "Welcome home, sir," he said.

Papa took no notice of him, hanging his jacket on a coat hook and proceeding to the study. He entered the musty, dark room and lit a lantern, then made for the bar. He poured brandy, not yet noticing the canvas in the middle of the room that rested upon the easel. Nikolas waited at attention in the hallway outside the study.

After drinking the brandy in one swig, Papa poured another and turned to Nikolas. "Aren't you supposed to be in bed?"

Nikolas said nothing, instead looking past his father at the painting, then back. Papa turned to where Nikolas glanced, seeing the painting.

"I spent weeks on it. I wanted it to be a surprise." Nikolas beamed with pride. "Happy birthday, Papa."

The words that left Papa's mouth in response were not what Nikolas expected.

"You came into my study."

Nikolas watched his father tense, his right hand tightening around the glass, his left hand making a fist.

"I know I'm not allowed, but I wanted you to see it when you came home."

Papa turned toward Nikolas, eyes cold and angry.

What followed was the beating to which Nikolas learned to

compare all future injuries. Mercilessly, the fists that came down on his ribs and face were all the more painful because they were imposters, traitorously replacing the hugs, kisses, and words of affirmation that Nikolas had hoped for. He'd expected "You are such a good painter," and "I love you, son." Instead, he endured "You worthless fool," and "How dare you!"

Papa dragged him, bleeding and broken, into the backyard and forced him to burn the painting.

Nikolas spent weeks in bed as Mother tended to him with bandages, salves, and gentle songs. She fed him pudding and soups until he could eat solid food again. The pain in his jaw lingered long after the rest of his body had healed, but his back was never quite the same, the pain of standing upright forcing him to walk with an even more unusual gait than he already did. Nikolas didn't enter the study after that, didn't meet his father at the doorway when he came home, and no longer called him Papa. When the man died, years later, Nikolas shed no tears.

And he never painted again.

Minister Vorick turned from the art, recalling the pain of his father's discipline as if it were the seeds of greatness. The day he received that beating was the day he received the only thing of value his father ever gave him. A gift of truth, a forced awakening, a devastating hammer of practicality that shattered idealism and dispelled foolish ambitions. It had freed him to pursue better things.

"Minister?"

Vorick turned to find a page at the entrance to the spacious throne room.

"Thank you for waiting," the page said. "She is ready to see you now."

When Vorick entered the room, Queen Mellice was standing in front of her throne, speaking with a girl in a red dress. The queen herself wore a lavish burgundy gown that stretched at the seams to accommodate her generous form. A modest silver crown adorned her head, failing to hide her thinning hair, or distract from the many wrinkles upon her brow. A tray of cheeses, chopped apples, and honey sat on a small table not far away, along with cups, saucers, and a pot of something that was steaming. As Vorick approached, he recognized the youth's delicate features. It was his daughter, Kayna. It had been several days since he'd last seen her. He chided himself for his inattention to the girl, but his brief self-deprecation was quickly overcome by new questions.

Why was she here with the queen, and why had she dyed her hair black?

"Ah. Minister. Thank you for coming. I was just speaking with your daughter," said the monarch. Vorick gave Kayna a puzzled look. "I invited her to tea, and she accepted."

Kayna smiled wryly in his direction and performed an abbreviated curtsey, then moved away to stand near the table.

"Walk with me," said Mellice as she grabbed Vorick's arm.

They strolled across the cavernous room as fast as the queen could manage, far enough to avoid eavesdropping. The queen released Vorick and gestured for him to stop.

"I have heard some disturbing news," she started.

"I'm sorry, Majesty, how may I help?"

"The Frozen Lands. I'm told that Roska barbarians have taken Bann."

Vorick had discussed the matter with the queen weeks ago, but her growing dementia must have stolen the memory. She was becoming politically irrelevant but still held significant social influence. Embarrassing her was no option.

"I'm sorry, my liege. I sent word when I first heard and have not spoken with you at length about the matter." He gritted his teeth in frustration at the charade he was forced to play. "Please accept my humble apologies."

"What are you doing about it?" she asked.

"General Cross has surrounded Bann and is holding it under siege as we speak." Cross was a fine leader, and success was assured, although Vorick had not yet received a dispatch saying as much. "That upstart Magnusson will be defeated within a fortnight, my queen."

"He better be," she said. "When I let you adopt Carris' duties, I didn't expect you would adopt his incompetence as well."

The queen was referring to the former minister of war, Torre Carris, one of the laziest leaders in the Great Land. He had grown fat and happy on high living, and when Vorick decided to clean house, it was easy to concoct evidence of treason. The fall of Carris, the many arrests and executions, and the assimilation of the bureaucracy into the Ministry of Justice was something about which Vorick held great pride. He found it humorous that she claimed to have 'let him' adopt Carris' duties. That was entirely his own idea, and he had not sought permission.

"I assure you, victory is imminent. I would not think of disappointing Your Majesty." Vorick gave a slight bow.

"That's not all I wanted to speak with you about, Minister."

Vorick raised an eyebrow in curiosity.

"Your daughter."

This was a gentle subject, and Vorick was ill prepared for it.

"The girl is remarkable," she said.

You have no idea, he thought.

"I'd like her to attend to me, along with my other ladies."

"Um. Of course, Your Majesty. But she has school and other duties, so I don't know where she'll find time."

"She will make time. I have tutors. Her schooling will be better than ever. She will have a room in the castle, and I will expect her to stay several times a week."

Vorick needed to have a talk with the girl. She maintained a strict schedule at the university and was tired at the end of most days. How had she found time to weasel her way into the queen's good graces? Kayna at court could be a disaster for him.

"Certainly, Majesty. I'll let her know."

"Oh, don't bother. I already did," the queen said as she walked away. "And now it's time for my tea."

Vorick took the queen's sudden departure as the dismissal it was, and on his way out walked close enough to Kayna to give a disapproving look. The young woman returned his gaze unflinchingly, along with the same devious smile she had used to greet him a few moments earlier. As if to accentuate her defiance, Kayna welcomed the queen to the table by grabbing the crook of the woman's arm, smiling delightfully, and leading her to a seat. She then tossed a wink back in Vorick's direction.

That girl was too smart by half. And twice as bold.

13

SEEING

Crone's Hill, near Eastway

E vening came, and the old woman prepared her dinner alone in the cabin. Well, sort of. *He* was often there. Other than her mostly silent companion, however, she had found herself alone in recent years. He first came to her long ago, and at the time she wondered if He was merely a product of her imagination. A periodic respite from the centuries of solitude. Sometimes she still wondered.

And oh, how loneliness now permeated her days. Even when she attended to her duties at the nearby abbey, she rarely interacted with the clerics there. The holy men paid scant attention to the slow-moving groundskeeper who did no more than trim the hedges and rake the leaves. It wasn't just that she looked old. Her hair had gone silver as a young woman, but it wasn't the only characteristic that betrayed her longevity. Her frame had sagged and her face was riddled with wrinkles. Her left eye was deformed, shrunken, and perceived nothing. Her right eye was cloudy and did not see well anymore. Long ago, she had taken to wearing a patch over the left eye, more for the comfort of others than for herself. Beyond her appearance, however, she *felt* old and found it difficult to hide the feeling from others. Her movements were slow and careful, and her manner conveyed a fatigue residing deep within.

She told herself that she wasn't old; she was seasoned. A chuckle escaped her throat as she rubbed salt on the bits of squirrel meat, then dropped them into the pot on the wood-fired stove. Thinking back over the years, she pondered her place in the world and how she came to be here, waiting. Waiting on Him. How much longer could she continue?

She harrumphed, chiding herself for allowing such a melancholy mood and dismissed the self-pity as she stirred the carrots, potatoes, and meat. Still, a quiet fog of depression lingered a bit, in her heart if no longer in her mind.

She carried a bowl of stew to her table, then returned to the cooking stove to check on it. Opening the loading door revealed that it had cooled; the wood burned to ash. It was her only source of heat, and if she didn't rekindle it, she would awake to a cold house in the middle of the night. She took a bite of potato, then went to the front porch to bring inside more birch logs to stoke the flames. As she opened the door, the wind blew at her fiercely, and her shoulder-length silver hair danced about in the gust, straining against a bone hairpin that kept it swept up on one side. Then, her eyes opened wide and her body went rigid as a seeing struck her. He spoke.

Anne.

Weeks had passed since last hearing His voice.

They are coming.

She stood in the doorway a moment, rigid, gazing out at nothing. In her inner eye, she saw travelers in need of her guidance and protection. After a time, she recovered from the vision and closed the door. She shuffled back to the table and took a seat.

"So you finally sent them, did ya?" She spoke to an empty room.

You are ready.

"I am old! My strength is gone!"

Her shoulders slumped as she stared into the bowl of food. A hard time was coming.

"You should have sent them long ago."

In my own time. Do as you're told.

"Or what? You'll let me die?" She stirred the food with her fork but didn't take a bite. "I've been asking for years to rest, but you've left me to rot here."

He didn't respond. So be it. Such a long wait, but perhaps she could finish things now. It was a good thing He gave her to do, or so He had always said. She had prepared long ago with the expectation that the task would have been completed by now. She had never expected to wait so long, and resentment had long since replaced her enthusiasm. She often wondered if she had been forgotten, or if the delay had been intended as punishment for her past sins.

So, they are finally coming. She had yearned to hear those words ages ago. All the years, all her adventures, all her mistakes.

"You better help me with this. I mean it."

Hunger pangs sprang up within. Not only would she need her own strength for what came next but all the strength He could send her as well. She hoped He would be true in this. She did not have what this task required, but of course, that had always been His way. They were coming to her in the twilight of her days, requiring her to depend all that much more on Him. It made for a scenario where He got all the credit, robbing her of any glory for the accomplishment.

She ate the bowl of stew, then served herself another. As she chewed her food, she carved an ornate design into the wood of the table with one of the tines of her fork. Light. Yes, that was it. She carved another. Earth. Harder, but still one of the easy ones. She carved a third. It was wrong, and she bit her lip in frustration. She tried again, much more slowly, deliberating with each stroke, and eventually revealed a design in the wood far more complex than the previous two. "That's protection, isn't it oh majestic procrastinator?" She looked up, but He didn't respond to her irreverence.

She would remember. Then she would teach. But there would be pain.

PART TWO

The discovery of the receptacle as a reservoir of power has been both a blessing and a curse. With it, the ceppit could be constructed, the gifted identified, and the dominance of the Great Land established. But it has brought strife. The holy power of Dei should be cherished and preserved. Instead, the throne and the church have loosed it for their own purposes. Evil acts by evil men.

The Oracle on the eve of her execution, Ankar, 305 PB

14

ROADS

W hen Mykel awoke, he was in a bed, looking up at the ceiling. Sounds of activity came from outside an open window. Where was he? He looked at the back of his right hand, expecting to see a gaping wound from the ceppit but finding nothing but a thin scar. He looked to his right to see Nara by his side.

"My hand. Healed. How long was I asleep? And where are we?"

"Four days," Nara said. Her bright-green eyes glowed even more than usual as her smile grew. "And we're in Junn."

In a city? Why?

He reached for Nara's right hand, only to find it wrapped in a bandage, clearly still healing. "I remember Father Taylor stabbing my palm. It hurt, but I thought I would be fine." He looked into her eyes. "Then the darkness. And the cold. I thought I was dying, but I saw your face. What happened, Bitty?" He normally used the nickname when she was vulnerable, not when he was suffering himself. She squeezed his other hand affectionately, and he suspected that the reversal was not lost on her.

"It drained you, Mykel. You were dying, and I ran to you. When I kneeled to help, it was draining me too. But then Dei came, a great light, and filled us both. He saved us."

"But how could that happen? How could it kill me unless..."

"Yes," she said.

"...I'm a cursed?" The thought of it struck a chord deep within him. It was the worst thing that could happen at an announcement, and it spoke much about what his future would look like. Cursed. Destined for death, or to be on the run forever. That must be why they had left Dimmitt.

"I don't like that word," she said, squeezing his hand again. "And you didn't die. You're fine."

But he wasn't fine. His hand might be healed, but he was far from fine.

As if oblivious to the effect that the news had on him, or perhaps deliberately trying to distract him from it, Nara explained how Bylo wasn't her father but instead a kind man who had adopted her from an orphanage in Fairmont.

"And I have my own magic. Magic that I never told you about."

"What?"

"Yes, Mykel. I'm gifted, or something like that. Bylo swore me to secrecy."

She went on to explain that her magic came long before the announcement ceremony, and that she could see things, and imbue ink. Magic that she had kept secret from him and from everyone in Dimmitt. She explained that she didn't understand it, nor did she really know how to use it. His eyes widened in amazement at her tale, and with shock that she had kept such things from him.

"I wanted to help them. Our village. I really did, Mykel. But I didn't know how, and Bylo wouldn't let me. I showed Sammy where to lay his traps, though. Where all the coneys hid. So you could both eat."

So that's how Sammy always got so lucky.

"It's ok. It's not your fault, but why didn't you ever tell me?" he asked.

"Bylo wouldn't let me say anything. He was afraid, somehow. Of me, perhaps. Or what they would do with me. *You* aren't afraid of me, are you?" she asked.

"Of course not," he said, but he wasn't so sure. Exactly what magic did she have? More than one gift? "So, you're a blessed?"

"I don't know. Neither does Bylo."

"Don't worry. I could never be afraid of you even if you had a dozen gifts. Just don't turn me into a frog, okay?"

But they didn't laugh. No joke could banish the tension that was now in the room. Nara had magic. He did not. On the contrary, he was a cursed. What had he done to earn such a horrific fate? In his life thus far, he had lost his mother, been unloved by his father, been separated from Sammy, and would now be pursued by the church as an abomination. If he had ever felt unworthy of her before, it paled in comparison to how he felt now. She was destined for wealth and power, but he was destined for execution. Had he displeased Dei so much that he deserved this punishment? Or was there some dark power at work in him that required destruction?

"And there's more, Mykel. Much more. Magic runes. Bylo has been studying them for years. I could never tell you before. Bylo forbade it. But now..." Nara stopped and bit her lip. "I'm sorry, I shouldn't have said that. Bylo wanted to tell you, and he should. It's his secret, not mine. I hate secrets."

Mykel dismissed her words, still lingering on his own flaws. "Nara, if I'm cursed, what does that mean? Am I a danger to you or Bylo? And why didn't I die? Cursed always die, don't they?"

"You could never be a danger to me, and you're alive because Dei saved you. And because Bylo carried us."

"Carried us?"

"Yes, if you can believe it. He'll tell you."

"What will happen if the church finds me?"

"Let's not talk about that."

"They'll kill me, Nara. They have to."

Nara's eyebrows furrowed, and her lips pursed in irritation. "They will never find you," she said. "Say no more about it."

Bylo entered the room and closed the door behind. When he came closer, Mykel forced a smile, but anxiety made it difficult to be truly grateful for the man's efforts.

"Nara told me how you carried us, Bylo. Thank you."

"I'm sure she didn't tell you everything," Bylo said, moving a chair to sit near the bed where Mykel rested. He spoke about runes as a preface to his own confession about a tattoo he had placed on Mykel's hip. He talked about scripture and margin illustrations, and how imbued ink gave power to those symbols. He told how he had inked Mykel's tattoo in the dark, on the run. He made excuses for the permanency of it, talked about trying to heal him with a surface rune, and how time and light were running out. He apologized multiple times.

Mykel interrupted him. "It's okay, Bylo. I forgive you. You saved me. Thank you."

"I worried about the effect it would have on you, son, since you're a cur—" He cut himself off.

"Since I'm a cursed. I know."

"He didn't mean—" Nara said. Bylo gave an awkward expression.

"Yes he did, but it's okay," Mykel gave Bylo a charitable smile. "I don't know what to call me, either."

Mykel reached down with his hand to rest it on his hip. There was something there; he could sense it.

"I have two of those now," said Bylo. "One on each thigh. It's easier to hide on the hip, but when I tattooed myself to test the strength rune, it was difficult to reach higher." Pride seemed to lace his voice as he described his work. "They do nothing once they lose their magic. The larger they are and the better the ink, the longer they last. But when the magic fades, they are just decorations."

"I'm not so sure," Mykel said. "It feels alive."

Mykel closed his eyes, still holding his hand on his hip, and thought of the tattoo. A bright pattern appeared in his mind, alive and hungry. His eyes snapped open in surprise.

"What happened?" Nara asked.

"An image appeared in my mind when I closed my eyes and thought of the tattoo. It seemed... hungry."

Mykel pulled down the cloth of his trousers, exposing the tattoo, his hand shaking with anxiety.

The design on his hip bore the same symbol as the one from his thoughts. He had known what it looked like before ever actually seeing it. Chilling. Something odd was going on here. Although surely with good intentions, had Bylo wrought some sort of dark magic? Alert now, Mykel sat up in the bed. Strange things were happening, and if people chased them, strange things might become terrible things. News of being cursed, Nara's gifts, and now a magic, hungry tattoo all spurred Mykel to action. Staying here was not an option, and although he might not escape these circumstances, he felt determined to go somewhere. Despite the emotional exhaustion, his body felt strong.

"Bylo, can we leave tonight?" Mykel asked. "I can travel."

Nara, still kneeling next to the bed, looked at Bylo, who glanced back at each of them.

"Let's go, then," Bylo said.

Bylo assembled their things and visited a nearby mercantile that sold them another pack, some salted pork, blankets, a thin tarp, and some socks. Bylo placed the pack on Mykel's back, and they set off to the north.

"I want to go to Fairmont, where you found me," Nara said. "I want to find my sister."

"Nara, we can't," Bylo said.

"Why not?"

"You know why. Soldiers. The church. They will have a description of you and Mykel even before we could arrive. You'd be conscripted into service, and Mykel would be executed."

Executed for being cursed.

"We're going to Eastway," Bylo responded. "I know someone who might help us at the abbey there. Brother Alen, who is now the abbot."

"You know an abbot, Bylo?" Mykel asked.

"Yes, well, I used to. He was one of the brothers at the monastery where I worked. Long before I met Nara."

"But an abbey is like a church," Nara said. "Won't they be chasing us?"

"Alen won't," Bylo answered. "At least I don't think so. If he won't help us, or can't find a safe place for us to live, we'll just go east. To the Yukan."

"I can't leave Sammy," Mykel said.

Bylo sighed. "I don't think you have any choice, son."

"Because I'm cursed. I'm a danger to him, is that what you're saying? That the church will come after me and Sammy could get hurt?"

"I don't know," Bylo said. "But for now, you should stay away."

Mykel looked to Nara, and there was compassion in her eyes, but she said nothing.

"Do we just hide forever?" Mykel asked. "That doesn't sound like much of a life."

"We'll talk about it later. For now, both your safety and Nara's depend on getting far away from here."

Although he didn't disagree with that, Mykel didn't like the sound of heading toward an abbey filled with church folks. Not with his new status as a cursed. Nor did he like heading out toward the Yukan, far from his home. He thought of the Windblown Wastes out west where criminals and loners were known to dwell. Would that be a better place to find sanctuary for a time? Perhaps Bylo was right. Mykel was ill-prepared for big decisions such as this, and there didn't seem to be any good choices.

As they walked through the streets of Junn, Nara stayed close to him. They looked about and spoke of the wealth that surrounded them. Wagons and horses moved along the roads, laden with goods and people. Many folks wore nice clothing, the children looked healthy, and the delicious smells emanating from taverns and inns invited them inside.

"Mykel, they all have shoes," Nara said. "Every child."

"I noticed that."

"We need to go back to Dimmitt. As soon as we can," she said.

"For Sammy."

"Yes."

They walked for several hours that night, stopping when they could no longer see the lights of Junn behind. They set up camp well off the roadway but did so slowly. Despite years of manual labor, fatigue from the walk seemed to have affected Bylo more than it had the youths, and the old man complained more than once. After a fire had been started, Nara rummaged through the packs to assemble a modest meal of lard and biscuits while Mykel gathered water from a nearby brook. They bedded down without interruption, and despite the fatigue, Mykel was grateful that they had made good time. If someone was after them, as Bylo suspected, Junn might not have been a good place to stay for long.

The next morning ushered in a full day of travel. They passed merchants and nobles, and even an entertainment troupe that rushed along as if late for a show. Whenever they saw someone on the road ahead, or heard footsteps or hooves from behind, Bylo directed them to cover themselves with their hoods and mind their own business. He explained that the delay in Junn had given pursuers from Dimmitt a chance to catch up to them.

In the late afternoon, as they saw soldiers approaching, Bylo urged Mykel and Nara to be particularly quiet. Once the men got closer, however, it was clear that they were battered. Some had bloody tunics; others wore bandages around their heads. In the bed of a wagon that accompanied them, several more could be seen lying prone. Wounded, or dead? Perhaps they were returning from a battle on the fringes of the Great Land. Everyone knew about the barbarian incursions, but Dimmitt was isolated, and Mykel had never seen the evidence of war up close. The fatigue and despair on the soldiers' faces remained on Mykel's mind through the rest of the day.

They could have walked longer that day, but Nara had begun to slow significantly, and stopped talking. Neither Bylo nor Mykel needed to ask if she was enduring a headache. Assured of their safety for the time being, they stopped well before sundown to prepare a camp on the back side of a hill. While far enough off the road and sheltered from direct observation by other travelers, they weren't so far away that they couldn't hear the occasional horse or wagon as it ambled by. Despite the obvious fatigue from hours of walking, Bylo seemed to find the strength to go fishing while Nara slept, and he collected several good-sized trout from a nearby lake. Mykel tried to duplicate the effort, but recent events had rattled him, and while his thoughts were elsewhere, he sliced his finger open with a hook. Bylo gave him a clean rag to wrap around his finger, and Mykel abandoned his fishing efforts to gather more firewood.

Bylo's fish made for a wonderful dinner. As they talked and joked around the campfire, feeling content considering the circumstances, Mykel wondered about the announcement ceremony, about Sammy, and the growing distance between them and their home. He looked at Nara, who sat next to him at the fire pit. A nap had helped her recover from her headache, and she cheerily bantered back and forth with Bylo.

———

Nara's heart broke for Mykel. He was cursed, he had been carried away from his home and his brother, and he'd had no choice in any of it. She, on the other hand, was with both Bylo and her friend. Although things were far from normal, she had the most important people in her life. Mykel did not. Sammy was far away, and although they had plans to go back, it wouldn't be any day soon.

Something else nagged at her though. Since leaving Dimmitt, she had thought more often about Dei, her subtle curiosity about the deity swelling to a powerful suspicion that He was much bigger than before. Or much closer, perhaps.

It seemed as if the talents she had been instructed to keep secret were endorsed by Him. True gifts, like those Father Taylor talked about. As if by saving them, giving her the energy to pour into Mykel, Dei had voiced a blessing upon their lives. The event had convinced her to dispel any worries about her magic being demonic in nature. She wanted to explore her talents further but didn't know quite how to begin.

Bylo's runes had received a similar endorsement in her mind. Dei had blessed Bylo's efforts when he healed Mykel with the health rune. She dwelled on it a bit. Feeling bold, yet trying to be discreet, she engaged her special sight for a moment and looked at Mykel.

He glowed with magic, just a touch. He looked different than before the announcement ceremony. Brighter, and with an odd color to him. Oh, it was muted compared to the ceppit, for sure, but much brighter than a normal person. She looked at Mykel's hip, and she thought she could sense the tattoo despite it being under several layers of clothing. She glanced over at Bylo, at his thighs, but sensed nothing. Why the difference? They had both been marked with the magical ink, so shouldn't she sense Bylo's tattoos as well?

"Nara?" Mykel had clearly caught her staring at their hips.

"Yes?"

He raised an eyebrow, obviously wondering what she pondered.

"Mykel, back at the inn when you saw that pattern in your mind, didn't you say it was hungry?"

Mykel nodded, and Bylo peered up from his dinner.

She continued. "Did you feed it?"

Mykel made an odd expression.

"The way you described that pattern reminded me of things I've seen. Never mentioned them, I guess." She was having a hard time articulating her thoughts. Feelings like this were not easily put to words. "I guess I didn't pay them much attention, but they've always been there."

Mykel stopped eating and looked directly at her. "What does the pattern look like?"

"Not just one. I have seen several, but only when I use my talents. They look like Bylo's designs, at least a bit."

Bylo stopped eating as well. "You see runes, Nara?"

"Kind of. I'm not sure."

Nara paused, her face flushing as they gaped. She scrambled for words to prove this wasn't something she made up. She paused for a moment, then continued. "If I close my eyes when I use my talent, sometimes it's like Mykel said. There's a pattern. I feed it and something happens."

"Feed it?" Mykel asked. "What does that mean?"

She struggled to absorb the fact that other people didn't see patterns. They had been apparent to her for so long, part of who she was. She often forgot that she differed from others in fundamental ways. "I guess it's like breathing on it. Or blowing on it. Hard to describe."

"Mykel. The rune on your hip," Bylo said, putting down his bowl. "Can you close your eyes and picture it again?"

Mykel closed his eyes.

"Feed it, like Nara said. Just a little."

Mykel gave them both an awkward look, then sighed and closed his eyes. Nara engaged her sight and saw Mykel's health rune flare hot and bright then fade back to its normal, subtle glow.

"Check your finger," Bylo said, pointing at Mykel's bandage.

Mykel removed the bandage, and the cut caused by the fishing hook had vanished, replaced by a thin pink scar. "It's gone." Mykel stared at his finger for a long time, his expression betraying both fear and amazement.

Nara wondered what this could mean. Bylo possessed no such ability, but he had been tattooed with strength runes. Was this what happened when a tattoo was inscribed on a cursed rather than a normal person? Would other runes behave in a similar fashion?

Nara did not enjoy the silence that dominated the rest of the evening. They finished the meal and prepared their bedrolls, but she was afraid to speak of what they had discovered, not knowing what it meant. The others apparently felt the same because few words were exchanged.

Bylo washed the dishes and Mykel lay down, while Nara sat

alone on the top of the nearby rise, watching out over the dark and silent road. She wondered what kind of strangeness would announce itself tomorrow, and what Mykel's announcement really meant.

Cursed. Was that a word they attached to people like him because they didn't know what else to think? He had done nothing wrong, nothing to insult Dei or the church, so why would they want to execute him? Could it be that he was just special, like Nara, but in a different way? A way they didn't understand?

After more than an hour sitting without Mykel, disappointment flooded her. She had hoped he would join her and keep her warm. In his absence, she drew her tunic tight to repel the chill, hugged herself with her arms, then glanced across the landscape again. Such a cold world this was, and she felt it more now than she ever had. They were on the run, fearful, and she could not defend them. Bylo's admonishments about her magic over the years seemed like a handicap now, and she wished she had defied him to practice her powers. If they were pursued by those who meant harm, skill with her magic would help face those challenges. Instead, she had been hidden and told to be quiet, never to call attention to herself. Foolishness.

She looked out upon the dark landscape. On a nearby hill, a hundred paces to the north, she noticed the glow of another person sitting at the base of a tree. She stood and walked a few steps toward the person, trying to get a better sense of him. A fellow traveler? The glow at once dimmed, and she almost lost sight of it. Odd. She wondered if she should alert Bylo and Mykel, then dismissed the notion; the person was causing no harm, and she shouldn't be afraid, should she? Instead, she thought of the stranger's needs. What might it be like to travel alone, sleeping on a hill in the dark, open wilderness? She was grateful to have companions and considered inviting the stranger to their campfire, then remembered how Bylo talked of pursuers and decided against it. She returned to the camp, found her bedroll, and lay down.

"Good night, Bylo."

His only response was a gentle snore. She looked at Mykel.

"Good night, Mykel."

More silence. A wind stirred up and whipped through the trees over their heads. Nara sighed, closed her eyes, and waited for the sounds of the night to coax her into a slumber.

Despite Gwyn's best efforts to suppress her own aura, the girl had still seen her. Was she a watcher, too? The camp remained quiet now, so she clearly hadn't alerted her companions. Either Gwyn was mistaken and had remained undetected, or the girl was naïve to the dangers that faced her. The latter thought invoked concern. The child would be easy prey to anyone who wished her harm, no matter what talents she might have, and getting her safely to Fairmont might be a challenge.

Gwyn thought back to her entry into the harbor at Junn. Having abandoned her boat on the docks, she had made her way to the nearby street and watched as they carried the young man into a nearby inn. That evening, she had dropped a note to Vorick from the local post office, updating him that they had arrived in Junn. She had written descriptions of the girl's companions but gave no details of their magic or the botched announcement ceremony. Even now, she wondered why she had left that out; such information would certainly be of value to the minister. Was she feeling protective of these strangers? If so, why? Perhaps it was because they seemed so different from previous enemies she had sought to capture or kill. They weren't royals or soldiers. Not killers or politicians.

Who would Vorick send to help retrieve the girl? She might be young, but her companions had talents and could be dangerous. She wondered again about the nature of their gifts. Although she hadn't seen the old man flare up since running from Dimmitt, she saw something strange from the younger man tonight. Sitting at the campfire, he lit up briefly, but there was an odd nature to the light. She had never seen a cursed survive an announcement. When they did, which was rare, the church put a quick end to them. Why were they so afraid? It seemed like their only talent was the ability to die on an announcement stage.

Gwyn ceased her ponderings and pulled a blanket from her pack to nestle under it for the night. Rest would be welcome, for tomorrow would likely bring another long day of sneaking and stalking.

15

ASUNDER

Fairmont
Ministry of War and Justice

Vorick's recent ambitions to expand the Great Land were reaping chaos, provoking barbarian incursions that grew in both frequency and severity. As he sat at his desk, the minister now wondered how he would manage the challenges. He looked for direction but settled on nothing, both his mind and his gaze wandering about.

Few decorations graced his cavernous office. The room had been designed with simplicity, allowing no distractions from the three large paintings set on each of the windowless walls. The murals depicted major cities in the land: Junn, Ankar, and, on the north wall, Fairmont. The remaining wall featured a single, large piece of glass and a beautiful view of Fairmont's wealthy garden district. The twin peaks of Mount Fi were visible in the distance—the room had been designed with the view in mind. He often gazed upon the mountain, hoping its majesty would inspire him to reach similar heights.

Despite the responsibilities of war and politics that required his attention, he was having a hard time focusing on them just now, his thoughts now wandering to the problem that Kayna was becoming. After seeing her with the queen, defiant and manipulative, he knew his control over the girl was slipping. When she was young, keeping track of her was simpler. Nothing about that girl seemed simple anymore.

Kayna had begun as a great project of a colleague, fifteen years ago. Bartholomew Lar, a renowned knitter, was the chief surgeon at the university hospital. He was an excellent physician and had been paid well for his efforts over the years—wealth that he spent on food and wine, often to excess. His wealth had led to boredom, however, and he had required an outlet for his restlessness.

Lar learned of a woman in a lower district of Fairmont, an impoverished region of town avoided by nobles and frequented by bandits. The woman was pregnant and anticipated a multiple birth. Her midwife believed the babies were breach, but when she tried to adjust them in the womb, they wouldn't budge. Conjoined, most likely.

The church viewed conjoined twins as an abomination, but Lar cared nothing for religion, was bored with his success, and held a reputation for trying new things.

He came to the laboratory while Vorick was performing an autopsy on a young lad who had dropped dead in the middle of the workday. Lar insisted on interrupting Vorick during the procedure, and Vorick cursed him for his audacity.

"Now, Nikolas. I need you now."

Vorick suppressed anger long enough to hear Lar's proposition, and the indiscretion lost its sting once Lar was given a chance to explain.

They left the laboratory and proceeded to where the woman endured a difficult labor. She was young, had no family with her, and they had asked no questions on the matter. This was an experiment and the lack of entanglements was ideal.

During the surgery that followed, Lar's suspicions were confirmed: the infants were joined at the spine. While each had their own spinal cords, many of the vertebrae were fused, and separation of the delicate bones would be difficult work indeed. Difficult work was Vorick's specialty.

Vorick cut the woman deeply, deliberately giving her no chance of survival. The subsequent surgery on the twins took hours, even with Vorick's skill, precision cutting that could not have been performed with normal tools. Between Vorick's cuts and Lar's knitting, they stopped the bleeding and repaired the separated tissues, blood vessels, and nerves along the backs of the tiny red-headed babes.

It would have been heralded as an astounding medical achievement of the age if not for inevitable condemnation by the church, which forced them to keep their elation secret. For months afterward, Lar and Vorick would meet over brandy to discuss the surgery, reliving their accomplishment in secret. It wasn't until several years later that the true consequences would become apparent.

Immediately following the surgery, a private nurse had cared for the infants in a secluded section of the university hospital until they could be transferred to another facility. It would have been foolish to put identical twins in the same institution with the scars they bore. Even an imbecile would recognize them as having been conjoined and permitted to live in defiance of everything holy. Vorick thought on how the discovery would have invited the wrath of the church, unraveling his own good standing with the archbishop of Fairmont. He had suggested they destroy at least one child to ensure no evidence of their sacrilege. Lar refused, and they sent each to an orphanage: one in Fairmont, the other in the Barony of Took to the southeast. Vorick wondered if Lar was being merciful or simply wanted to preserve his trophies.

It was later that the trouble began. About a year later, Vorick had attended a summertime dinner party where he spoke with a very drunk cleric. The old priest worked as a scripturalist for the archbishop, engaging in research efforts. The man specialized in the study of prophecy, particularly the book of *Cataclysmos*. Vorick and he talked about ancient scriptures, and Vorick tried to hide his disdain for religion. But the cleric's words startled Vorick, telling of ancient manuscripts and the illustrations in the margins. How runes changed the meaning of scripture text, something scholars were just beginning to understand in more detail. He spoke in quiet tones about twins, between generous gulps of wine, as if hiding an elaborate secret.

Vorick's interest was piqued when he learned that the archbishop had borrowed soldiers from the queen to scour the Great Land, gathering up old manuscripts and locking them away until they could understand the ramifications. Apparently, they didn't want someone professing to understand Breshi in a new way, then preaching a gospel different from the message they had practiced. Such an event could spell the end of the church, with splinter sects fighting for control of the hearts and coin purses of the people. The skullduggery of secret searches by soldiers to find potential treasures kept Vorick's attention. Nikolas Vorick collected things of value, and if these old books were sought by the archbishop, they must be precious indeed.

The conversation with the priest sparked a new interest in Vorick for all things religious. He hadn't found faith or anything so daft, but few things in the realm were able to manipulate human beings more than religion could.

He acquired manuscripts of his own, although he doubted their fidelity to the originals, and learned of errors in the standard theology of the church. The most profound of these was the well-known prophecy regarding the separation of the twins, found in *Cataclysmos*. Assisted by the words of the drunk priest, Vorick unraveled that the foretelling pertained to the expected destruction of the twin-peaked mountain southwest of Fairmont. Locals called it Mount Fi, but its official name remained the Mont of Phyili. Named after the Breshi word for twins, it was a central part of the apocalyptic eschatology ever present in church sermons.

The translation error meant that the separation of the twin peaks of Mount Fi had been misunderstood; the scripture actually pertained to the separation of a human being. At first, the error regarding the twins seemed of little significance to Vorick, regardless of the scholarly implications. Vorick didn't believe in Dei, Kai, prophecy, or any of that nonsense. But he acknowledged the power of superstitions. Of dreams. He had read the histories, and how seers often guided powerful men through visions.

As Vorick pondered the surgery more, thoughts of the twins came back in disturbing frequency. Perhaps some in the church had suspected the translation error and forbidden the separation of conjoined twins as a precaution to avoid fulfilling prophecy? Eventually, he suffered his own disturbing daydreams about the mountains and the babes, and the matter began to take on an urgency in his mind.

He tried to ignore the matter for four years, but the dreams continued and he was compelled to attend to them. It would take little effort to locate two orphaned children, scarred as they were. He started by going to the orphanage in Fairmont where they had placed the one child, only to learn of her abduction by an unknown party more than two years before. He became infuriated with his own delay, and even more angry at the orphanage. They had conducted little investigation and found no culprit, nor any leads he could pursue to find the babe. Apparently, losing an unwanted, scarred toddler was more of a blessing than a nuisance to such a place.

The disappearance of the first girl forced urgency upon Vorick, and he left the same day on horseback to Took, finding the other twin straight away. When the clerk demanded more money to allow the adoption, Vorick dropped a sack of coins on the desk and walked out of the building, meeting no further resistance.

He floated the story of the girl being his long-lost daughter, Kayna, stolen from him years ago by the father of his young bride who had died in childbirth—it had taken him years to find her and bring her home. Lar had recently died of heart failure, and there was nobody in his social or political circles who challenged the account. None who cared. They valued Vorick for his wealth and power, caring little about his personal life.

When Kayna reached age six, the first signs of trouble arose. She didn't mix well with other children, often sitting on her own, away from others. Seeing how she didn't make friends well, he thought a pet might be appropriate and instructed the nanny to buy a cat. One day, he came home from his office and found the girl in the backyard, the pet on her lap. As he approached, he noticed the kitten was motionless, but Kayna was examining a small cut on the top of her hand, blood evident.

"What happened to your hand?" he had asked.

"It scratched me," she said dispassionately. Vorick leaned down and picked up the kitten. Dead.

"Kayna, why is the kitty dead?"

"It scratched me," she said again and went inside the house.

Upon inspection, he noticed the animal's stiffness. The skin was dry and desiccated, eye sockets empty and black, as if it had been sucked dry of all life. Harvested?

In the months that followed, there were other manifestations. A boy who lived nearby made fun of Kayna. One day, the school sent her home after she punched him in the face. The next day, the boy's home burned to the ground and his family had barely escaped the conflagration.

In response, Vorick pulled her out of school, hired a full-time tutor, and spent more time with her. When he could pull himself away from his duties, he took her to a cabin on the outskirts of Fairmont. There, they would explore the things that made her unique.

At first, he thought she was blessed and became excited for her prospects. By the time she reached seven, she could store magic in a cepp. By eight, she generated heat like a flamer. It awed him that she possessed powers with no announcement, and requiring no receptacles of stored energy, instead using energy from within her own spirit. It was a chilling discovery for one who wielded no such advantage. He also found she could replenish her own energies by drawing them directly from living things: plants, trees, and animals. After doing so, she would sometimes be energized, manic with enthusiasm.

Vorick was unaccustomed to jealousy such as this. As the only blessed in a hundred years, with two magical gifts, his acclaim had been taken for granted, and his rise to power came as no surprise to anyone. Kayna's ability to exhibit power without a cepp, however, made his own talents look mediocre by comparison.

Little did he know at the time, that was just the beginning. By age ten, she manifested flashes of extreme strength, and by twelve she could see sources of magic, like a watcher. Vorick taught her to hide her aura so that she would not be easily spotted by other watchers. She was counseled to keep her magic secret, speaking of it with nobody. She took his advice so well she even stopped sharing with him.

But he did not envy her headaches. The pains would be triggered by activity or stress on her body, even hunger. The result was pitiable; the child would be paralyzed with pain and spend entire days in bed. Kayna's power came at a price.

Soon, Vorick added the Ministry of War to his control, a coup that fed his search for power far more than surgery, executions, or painting ever had. He wielded two gifts, and now he commanded two ministries. The additional influence allowed him to keep Kayna away from an announcement ceremony—he was fearful of what might be revealed in such an event.

Kayna's early troubles fitting in with other children evaporated as she learned social graces. She practiced how to give presents and how to make friends. She gained popularity with her peers, partly because of her beauty and partly because she always knew what to say. Kayna had developed skill in the delivery of compliments, and people were drawn to her for both her wit and her generosity.

But Vorick knew better.

Kayna had stumbled as a young child in her attempts to charm people, and he knew the charisma she exhibited at a later age was engineered by a mind becoming adept at the manipulation of others. She had learned these skills from watching him, replacing her clumsy, childlike imitations of his own repartee with more refined interaction. But Kayna had become no skilled socialite; she was a mimic. She was good, however, and it was difficult to tell the difference between the two.

It therefore came as little surprise that she was able to charm the queen. What vexed Vorick was that she had done so without him knowing. How had she gained access to the old woman? He thought Kayna was buried in scholastics, having little time for climbing social ladders.

Despite his frustrations, Kayna's manipulation of an old woman who had scant years until her death would make little difference in Vorick's own plans. The queen was demanding and proud but retained little real power. The establishment of the ruling council a decade ago—Vorick's idea—had all but removed the need for a monarch in practical matters. The queen still received updates on important events, had a representative on the council, and exerted social influence, but she no longer carried significant political concern. The heavy lifting of policy and government was now undertaken by the council.

In recent days, it was the chancellor who had become Vorick's biggest problem. Lord Archibald Holland held the highest position in the land and wielded more political power than Vorick. But the now-lengthy siege at Bann remained an open political wound, undermining Holland's policy record. The displeasure had trickled down, and just yesterday Vorick had received a reprimand for recent failings.

It was with Holland on his thoughts that Vorick penned a dispatch to General Cross using poignant words about urgency and decisiveness. He intended to convey no tolerance for further delay; victory in Bann was needed now. Mid-sentence, a loud knock at his office door startled him, and his hand faltered on the page. Irritated at the interruption, he dropped the quill. "Come in."

The door opened to reveal a tired-looking young man, clearly a messenger, holding a battered note. "Post from Dimmitt, m'lord."

Dimmitt? Where in damnation was Dimmitt?

Vorick took the post from the boy and set it aside, then reached into a drawer for a coin. He tossed a silver drachma, dismissing the intruder with a wave of his hand. Vorick then picked up the quill, intending to finish the message to Cross. Halfway through the effort, he looked aside, the messenger's battered note nagging for his attention. Dimmitt? With a frustrated scowl, he dropped the quill a second time and opened the note.

I found the girl.
Child of a laborer.
Island on the southeastern coast.
Dimmitt.
—GK

Vorick's eyes locked onto the first four words. All concerns about Cross' work in Bann, all his frustration with Chancellor Holland, even the irritations about Kayna and the queen vanished in the light of this revelation. He had been sending watchers to look for Kayna's twin for years but had held little hope that any would succeed. If the girl was anything like Kayna, she could grow to become a force he must have under his control, or his ambition would be for naught. Who knew what powers the girls possessed or could unlock for him? And what would happen if they fell into the hands of an enemy? To have a rival in control of such magic was unacceptable, and he vowed to act quickly. This new girl must be won, or she would be destroyed. His goals would not be unraveled by a misstep here, and there was only one man he could send on such a task.

He grabbed the incomplete message to Cross, crumpled it, and dropped it into the trash bin. After retrieving another sheet, he penned four words, affixed his signature then placed the message into a scroll case for immediate delivery.

16

STRANGERS

On the Road to Eastway
Eight Days after Announcement

M ykel found little joy on the dusty roads—long, boring days with many steps. They passed plenty of travelers, including more weary-looking soldiers that were likely returning from some campaign. Bylo moved slowly but had somehow found the endurance to walk well past sundown today, and when they finally stopped to set up camp and pull items from packs, they were forced to light their campfire in the dark. Dry firewood was hard to find, and the fire struggled, weighing down the mood of the travelers as it failed to dispel the chill in the air. Then the wind picked up and the flames danced sideways, disappearing from time to time into the wood that fueled them.

Mykel moved his bedroll closer to the warmth and adjusted the small logs, nudging them closer to one another and hoping to develop a good coal bed to last the night. Concerned the fire would go out, he found trouble sleeping. Poking the logs from time to time, he considered Nara, who lay only a few feet away.

So full of life, and everyone could see it. Bylo mentioned it often and would nod or wink at Mykel as she chattered away about something inconsequential to them but monumental to her. Trees swaying, clouds passing, or even a simple rainfall were so important to her. She was enchanted by the wildlife as well, even focusing on shrews that crossed their path, and he and Bylo smiled as she chased the tiny things. At one point yesterday, a bluebird lit upon her shoulder, pecking at the cloth of her tunic. Mykel had moved to shoo it away, but Nara stopped him with eyes of cold irritation. She then whispered something soft to the little creature and fed it a piece of biscuit from her pocket before it squeaked at her gratefully and flew away.

Lying by the campfire now, his thoughts wandered from Nara to the tattoo on his hip and the magic it carried. Its nature was not what he had expected; it was more like a tool. He was the source of power, and it was just a conduit. He wondered if Nara's magic was just as confusing to her. This was all so new to him, and he didn't know what to think. Could he heal just himself, or could he heal others, too? How badly could he be wounded and still survive? And what other tattoos might Bylo decorate him with?

He heard a sound, then saw two shapes approaching quickly from a copse of trees.

"Bylo! Nara!" He lunged at the fire to grab a stick partially buried in the hot coals. His night vision was ruined by the flames, so he didn't see the sword when it sprang out of the shadows and bit his belly. The pain was deep, and panic struck him like a second blow. The figure pulled the sword back quickly and dodged Mykel's clumsy attempt at a counterblow using the stick. The man lunged a second time, and Mykel ducked to avoid the swing of the sword as it nearly missed his head, but he failed to dodge the backhand move as the flat of the blade came at him. The impact of the steel sent pain exploding through Mykel's head, then everything went dark.

As she rose at the sudden alarm, Nara felt sympathy pains lance across her midsection, then she saw Mykel fall to the ground. She dropped to her friend and saw blood flowing from his belly. "Why?" she screamed at the man. The man smirked, sword down at his side, seemingly fearing nothing from Nara or Bylo.

What had they done to deserve this?

Bylo stood nearby, mouth agape, and Nara looked to him for help, but he didn't move. She then grasped at the nearest blanket and pushed it hard against Mykel's abdomen to slow the bleeding. Her friend's face was expressionless, his eyes partly open. Unconscious. She didn't know what to do and felt trapped between fear of Mykel's horrible wound and a desire to lash out in anger at these cruel strangers. Her heart pounded painfully. What should she do? What *could* she do?

She had magic if she could figure out how to use it. But she'd have to leave Mykel's side to do so, and she was not ready for that. The stress of the moment, the indecision, produced the beginnings of a headache growing behind her eyes.

Six men had now come into the half-light. Rough-looking, they bore the stench of men who had gone too long without washing. Several grinned cruelly, displaying mouths with few teeth.

Bylo fell against her, shoved by a man from the other side of the fire. "Take whatever you want," Bylo said. "Please."

Bylo applied pressure to Mykel's gut with one hand against the wadded-up blanket. He used the other to check Mykel's pulse, nodding to assure Nara that he was alive.

Nara focused on Mykel. "Wake up," she said, hand on the side of his face, not knowing what else to do. "Mykel, please."

The men rummaged through the camp casually. One of the ruffians—probably the leader—barked orders to search the surrounding area in case valuables were hidden close by. The men robbed them of their food and bedrolls, then searched them. One found Bylo's meager purse of coins and shook it with a disappointed expression on his face while another pulled Nara away from Mykel forcefully, then searched her far too thoroughly. The man's wandering hands disgusted her, and Bylo barked in protest, only to get a fist in his belly for the effort.

The one who searched Nara yelled out toward the trees. "Raq, when you get done over there, I have a present for ya." He grinned at Nara. "I know how you like redheads." A happy shout came out of the darkness. "Dibs!" but it was followed a moment later by a painful cry, a burbling sound, and a thud.

"Raq?" said the man next to Nara. Out of the corner of her eye, Nara made out a glint of steel in the darkness, and she heard another body fall.

The leader of the group came close to the fire, an irritated expression on his face. Not tall, but widely built, the man sported a shaved head that shone in the firelight. It was the only sign of personal grooming undertaken by any of the bandits. A dark, bushy beard and squinty eyes added to his menacing visage as he pointed at the man next to Nara.

"Go check on what's going on out there, Frank."

Frank gazed fearfully in the direction of where Raq had been searching the trees. "But…"

"Go!" ordered the bald man.

Frank did as he was told, but after a moment there were more sounds of struggling. The bald man shouted to another that Nara couldn't see in the darkness, more concern in his voice.

Nara glanced back and forth between Bylo, Mykel, and the bandits, confused as to what she should do. She engaged her sight to search the darkness, spying a single glow approaching from off to the left. It had the same appearance as the traveler that had camped on the hill last night, and she wondered if the person had been following them. She realized that she was staring and feared giving away her potential rescuer's position, so she turned back to Bylo and Mykel.

A cold, sharp pressure came upon her neck. The bandit leader, with a knife to her throat, yelled out, "Whoever you are, come for me and the girl gets it." Nara imagined the evil grin he must have been wearing on his face as he spoke. His warm, rancid breath washed across her cheek.

The man pulled Nara back, leading her away from the fire and into shadows, causing her to stumble on rocks and bushes.

Reluctant to cause pain but knowing that these men intended to deliver it upon her and her companions, Nara resolved to act, but as she closed her eyes, the blade cut further into her neck. Her concentration fled, replaced by terror. He pulled her back again, and she almost tripped trying to keep up with him.

"Let go of me," she screamed.

He laughed mercilessly and applied more pressure to the dagger against her skin. Nara squeezed her eyes shut against the pain, feeling blood drip down inside her collar, then down her tunic. She pictured the first thing that came to her mind: the rune she had seen on Mykel's hip. It snapped to the front of her thoughts, and she channeled energy to it.

The wounds on her neck and her palm warmed and tickled, flesh knitting together. She healed, and without a tattoo!

The neck wound had been shallow, certainly not life-threatening, and she had wasted time in the middle of this emergency. Eager to try something else, she looked at the ground beneath the feet of the man who held her fast. She reached to her inner power and willed the soil to rise and trap him in place. The earth ignored her call, cold and deaf to her summoning, leaving her with a sense of foolishness and a lingering fear that he would cut her even deeper for her secret defiance.

Nara looked over at Mykel, who remained motionless, in a fetal position next to Bylo. Her focus on him renewed the ache in her gut, sympathetic pains that throbbed with each of Mykel's heartbeats. Her friend was defenseless, in a dangerous place, when he should have been home, safe in Dimmitt. He was here, hurting, because of her foolishness. Because she had imbued the ceppit and nearly killed him.

She closed her eyes and reached her thoughts out to the man who held her. They came quickly back to her, and in a moment, she was feeling what he felt, a growing and odious combination of anger and lust, greed, and hunger. Raw, like that of an animal, but familiar, somehow.

Like an animal.

A flash of memory moved toward the front of her mind, of an encounter in the woods several years ago. An injured wolf and the anger and pain it had felt. And how she had calmed it with her own emotions. Did she dare try that now? Would that be an invasion of his privacy, a line she shouldn't cross? Then the cold steel touched her neck again, and she realized the foolery in her misgivings. If she didn't act, this man would continue to do far worse than invade her privacy.

Nara closed her eyes and sent feelings out to her captor, feelings of calm, of quiet, of stillness. It was difficult at first because she was experiencing none of those things, but after a moment, she was able to manufacture them. Thoughts of peace and fatigue, a desire to rest and to sleep. After a moment, the arm around her relaxed, the knife blade moving away from her neck.

"I... I'm dizzy," he said as he loosened his grip. "I'm so sorry," he said, confused, but no longer agitated. "I don't know what came over me... I... uh..."

Just then, Nara heard a sound of something whipping through the air nearby. The bandit leader shouted, dropping the knife from his hand and releasing her. She heard the sound of steel against bone as a groan escaped his throat and he hit the ground at her feet.

A strong hand gripped her by the upper arm and pushed her to the ground near Bylo. It was a woman!

The stranger stood in front of her, the grips of two swords visible in scabbards strapped to her back. She had brown, wavy hair with a few strands of gray. Wearing a harsh expression, her high cheekbones and blue eyes were illuminated by the dancing firelight, almost as biting as they were beautiful.

"Let me look at that," she said. She had a deep voice for a woman, and distinct, deliberate speech. She put her hand to Nara's neck, then shifted Nara's clothing, looking for a wound and finding none.

"Did he cut you?"

"No," Nara lied. "Who are you?"

"I'm Gwyn," the woman said. "And it looks like you are fine. Must have been his blood." She turned to Bylo and glanced down at Mykel. "What about him?"

Bylo lifted the blanket he had been using to apply pressure to Mykel's abdomen. The bleeding had stopped but the wound still gaped, a deep and dangerous cut. The edges of the flesh were splayed open, and severed muscles could be seen beneath. Nara cringed at the sight of Mykel's horrific wound and rushed to his side.

"He won't make it," the woman said to Bylo. "It's a gut wound; he won't be able to travel, and it's sure to become infected. I'm surprised it isn't still bleeding."

The woman grabbed a log from the fire and held it up high, one end flaming like a torch. Nara looked about to see several still forms within a dozen paces of the firelight. They were surrounded by dead men.

The woman turned to Bylo. "Help me get rid of these vermin."

"I'm staying with the boy," Bylo said. There was frustration in his voice.

"It's okay, Bylo. I'll stay," Nara said, laying a hand on Mykel's chest. After a moment by his side, her face went flush, her headache came on stronger, and her belly throbbed again with the pain of Mykel's wound. She rose and moved away a few steps to retch her dinner into some nearby bushes before coming back to his side.

Nara watched Bylo and the woman drag the dead ruffians away from the camp. Dead human beings. They were breathing just moments ago, and now they were silent. The contrast was horrible, demonstrating how easily life was snuffed out, but it could just as easily have been Nara, Bylo and Mykel that were being thrown into a pile. The weight of the moment hung heavily on her, tears threatening to make their presence known.

Bylo returned, gathered logs in his arms to stoke the fire, then sat to attend to Mykel. He tried to dress his wound but grunted in frustration. "Bandages will not be enough. I need dried gut. Or thread. To make sutures."

The woman shrugged and produced nothing to help. Did she have no materials, or simply not care?

"My friend is dying," Nara said. "Please help!"

"I have no suture material. Not that it will matter. It will be a blessing if he doesn't wake, trust me. It's over for your friend. And... I'm sorry for your loss."

Bylo looked at Nara, lips pursed, clearly sharing her sense of loss. "I'll bandage him tonight," he said. "In the morning, we will try to wake him. If he can wake."

Nara nodded. If Mykel woke, he could heal himself, as he did with his finger. But what if he couldn't wake? Could his new magic work while he slept? What if it didn't? She would heal him herself if she could. Knitters could do it, but she had never practiced such a thing and had no idea if her magic could work this way.

She closed her eyes and placed her hand on his hip. Through the dull pounding of the pain she shared with him, she sensed the health rune, blurry and indistinct. She tried to feed it, but it refused her, dancing away from her vision as if to tell her that it belonged only to Mykel. She poured more energy into it, but it refused her again. How did knitters do it? What pattern did they see when they practiced their craft? Oh, if she had practiced her magic instead of listening to Bylo's warnings, she might be able to save Mykel now. Gentle words meant for his ears escaped her lips, and she clung close to him, her hand remaining on his chest. His light was strong, so she took comfort in that, but this was far more serious than a finger sliced open by a fishing hook.

"Who are you?" Bylo asked of the woman who had saved them as they returned to the fireside.

"Another traveler," she said. "Headed north. I was camping a little to the south when I saw these men sneak toward your camp."

"Thanks for your help," Bylo said. "You can join us if you wish."

"I think I will, actually," she said, "Thank you." She then scattered the logs and began to stomp out the flames that were keeping them warm. "No fires at night. You're asking for trouble."

Bylo sighed, then covered Nara and Mykel with a blanket.

"Thank you," Nara said. She snuggled closer to Mykel, hoping to keep him warm now that they had no fire, and thought of the danger she continued to present to him. This journey had been to protect them. To hide them. She couldn't bear to think of being apart from Mykel. To lose him. For as long as she could remember, he had been near, by her side. Other than Bylo, he was the only one who listened to her when she was weak or laughed with her when she was strong. Was he now dying by her side? Was it her fault, somehow?

Her mind wandered back to Dimmitt and how Dei had saved them both on the announcement stage. If not for Him, they would both be dead.

Help us now, she prayed. *If you're there, please help us now.*

Imbuing the ceppit had set a chain of dangerous events in motion. When would the pain end? She adjusted the blanket and cuddled close to Mykel, eventually closing her eyes and falling asleep.

Gwyn placed her bedroll near the foolish travelers. She had not initially planned on breaking her cover, but when the bandits approached the girl and her companions, she had little choice but to intervene and save the minister's prize from calamity. As she now scanned the darkness for more unwelcome visitors, she spied the light of someone coming close. The figure moved slowly but deliberately, making no effort to hide their approach. Gwyn sprang to her feet.

"Gwyn," the stranger said in a low tone, not waking any of the others. It was a female voice. "Follow me."

The woman moved as if she was old or crippled, aided by a walking stick as she headed toward the nearby trees from which she had emerged.

Wondering how the stranger had known her name, and concerned about the implications, Gwyn followed. As they approached the trees, Gwyn considered drawing her swords.

"That won't work out well for you, Gwyn Khoury," the woman said.

Gwyn hesitated. How had she known her intentions? Or her name? Did she also know her mission? Gwyn could not allow it to be revealed it to the others. The woman must be silenced.

Gwyn stepped more quickly, intending to charge, but just as she came close to her target, the woman used her walking stick to lift a loose root in Gwyn's path. Gwyn tripped forward, a twist midair preventing the collision of her head on a rock. Just as she thought she had avoided injury, the walking stick came down on her nose with brutal force.

Gwyn shrugged off the pain and rolled to her feet. She touched her nose—it was bleeding and probably broken, the stinging pain affecting her vision. She wiped the blood on her shirt, then focused on her target. The woman stood calmly in front of her, a smug smile on her face. Gwyn planned a charge, intending to grab the woman's arm and take her down to the ground. She stepped lightly to one side, then to the other, using a fast but circuitous approach to keep her opponent guessing. The confusion would contribute to the chance of taking the woman off her feet once she finally closed the distance and swept her legs out from under her. Or so it usually went.

But this woman made no changes to her stance as Gwyn approached. She simply stood, knees bent, arms and shoulders relaxed. When Gwyn finally closed in, she reached for the woman's shoulder in an attempted to follow with a leg sweep. To her surprise, she grabbed nothing but air.

As Gwyn sailed by, the woman deftly pushed Gwyn aside, altering her trajectory into the side of a tree. The blow against Gwyn's rib cage knocked the wind out of her.

So little effort by the woman, and now Gywn was in heavy pain. This woman far outmatched her, even without a weapon.

"You fail to react to changing circumstances," she said. "You don't anticipate your opponent. You ignore your surroundings. The root and the tree have caused you pain." She chuckled. "Living things have always given you trouble, haven't they?"

The stranger's admonishments sounded like the scoldings of a master. Gwyn had seen weapon masters duel in Fairmont, but she herself had never approached the level of skill necessary to train with them.

"You intend to betray them," the woman said. "To give them to a dark man."

"How could you…?"

"Worry not. I won't tell."

Gwyn didn't know what to say. She engaged her sight and confirmed what she now suspected. The woman was gifted.

"Gwyn Khoury, you are not a very nice person today. Probably won't be tomorrow either. Just do me a favor."

Gwyn paused. It seemed as if the woman could easily kill her and still might. "Who are you? Who sent you?"

"Does it matter?"

"I want to know." Gwyn stood and brushed herself off.

"We don't always get what we want, do we? All you need to know is this: I mean you no harm. I won't interfere with your plans. Betray them if you must. Tell the minister what you will. But don't kill them yourself."

Gwyn considered the terms of the agreement. She had no intention of killing them, anyway. Her mission was to retrieve the girl. There was nothing to lose in this bargain, was there?

"They will suffer enough pain by your hand without you stabbing them in the back on top of it," the woman said. Then she walked away.

Mykel woke in the middle of the night to darkness, Nara's arm draped across his chest. A familiar snore revealed that Bylo was sleeping nearby. Mykel removed Nara's arm and put a hand to his belly only to find loose bandages. A dull, pounding pain in his gut grew intensely, bringing back memories of the recent attack and the blade slicing him open.

In the darkness, he carefully pulled up the bandages, sharp pains joining the dull ones as he did so, and his fingers found loose flesh and wetness beneath. Blood. He put his fingers over the tattoo on his hip, even as dizziness came over him. Then he felt foolish; touching the rune would accomplish nothing. That's not how this magic worked.

He dropped his hands to his sides, rested his head back on the ground and closed his eyes, trying to remember the shape of the tattoo in his mind. It snapped into his vision instantly. He gathered his resolve and fed the symbol some of his energy, breathing on it, as Nara said. He then reached down to his wound, the pain now less pronounced than before, but damaged flesh was still apparent. He laid his head back again, summoned the image, and fed it much more, so much that he felt lightheaded. He waited for the vertigo to pass and reached down again. The wound had closed. Healed. He pushed against it, feeling the taut muscle underneath the skin. There was no pain at all. Incredible.

A few rays of sun over the horizon announced the coming of morning, and a noise from the trees about fifty feet away caught his attention. Mykel extracted himself from the blankets and rose, feeling strong, if a bit sleepy. Was someone watching them? He walked in the direction of the sound, reaching down to grab a small log. If another ambush had come upon them, he would not be surprised again, though he would have preferred a sword or a club over this piece of wood.

A woman walked out of the woods just as he approached—a small woman, Nara's height but much older. She had short silver hair and a patch over one eye.

"Who are you?" Mykel asked, brandishing the log.

"He's doing fine without you."

"What are you talking about?"

"Sammy. He caught two coneys today."

Shock at hearing his brother's name stopped him in his tracks. He had dared not think of Sammy at length for fear that the grief would tear him apart. Fear of the authorities and the church barred Mykel from returning for Sammy, and confusion was now added to Mykel's angst.

"Who are you?" he asked again, his voice cracking with the effort, anger and frustration rising at once.

"My name is Anne. I'm a friend, Mykel," she said. "I'll help."

"I don't trust strange women who hide in the trees late at night and talk about my family."

The old woman chuckled. "Son, you don't trust anyone; it don't matter about the trees."

Mykel didn't know how to reply and took a moment to compose himself. "Have you come from Dimmitt? Are you sure Sammy's okay?"

"After your announcement, Lina Tibbins spent the whole day with him. He cried a bit. Then she kissed him." The woman smiled.

Mykel wiped a tear that raced down his cheek, and he failed to restrain a curious grin. "She kissed him?"

"He worries for you, but he'll be fine."

"Will I see him again?"

"Do you want to see him again?"

"Of course!"

"Then make it happen, young warrior. Nobody holds you back."

Young warrior? The woman turned to walk away.

"Where are you going?" he asked.

"I'll be back tomorrow."

"But wait, uh, I wanted to…" His words trailed off, mouth open. He dropped the log at his feet as she disappeared into the woods. What had just happened? Who was this stranger, and how dare she come into their camp like this, drop news of Sam she couldn't possibly know, then leave again? And how did she know about Lina, about Sam's traps and the coneys he caught? There was something odd yet powerful about the woman that seemed in character with his life of late. A new life of craziness. Of magic and fear and wonder. And danger.

After a time staring out toward the woods where the woman had departed, Mykel turned in a direction of his own. He found a fallen tree and sat on it, inspecting his belly in the growing light. A thin pink scar could be seen where the wound had been. He touched his mouth and wondered. Could he heal his scarred lip as well? He kept his fingers pressed to the lip and summoned the rune again, feeding it and hoping it would take away the blemish.

He moved his fingers over his lip. The tight, inflexible flesh had not changed; the scar remained. So, his magic could heal wounds but would not remove scars. Scars would always be a part of him, it seemed, a record of pain for others to see. His life would be very different from that of other gifted folks.

He didn't know how long he sat there, but as the sun began to fully illuminate the morning, he made his way back toward the camp to lie by Nara's side. She stirred as he came close, and she reached out to him. He grabbed her hand in his. "Go back to sleep," he said. "I'm fine."

They slept.

17

BARBARIANS

Bann – Frozen Lands
Northernmost Fort in the Great Land

General Zebediah Cross stood proudly at the front of his army, resplendent in the dark, plate-mail armor. He was a giant, well over six feet tall and almost three hundred pounds of muscle and bone. He stood out among men, even soldiers. With olive-toned skin, sporting long sideburns, even in his mid-forties he remained intimidating, holding the loyalty of his troops through action and violence.

Bann was the largest fortification in the Frozen North, a region known for tundra, mosquitos, and barbarian incursions. The siege should only have taken a few weeks, but these crafty, spear-wielding fiends had held on twice that long, led by a fierce chieftain who called himself Cnut Magnusson. Cross had better things to do than sit and wait for the light-skinned hairballs of the north to starve, so he had taken drastic action today.

Moments ago, he had sent most of his forces at a central tower, attracting the enemy's archers away from the nearby walls. It had left his true target unguarded. A single young flamer had then been used. She was a girl, no more than seventeen, and was guarded by shield men as she attacked the exposed tower while the enemy was distracted, destroying the fortification in a cataclysmic explosion that consumed the soldiers and, sadly, the flamer. But the cost had proven worthwhile when the stone wall came tumbling down.

With the breach now accomplished, Cross ordered his entire force toward the opening, flooding his superior troops into the now vulnerable fortification. He followed on foot.

Wherever the royal troops went, destruction followed. Without having to face an enemy on high walls, Cross' better armed, better-trained men in superior numbers were unstoppable. They suffered few losses as the enemy retreated or surrendered en masse. A small force of more experienced warriors was holding out in the inner keep, but in short order, Cross' men battered through the heavy wood barrier and exposed them.

As they entered the inner chamber, Cross spied six of the chieftain's private guard protecting him. They wielded spears, swords, and defiant expressions on their faces, but were vastly outnumbered.

Sunlight from windows high atop the chamber walls provided the illumination, showing a circular throne room. Fifty feet across, the room held a crude wood-and-stone throne in a well-lit area to one side. Magnusson stood in front of the throne, feet planted firmly and his eyes locked on Cross.

In his mid-thirties, the barbarian chieftain was easily a decade younger than Cross and stood a head higher, almost seven feet. He was thin but well-muscled and wore a brown beard and long, brown hair. His braids reached mid-back, and scars and tattoos festooned his bare torso. Studded-leather greaves covered his legs, and a bone crown sat upon his head. Ornate Roska battle symbols were painted in red, blue, and yellow on his face, shoulders, and arms. In his left hand, he carried a ten-foot spear, the head of which appeared to be fashioned from fine steel and must have weighed twenty pounds.

Cross stood fifty feet away across the large chamber, head to toe in dark armor, a two-handed sword resting in a giant scabbard across his back. His black-enameled helm, the visor flipped up so he could see, completed the contrast between the civilized general and the barbarian chieftain. For a moment, they stood and looked at each other, and Cross' heart began to beat faster in anticipation of the impending conflict.

Cross intended to meet his enemy on equal terms. There would be no surrender here. He would take the chieftain's life, but he would allow him the dignity of dying in combat before his men.

At Cross' direction, his soldiers stripped away his armor, piece by piece, while Magnusson watched, alert but unmoving. When the final piece of armor was removed, the men retrieved Cross' sword. Despite its monstrous size—six feet in length—Cross held the blade in his right hand unaided. Few men could wield such a sword two-handed, much less with only one, and Cross' strength was apparent to all.

The two leaders stood, each bearing his weapon of choice, ready to begin a contest of mighty men. Smells of blood and sweat filled the room, and Cross could still hear the occasional shouts from soldiers outside as they searched through the bodies of the fallen, looking for treasures.

Magnusson grinned. The barbarian lord took several steps forward, pointing his spear at Cross and shouting unintelligibly what was obviously a challenge, probably filled with profanity and several insults. Cross stood still.

Magnusson sped forward at a sprint, bellowing as he did so, holding his spear with both hands in a direct charge. He closed the distance between the two rapidly, yet the general stood his ground. Soldiers backed away as the giant men appeared destined to clash in outrageous fashion.

In the last moment before impact, not yet having moved an inch, Cross stepped deftly to the left, turning his torso as he dodged not only the spear but Magnusson's entire body. The chieftain passed by, missing his mark, and as he did so, Cross' left hand came up and pushed the chieftain's shoulder, throwing him off balance.

The chieftain tumbled forward, the tip of his spearhead catching between two wooden floorboards, wresting itself from his grasp. The entire maneuver took a fraction of a second and showed Cross to have a speed that far outstripped that of the taller, younger man he battled.

Cross took a single step back in line with his opponent, still holding the massive sword in his right hand. His smile invited Magnusson to try again.

The chieftain stood, retrieved his spear, and somewhat more apprehensively mounted another charge. Just before coming in contact with Cross, he slowed instead of continuing at full speed, then thrust forward with his left hand, sending the large sharp spearhead toward Cross' chest.

Cross sidestepped.

Magnusson thrust two more times.

Miss. Miss.

Magnusson swung the spear in a huge arc over his own head, then at Cross, aiming for the general's head. Cross ducked enough to dodge the spearhead, and the attack missed by less than an inch.

To an unskilled bystander, it might have appeared that the blow had come close to hitting its mark, but the men in this room were not fooled. They could see that Cross was so skilled, so in tune with the weapons and bodies in this fight, that every move was planned with no wasted motion or effort. It was a result of years of practiced battle, training, and a talent for death that defied reason.

The battle continued this way, Magnusson thrusting and swinging his spear, missing every time. Sometimes he fell because he overextended himself. Other times, Cross nudged the spear a certain way, or bumped the chieftain's leg, shoulder, or arm, forcing him off target. The bout was working perfectly for Cross' purposes, and he reveled in the action of it. Standing outside a wall for weeks, waiting for people to starve was mind-numbing. The action of this moment, however, was thrilling. It had the additional benefit of providing a reminder to his men of why he was the general and they were his soldiers.

In a demonstration of great endurance, it took nearly ten minutes of assaulting the air near Cross before Magnusson was exhausted, and then Cross decided to end the fight. The chieftain must have known that his end was near; he charged with his remaining strength, directly at Cross, spear aimed at his opponent's midsection.

Cross sidestepped, this time to the right. He twisted his torso as the spear passed by harmlessly, then leaped into the chieftain with his left hand balled into a fist. The thunderous impact of Cross' haymaker hammered the chieftain's head back unnaturally, the rear of his braided skull impacting his upper back, neck snapping. As the man's carcass fell to the ground, the bone crown launched from his head and skittered across the wooden floor to stop on the floorboards near the throne.

Not once in the duel had Cross used the giant sword held in his right hand.

The general walked to his men and directed for his armor and sword to be put away. Victory was complete, and he demanded an update as he made his way through the fortification, heading back to his command tent. "How many did we lose?"

A nearby officer responded. "Eleven infantry dead. And three shieldmen."

"Not bad. Fourteen and a flamer. Time to go home. We should have done this a month ago," Cross said.

Cross departed the scene, wearing only his tunic and trousers, and left the looting of the enemy to his soldiers and commanders. While he enjoyed the visceral thrill of combat, the puzzles of strategy, and the challenge of military leadership, he didn't like this part of war. The raping of defenseless women and beheading of their husbands and fathers held no joy for him, but his men had been obedient and deserved their rewards.

Upon arrival at the rear of the encampment, he entered his command tent and washed his hands and face.

"Letter, sir. Urgent. From Fairmont."

Cross turned to see a young messenger in heraldic garb tossing aside the drab green tent flap, a scroll case in his hand. He grabbed the case and waved a gesture of dismissal while drying his face with a towel. Once he had emptied the case of its contents, he noted a familiar seal on the enclosed scroll. The message inside was unusually brief.

Found her.
Return immediately.
—Vorick

Cross stuffed the scroll back into its case, then grabbed his travel pack and found a nearby soldier, inflicting orders on him to make rushed preparations. "I leave within the hour."

The army would follow in time, but this was something that required haste. All thoughts of triumph and glory from his victory were banished, inconsequential in comparison to this new task.

He must collect a little girl for his Lord.

18

KAYNA

Fairmont
The Estate of Lord Vorick

K ayna sat at the writing desk in her room as she perused her journal, a thick leather-bound tome given to her by Papa on her tenth birthday. Reading seemed like a fitting thing to do on a dreary Sunday evening.

Papa was nowhere to be found; he'd left her to find her own entertainment in this big house. Again. She was surrounded by fine things but no real people. There were just servants about, but according to Papa, they were small folk and didn't matter. They rarely spoke and didn't seem very interesting, so maybe he was right.

Porcelain figures of animals decorated the top of her armoire, perfectly straightened and meticulously polished. Gowns and night-clothes hung in an expansive wardrobe, with fine jewels in a nearby oak cabinet. The estate was grand and opulent, with high columns on the outside and expensive furniture within. She needed nothing, was challenged by little, but was growing increasingly aware that she was meant for something greater. The ambition had grown into a poignant dissatisfaction with her circumstances.

As she read, she relived the record of her thoughts on the thick vellum pages. An account of her life thus far - how odd it must be when compared to that of most young ladies.

"You're different from other people, Kayna," Papa had once said. "Keep those differences to yourself."

It was good advice and had caused her to season her appetites with a dash of caution. The stories about those who became enemies of the church or the throne were known. Stories of being different and standing out from the crowd. Stories that ended in death. Having a father who was in the business of delivering justice made those concerns even more salient, so she learned to keep secrets, even from him. Oh, she would answer his questions about her magic from time to time, absent the details. He took the hint and stopped asking. The distance in their relationship was not just because of magic, however. Although Papa's parents had apparently died years ago, he never mentioned Kayna's mother or any other relatives, and she often wondered why. Not that she needed family. Yet, she was curious, she had asked, and he had avoided the topic.

The only family she had was Papa, who was one of the wealthiest and most powerful men in the Great Land. When people talked about him, they did so fearfully. At first, she had thought such concerns silly. He made sure she had everything she needed, and she thought him to be a generous person. After a time, she came to believe that his care of her meant no such kindness. He was keeping her as one would keep a treasure. Or a trophy.

But the respect he held in the eyes of others had been earned because Papa was quite powerful. She remembered when they were on a walk one day, and a stray dog charged at them. He killed the animal from twenty feet away with merely a look. She didn't just see the power, she *saw* it. Papa flared with light, bright and blinding. A bracer on his left forearm, hidden under clothes, dimmed a little after his effort. Magic spent. But magic that could run out.

Kayna needed no such bracer, and this seemed to bother him. It had been apparent in his eyes when she practiced her talents as a little girl. She would throw fire or run quickly, lift something heavy, or summon the air. He would applaud her with his hands, but Papa's eyes held no such praise. Fear dwelled in them, and it was a transformational experience for a child to see that the most powerful man in the world was afraid of her.

Kayna thumbed through more pages, reading the words that once had seemed important enough to write down. Yet the pages had an emptiness about them. Things she could never write down because she had no memory of them. Things only Papa knew.

Her earliest memory was of riding on a wagon. It was a long trip, and it was cold. When it ended, she was in a warm house. That's all she remembered of the experience. Years later, she had asked about the trip, and Papa said it was to visit a dying friend, but Kayna wasn't so sure. It had been more important than that, but he wouldn't tell, and she might never know.

She moved forward a dozen pages and read some words she had written years later, at age thirteen.

I drained the life out of a tree in the neighbor's yard today. It took longer than I would have liked, but felt good. I hope nobody saw me.

Early on, she had learned that although she required no cepp, using her talents made her weak. Vulnerable. She loathed the feeling and learned to replenish herself by taking the energy from plants, but that was like drinking water through a tiny straw—too little energy and far too slowly. She moved on to small animals. Rats, cats, and a stray dog here and there. The rush of joy that came with the energy invigorated her, producing an emotional and physical high without equal. At first, she would shake uncontrollably after a draining, twitching with strength and fervor. Often, she would drain a creature even when needing no replenishment, merely for the joy it brought. And the drainings served to heal, lessening her headaches better than anything provided by Papa's doctors.

Sucking the life out of animals would be perceived by others as barbaric, so she took pains to absorb them quickly, rather than drawing out the affair to savor the pleasure. A quick death was better, wasn't it? Merciful? It was difficult to judge such things. In her classes, she heard stories about heroes, their trials and struggles, and the inevitable defeat of the villains who opposed them. The stories would depict the enemy as some dark force that preyed on the weak, delighting in suffering or some such nonsense. If anyone witnessed Kayna draining a stray pet, they would surely label her as one of these monsters. But the tales in books told it wrong. Perhaps Kayna's actions seemed villainous, but not like the stories depicted. Kayna didn't wish pain or suffering on others—what could be gained from that? Perhaps the villains in stories didn't feel anything at all; they were simply not hampered by the guilt and fear that plagued others. They shouldn't be despised, but rather envied for their freedom.

Then she would think of how much joy it brought her to drain living things and would become conflicted. Perhaps she was a dark thing after all, but if so, she carried no guilt in it. She hadn't created herself and therefore bore no responsibility for her nature.

But oh, how she differed from others. When other children had fallen and skinned their knees, they had cried or gotten angry. When Kayna incurred injury as a child, she experienced only pain, not anger. Although she hadn't enjoyed the pain and took measures to prevent it from happening again, she experienced little emotion about it. If another child tormented her, she simply made them stop. That may have meant causing them pain in return, but it wasn't to delight in their suffering, merely to bring an end to her own.

Kayna came to a section in the journal where she had written about an argument with Papa. About how he had called her dull. That was the word that bothered her.

Papa said something today. I didn't like it.
"You're dull, Kayna. Try harder to get along with people. They expect it of you. I expect it of you."

Dull. How cruel a word that was. It implied a lack of importance. A lack of passion. A lack of life.

But was he was right? She sometimes felt dull, as if she were a weak candle, with little flame, little power of her own.

Papa didn't want a dull daughter. He expected her to fit in with her peers and to advance among those in his social circles. He wanted her to rub elbows with elite friends and their children. There were indeed advantages to having people admire her and want to be around her, so she had complied with his wishes, if for no other purpose than to avoid being dull.

Learning how to be likable presented difficulties, however. She had to learn the many subtle hints and implications young ladies weaved into their conversations. She learned body language and noted how it often conflicted with the content of the words people spoke. And the power she held over boys. Oh, not every girl carried such power, but Kayna was beautiful, and the boys came around early and often. When a boy took a fancy to her, she could make many errors and still not lose his affection. She enjoyed having such power over people. It provided a sense of security. A sense of calm. It paled in comparison to her magic but was notable, nonetheless.

Kayna's dispassionate manner soon became an asset rather than a liability as it was easy to control herself. She never betrayed her feelings unintentionally because they simply didn't bubble to the surface uncontrolled. She experienced them from time to time, but like fish hiding at the bottom of a quiet lake, they rarely broke the surface.

A lack of passion would not suffice for Papa's ambitions, so from her early teens, she practiced her emotional reactions every day in a mirror. She learned to feign surprise, bashfulness, admiration, or outrage. She mastered delight, frustration, and sadness, and could soon cry on command, shedding as many tears as she liked.

Soon her reputation for being the witty, beautiful, charming daughter of Lord Minister Nikolas Vorick began to grow. Her influence grew along with it, and she received invitations to tea, to lavish parties, and to ride about the countryside with young noblemen bewitched by her beauty and charm.

Darin was just such a fool.

Albion Ripowski, the Earl of Katch, was an old man waiting to die far away in the southeastern part of the Great Land. Albion was a crafty man who rose from street rat to powerful merchant, then purchased enough land and bribed enough churchmen and government officials to become an earl. At the age of sixty, he acquired himself a young bride from the queen's court and produced a handsome young heir, Darin Ripowski.

Darin loved riding, hunting, and spending money on pretty girls. It made him an easy mark. They met at a spring social held by a new baron in the outskirts of Fairmont who wanted to make a name for himself. It was a lavish party with a juggler, a grand orchestra, games of croquet, and a card tournament.

Kayna had seen Darin playing croquet badly and poked fun at his failures while sipping sweetberry punch. After he abandoned the game and came to her side, he attempted to charm her with good looks and fancy clothes. Tall, blond, with a strong jaw and broad shoulders, he cut an impressive figure, even for a nobleman. Although only a few years older, he towered over her in height, yet despite his imposing physique, he was putty in her hands. She teased him and refused his overt advances, but eventually sat and had tea with him. Her coyness emboldened him, and following the event, he became relentless.

The flowers and expensive gifts arrived without ceasing. He invited her to countless gatherings, and she almost always refused. From time to time, she would bow to his request and attend a party, but would never be alone with him and would leave after a short time, hiring a carriage to take her home. Darin had recently invited her to a lavish ball, and she had accepted. She had dyed her hair black in an effort to look more mysterious. It suited her.

When the night of the ball arrived, she showed up in a beautiful but modest gown, her straight dark hair down to the middle of her back, a blue forget-me-not flower in her hair. She was stunning, and Darin had surely fallen in love. Yet she only danced with him once, then wandered about, talking briefly with others, including young men she knew to be his rivals.

Leading Darin on was entertaining. A growing cadre of lady friends encouraged her to refuse his advances most of the time but accept invitations often enough to keep him interested. Accompanying him to court functions, she had recently even managed to meet and charm the aging queen.

But in the end, nothing held the priority in her heart reserved for her true love, her magic. As she got older, she discovered more abilities but hadn't acquired much skill with their use and didn't know how to improve. There was no book that could help her with this so she remained alone in her efforts.

Early in the mornings, she would rise and go into the backyard to practice. Papa owned a spacious estate in the heart of Fairmont, including a high-walled garden where all sorts of flowers bloomed. It was there that she explored her gifts. It was only a year ago that she had written about her efforts to uncover these mysteries:

When I close my eyes, I can see the magic. And life. Plants are dim, but people are brighter. Papa glows very brightly, more than anyone else. I've heard of watchers and how they have a special sight. Am I a watcher, then?

But she was not a watcher. She was much more than that. She could float above the ground, closing her eyes and concentrating on the surrounding air to drift above the grass. What a wonderful feeling! Unfortunately, although the energy required was moderate, the mental effort of controlling the air currents exhausted her quickly. She wondered how high she could go, but feared a fall if distracted.

Fire was easy—pure energy that required little mental control. She would simply channel her strength and burn something. An overt act, absent of any skill or challenge, using fire seemed more like screaming than practicing the fine art that her magic was becoming for her. Besides, it would be difficult to hide the evidence of such efforts. Smoking, blackened things left quite an impression on folks.

Cutting was difficult. She would try to cut the branch of a small tree or a flower and would invariably destroy it. She could damage things, but she would bruise them badly or turn them into a sloppy goo in her hand rather than executing a fine cut. Everyone remarked on Papa's legendary work in the laboratory and on the battlefield, and Kayna envied the skill he held regarding this talent. She once considered asking him to train her in cutting, but had dismissed the thought. It was preferable that he didn't know about her ability in this area.

Kayna closed the journal and sat back in her chair. She wanted to learn more about her magic but didn't know what else to practice. In the past, she would sit in the garden for long periods of time, closing her eyes in a semi-meditative state, trying to explore what other talents she might have. She found it like stirring through a pot of soup while wearing a blindfold, feeling the bumps of potato or carrot or meat against the spoon. The talents were down there, but she couldn't quite get them on the spoon to taste them. Or perhaps it was like trying to wiggle her ears as a child. She couldn't quite make them move. She would work her eyes and jaw but was at a loss how to find the muscles that worked those ears. Then one day she found her ears, and they wiggled. The same would happen with her talents; she just needed to find them.

It was with this idea in her mind that she stood from her chair and left her room to go downstairs. Papa was gone, his rooms empty, but perhaps he held some clues therein. She descended the staircase into the foyer, then down the long hallway. She came near to a maid who was sweeping the floor, but the woman moved out of the way as Kayna passed by.

The hallway ended at two tall wooden doors. She tried the handle, only to find that the doors were indeed locked.

She knelt to look inside the keyhole. The lock mechanism seemed old and simple. She wouldn't be able to open the door without a key and forcing it would surely invite Papa's anger. He'd never struck her, but she didn't want to tempt his wrath. Papa was capable of things far worse than a slap across the face.

She walked back down the hallway and went outside. It was nearly dark, and the cool air was welcome after being inside most of the day. She moved slowly around the side of the house toward the windows of Papa's rooms. The windows were too high to reach, especially for someone as short as Kayna. But she was not limited by her height.

She looked about to make sure she was not being watched, then closed her eyes and summoned the air, just a little at first. It billowed her dress and blew her hair back, then she lifted a foot and felt the air become solid under her toes. She stepped down on the firm air and strengthened the summoning, then began to rise toward the window, holding her hands against the side of the house and walking them up the wood siding to keep her balance. When she arrived at the window, she reached for the sill and tried to lift the panel of glass. It didn't move. She peeked inside to see that the latch was fixed in the locked position. There would be no opening it from here.

Still using the air to support her, she moved laterally, looking at each of the latches. The second window was locked as was the third. But the latch on the fourth window was only partially moved into the lock position.

The wind faltered under her, and she realized that she had let her concentration slip. A fall from this height would do little more than twist an ankle and dirty her dress, but it would be unpleasant, so she closed her eyes and refocused the summoning, then looked again at the window.

If she pulled on the window, would it move? She tried, straining with all her might, and the window wiggled a bit but held fast. She looked through the glass at the latch again and noticed that the flat edge of the latch handle was wide. Like a sail.

She focused on the handle and summoned air, but this time, she commanded the air *inside* the room. She told it to blow up against the latch handle and focused it tightly, pulling up on the window as she did so. She strained and summoned and focused. And hoped.

The window slid open suddenly, and the surprise of it caused her to lose focus. The air left her, and she fell several feet to the grass below where she landed awkwardly on her backside. She stood immediately and brushed the leaves and grass from her dress. She was unhurt. Then she looked up at the window and smiled.

The air carried her up again, and she slipped into the room, closing the window behind her. Papa's bedroom was large and there were paintings on all the walls. She walked into the next room, his attached study, looking behind her to make sure that she wasn't dropping bits of grass or leaves from her dress. He had never allowed her in his study, and she felt a bit of a thrill as she committed the secret intrusion. She saw a big leather chair sitting prominently next to the window and imagined Papa sitting there, reading his important papers by the light of the sun.

She looked about the room and saw cabinets under the many bookshelves that adorned the walls. New tomes graced the shelves. She grabbed one to take a look. The pages were crisp and clean, with the smell of new paper, as if they had never been opened. She replaced it and grabbed another new book and perused the contents. Something about anatomy. She replaced it carefully.

Under the bookshelves were display cases, with velvet cushions and glass tops so that one could see the contents but not touch them. One case displayed a collection of pretty knives. Another had beautiful coins. A third had fine jewels: blue, red, purple, and several in varying shades of green. Some were cut, others were jagged and raw, but all were beautiful.

Papa collected things. New things. Pretty things. And he locked them up in places where he could see them but where nobody could touch them.

A wood table stood against the wall near the leather chair. On it rested three tomes and a map of the Great Land. On one end of the table, a silver goblet sat next to an amulet, its gold chain hanging off the side.

Kayna picked up the goblet to inspect it. Bronze wire was pounded into the sides of the metal in an odd pattern, and wine stains were evident inside. She set it back down and reached for one of the loose tomes. There were no words on the spine, but a peek at the contents quickly revealed it to be an account of council proceedings. Politics. Boring.

She put the tome back in its place and looked at the map. It depicted troop locations and notes about barbarian incursions. She recognized the scribbles in some parts as Papa's handwriting.

Her eyes scanned the room for something of value, but there seemed to be nothing of interest here, so she sat in the big leather chair with a huff. As she looked around the room again, the chain hanging off the table caught her eye. She leaned forward to grab it and dragged the attached amulet across the table until it fell into her lap.

The amulet was made mostly of silver, an ornate symbol in gold filigree on the face. The symbol looked like the runes on scripture scrolls or the icons hanging on the walls of the church. She remembered it now, a gift given to Papa by the archbishop a few months ago. She had attended the church service with him; he insisted that she be there. The old priest had preached about how Dei was the light of the world and brought heroes to protect the people. He mentioned Papa and his work to keep the barbarian invaders from destroying the Great Land and bestowed a special ordination on him as a protector of the faith. As the archbishop did so, Papa stood next to him on the stage, grinning proudly while the cleric draped the amulet around his neck.

She focused on the gold symbol on the front of the heavy ornament. It didn't seem quite right.

She sat in the leather chair to contemplate it further. Amulet in hand, she closed her eyes and held the symbol in her mind. Somehow, she knew that a squiggly line on the bottom was too ornate and the top bore too many dots. She pictured the rune how it should have been, and it snapped into her mind, hungry and longing for energy.

At first surprised, she calmed herself and fed it a bit of her power, only to feel the symbol come alive. She opened her eyes. Her hand glowed with a bright, scintillating multicolored light. There was no heat, only a tingling sensation as the colors danced about, making designs upon the walls of the study.

Her heartbeat quickened, and her face flushed with the thrill of it. Fearing she might be discovered, she shut the image out of her mind, and the light winked out. She whirled to look out the window, hoping she had not been seen. There were no onlookers beyond the high garden walls and her gaze turned back to the faulty symbol on the amulet's face. The symbols were keys that unlocked her magic.

I must have them all.

19

SANCTUARY

On the Road to Eastway
Nine Days after Announcement

Nara woke to the sound of someone rustling about the camp. She rubbed her eyes and sat up, yawning, then noticed Mykel doing the same. She then remembered his wound.

"Lie back down, Mykel. You're hurt!"

"I'm fine," he said, lifting his shirt. "I healed it when I woke up."

She moved her hand across the skin of his belly. Dried blood crusted in a few spots, but all that remained was a long pink scar. He could heal himself whenever he wants. And not just fingers!

"Wow, you really are a gifted, Mykel."

He gave a wide smile.

"Good morning," a strange voice said from behind them.

Their heads spun to face it. A woman with short silver hair at their campfire sat stirring something in a pot over the crackling logs. A patch covered one eye.

Bylo rose from his bedroll. "Who are you?"

"My name is Anne."

"I met her last night," Mykel whispered to Nara.

"I wasn't asking your name," Bylo said to the woman.

"Your questions will be answered soon enough. For now, have something to eat. Then we should go."

"We're not going anywhere with you," Bylo said, continuing his protest.

The woman looked away, staring at nothing for a moment. "Of course he's afraid," she said. "In your supreme wisdom, you swept him and the children up in a maelstrom and left me to deal with it."

Who was she talking to, by Dei? Was the old woman cracked? Nara looked to Bylo for direction, and he shifted nervously.

The woman turned back to Bylo. "You're being chased, young man."

Young man? Bylo was old. She really *was* crazy.

"If you don't hide yourselves better, he'll have you all."

"Who will have us?" Bylo asked.

"Does it matter? You're slow. Complacent," the woman said. She nodded her head toward Nara. "And you'll lose your girl if you're not careful."

Lose me?

They had all been on the edge of anxiety since escaping Dimmitt, and the ambush last night had rattled them even more. Now they had to contend with another stranger?

"We're just fine without your help, thank you," Bylo said. "And I don't appreciate you coming into our camp and starting a fire as if you belong here."

"You should stay off the roads, and it would do you even better to come with me," the woman said. "It's entirely up to you, of course. But if you'll let me, I'll see you to safety. And I'll see the children trained." She stirred the pot again, and some liquid spilled out onto a hot rock, then sizzled and evaporated into the air. "Oh, look what I've done."

"Train them?" Bylo asked.

"Yes, Bylo. Without training, they will not survive what is coming their way."

"You couldn't possibly know what is coming their way. Besides, I'm going to hide them myself."

"And where is that?"

"Well, I... Somewhere."

"Exactly."

Bylo bent over and began to stuff belongings into a pack. "We don't need your help."

The woman sighed and moved away from the fire. With her stick, she drew a symbol and looked back at Bylo and Nara. Bylo dropped his pack and came closer to see what she was doing. The woman finished the scrawl, then motioned to the dirt and drew a straight line down the middle of the symbol, bisecting it. Nara watched Bylo as recognition grew in his eyes.

"Is that enough for you?" the woman asked.

"What is it, Bylo?" Nara asked.

The woman kicked the soil, obscuring the rune.

"The human rune," he said, slowly. "From the scriptures of Cataclysmos. Phyili. Separated twins." He looked to Nara. "Maybe we *should* listen to her."

The woman may have been crazy, but her knowledge of their circumstances seemed to have quieted Bylo. Strangely, Nara felt a burden lift. A burden of loneliness, or perhaps one of vulnerability. With just the three of them, traveling for days, they had been easily attacked, easily harmed. Now, they had a bodyguard, of sorts. And an old crone who seemed to offer help. There was comfort in having someone else who knew about their troubles, as odd as these circumstances were. Someone who could provide direction, and maybe some answers.

A few moments later, Gwyn walked into the camp. "I gathered some berries for the oatmeal." She turned to Mykel. "You're looking healthy today."

Mykel lifted his shirt to show her. "I'm full of surprises," he said and took in a deep breath, puffing out his chest. Nara chuckled. Boys.

He turned to Nara. "What?"

"Nothing," she answered. "I'm just happy that you're okay."

"Amazing thing," Gwyn said. "Never heard of a gifted who could heal himself."

"Feeling well, son?" Bylo asked.

"Yes, Bylo, I am."

Bylo looked at the strangers, then raised an eyebrow at Mykel, wordlessly inquiring about their new visitors.

"They seem okay," Mykel said as he kneeled to put another log on the fire.

"You're awfully trusting today," Nara said, quietly. "That's different."

Mykel stepped back from the fire so that he could talk privately, and Nara followed. They moved far enough away so their conversation could not be heard by the others. "I've had a rough time recently," he said. "Maybe I'm looking at things a little differently."

"Or maybe you have magic now. And you heard someone talk about training you and started thinking about swords and fighting and got all excited about being a big, tough warrior."

Mykel cracked a smile but said nothing.

"Thought so," Nara said.

"I can heal myself now. Does that mean I'm still cursed?"

"I really don't know what the church will think, but they are crazy if they think the power to heal could ever be a curse."

"Maybe they won't want to kill me anymore?"

"They'll never find you, Mykel. I won't let them."

"If I can learn the sword, they won't get either of us."

Nara chuckled. "I don't doubt you one bit, Mykel Aragos. You're the most stubborn person I've ever met."

Nara turned back to the fire to see Gwyn pass some berries to Anne, who poured them into the pot and continued stirring. No words were exchanged, and there seemed to be an awkward tension between the two women. Nara watched from afar, wondering about them.

"Had you two already met?" Bylo asked Gwyn and Anne.

"Last night," Anne said. "It was an interesting conversation, wouldn't you say, Gwyn?"

Gwyn flashed an awkward look.

Nara wondered about the appearance of the two women in such a short time and whether they were in cahoots with each other. Anne definitely had a sense of authority about her. Had she pacified Gwyn somehow and taken her into her confidence? Then she remembered how Bylo had been subdued by a few scratches in the dirt and decided not to dwell on it any further. Strange times, but no stranger than they had endured lately, and these people might actually help them, as Mykel hoped.

"I have a place near the abbey at Eastway," Anne said as Nara and Mykel stepped back toward the fire. "Where you can hide, rest, and contemplate your next move. If you want to follow, I'm leaving soon. If you want to risk your lives on these roads, so be it."

Nara looked at Bylo, shrugging her shoulders and giving him a questioning look. Bylo turned away and sighed. He was clearly undecided on the matter.

After they shared the berries and oats, the woman grabbed the cooling pot and dishes, then walked away. "I'll clean up," she said. "There's a little creek this way."

Once the woman was out of earshot, Gwyn spoke up. "I don't like her."

"We're grateful for your help, Gwyn," Mykel said. "We really are, but I don't think this will be your decision."

"She is a bit off," Nara said. "Did you see her talking to the air? But she's interesting. And if she has some sort of hideout, maybe we should join her. Couldn't be worse than wandering in the wilds and getting ambushed again."

Mykel turned to Bylo. "You keep saying that someone is following us. The church or the authorities. We were going in this direction, anyway. To Eastway, right?" Mykel turned to Gwyn suddenly as if he just realized that he had said too much.

Bylo said nothing, but neither did he offer any protest. It was enough of a consensus for Nara, who hurried after Anne. "Wait," she said. "I'll help. And we're coming with you."

Bylo urged them to pack up camp quickly and they continued north, parallel to the road. It was slow going as they trundled through the brush, avoiding heavy woods and swampy marshes. Bylo had more difficulty than the others. Nara stayed close to him at first but soon after wandered ahead, becoming distracted with a conversation Mykel was having with Gwyn at the front of the group.

"Where are you from?" Mykel asked.

"The Barony of Took," Gwyn said. "It's near Eastway, actually."

"So, you were heading this direction before you met us?"

"I was going home to visit."

Nara wondered what sort of place such a fierce woman might call home.

"And where did you learn to use those swords?" Mykel asked.

"I was employed by the Baron of Took for some time. It was there that I received my training."

"You're a mercenary, then?"

"Something like that. More like a bodyguard, I would say."

"I would love to learn the sword. How long will you stay with us?"

"I suppose until you get where you are going," she said. "I'm not expected home for more than a week, and it isn't out of my way."

"We appreciate your help," Mykel said.

"You're welcome."

Nara hung back to report some of the conversation to Bylo.

"She's a bodyguard, Bylo. And used to work for a baron or something."

"Might be handy," he said. "But too much is happening, and too fast." He looked at Anne, who trundled along a dozen paces behind them. "Keep an eye on both of them, Nara. They might be helping us, and they might not. Hard to be sure."

Bylo was clearly still suspicious, and he had always been that way, but Nara was satisfied. With new allies, and Mykel's ability to heal himself, they would better be able to avoid capture, wouldn't they? And this strange old woman had offered to train them. Did she mean to teach them to fight or to use magic? She seemed to know about Bylo's runes, but did she also know about Nara's talents?

What would it be like to learn about magic? What would such training require? Bylo always seemed worried that Nara would be put into combat, forced to use her magic for war. But this woman seemed nothing like a warrior, and Nara wondered what it would be like to explore her magic in a way that didn't hurt anyone.

But they couldn't hide and train forever. Afterward, they'd have to do something, to go somewhere, to live. What would that life look like? Nara thought of her sister and wondered if she still lived. Perhaps she should go to Fairmont, to the orphanage where Bylo had found her, and begin a search for her sister anew. If she gained skill with her magic by then, maybe she could defend herself enough to avoid capture or being placed into the armies. Bylo seemed to think she was powerful, and hadn't he said exactly that?

"Nara, you aren't gifted. And you aren't blessed. I truly don't know what you are."

What could she do with her talents? She thought of how people in villages like Dimmitt starved while rich folks lived such happy lives. Could she change that somehow? There must have been a reason Dei had created her, a reason that was bigger than running and hiding, but it all seemed overwhelming, and she wondered if she could embrace it. Whatever it was that she was meant for, perhaps training would be the first step.

As she turned her thoughts to Anne, her curiosity was sparked. Who was the strange woman who wandered into their camp today, fed them some breakfast, and was now leading them off somewhere? How did she know things, and what was she getting out of this deal?

Nara hung back to speak with the old woman. "Where are you from, Anne?"

"North."

"How far north?"

No response. Nara hoped she wasn't annoying the woman. "Do you live alone?"

"Yes."

Anne clearly wasn't accustomed to having people around.

"I was just wondering about you. I hope you don't mind."

Anne turned to her and cracked a smile. "I don't mind. Go ahead with your questions, little one."

Nara warmed at the smile and saw Bylo slow his pace as if to hang back and eavesdrop on their conversation. He worried about everything, even an innocent conversation with an old woman in the middle of nowhere. Silly man.

"You live near Eastway?"

"Yes, I have a little place on a hill near the abbey."

"Do you work at the abbey?"

"Sometimes. They let me tend the grounds. Raking leaves and trimming trees... that sort of thing."

"Do you have a husband? Friends?"

Anne turned to her with an odd look, which turned into a smile.

"I'm sorry, I don't mean to pry, I just..."

"It's okay. You are the curious one, though, aren't you? No, I'm not married. And I don't have any friends."

"That's terrible. I mean, aren't you lonely?"

"It's not so bad."

Nara wondered what had possessed this lonely old groundskeeper to walk so far to meet travelers and guide them north. To train them? Keep them safe? It seems that Anne was keeping secrets.

Nara stopped asking questions and let the conversation die. After a few moments, she turned to look at Anne with her *other* sight. She looked different. Her light was brighter than a normal person. She was clearly gifted.

For most of her life, Nara had lived in a quiet, poor village, uninvolved with anything interesting. In the last few days, however, she had become surrounded by strangeness.

"Thank you for talking with me, Anne."

"You're welcome."

Nara moved faster to catch up with Bylo. "How are you faring?"

"I'll be okay," he said. "Have an interesting chat?"

"She's odd, but she seems nice. I kinda like her."

Bylo said nothing, and Nara didn't know if it was because he didn't like Anne or he was feeling discomfort from the endless walking. It didn't get easier for him, and he often mentioned the ache in his old bones, seeming to welcome every short break they took.

They passed the first night in a dark wood that was free of any significant underbrush. At Anne's guidance, they had placed their bedrolls close together for warmth but did not start a fire until they woke. "Too dangerous," she had admonished. After eating oats boiled with water from a nearby creek, they set about again.

It went on like this for many days. They were never more than a mile from the road but rarely came close to it, and occasionally they heard travelers and horses passing in the distance. They followed rivers and walked through woods, avoiding open meadows or flat plains where they could be spied from afar.

One day, Mykel stuck close to Nara, who had been unusually quiet. When she tired, Mykel reached out and held her hand, but she eventually stumbled and would have collapsed if Mykel had not caught her. She had succumbed to the pain of another agonizing headache, and Mykel must have sensed it long before she fell. She was grateful.

Mykel carried her for several miles to the shelter of a hollow near a creek where they finally rested. The pain in his arms and back must have been grueling, but he did not complain.

During each day's travel, Nara continued to have conversations with Anne as she gently probed the woman's past. Anne was resistant at first but eventually warmed up to Nara, engaging her on a deeper level. Anne told of the clerics in the abbey at Eastway and how she tended the grounds there. By the way she talked about the people she watched grow up in the area, Nara figured that she must have been employed in that capacity for a long time, but Anne didn't say exactly how many years. Anne also told stories of a young woman in Ankar, far away. She spoke of the peaceful, native peoples in the Windblown Wastes out west, the barbarians of the north, of old kings that never existed and more recent ones that had. Nara couldn't decide whether Anne fancied herself a storyteller or a historian, but there was much more to her than Nara originally deemed.

Through it all, Nara spent more time listening than talking. She did ask some questions, however. Questions about Dei, Kai, and the church. Others were about heroes and their sweethearts. Anne occasionally chuckled with a warm, hearty laugh, and Nara smiled whenever she heard it. Other times Anne would disturbingly talk to the air, or the sky, or a tree, with words that were alternating with irreverence, scorn, or resignation. Odd woman. As she talked, Anne would often go off on a tangent about a particular person, detailing what they liked to eat or who they often argued with.

After more than a week of traveling, they finally arrived at their destination, walking up the side of a large hill to a cabin set above the trees. "I built it here so I could see the horizon," Anne said to them. "It's breezy, but the view is worth it."

And it was. It bore a northern exposure that Bylo said would hinder growing crops, but the landscape took their breath away. To the northeast, one could see the Abbey of Eastway only a few miles away. Didn't Bylo mention that his friend, Brother Alen, was an abbot there? Anne had directed them to Brother Alen's doorstep, Bylo's original destination. Coincidence?

To the northwest, one could see the Twins, a grand sight. One mountain was flat at the top, the other sharp and pointed. Both were covered with snow and somewhat obscured by high clouds. They couldn't make out Fairmont from here, but the mountain peaks reminded Nara of how dangerously close they were to the seat of power in this land. Probably less than a week of travel and one could be in the capital with the queen, the archbishop, and much of the army. Just as quickly, those people could come here.

"On the south side of the hill there is a broad meadow where I plant," Anne said. Her manner seemed more youthful than when they had first met. "I could use some help tending it if anyone is willing. Green beans, squash, carrots, and potatoes. Lots of taters." A groan at the end revealed she had been overwhelmed with potatoes of late.

"Enjoy yourselves," Anne said, "but don't leave the hill. We sleep in the cabin tonight, and tomorrow we begin."

"Begin what?" asked Nara.

"You'll find out," she said, grinning.

After Nara left to wander the woods on her own, Mykel's curiosity about Anne moved him to spend some time with her. The two didn't talk much as they tended her garden, low on the southern side of the hill. He had always been drawn to physical activity and silence, and gardening provided both. Pulling weeds, he quietly pondered the differences between him and Nara. Not merely the contrast in their appearance and stature but in their manner as well.

"She can't love you yet, Mykel." It was the first thing he heard Anne say in over an hour. "Not like you want."

The sudden personal intrusion brought him pause.

"I know," he said. "I'll wait."

Over the days of travel, he had come to learn that Anne knew a lot. About everyone. Although he couldn't articulate why, he knew Anne was right about this, too. He and Nara were both young, but not as young as some lovers were. It wasn't their age that presented the problem, it was something more.

"What is it about her?" Mykel asked, eyebrows raised. "How is she so different?"

"Good question, and it's hard to put a finger on. Yet the separation of Nara from her twin has left a void in her. A brokenness."

"Yeah, she told me about a twin. She just found out recently. Bylo kept that from her for years."

He wondered what it had been like for Nara, so many years of wondering on her past, but Bylo refusing to share it. She hadn't spoken of it often, keeping her frustrations quiet. And her magic even more so. Magic! The friend he had spent so much time with had kept big secrets from him.

He wondered if he was untrustworthy in her eyes. Was there was something he could have done, or said, that would have encouraged her to share her burdens? Instead, he had been oblivious, always interested in their island adventures, or swimming, or climbing mountains. He should have listened to the concerns on her heart. He had been a fool.

"Sometimes she feels the pain of others," he said, returning to the work. "I've seen her tend to the hurts of animals and village kids. When they suffered, she flinched, as if she felt the pain herself. Is that part of her magic?"

"Yes. And it may be why she is slow to defend herself. As if she would suffer the pain either way and refuses to be the cause of it. You must protect her during this time."

"Will she ever be stronger?"

"It's not about strength, Mykel. In some ways, it makes her stronger than any of us. But I understand what you mean, and I don't know what to tell you."

It was the first time he had heard Anne say she didn't know something, and Mykel wondered if she really didn't know or simply wouldn't share it with him. "She's special," he said.

"I like her too," Anne said, smiling at him.

Evening approached. The sun dipped low on the horizon, and he and Anne had finished their work in the garden patch. They returned wordlessly back to the cabin. Mykel hoped for an early bedtime—the work had fatigued him, and he longed to sleep. As they walked up the hill, he thought again about Sammy, hoping his brother was not suffering Pop's wrath in Mykel's absence. He would return to Dimmitt someday. Soon, if he could.

20

PURSUIT

Kayna was sitting quietly on a landing above the queen's throne, thinking what it might be like to sit in the grand seat. How would it feel to rule the Great Land? Kings and queens of old had reigned supreme, and though political power largely rested with the council now, would it always have to be that way? The position of monarch, Queen, grand mistress over all, could it be hers? It presented an interesting temptation.

But Papa was in the way. Rich and powerful, the only blessed in the land would be an obvious barrier to her rise, and it would be years before she could surpass him. She didn't understand her powers very well, didn't know how to find more symbols, and there was nobody she could ask.

She would be greater than them all, eventually, and it was difficult to shake that ambition and find the patience she needed. And that was if Papa didn't have some purpose for her that she had not yet fathomed. She didn't know what plans he had, or really if he had any plans at all. He seemed content to keep her, as he did many other things. Art covered the walls of their home, he owned many businesses, people owed him favors, but he seemed to do little with any of it. It was almost as if the joy for him was simply *having* things of value. Was Kayna just another treasure in his collection? Another trophy to make him feel important?

As she sat there, a side door opened and Papa came in, looked about, but didn't see Kayna on the landing. She held her breath and instinctively suppressed her aura, hoping Papa wouldn't discover her. He walked over to gaze upon the throne from the floor below. After a moment, he looked about again, then walked up the three small steps and sat in the ornate chair, hands moving across the plush velvet cushion and gold-inlaid arms.

A few moments later, the main doors opened and General Cross came in, the large man walking quickly toward the throne as Papa stood.

"The latest message from Gwyn Khoury reports that they left Dimmitt and went to Junn eight days ago," Papa said. "The girl is accompanied by an old man and a young one. Find her. Bring her back. I don't care what it takes."

Kayna wondered what girl they spoke of. Who could be so important that Papa and General Cross had met in secret to speak of her?

"Minister, why not just have the watcher bring her back?"

"I'm not confident she would succeed, General."

The odd tone accompanying Papa's response struck Kayna. He had sent a gifted after a girl, but that wasn't enough?

"Understood. I leave in an hour. I'll send word to the windblown garrisons; many have tried to hide in the wastes. I'll order the garrison at Ankar to send men along the coastal trail in case they went west from Junn," Cross said. "I'll take the southern…"

"No!" Papa said. "Send no word to any of our outposts. Tell nobody. Take one man with you, no others."

"Yes, Minister."

———

After Vorick left the hall, Cross was left to wonder still more at the odd circumstances. He began to have the feeling that he was not alone. He looked around the room, then up. He found the culprit sitting quietly on a landing that led to an upper passageway. It was the minister's daughter.

Upon discovery, Kayna stood and gave a shallow smile, clearly having overheard their brief exchange. Did she know he intended to retrieve her sister? Vorick had voiced his interest in the twin years ago but had sworn Cross to silence on the topic. The secrecy, coupled with his concern that Khoury could not handle the mission alone could mean that the girl was important and not just because she was his daughter. She must also have magic. Did both girls have magic?

Cross gave a nod to Kayna, then turned to exit the room.

The trip south would be at a breakneck pace, for he had lost much time. He selected Lieutenant Jordan Almit to accompany him. Almit was the son of one of Cross' captains and one of the more obedient young soldiers assigned to the garrison at Fairmont. He was also an excellent rider, and Cross could not suffer a laggard on the road.

On the first day, they made more than forty miles before camping and the horses looked as if they would expire if they took even one step more. On the second day, they made another thirty miles before exchanging mounts with a farrier in East Junction.

They inquired along the way with everyone they met but gathered no evidence of their quarry. Cross remained confident that the watcher's information was solid, but circumstances could change and they were days behind.

Day three brought trouble. After Cross' horse threw a shoe, bad weather overcame them. Winds whipped through the trees and along the road, chilling both men and beasts. They limped into Took, but Cross necessarily took pains to avoid being noticed by anyone in the local baron's employ. A low profile was necessary; he had no desire to invite the minister's anger by raising suspicions among local nobles on what was supposed to be a discreet errand.

Cross sent Almit to the local post office to check for a dispatch from Gwyn Khoury, but the soldier found nothing. In an attempt to remain undetected, Cross spent time in a dirty inn on a bad side of the city waiting for the weather to clear. He remained secluded for two days, wary that his distinctive size and bearing would give him away. He was ill-suited for work such as this and cursed Vorick for sending him on this errand.

Almit made inquiries about their target but found no indication that Khoury or her companions had passed this way. When the weather persisted, Cross directed Almit to replenish their provisions and prepare to continue south, despite the hardship it would be with the wind and cold.

Even with new horses and gear, the weather slowed them significantly, and it took three days to travel to a small town called Glennway. Upon arrival, they headed directly to the post office, where Almit retrieved a dispatch that awaited them. Finally! In the note, Khoury disclosed that she was still following the group and that they were traveling north.

Could they have missed the travelers? Passed them in transit? They had closely scrutinized all on the road, but perhaps the group had stayed in the wild as they journeyed? That would have slowed them considerably but would also make them hard to find. Cross doubted this was the case—the watcher would have alerted him to that in the note, wouldn't she? Unless Khoury was not as loyal as Vorick hoped.

If they were going north, they may have veered east. Could they be going to Eastway? The abbey at Eastway was built around the oldest cathedral in the realm. Educated people knew of the early church's work with the translation of the Breshi language at Eastway. Perhaps the old man was a scholar—or maybe a cleric?

Cross decided to take the road to Eastway, which was less than a hundred miles away. He ordered Almit to send a note to update Vorick on their progress, then he resupplied for the next few days of travel. He would find the girl and take her to Vorick. Then he could return to his army and be rid of this bothersome errand.

21

TRAINING

Crone's Hill
Twenty Days after Announcement

The sun had not yet risen when Mykel was awoken by Anne.
"Today you run," she said.

"I don't understand," he said. "What do you want?"

"I don't want anything. Do you know what *you* want?"

It was a good question, and it took a moment to spur his sleepy thoughts into action. Running away from Dimmitt had not been his desire and had seemed like a reaction rather than a decision. She was offering him a choice? He missed Sammy but couldn't bear to leave Nara's side. He had magic, but it seemed of little use other than to keep him breathing. If he could learn to fight, with armor and weapons, to protect those he cared about, that would be something. Yes, that's what he wanted.

"I want Nara to be safe. I want to go back to Sam and keep him safe. People chase us. They hurt us. I try to fight back, but I don't know how. I can hunt, I can work, I can run and swim and climb mountains, but none of that matters because I can't *fight!*"

The exasperation in his voice drew a chuckle from Anne.

"That's better. I wondered when the warrior would show up. Would you like to learn to fight, Mykel?"

"Yes!"

"Then you run."

They ascended to the top of the hill above the cabin, where a few windblown birch trees stood at the center of a wide, flat area. They watched the first few rays of light from the sun illuminate the plateau, the hardy trees silhouetted against the orange and red colors growing on the horizon.

"Take off your shoes," she said. "You won't ever need them again."

He cocked his head with a quizzical look as he removed them, then gazed at the ground below. Sharp rocks and sticks were scattered throughout the windblown landscape. Did she plan on gentle exercises? He would hate to tear his feet up on this stuff.

"Now run," she said.

"Run?"

"Do you understand the word?" she asked.

"Where?"

"Around," she said, directing him to run around the trees. "Until I tell you to stop."

He started running around the trees, his feet occasionally landing on a sharp rock or stick. Sometimes it was merely uncomfortable, but other times a toe or his heel would hit something sharp, and pain would lance up his lower leg. The pain grew with each step.

"Wider," she told him. "Bigger circles."

He skirted the plateau's edges, continuing to run, pain increasing. This was training?

"Faster!"

He ran faster, limping as his feet bled from multiple wounds, and the pain invited doubts, doubts that threatened his success. Every young man sought glory, but that didn't mean they were worthy or capable of it. Could he really do this? He began to doubt that Anne was an ally and wondered if she was injuring him on purpose through this supposed training session. But his eagerness to learn how to fight overcame his misgivings, and he continued.

"Wider," she said again, and he made bigger circles, but he now encountered the descending edges of the hill, and his ankles strained to manage the angled slope.

"Faster," she said again.

Mykel began to tire, his ankles weakening under the burden, the soles of his feet hot with pain from the repeated impacts and cuts.

"Turn around," she ordered.

He turned to run the other way, straining his ankles in the other direction. Although the change was welcome at first, after a few moments his ankles began to throb again. Red stains marked the ground from previous passes over the same rocks with bleeding feet.

"Faster." She raised her voice. He had descended so low on his route around the crown of the hill that he occasionally lost sight of her standing on the plateau above.

"Wider!"

His lungs heaved, his legs weakened, and the ache in his ankles grew. Then he stumbled and fell, his knee impacting squarely against a rock, tearing his trousers. Blood flowed from the dirt-encrusted gash. He wanted to take a moment to catch his breath and recover from the pain screaming up his leg, but Anne sprinted to him, leaning over the edge of the hill, her face tight and angry, shaking her walking stick in the air. "Did I tell you to stop?"

"My knee," he said, protesting. "And my feet."

"Then fix them!"

The tattoo. Of course!

"You should never fear pain again, boy. You have a gift that reduces injury to mere annoyance. Few wounds will slow you again. Keep running!"

Anne's mention of his gift renewed his confidence. He wasn't cursed; he was gifted. And someone besides Nara now recognized that. He could do this; he was worthy. He had to be. Mykel started to close his eyes to summon the image and feed the rune but was startled by Anne's scream again.

"Go!"

"But I was going to…"

"*Now!*"

He ran. Bleeding. Ankles aching. Feet hot with pain. She followed from her vantage point on the edge of the plateau, screaming at him.

"*Fix it!*"

He closed his eyes to heal and lost his footing, crashing again to the ground, the wind knocked out of him.

More yelling. The stress was overwhelming his ability to focus on running, and confusion swarmed him as he struggled to understand what she wanted. He wanted to learn to fight. To protect Nara. He accepted that training would be difficult and was grateful for Anne's efforts, but he couldn't understand what she now expected, and this felt more like abuse than training. How could he heal if he couldn't stop?

An idea floated into his thoughts, pushing past the pain and confusion.

Perhaps he didn't need to stop.

He picked himself up again, running despite the agony, and tried to summon the image of the rune as he continued the path around the hill. It hid at the edge of his vision, and it was hard to visualize with his eyes open.

She compelled him to run faster, along an ever-wider path around the hill, descending as the incline increased, his lungs heaving with pain. Sweat dripped down his brow. He was accustomed to working; he often lifted heavy burdens for hours on end, but this was different.

He tried to feed the rune again, as much as possible while still concentrating on running around the hill, avoiding the trees, bushes, and rocks. He gave the symbol some energy, and it flared ever so slightly. The pain in his knee faded, evidence that his efforts were bearing fruit. The ache in his ankles then lessened. He ran faster, continuing to feed the rune, and the ache in his lungs let up, despite the fervor in his exertion. The sharp pains in his soles abated entirely.

Her voice cracked as she shouted at him, but she was far above him now. Anne's admonishments were pushing him to go longer than he thought possible, incurring pain and injury, but then healing himself. He learned that by flaring the health tattoo, he could work himself harder than ever before. Not only did it heal the pain in his feet and legs, it removed the pain in his lungs as if he had not been running at all. Could he run forever? What a feeling! He was not a boy anymore; he was a man, with magic and power.

He ran faster, descending the hill, and after a time he realized that several moments had passed since Anne had given any commands. He enjoyed both the silence and the wind on his face as he dashed up to the windblown trees on the plateau and back down the other side. He leaped and sprinted, and when he tired, he flared the health rune and became replenished. When he twisted an ankle or tore open his heel on a rock, or fell and crushed an elbow, he repaired himself. He didn't possess unlimited endurance, but those limits were no longer measured in the way a normal person would. He began to feel a mental fatigue, a spiritual emptiness growing within. When this reservoir ran low, only then would he stop. But not yet.

He marveled at the implications of his gift. Injury no longer presented great risk, as Anne said, and pain would no longer carry the same sort of fear for him. Mykel thought back to the lessons from school about the different gifts people might receive, but he remembered nothing like this. Could he be unique? He wanted to share this moment with Sammy, to tell his brother he had a real gift. He may not have become the bear his brother had hoped for, but in many ways, this was better. Maybe he really could protect Nara. He may not yet know how to wield a sword, but he would learn soon. No matter who came for them—the church or the army—it would be hard to kill him now, wouldn't it?

Eventually, he and the others could return to Dimmitt together, save Sammy, and find a place to raise him away from Pop.

Mykel smiled wide and ran ever faster.

Nara rose and walked out the cabin door, then stretched and inhaled the cool morning air. After a few moments, Anne stepped up onto the porch and stood with her, looking out to the northeast, taking in the sun.

"Hungry?" Anne asked.

"Oh, thank you, but no," Nara said. "I just woke." She squinted at the brightening landscape, and pain lanced across her vision.

"Noise and light are the worst, aren't they?" Anne asked.

"They are," she said. Especially in the morning. "Is it so obvious?"

"You don't hide your emotions very well."

"So Mykel says." Nara chuckled. "Sometimes he knows what I'm feeling before I do. Um, did *you* want to eat? I can get you something."

"Oh, I don't eat much anymore. Or often," she said. "*He* gives me strength."

"Dei?"

"Something like that."

"What do you mean?" Nara asked.

"He never told me His name."

"You mean, He talks to you?"

"Sure. He doesn't talk to you?"

"Nope," Nara said, disappointed.

"Maybe you're just not listening," Anne said.

"Yeah, maybe."

The light from the rising sun grew ever brighter on the horizon, and the Twins stood tall in the distance.

"Anne?" Nara asked.

"Yes?"

"Why am I so different?"

"You are quite the creation, little one," she said, putting her hand on Nara's shoulder. "Some of His best work."

"I used to think I was a demon."

"Nonsense. But you *are* different."

"Tell me," Nara said. "Please."

"Of course." Anne gestured to a couple of stools on one side of the porch, crudely made of sections cut from a tree, the thick bark surrounding the stools were distinctive of cottonwood. There were many cottonwoods in Dimmitt, and the sight of the wood made her homesick. They sat.

"Magic is from Heaven, Nara. It is divine energy."

Nara focused intently on the old woman as she explained.

"In the scriptures, you have heard how Dei and Kai made the world together, but Dei wanted to make humans as well."

"Yes," Nara said. "He did so over Kai's objections. Father Taylor taught this in scripture classes."

"Well, I am not so sure about all that scripture stuff. They get a lot of that wrong, but I am confident of this," Anne said. She adjusted herself on the stool. "Dei, Kai, whatever you want to call the Creator; He made us from Himself. We are part of Him."

"Okay."

"But He gave us bodies. Bodies to keep His magic, His self, His energy contained."

Nara was intrigued with Anne's different perspective on Dei, her maverick brand of faith. It seemed so different from what she'd heard before, and she was eager to hear more.

"But some of us are broken," Anne said.

"Well, lots of folks have problems, right?"

"No, I mean some of us are really broken. Flawed. Physically."

"Oh. My scar. My sister."

"Exactly. You were literally broken in two, by a surgeon. A single human being, in a sense, divided into two. Few could understand the significance. That body of yours is meant to contain the god-stuff inside you, but it has cracks. Leaking."

"I often feel broken inside. Is it that obvious?"

"I am broken too. Blind in one eye, and my other functions poorly at best."

"And Mykel. His mouth."

"Yes," Anne confirmed. "A cleft palate."

"So, only broken people have magic?"

"No. Everyone has magic, Nara. Everyone has a piece of the divine inside them. We are all of equal value, from the tiniest babe to the grandest king."

"But only the broken leak it."

"Yes. And just because someone has a physical ailment, defect, or disease doesn't mean they will bear magic. Gifted are rare."

"Will it all leak out eventually?" Nara asked.

"Oh no. If that happens, we die."

"That almost happened to us. In Dimmitt."

"Yes. At your announcement ceremony. But you didn't die. You and Mykel recovered. Although it takes time, you will recover the magic."

"Does Dei give us more when we run low?"

"Perhaps. I'm not sure how that works."

Nara looked out across the trees below, and Anne followed her gaze. Some birds flitted across their field of vision, chasing each other and chattering as they glided about. She wondered what Mykel and Bylo were doing, what they might think of Anne's words, and if it would change their view of Nara. Would they see her as broken, or did they already?

"I don't have a single gift," Nara said.

"No, you don't," Anne said. "You leak so much that your magic can take almost any form you wish."

"Does that make me dangerous?"

"You may be whatever you choose. Yes, you could be dangerous if you wanted."

"I don't want to. I don't want to hurt anyone. Ever."

"I know."

"Anne?"

"Yes, Nara?"

"What is *your* gift?"

"I'm very old."

"How is that a gift?"

"To be honest, I'm not sure," Anne said. "I've thought of it more like a curse."

"It's not just that you're old."

"No, I can see things."

"You don't use a cepp, though?"

"Look closer."

Nara looked, then noticed something glowing in Anne's hair. The hairpin. Nara reached for it tentatively, asking permission without using words.

"Go ahead," Anne said.

Nara removed the hairpin and held it gently.

"So faint, I barely noticed," she said.

"I don't need much at all. I don't need a harvester."

"How did you make it?"

Anne pointed at the pin, which was made of three small sharpened bones tied with twine. "See the middle bone?"

Nara nodded.

"A leg bone from a rabbit. I take the bone after a fresh kill, sharpen it, and put it in the middle. It lasts quite a while, and I don't need much for my talents."

"Wow."

"Seeing doesn't take much, and neither does long life. Once you learn to use your own talents well, you'll also be more efficient." She reached for the pin to replace it, but Nara stopped her.

"Let me," Nara said.

Reaching up, Nara combed Anne's silver hair with her fingers, preparing to replace the hairpin. She wondered how long it had been since Anne had felt the touch of another human being. She imagined that living here in this cabin had to be quite lonely, and Nara took an extra moment getting Anne's hair just right.

"Exactly how old are you?" Nara said as she finished. She placed the pin neatly and patted Anne's shoulder, then sat back on her stool.

"Very old."

"Gifted with long life, you must be an ancient, then?"

"Yes."

"Wow. I've only heard of them in stories. Old and with a special sort of vision," Nara said. She looked out at some tree branches that rustled as a squirrel jumped between them. "If you are an ancient and you have vision, you must be a blessed. Reminds me of the Oracle of Ankar."

Silence.

Nara turned back to her.

"*Are* you the Oracle of Ankar?"

Anne delayed before answering. "Not anymore. I'm just a groundskeeper now."

Anne's admission shocked Nara, silencing her for a moment. How had she survived her famous execution those hundreds of years ago? A longer silence came between them, then stretched and hung about the two as they looked out at the trees.

"The resurrection of Breshi," Nara finally said. "Here in Eastway. At the abbey."

"Yes. I helped a bit."

"Do they know?"

"The clerics at Eastway? No."

"Wow, Anne. They just think you're the one who trims the hedges."

"I do trim the hedges, and I'm darn good at it!"

They both chuckled.

"What do you see?" Nara asked, looking directly into Anne's one good eye. How did she see so much, and what were her limits?

"Sometimes I see what has happened... sometimes what is happening... still other times what will happen."

Nara shifted on her stool.

"You've seen things too," Anne said, "haven't you?"

Nara nodded. "But just a feeling. Not like you."

"If you practice, it will be clearer. I can show you."

"Maybe," Nara said, turning away. The curiosity of her magic's limits had grown in recent days, but it came with fear. Fear that she would hurt others, the way her actions had hurt Mykel at the announcement. And fear that she would be different. She was already different enough. The indecision was frustrating. Indecision borne of fear. Fear learned from a father who had sought to keep her hidden. Perhaps he was right and the fears brought safety, to others as much as to herself.

"You can't escape it, Nara—your magic. Your destiny is an important one. You can't run from it."

"I can try," Nara said softly, almost to herself.

"Yes. You can try."

They stopped talking, instead watching the sun finish its rise, full daylight flooding the sky and the earth below. Without another word, Nara left the porch and wandered into the woods, kicking at the twigs and underbrush. Anne had waited here for centuries, but for what? Or for whom? For Nara? Anne's words about Nara not being able to escape her role in the world seemed true enough. But they were also a call to something Nara was not yet ready for. She was more than a blessed, and much was certainly expected of someone like that. But she was just fifteen and shouldn't have to shoulder such a burden, should she? It didn't seem fair.

She thought of her history lessons in school. The Oracle of Ankar had counseled the most powerful nobles in the realm and was thought to be largely responsible for the reconstruction of the Great Land after the mysterious end of the Breshi civilization. There were stories written about her and her lover, the Guardian, the battles they led, and the peace they had finally achieved. Many feared she would take the throne and rule the Great Land herself. In the end, her enemies rose up and executed her for heresy. Or so the histories said.

The histories were wrong.

Anne may be the oldest person on the planet, a figure of the ages, mentioned in scripture and who once sat at the right hand of kings. How wise is she? What things has she seen?

Nara wondered why Anne was spending time with her, why Nara warranted the attention of such a person. She thought on her own magic and how it had always set her apart from others. Just how strong was it? What could it do?

As she walked deeper into the woods, she thought again of the night, not so long ago, when she snuck into the church and imbued the ceppit. She couldn't seem to let go of her regret over that foolish act, the act of a silly girl who thought she could save her village from poverty. She now knew that she had tampered with powers that she could not understand.

22

FLAY

Fairmont
Ministry of War and Justice

Vorick sat in his office, frustrated with the day thus far. Efforts fared poorly on the frontier, and the town of Kavalin had now fallen to barbarian incursions. Chancellor Holland had learned of it first and had just spent half an hour in Vorick's chambers berating him about incompetence, poor leadership, and no vision for protecting royal resources. Vorick had been required to summon all his will to restrain from cutting the chancellor down for his foolish impertinence. The man may be chancellor, but he continued to breathe only because of Vorick's ability to manufacture patience.

What might have happened if he had murdered Holland as the man stood there, red-faced and screaming? The queen would not have been pleased, nor would the council, but what could they really do about it? If they brought him up on criminal charges in a civilian court, Vorick would tamper with the proceedings. Wielding so much influence, it would be easy for him to sway the jurors. If they chose to charge him in a royal court-martial, the council would serve as the jurors. That would be even easier—many of the council ministers owed Vorick substantial sums of money.

Vorick had been patient in recent years, but suffering lesser people was increasingly difficult and he often engaged in fantasies of forcefully seizing the chancery, or even the throne.

His vainglorious daydream came to an abrupt end as he remembered the problems out west and the fact that his general was indisposed, unavailable to lead the troops. Vorick would be required to attend to Kavalin himself. Frustrating.

Tired of dwelling on problems of state, he chose to think on more encouraging things. Perhaps this would be a good time to check on his latest project?

He left the ministry hall and grabbed a chestnut palfrey from the hitching post outside. He hopped up onto the saddle and kicked the mount to a gallop, heading straight into Fairmont. A few minutes later, he arrived in front of a small, stone, single-story building in the craftsman's district. No sign adorned the front, its windows were boarded up, and the edifice looked scarcely bigger than a storage shack. Trusting this project to a single unguarded man was risky, but secrecy was paramount. Neither court nor council could know what they built.

He tried the handle, but it was locked. He pounded his fist against the wooden door, announcing his presence. Moments later, it swung open, and a bearded, dust-covered man in his fifties held the door with one hand, an oddly shaped, steel tool grasped in his other.

"Check before you open up!" Vorick pushed his way inside. "Don't just admit anyone who comes knocking!"

"Sorry, sir."

"Finished yet?"

"Pretty close, Minister," the man answered, then latched the door after Vorick stepped inside.

The work area comprised a single room. The only illumination came from a few strands of sunshine peeking through cracks in the boarded windows, assisted by a flickering lantern on a worktable.

Vorick strained until his eyes became accustomed to the dark scene. Months had passed since he had last checked on the man's progress.

"It's been a long time, sir," the man continued.

"I'm here now."

Vorick retrieved a piece of coral from a worktable. It was very light.

"I hope you haven't wasted any more material," he said, putting the coral down again. "This stuff is hard to come by."

"I've wasted a lot." He pointed to a bin in the back of the shop.

Vorick stepped closer to notice oddly shaped pieces of bone and coral, along with piles of powder and shavings. He sighed, hoping the expense would be worth it.

During his early efforts as a harvester, Vorick had learned that charging a cepp with energy drastically reduced its weight. He took to researching the matter at length to learn that a one-pound bone cepp lost more than ninety-five percent of its weight when fully charged, and that was just the beginning. The same cepp, when charged with energy, became as hard as steel. Rocks would shatter against the resilience of the imbued receptacle, and blades would glance off without leaving a mark.

At first, he was amazed that nobody had exploited this before. Such a find would give one the ability to construct armor or fortifications of unspeakable strength. Then, the economic realities came to bear, and he understood the problem. Imbuing an entire suit of armor would take so much energy that one would be required to kill many human beings, a herd of cattle, or hundreds of trees to fill it. Harvesters would charge a fortune to complete such a task.

A suit of imbued armor would weigh almost nothing, however, providing invulnerability and unlimited energy for its wielder's magic—a dream for one such as him. His own physical shortcomings prevented him from bearing the weight of chain or plate mail, but a light suit made of charged materials might be possible. Such power and legitimacy this armor might bring him. Not only in the minds of his peers, but in the eyes of his army.

But he faced no mere engineering challenge. There was the issue of how to maintain the charge. Cepps leaked, and so would armor.

He experimented with materials for receptacles, learning that although crafters employed bone most often as a base material, which was far superior to wood, it still leaked too much. A simple unadorned bone cepp lost half of its energy in under a week, even if unused. Petrified wood cepps, although stylish in court, retained the energy no better than bone.

But coral was different. Although brittle when initially cut from the reef and remaining so until charged with power, coral became more resilient than bone once filled with energy. And coral retained the magic. Once filled, coral cepps lost very little energy over time, maintaining most of their magic even a month after being charged.

Unfortunately, coral was more precious than gold. Prized as a premium material for manufacturing cepps, the richest of the gifted nobles snatched up the material when available, making it exceedingly rare. Vorick purchased some but never found large enough pieces to fashion armor plates and soon realized he would have to hire someone to search for a fresh source. Five years of costly exploration passed before his contracted divers found a generous reef off the southern coast and cut the materials he needed. Fortunately, Vorick had acquired a vast fortune, accumulated over the years, initially through his harvesting efforts, but later through his business ventures. When the only blessed in the land declares himself your business partner, wealthy men comply and fork over their profits.

As the Minister of War and Justice, he had access to the best craftsmen. This was detailed work, however, and choosing the right armorer for this project was imperative. Fashioning a suit of coral armor would seem like madness to most men, and Vorick took care with those he had approached. After much deliberation, he chose Master Declan Triff, a hairy, unmarried, middle-aged man who had opened his own shop years ago. Lords and knights knew Triff not only for his hardy suits of armor but also for the beauty of his work. In Vorick's estimation, the man thought of himself less as an armorer and more an artist, displaying patience for fine craftsmanship that Vorick could take confidence in. He had not been disappointed.

Through trial, error, and the waste of thousands of gold crowns in discarded materials, Vorick and Triff worked in this secret location with large chunks of red coral that the minister charged with a small amount of power. They sought a delicate balance, charging the materials enough to withstand the crafting process without breaking, yet still brittle enough to be shaved and molded. After several years, the armor was nearing completion.

The crafting process had not come without frustration. While Vorick wanted his treasure to be completely fashioned of coral, practicality had intruded. Triff complained about not having enough access to Vorick, who traveled often on ministry business, making him unavailable to charge or drain a certain piece to the level necessary for the work. When fastening pieces together, there was often a part that needed to be installed and some shaving that needed to be done. To accommodate this, Triff used uncharged bone pieces, primarily around the edges where the plates of coral met one another in hinges, hooks, and catches.

Then there was the undershirt.

One could not wear any sort of armor without a layer of protection beneath. A layer of heavy padding guarded the wearer against the chafing and damage caused by chain or heavy steel. The sharp edges of coral presented an even greater threat. Unfortunately, the padding required would need to be thick and cumbersome. If not overcome, the genius of Vorick's project would be for naught.

Silk was the answer.

Soft and comfortable, tailors employed the costly material to craft the most elite fashions. One would find silk dresses and shirts on the richest of nobles, but it was far too fragile to withstand direct contact with coral. Unless it was charged with magic.

Silk was a natural material produced by living things—worms. In that, it shared a similarity to wood, coral, or bone, and its nature allowed the storage of energy. That energy then strengthened it. Silk bled out quickly and needed to be charged often, but that presented no problem for a harvester like Vorick. The armor itself was capable of holding so much power that bleeding small amounts to keep the silk strong would be of little consequence.

In the end, they had fashioned a devastating tool that would be nearly weightless, yet impervious to physical blows. And comfortable—or at least they hoped so. When Vorick first donned the armor, they needed pulleys and ropes to bear the weight of the thing so he wouldn't be crushed underneath.

"Is it in the closet?" Vorick asked.

"Yes," Triff said, pointing to a locked door in the back of the shop. Vorick worked the hasps to pull the door open. Triff brought the lantern closer, illuminating the small room.

"Took me an hour to move by myself," Triff said.

The suit hung on pegs drilled into the stone blocks of the back wall. The light danced in the chamber, flashing off the plates of armor, caressing the red coral, unveiling hints of the skeletal armature and giving an ominous appearance. It was armor like no other, the most powerful protection in the realm. And easily the most expensive.

But it remained heavy. Vorick wondered if it would be possible to don the armor and walk anywhere at all under the load.

Reaching out and touching the plates, he sensed the magic inside. There was some magic, but the armor was mostly empty. He had drained the stored energy in his bracer cepps many times to fill the coral plates enough to work with them but not yet enough to make the armor wearable. Filling it completely would take a huge sacrifice. Perhaps he could march into a poor district of this town, slaughter thirty or forty beggars, and the deed would be done.

But he would suffer a cost for that kind of slaughter—a blow to his reputation and perhaps even the loss of the church's approval. That was unacceptable. A legitimate way to harvest human beings would be difficult to find, however. Then he realized his foolishness. The perfect opportunity was staring him in the face.

War.

He would take the armor out west, lead the charge against the barbarians in Kavalin, and the project would be finished.

"It's ready," Vorick said, still looking at the armor, Triff at his back. "And I'm taking it."

"Sir, there are still too many bone hinges and hooks. I have been replacing them with coral, but you said…"

"It's ready!" Vorick cut him off, still staring at the majestic suit of armor, imagining its potential.

Triff put down the file and the piece of coral he was working on. "Yes, sir."

Vorick turned around and faced Triff. "And the sword?"

"In the corner."

Vorick turned back with the lantern and moved to the corner of the armor closet. A blade and scabbard leaned against the wall.

As beautiful and powerful as the armor had become, this was the prize that seized Vorick's fancy. A sword symbolized strength, and men wore swords to assert their authority and station. While he often carried a thin rapier at his side, Vorick was useless in sword-play. He couldn't move quickly enough, couldn't leap forward to direct a thrust or dance sideways to avoid one from an opponent. His sword served primarily as an ornament, and he would lose a duel with even the most incompetent of swordsmen unless he employed magic.

But this sword was different, having been decorated with a special rune.

He came upon the rune years ago after acquiring an old copy of the scriptures *First Light*. In that manuscript, he found a design that looked familiar to him. The text of the scriptures spoke of how Dei and Kai formed the earth from the darkness of chaos. In the margin near this passage stood a beautiful but simple pattern, inked with a fine pen. It wasn't a perfect analogue, but it had been very similar to the pattern he often saw in his mind when he used his cutting talent. The chaos rune.

One day a few years ago, he was experimenting with the resilience of magic-infused bone and marveled at how well bone knives held an edge after being filled with energy. On a whim, he drained the knife of energy and carved the rune from *First Light* into the side of a dull blade. The rune was not complex, and although he had not developed a marked skill with inscription, he had seen the design in his mind for years and possessed a strong sense of how to shape it.

Etching the pattern on the blade did nothing at first. Once the blade was charged, however, the dull knife became devastating. When pressed against a surface, it destroyed flesh, wood, and even iron. He had transferred a gift to a physical object!

Oh, it wasn't refined in its effect. The blade didn't cut like a razor, not the way Vorick had learned to employ his talent. The weapon didn't cut at all, actually. Without a mind to direct the power, the knife simply disrupted everything it touched, tearing materials apart, and leaving destruction behind. The damage it inflicted reminded Vorick of early experiments with his talent as a teenager when he would bruise flesh or objects, or even liquefy them. Still, steel breastplates and leather cuirasses would become like butter under a blade such as this.

The implications of the discovery were at first wondrous but rapidly became a concern for him. If such weapons were created, they would make an adversary much more formidable, minimizing his own advantage. He resolved to keep this a secret and promptly destroyed the experimental blade.

Now, however, he had need for a sword to complement his suit of armor.

Although Triff was no weaponsmith, he was wonderfully talented, and Vorick had come to trust him to a degree. Besides, revealing these secrets to another craftsman was a risk; Vorick wished to bring no more into his confidence. One really should hire a weaponsmith for sword-making, but the challenges associated with crafting a powerful sword were more often in the development of alloys, of weight and balance, and the ability for the steel to maintain a fine edge. None of these would be a problem with this sword, so Triff's skills were sufficient.

The craftsman's attention to fine detail was a blessing, and the ivory sword he fashioned was a beauty. Almost three feet long and carved from the tusk of a walrus, it was a work of art. A giant ruby graced the pommel, and ornate scrollwork danced along the slightly curved blade above the rune that was engraved near the hilt.

Vorick set the lantern down on the stone-tiled floor, then reached for the sword in the dim light and tightened his hand about the grip. Little magic remained in the blade, and he would have to be careful for fear that it might become damaged. Gingerly, he pulled it from the scabbard, revealing the ornate scrollwork and the imposing rune inscribed on the white gleaming surface. *His* rune.

After stepping back into the room, he rested the scabbard on a nearby table, then made some sweeping cuts at the air with the blade. It was heavy, and his arm tired under the strain. He was tempted to slay Triff right there, which would allow him to charge the blade and reduce its weight to that of a feather, but he still needed the man. Instead, he channeled power from the bracer on his arm, fed it into his sword, and felt the weapon lighten immediately.

Much better.

Moving the magic gave him a thrill, as it always did, but the feel of the ivory blade in his hand gave him an even greater pleasure. If a real man carried a sword, what would you call a man who carried a talisman such as this? Perhaps Vorick was becoming much more than a man.

The blade needed a name. He thought of what would happen when this sword faced battle against normal soldiers—or even knights. Armor would be rendered useless. Shorn apart. Torn. Their skin would be pulled from their bones. Render? Shatter? Then he had it.

Flay.

He smiled with pride.

"I'll be back later today. Box up the armor and get it on a cart." Vorick tossed his rapier aside, tied Flay to his belt then walked toward the exit. "And pack your things, Triff."

"Where are we going, Lord?"

"We're going to war."

23

TRUTH

Crone's Hill
Twenty-One Days after Announcement

When Bylo rose, a knot in his lower back complained loudly. Anne came into the cabin a few moments later.

"How are you doing?" she asked.

"I'm tired, Anne. Walking for so long these past days. I'm not accustomed to it."

"You've done well," she said. "But there is more to do. Please come. I want to show you something."

They left the cabin and walked up to the plateau. As he followed her, Bylo thought of Phelan. It had been a long time since he had a friend. Perhaps Anne could be one. At first, he hadn't trusted her, but she had done nothing to harm them in the recent days, and much to put them at ease.

She took a seat on a large rock and looked over the north side. Bylo sat next to her. The Twins were in view, but he wasn't gazing upon the peaks. Instead, he fixed his eyes on a figure running through the trees below at a full sprint. It was Mykel, and Bylo watched for several minutes as the boy raced about, moving up and down the steep slope. Despite his speed, he didn't seem to tire.

"Impressive, isn't he?" she asked.

"How is he doing that?" Bylo asked, amazed.

"He's a different sort of person than you have seen before."

A couple of times Mykel leaped off a high rock or precipice, then crashed onto rocks or fallen trees in what was clearly an intentional, seemingly suicidal leap. He would then rise, walking slowly for a moment, then race off in another direction, having already recovered from the fall, disappearing into some thick trees, only to emerge later at breakneck speeds.

"The health rune," Bylo said. "It's become permanent."

"Yes," Anne said. "But he needs another."

"Another?"

"I am hoping that you will give it to him."

"Which one? I'm only good with a few. It needs to be perfect on the first try, or it fails."

"A new one." Anne said, smiling.

Getting Mykel's health tattoo correct had required a combination of lots of practice and plenty of luck. She wanted him to learn a completely new one?

"And it will be the hardest one you've ever done," she said. "Don't worry, you'll have plenty of time, and you won't be inking in the dark after running scared for miles, either."

How did she know about the escape from Dimmitt? Had Nara told her? What else did this woman know?

"Please find Nara and bring her to the garden," she said. "I have something to show you both." She started to walk away, but then stopped and turned. "And Bylo…"

He turned to face her.

"You should tell her."

"Tell her what?"

"About the tavern keeper."

Bylo's blood went cold.

"Nara should hear it," Anne continued.

"It'll crush her," Bylo protested.

"She deserves the truth, Bylo. Especially from you. You're the only father she's ever had. Don't let her remain deceived."

"That will be hard, Anne."

"No, it won't, it's truth. Truth is easy. Give it to her, Bylo." Then she walked away.

His heart skipped a beat with the familiar words. Did Anne really believe that truth was easy or was she using the words to remind him of Nara's request? To echo the child's desire for truth, or perhaps to demand it on her behalf?

In so many ways, this woman reminded him of Nara. They were pragmatic in their views, so simple in how they looked at life, and there was a power in their personalities Bylo found compelling. He continued to sit for a time, then stood and slowly descended the incline toward the cabin. After a few minutes of searching, he found Nara sitting on a stump in the woods nearby, twisting a twig around her fingers and whistling.

"Hello," he said.

"Good morning," she replied, turning and smiling at him. "How did you sleep?"

"Well enough." He joined her, sitting on a nearby fallen log. "What are you doing?"

"Just thinking."

"About?"

"Nothing, I guess."

"I do that sometimes," he said, waving a hand in front of his face to ward away a mosquito. "Anne wanted to show us something. She's waiting at the garden."

"Okay," Nara said, but didn't rise. Bylo took the hint and waited with her.

"Bylo?"

"Yes?"

"On the boat, when I told you about how Dei saved us."

He braced himself as Anne's words hovered in the back of his mind. Nara looked up at him, but Bylo said nothing, raising an eyebrow in feigned curiosity.

"You didn't answer and told me to go to sleep. As if you didn't believe me."

"It's not that," he started to say, wanting to shut down the conversation. "It's just that..."

He stopped talking, not knowing how to proceed. Fear of crushing Nara's spirit stalled him, but Anne's appeal now urged him on. That amazing woman had foreseen this conversation. "It didn't happen like you said."

Quietly, as if she was expecting this, Nara whispered. "Tell me."

Bylo took a deep breath as he steeled himself to this task, despite the pain he was feeling for her. She did deserve the truth. She had always deserved the truth, and he had repeatedly chosen to keep it from her.

"Amos, the tavern keeper. He reached down to help you and Mykel when you fell," he said. His voice cracked as he spoke, grief for his little girl welling up inside him. "You touched him, and..."

"Amos is dead, isn't he?"

A tear rolled down her cheek as she looked up at him. He would have given anything to ease her pain, but this wasn't a skinned knee that he could bandage. "Nara, I..."

"When I thought it was Dei, it wasn't. It wasn't Him at all."

She buried her head in her hands. "I killed that lovely man."

"It's not your fault. Bad things happen, and we can't always stop them."

"Then whose fault was it?" There was anger in her voice.

Bylo could find no words. She had killed to save her friend. She had stolen an innocent man's life, leeching it like some sort of monster, and it had been horrible to watch. Had she suspected the truth but failed to admit it to herself? Did she now think herself evil? He remembered the conversation he'd had with her back in their cottage when she had asked if she was a demon. How she must now be suffering, her faith in Dei shattered and old fears rekindled. He felt his own faith shake a bit. Dei had never seemed like a warm, close friend. Years in the monastery, years of study and reverence had given Dei an aura of majesty in his mind, but He had remained a distant figure. A powerful god who was worthy of worship, but not warm. Never warm. In a way, he had been envious of Nara in this. She had always seemed to have a simple faith as if she saw Dei as a father. Or a friend. Perhaps her feelings about Dei would change, now.

She stood, and Bylo also stood. She made no noise, but a flood streamed down her face. She moved in for an embrace, and his arms were ready to receive her.

"I know it hurts, dear. I am so sorry." They stood there a moment, quietly. "I love you, my dear. Truly. You are an angel, a divine blessing to me. Amos' death was an accident. An accident that saved you and saved your friend." He hugged her tighter, then continued. "You lived, Nara. Mykel lived. A horrible, unfortunate day, yet you both lived! Maybe Dei was involved after all. Maybe He has more for you to do in this world, and Amos' sacrifice was part of that, somehow."

Bylo wanted to share his own feelings about Dei at that moment. He wanted to communicate that, despite his own desires, the Almighty always seemed to be working on something bigger than Bylo's own petty goals. That even as a grown man, he had felt like a leaf blown about by a raging wind. He had never possessed control over his life and had come to believe that control was just a fantasy. Humans played a role written for them long ago—none had a choice in the matter. Instead of talking, however, he just held her. After a time, she pulled away.

"Anne asked to see you," he said.

"Not now. I need to be alone."

She looked directly into his eyes as if pleading for help. The misery on her face tore at him, then she turned away.

Nara walked deeper into the woods, away from the hill, the cabin, and everyone else, eventually finding her way to a stream. She took off her shoes and dangled her bare feet in the water, which was unusually warm.

So, Dei didn't save her after all, and she was a killer. Why couldn't she have seen this without Bylo's help? Had she longed for contact with the divine so badly that she had let her vision be clouded? Had she invented Him in her own mind to find peace? Perhaps Bylo's efforts to keep her magic secret were born of wisdom after all, and fearful thinking was safe thinking. The thinking of good people rather than that of foolish children.

Amos Dak—he was the life of many village parties and had been loved by many. She had spent no time in his tavern, and certainly didn't know him well, but his bouncing belly and loud jokes had wrangled more than a few laughs from her. Taking his life hadn't been her intent, and Bylo's words helped ease the pain. At least *he* didn't think her to be a demon.

She wiggled her toes in the moving water, the smooth stones warm and pleasant under her feet. The combination of the water and the quiet sounds of the forest refreshed her and she lay back, resting her head upon some soft moss on the creek's side. Sunlight filtered through the leaves high above, flickering as the breeze moved the trees and branches, changing the way the light fell upon her.

Are you up there, Dei? Or are you just a figment of my imagination? A silly tale for children and fools?

She didn't expect Him to answer, and if Anne was right, she didn't know how to hear Him, anyway.

Just then, the wind picked up, and the high tree branches separated. With no leaves to block the sun, the light streaked onto her face, startling her, but she dared not move away from the brightness. On the contrary, she wished she could move closer to it, so hungry was she for the comfort. She closed her eyes with the pleasure and felt a peace come over her. Her body relaxed. A tingling sensation started behind her eyes, moving to her spine, slowly, then along her arms and out to her fingers. She felt her muscles relax, and she sank into the mossy bank of the creek, anxiety slipping away. Then it was over. The wind was gone, and the light faded. She opened her eyes to see that the sun had resumed its flickering dance among the leaves.

Was that an answer? She lay in place for a while, but the wind did not pick up again, and she wondered if it had been her imagination. So short was that moment, so brief that joy, and she longed for it again. Was that what Anne was talking about? Had Nara just listened to Him?

She didn't want to leave the creek just yet, but she heard the voices of Bylo, Anne, and Gwyn moving through the woods far upstream. After putting her shoes back on, she stood. She looked about, not knowing why, but reluctant to leave this place. But there was nothing here but water, moss, and trees. She smiled.

"Thank you," she said out loud.

It was a steep hike, but she found them up at the creek source, a hole in the ground where the water bubbled up under a sheer rock face. The stone wall above was in shadow, covered with layers of moss and vines.

"Sorry," Nara said. "I needed some time."

Bylo smiled tenderly.

"Where is Mykel?" she asked.

"He'll be along soon enough," Anne said.

"I brought some snacks," Gwyn said, reaching into her pack. She produced a couple of bread rolls with cheese and warm meat stuffed inside. They smelled great, but Nara wasn't hungry. "More coney," Gwyn added. "Fresh from this morning. They are all over the area."

Bylo grabbed a roll, but Nara refused. Instead, she turned to Anne. "You had something to show us?"

"Yes, I do," she said. "Right here." Anne smiled and turned toward the flat wall. "Now, where were they?" she said, peeling moss and pulling vines away from the side of the hill as if looking for something.

Gwyn drew a sword and helped Anne scrape away the vegetation, revealing a crack in the rock. No, it wasn't a crack; it looked like a seam. Manmade. Nara moved closer. The vegetation was so thick, it must have taken decades or longer to grow.

Gwyn continued to scrape away the moss and pulled on the vines, revealing a recessed stone door with no hinges. Might it slide to one side and disappear into the wall? Nara saw no handles, so how could one move it? The slab would be very heavy. Then she noticed two ornate runes, one to the left of the door, the other to the right. A white-colored grout filled the etchings.

"This one opens the door," Anne said, pointing to the left rune. "This one closes it," she said, pointing to the rune on the right.

"Bylo, this should interest you. The door is powered by water pressure in a chamber carved deep inside the rock." Smiling with satisfaction, Anne turned to her companions, then tapped a rune and looked at Bylo. "Remember this. This is what it looks like."

Bylo stood slack-jawed. "The water rune," he said, clearly amazed. Nara remembered how often that design had frustrated him in his studies, and she shared his joy at the discovery. What other secrets did this place hold?

"Anne?" Gwyn asked.

"Yes?"

"How do we open it, and what is inside?"

Anne's face screwed up with disapproval. "We don't open it, Gwyn. Nara does." She turned to Nara, expectantly. "And I'm not going to tell you what's inside. You'll have to see for yourself."

The look on Bylo's face showed that he was wondering how Anne could know what was in there. Clearly, nobody had been in this cave, or whatever it was, for many decades, perhaps even centuries.

"Anne," Nara said, "how long has it been since you were in there?"

"A long time."

Nara then turned to the others and raised her eyebrows, wordlessly bragging that she had been privy to Anne's secret.

"Young man..." Bylo said, clearly putting it together. "Nara, you knew?"

Nara smiled then looked to Gwyn, who held an amazed look on her face, mouth open.

"You're an ancient?" Gwyn asked.

Anne smiled humbly but said nothing in response, turning to Nara. "Get to it, girl."

Nara knew what was being asked of her. The rune somehow opened the door, and she was to imbue it. Anne wanted her to use her magic, the same magic she had used to kill Amos Dak. But nobody would die today. This was just a door, and she was the only one who could open it.

She moved to the rune on the left side, then placed her hand against the cold stone, feeling the emptiness within. She closed her eyes and poured out some of her energy.

The ground shook with vibration as the sound of grinding rock startled them. Nara pulled back, moving closer to Bylo. The grinding stopped, leaving only the sound of the stream behind them.

"More," Anne said. "Don't be shy."

Nara moved again to the rune, closed her eyes, and gave it a solid push of power, much greater than before. Only partially covered by her hand, the design began to glow brightly in response to the surge of power flowing through it. The ground shook again, the vibration continuing much louder now, and the four of them took a step back as the door slid to the right.

The sounds of water rushing beyond the wall reached their ears. Nara expected cool air, dust, and the odors of centuries of silence, but instead, the group was buffeted by a warm wind. Fresh aromas of flowers and grasses filled Nara's nose as if there was life within. A long hallway carved from the rock was visible. It was not roughly hewn, but instead, smooth. Expertly crafted. Runes in the walls faintly illuminated the tunnel.

"Amazing," Nara said, looking at the glowing symbols. She had never heard of such a thing, not even in stories. "Where do they get the power?"

"Come," Anne said, stepping into the tunnel ahead of them. "I'll show you."

24

LIBRARY

Fairmont
The Estate of Lord Vorick

I t had been several weeks since Kayna discovered the light rune, and she was obsessed with the search for new symbols. Knowing that important images came from holy books, she now found an interest in religion, attending mass, and reading scriptures when she could. But her interest was born of ambition, not of faith. There was power to be had, and she would find it.

As she used her sight to visualize the runes in the margins of the holy books, she discovered they were often wrong. Most of them possessed more complexity than the one that generated light, but she couldn't discern the proper configurations in her mind and produced no results. She must have been lucky with the rune of light and her irritation was growing.

Although she had encountered problems with the runes, she was having success at church. Clergy had caught sight of her efforts, probably mistaking it for actual faith, and she had recently accepted an invitation to study with Father Todd, a junior priest in his early twenties. Twice a week, Kayna, Father Todd, and several older parishioners assembled to study in an office near the cathedral and talk about Dei. They used new manuscripts, but all the symbols were wrong. In fact, the newer the books appeared, the less precise the runes seemed. Where did they keep the old books?

One evening after a scripture study, she lingered with Father Todd when the others had departed, asking him questions about prophecies found in the holy books. It was obvious that he was passionate about the study of prophecy, and she used the interest to engage him in conversation. He took the bait and chatted with her as she followed him down the corridor between the church offices and the cathedral. They climbed two levels of stairs to the library to return several bound tomes he carried.

"But I don't understand the focus on the mountain peaks. I wonder where that comes from," she said, feigning ignorance.

The cathedral was massive, and she had never been above the main sanctuary. Paintings and sculptures adorned the sides of the broad marble staircase that circled upward to the library. Icons displaying the early saints were set between each work of art. On a platform between surrounding staircases, statues depicted Dei standing over a defeated Kai, pointing down at Him in a posture of authority and admonishment. Dei was strong and beautiful, carrying a sword held high in one hand. Kai looked demonic, with horns visible upon His forehead and fangs jutting from His mouth.

"Scripture clearly shows us that the twin peaks of Mount Fi will separate in a cataclysmic event, transforming the world as we know it, Kayna," Todd said, enthusiastically. He clearly held great love for this topic. "We know that pain will follow for some unfortunate souls, but traumatic events are often part of progress."

"That seems so scary. How can one prepare?"

They pushed past an imposing oak door, bound with thick metal bands which were ancient but sturdy. He continued, unwittingly escorting Kayna past signs forbidding entry to non-clergy. The library was lavishly furnished, and a plush carpet covered the hard stone tiles. A grand open area graced the entrance, with three levels visible from where they stood. Each level displayed shelving that held books, scrolls, and stacks of paper. Scattered throughout the library were tables, some of which held mounds of materials being perused by novices, monks, or other clergy deep in study.

As Kayna and Todd moved past the entry, several faces turned to see them, each wearing a look of disapproval. With shock, Father Todd clearly realized he had admitted Kayna to the archive without permission, and he blushed at his error.

"I'm sorry, you probably shouldn't be in here."

"Of course, Father. Thank you. See you next time," she said gaily. Smiling widely at him, she cocked her head in what would be seen as a flirtatious move by onlookers. "Bye!" Whirling, the flare of her dress added to the show before she walked out. Now that she knew where the library was, she had no more use for the man and wondered what sort of trouble she had just caused him.

That library, how grand! She must have access. Tonight.

As usual, Papa wasn't home that evening, which served her plans perfectly because he wouldn't hear her leave. She waited until the housemaid returned to her quarters, then grabbed a couple of apples from the kitchen. She climbed the stairs to her room, then latched her bedroom door behind her. If Papa came looking, he would run into her locked door and think she was sleeping. She changed her clothes, donning trousers and a warm button-down shirt tucked under a wide belt. She then retrieved a satchel from her closet, putting the apples inside but leaving plenty of room for books. Throwing the satchel over a shoulder, she moved to her bedroom window, then spread the drapes aside.

As she slid the window open, a cool, autumn breeze swept into the room, setting her ebony hair to dance. Some light drifted her way from street-lamps behind the garden but not enough to expose her departure to the neighbors.

Kayna looked at the ground below and felt a fright. She had never floated more than a few feet above the ground, and her room was on the second story. A fall would drop her straight onto a statue of a stag that decorated the lawn below. Oh, how that would hurt!

She moved to sit on the windowsill, then closed her eyes and fed power into the image that summoned the air. She called the wind slowly at first, so as not to bring a gust and lose control, then more until the breeze from below buffeted against her feet. It was warm when she summoned it, unlike the chill that usually came this time of year. Her air was always warm and comforting. At once, she slid off the sill and magnified the summoning.

It caught her up, but she didn't have time to close the window before falling. The wind clumsily supported her, almost twenty feet above the ground, turning her onto her back, her hair wafting upward in the drafts. She steeled herself against anxiety from the height, closing her eyes. Wresting control of the fear, she rotated upright with her arms held out at her sides. What a feeling! She could stay here forever, reveling in the power of her magic. She directed the wind to move her forward and down, setting herself on the grass below, but avoiding the statue. The air summoning was becoming easier with practice, and she found pride in her success. She made more progress in her skills when she found a practical application for them, something tangible to focus upon. Still, it drained her a bit, and she despised that feeling. She would want strength tonight, but a rat or dog would be insufficient—she would need something more.

After adjusting her clothing and satchel, she walked briskly out the back of the garden, through the gate, and onto the street. The library was a good walk from here, and she had not yet decided how she would enter.

She walked for a long time through the dark, but no ruffians bothered her. This neighborhood was safe, home to politicians and people of importance who paid many a soldier to wander about at night. One such sentinel stood in an alcove across the street, his armored breastplate reflecting light from a nearby torch lamp.

After a time, she approached the church district and spied the stables where the mounts of important clergy and their guards were kept. A big animal would be perfect to quench her thirst. Darkness cloaked her entry through the back door, and since a stable hand likely remained on the premises at night, she made sure to be quiet as she walked on the dirty floor between stalls. The animal smells hit her hard as she entered, and the sounds of snuffling and snorting made it clear that some creatures had noticed her. A piece of straw got stuck in her shoe, irritating her instep. With one hand, she braced herself against the gate of a stall as she removed the straw. A warm, wet sensation against her supporting hand surprised her, and she turned to see a large, chocolate destrier was rubbing its lips against her fingers. Looking for food or volunteering to be food for her? Such a large animal would be ideal for tonight.

Concern rose in her mind regarding the damage she would leave behind. She wanted nobody to be alerted to her presence, but it would be difficult to hide the evidence of what she intended. When she drained small animals, she often left them desiccated, with obvious and disturbing wounds on their dry, cracked skin. Sometimes the eye sockets emptied as the orbs drained of fluid. Such a sight on an expensive horse would bring unwanted attention. Perhaps a partial draining would not leave such a macabre sight. She would try to restrain herself.

"Come here," she said to the destrier, reaching into her satchel for an apple.

The animal came closer, reaching for the treat she held in her hand. She lured it, holding her arm back teasingly to encourage the creature to put its mammoth head across the gate. When it did so, she reached up with her left hand to the side of its jaw, closed her eyes, and began.

In her sight, the energy of the animal was greater than anything she had drained before but dimmer than she expected. It seemed to be covered in a shell, preventing her access. She steeled her mind and willed the covering to split, striking out with a malicious intent. The covering cracked, and she could see light and energy inside.

The horse started suddenly, letting out a shudder and losing all focus on the apple. It tried to pull away from her touch but was unable. She pulled the light into herself, making it her own. The energy caressed her, warm and strong and wonderful, with an intensity she had never sensed before. It was like her warm wind, but much greater in intensity. She almost lost herself in it, wanting to take it all, every bit, but she knew she shouldn't. She clamped down on the flow of energy and broke the link, opening her eyes in time to see the horse fall.

The noise it made was significant, and the surrounding animals whinnied and snorted in protest, as if in solidarity with their fallen brother. Up a small set of stairs to her right, she saw a light growing —someone approaching with a lamp. She moved to the exit and closed the wooden door with barely a sound. A moment later, the stable hand would come in, finding only a dying horse and an uneaten apple on the floor outside its gate.

A short walk carried Kayna the remaining way to the cathedral. The evening had grown completely dark. Even the torch lamps upon the street did little to chase away the shadows, which would be her allies tonight. She looked up at the cathedral, seeing the domed roof overhead, the sharp spires, and many windows on all sides. So high!

Even with the new strength coursing through her spirit, she wondered if it was possible to ascend that far. She walked around the south side of the massive edifice and sought an area where she could attempt it unseen. She found an open patch of lawn and hedges near an unlit lamp. Perfect.

She looked up, finding a window at the base of a spire near where the library might be. She found it difficult to judge such a thing from this distance and bit her lip as she contemplated her poor planning. Enthusiasm and ambition had driven her here, and her haste might bring failure to this outing. The window appeared to be more than a hundred feet up, far higher than she had ever attempted. Falling from such a height would be the end of her, but she was oddly undeterred. The power coursing through her gave a strange confidence.

When she summoned the air this time, it came quickly, powerfully, and without the chaos that had accompanied her prior efforts.

Her command of it was absolute, lifting under her feet expertly without pulling much at her hair or clothing. It knew what she expected and endeavored to please her. Up and up she sailed, so smoothly that she opened her eyes without fear, traveling with confidence along the dome to the window that awaited. The buildings below shrank, and she wondered if anyone saw her rise above the cathedral. An apparition in the night, Kayna commanded the air to rise ever upward, her head held high. Who else could do such things?

Upon arrival at the window, she banished her grandiose imaginings, reached out with her left hand, and pushed. It gave way easily, to no surprise. There was no need to lock a window at this height. She climbed in and dismissed the air, a dutiful servant for which she had no more use.

The window opened into a long hallway that led to the main library chamber. Wall sconces with candles illuminated the way. It was very late and few clergy were present, hopefully making it easy to avoid discovery.

After a few moments of perusing the stacks and shelves on the second level, she found some manuscripts that interested her and tucked them into her satchel. Then something else caught her eye. On the third level of the library, the shelves seemed different. She looked about before moving down a hallway, then took an unoccupied stairway up. Upon arrival on the third level, she noticed that the shelves were slightly shorter but also more sparsely arranged. The books they held were behind small, sliding glass doors.

She stood in front of one section for a moment, then slid the glass door aside to peruse the books within. They were so old! Scratches and wear on the leather bindings were apparent, evidence that they had been well used. What wonders did they hold, and how would their runes look?

A sound from a nearby aisle startled her.

"Hey."

She turned to the voice.

"What are you doing in here?"

Of course. Such treasures would not go unwatched.

An elderly man, obviously clergy by the look of the robe and the amulet around his neck, pointed a finger at her.

"Who are you?"

She squared up with him, then closed her eyes. Black hair fell in front of her face, hopefully obscuring her features, but the candle-light must have illuminated her form for the old man, a faceless dark angel. Fire would be a poor choice here, so she made a more familiar one. The air swirled at her command, extinguishing nearby candles, then caught the man sideways. It flung him up and over the railing. His eyes went wide, and he reached out at nothing, scrambling in futility with his fingers and arms. He plummeted two stories down, where his head cracked open on a table, then his body flopped life-lessly onto the floor.

Kayna slid another glass door open, then grabbed several books in the crook of her arm, eager to return for more now that she had found their hiding place. Retreating from the library the same way she had entered, she escaped without further discovery. As the air carried her to the street outside, she chided herself for handling the cleric in such a manner. What a waste of life.

Draining him would have been delightful.

25

CAVERN

Crone's Hill

Nara waited at the cabin for Mykel. Anne had said he would tire from his training and come back soon, but it seemed to take so long, and Nara was eager to share the discovery of the cavern with him. She looked about the old shack, wondering how long it had stood here, and how long Anne had lived inside. The logs that comprised the walls were old, dry, and cracked. A few pots hung from pegs, but there were no chairs, only stools made from tree stumps, like those on the porch. It seemed odd that Anne would have lived here, rather than in the bright, warm cavern for all these years, as if she had chosen the modesty of the place for a reason. Humility? Or was she punishing herself for something?

She heard Mykel before she saw him, the sound of his footfalls coming down the path that led from the plateau. She left the cabin and found him looking flushed and sweaty, shoulders sagging, but a smile on his face.

"Mykel, come! You won't believe this!"

"What?"

"Trust me," she said, then walked quickly in the direction of the creek. Mykel caught up, walking at her side.

"Anne says you were training?"

"Yes, for a long time."

"Tired, then, eh?"

"Yes, but a different kind of tired. The health tattoo that Bylo gave me helps. I don't get tired the same way anymore."

It took them some time, and Nara almost got lost, but she eventually found the creek. "Feel the water," she said, leaning in to splash Mykel.

"Hey!" He stepped in and splashed her back. "It's warm!"

"Yes, it is," she said. "But that's nothing. Come up here."

Nara's feet hopped from rock to rock as she crossed the creek back and forth, making her way to the source where it bubbled up from the ground. Mykel came up beside her and stood in the middle of the creek, slack-jawed with his mouth open as he stared at the open doorway that led to the cavern tunnel.

"Come inside," Nara said as she stepped inside, where the walls were lit by the many light runes.

"How do they work?" he asked.

"Magic, of course. There are more inside. I'll show you."

Mykel hesitated.

"Don't worry, Mykel. I'll protect you," she said, teasing, then grabbed his hand and pulled. He cracked a grin and followed her.

The tunnel opened into a huge underground cavern, three hundred feet high and easily a thousand feet in diameter. Illuminated by thousands of the same glowing symbols, it was as bright as daylight. They slowed, and Mykel's gaze moved around the cavern to the many sights, his face expressing the same amazement Nara had felt when she saw all of this a couple hours ago. Birds flitted about, their nests visible on ledges high in the rock walls. A creek with blue-tinted water flowed through the center of a large flat area and pooled in one section, creating a reservoir; a big rock stood out in the center of the pool.

"Can we swim in there?" Mykel asked.

"I think so. Come over here," Nara beckoned. She led him to a huge patch of vegetation growing along the sides of the creek that flowed out of the reservoir. "Anne says these make it all work." She pointed to a large patch of plants. They looked like weeds with bright red-and-orange blossoms adorning the tops.

"How so?" Mykel asked.

"She calls them fire weeds, and they release these soft seeds into the air." Nara waved her hand over one of the blossoms. A fluffy white cluster of small seeds released, wafting up toward the ceiling.

"There are little plants that grow in the grooves of the runes above. They absorb the white seeds from these fire weeds," she continued. "Those little plants bring the runes to life. Runes of light, Mykel! It all works together. The water comes up out of the ground at the far end, pooling in the reservoir and heating the chamber. Fire weeds feast on the soil. Plants in the runes above use the condensation and the floating seeds to produce the energy in the inscriptions, and the magic runes provide the light that shines back down on the plants. All this majesty, hidden away in a cave."

"How did the birds get in here?" Mykel asked.

"I don't know, but Anne said the Breshi built this place eons ago as an act of worship to Dei. A sanctuary. Perhaps they brought the birds inside?"

Nara pointed toward Anne, who approached from the far end of the chamber.

"Finally tired, Mykel?" Anne asked.

He smiled and shrugged. "I have my limits."

"And we will test them, young man. Come. I have something you might wish to see."

She led them several hundred feet further and around a large pillar. Nara examined the pillar; it was sheer and tall, with no seams or joints, as if carved from a single piece of stone. On the other side, they found Bylo standing in front of a large flat rock wall. In front of the wall were a long bench and a wide table, made of smooth stone. Inscribed in the wall was a giant rune, twenty or thirty feet high, stuffed with the same vegetation that filled the light runes, but it wasn't glowing.

"What is it?" Nara asked.

"A rune of protection; it keeps this cavern intact. Strong. It will also serve as Mykel's new tattoo," Anne said.

"A new tattoo?" Mykel asked.

"If you want to be a warrior, to be able to protect Nara, you will need all the help you can get," Anne said.

"I don't understand," he said.

"It protects you, silly!" Nara poked him in the ribs. "From danger. Monsters and shadows and curses. That sort of thing."

Mykel chuckled.

"Come over here," Nara said, as she pulled him over to a patch of grass with a big fruit tree growing in the middle. It had broad branches, soft brown bark, and long, narrow green leaves that hung down several feet from each branch.

"Let's eat," Nara yelled back to them. "You must be hungry."

Anne, Bylo, and Gwyn joined them at the tree.

"Apples?" Gwyn asked.

"Something like that," Anne said.

They plucked the fruit from the tree and sat in a circle to eat. They were softer than apples, yet sweeter and more satisfying.

The evening was spent resting, swimming in the lagoon, and wandering about the cavern. Bylo sat occasionally on the stone bench and practiced his inscriptions on the table.

Mykel and Nara played in the water, occasionally diving to the bottom. Mykel could hold his breath much longer than she. Once, he sat on the floor of the pool long enough to bring her to a panic, but he finally surfaced and spit water in her face. She splashed him in return. As they played, Nara wondered how much time they would have in this place before calamity fell upon them again. How long before those who pursued them found their way to her? She hoped it would be a long time.

Little blue birds flew overhead as Gwyn watched the youths swim. She thought how easy it could be to forget about Vorick and hide in this place for a while. How easy it would be to join these people, live in this cavern, and pretend the outside world didn't exist. If they knew what was coming for them, they would be fearful right now, instead of playing, laughing, and splashing.

She wondered how Vorick would kill Mykel. As much as Mykel's healing powers were a nice trick, they wouldn't help him against the minister. How much training would the young man actually receive before he was tested?

And Nara. She was the unknown factor. Mykel wouldn't be able to stand up against Vorick, but maybe she could. In order for that to happen, she would need to grow up very fast, to embrace whatever strange talents she possessed. Gwyn thought of the way Nara had opened the tunnel door. The child had poured magic into the water rune, without a cepp, from her own spirit. As a watcher, Gwyn had seen many things, but never anything like that. What else was she capable of?

"Beautiful, aren't they?" Anne said.

Gwyn pivoted, surprised.

"Young, ignorant, and happy," Anne continued. "As happy as possible under the circumstances."

"Yes," Gwyn said. The unspoken admonishment was not lost on her. Anne knew Gwyn's intentions and was making her suffer in advance for the betrayal she intended to inflict.

"She doesn't seem very strong. Why does he care for her so much?" Gwyn asked.

"I don't know. You should ask him. Maybe he senses how much she needs him and, at least for now, how vulnerable she is. Mykel is drawn to people who need him, and he yearns to keep them safe. But maybe he also senses her potential, her greatness. Maybe he longs to be nearby, to be part of it. Why does anyone love another person?"

"I really wouldn't know," Gwyn said, then went silent for a time as her thoughts ran about on their own. There was something valuable happening here, in this cavern, and between Mykel and Nara. Something important, she was sure of it. Would Gwyn's betrayal disturb that? Would it destroy them? Or was it a necessary part of their story?

"Why do you not protect them?" Gwyn turned as she asked, looking intently at the ancient woman, betraying her own frustration with the circumstances. Gwyn's words fumbled as she tried to articulate her anger. "Why... why would you let me turn them over to Vorick?"

"I don't care to judge the ways of people," she said. "My role is to guide, to teach, and to watch."

"That's cowardly of you. I would think that someone so old and wise could come up with a better way to lead the rest of us." Gwyn gritted her teeth as she spoke, not sure if she was feeling frustration with Anne, or simply struggling with her own shame.

"You're one to talk about cowardice," Anne said. "You'd destroy these children to save your own skin."

"It's not like that. I don't wish them any harm."

"Then stand up to your master, woman! Put your neck on the line for another human being. You wear the trappings of a warrior as if you're brave and proud, but you're nothing but a scared little girl inside."

"You know nothing of me," Gwyn said.

After a time, Anne continued. "Everyone makes their own choices. Just remember, you're not defined by who you were yesterday. You're defined by what you actually do. Today. In fact, it's the only choice you ever have. What you do right now is all that matters."

The words hung in the air as Anne walked away. Gwyn had manufactured justifications aplenty for her actions in the past and continued to do so even as she planned to reveal Nara's whereabouts to the minister. She thought she had come to terms with her own role in the world long ago. Assassin. Soldier. A hired sword who followed orders. But she had never felt part of something before. Part of a family, like the bond these people seemed to have. Would the warmth of a family have helped her to become a different person? A better one?

As she watched Nara and Mykel emerge from the water, she discarded self-deprecation to return to her accustomed indifference. Emotional detachment she understood, and it had oft provided a haven for her.

The group made a trip to the cabin to gather their belongings and return to the large cavern. As they walked back, Nara wondered again how long they would be able to stay before they would have to be on the move.

They lay their bedrolls in a dark hall, tucked away in a corner of the cavern. Nara placed her bedroll near Anne, Bylo, and Mykel, but Gwyn placed her bedroll in a particularly dark section, apart from the others.

The sleeping hall bore a few small light runes; it was dark enough to sleep, but not so much that one stumbled into things. After they bedded down, Nara spoke up, finding her thoughts too busy to allow her to rest.

"Anne?" she asked.

"Yes, Nara."

"How did they make the cavern?"

"Earth shapers."

"Never heard of them," Nara said.

"You've heard of flamers. They control fire. Others can control earth or air or water. Earth shapers mold rocks, dirt, and stone. The stuff from which living things grow."

"Wow," Nara said. "Fire destroys, but these earth people could create such wonder. Beautiful."

"Yes, it is."

"Where did they all go?"

"Lost," Anne said. "Hundreds of years ago. Along with many other folks."

"The end of the Breshi?" Nara asked.

"Yes."

Nara had been nursing a growing headache. Although it wasn't strong, it was enough to keep her from sleeping. She lay alone with her thoughts, quietly pondering the Breshi earth shapers, how the land was without them now. She pondered the beauty they had created, and the power held by the earth. Mountains towered over all living things, grand and majestic, with massive stones and peaks one could see for miles. But earth was also pebbles and soil. Pebbles she had thrown into ponds, and soil that gave birth to potatoes one could eat, trees that provided homes for animals and shelter for people. Earth was big, and it was small. It was everywhere, and it was amazing. What would it be like to be an earth shaper?

She thought about the protection rune and the power it would unlock for Mykel. The water rune and how it commanded the doors in the cavern. Did the runes in Bylo's book each unlock powers?

She glanced about to ensure that the others had fallen asleep, hearing only the soft sounds of slow breathing. She peeled back her blankets, then looked about. In the dim light, she could see the outline of Bylo's pack against the far stone wall. She checked to make sure nobody was watching, then sneaked over and carefully unbuckled the straps. A moment later, her fingers gripped the leather of his manuscript. He had never let her read it before and certainly wouldn't approve of it now, but she needed to see the runes. Before she could talk herself out of it, she was out of the sleeping area and halfway across the well-lit cavern, manuscript tucked under one arm.

She exited the cavern, then ran through the woods, eventually finding her way to the top of the hill and the moonlit plateau. Nobody would think to find her way out here. Sitting under one of the birch trees, her fingers moved across the worn, brittle pages. Unable to read the text in the dim light, her focus was entirely upon the margins and the treasures inscribed there, but the moon failed her. In her haste to steal away, she was no longer in the cavern, where the light runes would have provided the illumination she needed.

Of course. The light runes.

She closed her eyes and pictured the shape of the light rune. It snapped into her mind, shocking her with the suddenness of it. She fed it some energy, and at once her headache was banished. Use of her magic often reduced the pains, but they rarely abated completely, and the relief was welcome.

When she opened her eyes, she was stunned to see that her hands were aglow with a scintillating, multicolored light, blinding in its intensity, lighting up the whole plateau. She shut down the energy with a thought and started again, eyes open this time, summoning the rune and feeding it only a trickle of power, like a soft exhale over a long moment. Her hands glowed ever so slightly, like a strong candle, just enough to read the book without hurting her eyes. The words and designs of the manuscript came to life with the light, and she turned her attention to the pages and the runes. So many were wrong, but she could almost tell how they should have been drawn. Imperfect, but close enough that Bylo's work to refine them now seemed important. Only now could she appreciate all the time he had spent with this book over the years.

Then she found the one she was looking for. It was ornate, with multiple sweeping strokes that crossed over one another. It had been drawn incorrectly, but it was close, and she closed her eyes to picture it more clearly. She set the manuscript on a nearby rock and pondered the pattern, moving it about in her thoughts until she found its true shape and it fell into place. She placed her palms down on the ground and fed the rune some energy, opening her mouth in surprise as she did so.

The earth was alive. She opened her eyes and grabbed a clump of dirt in her hand. It looked simple with her normal vision, but with the rune alive in her mind, she could sense the potential in the dirt, no longer inert and lifeless but like an extension of her body. Maybe a little toe. She wiggled it.

The clump of dirt came apart in her hand, becoming a cloud of particles that moved in a tiny whirlwind. It assembled itself into a pillar of dirt several inches high, then abruptly compressed into a tiny pebble. She inhaled deeply in surprise and stopped the wiggling. The dirt collapsed into a pile on her palm.

"That's earth-shaping,"

Nara started at the voice from behind her.

"You surprised me!" she said, turning to see Anne leaning against the tree in the near darkness.

"With time, you will get better. You won't carve a cavern with rivers and lagoons anytime soon, mind you. And you'll exhaust yourself many times before you figure out how to be efficient with your energies, but you've taken the first step."

"I sense power in there, Anne." Nara dropped her hands to the soil again and closed her eyes. "It's almost as if I can feel its heartbeat. As if there is energy inside the earth."

"There's life in everything, Nara. We all come from the same place."

"But power in dirt?"

"Yes, a bit. Not much. Not like living things, but if you reach deep enough, it's there." Anne started to walk back across the plateau toward the cavern.

Before she went far, Nara called out to her. "What else can I do?"

"Anything you want," Anne called back. "Keep practicing."

The next morning, Mykel awoke to the pain of something hitting him in the ribs.

"Ow!" he yelled, rolling away from the assault to spy Anne holding a stick in her hand.

"Get up! You have work to do," Anne said.

"Did you have to hit me?"

"Are you worried about some sort of permanent injury, little boy? Or does pain still make you shiver and cringe?"

Little boy. The term rankled his pride. This woman couldn't be as harsh as she pretended, could she? He agreed with her, however. Pain shouldn't be the obstacle for him that it once had been. After years of reacting violently to injury, as most people did, he found it difficult to overcome the habit.

"Don't worry, we'll work that fear out of you, son," Anne said. "Get dressed—you'll be training today."

Thoughts of wielding a sword motivated him to rise quickly. Swords were a symbol of power and virility in the culture of the Great Land, and he pictured himself walking around Dimmitt with a blade dangling in a scabbard from his belt. He wondered what Nara would think of him. Mykel the warrior. Mykel the blade-master. Thoughts of nobility and grandeur occupied his mind as he dressed and walked out of the alcove into the brighter light of the cavern. Gwyn greeted him.

"You're with me today," she said. "Anne has asked me to teach."

After leaving the cavern, Gwyn led him on a long run, forbidding him to replenish himself. Yesterday's endless running had done wonders for his conditioning, and he easily kept up with Gwyn's fast pace. "Why are you staying with us?" he asked between breaths. "I'm grateful, of course, but didn't you want to visit family or something?"

"They aren't expecting me yet," she said. "Are you already tired of me?"

"No, of course not! I just didn't want to keep you. You can stay as long as you like."

After a couple of rounds about the hill, Gwyn cut two long saplings, removed the small branches from them, and gathered vines. She then walked down to the creek bed. Mykel watched as she selected two heavy, oblong rocks. Kneeling at the side of the creek, she tied the rocks to the end of the saplings with the vines.

"Perfect," she said.

"What are they for?" Mykel asked.

"Your training."

Gwyn led Mykel back into the cavern, a rock-laden sapling in each of her hands. When they arrived at the training area in the center, she tossed one of the saplings to Mykel. She dropped the other at her feet.

"Hold the stick by the end," Gwyn said.

At first he gripped it by the rock in his right hand, but when Gwyn scoffed at him he switched to the other end, embarrassed. Apparently, she meant the stone to give weight, not to serve as a grip.

"Hold it out as far as you can to one side," she said.

He moved the long stick out to his right side and adjusted his stance to prevent from toppling over. It was heavy.

"The weight on the end makes it difficult to hold aloft," Gwyn said.

"No kidding," Mykel said. "It's a lot heavier than it appears."

"Carrying a sword, axe, or staff can be like this in a long battle," she said. "What seems manageable close to your body becomes unwieldy when held at arm's length. This is the first lesson."

His shoulder already began to strain under the pressure, and muscle failure was imminent.

"I can't go any longer," he said, dropping the stick to the ground, the stone at the end striking the surface of the training area.

"Again," Gwyn said.

"Give me a second," he said.

"*Lift it!*"

Her raised voice reminded him of Anne's admonishments yesterday during the runs around the hill. Then he remembered how he had conquered that challenge. Of course!

He lifted his arm, immediately feeling the pain of muscles failing under the extreme strain, but without closing his eyes he flared health, and the pain in his shoulder faded. Gwyn went over to the sapling, put her hand on the stone, and pushed down against him. Mykel matched her pressure, but the pain lanced through his shoulder and he flared health again. Gwyn's pressure did not relent, and she turned to him with a mischievous look. She was testing him and probably enjoying herself. He redoubled his efforts and flared health yet again to relieve the agony that surged.

It's only pain, he told himself. *Pain is just information, to be welcomed and not feared.*

He flared health again and lifted with all the effort he could muster. The stone at the end of the sapling rose with his effort even with Gwyn's downward pressure.

"Good," she said. "Now out to the front."

She directed the sapling in front of him, keeping downward pressure to work his shoulder in a different manner.

"Don't let up!" she encouraged.

The rotation engaged new muscles, allowing the tired muscles to relax. After a moment, the newly-straining muscles began to fatigue, and he flared health again. After a few minutes, Gwyn stopped him and directed him to put the sapling in his left hand. The training continued like this for over an hour, but the frequent healing replenished the muscles, and he knew he was getting stronger. Eventually, he held both saplings out to his sides, one in each arm.

"You build new muscle quickly, Mykel. Anne suspected this would be possible."

New muscle? Repeated activity could indeed make a man stronger, and Mykel thought of the dock workers who unloaded the crates of fish from the boats in Dimmitt's harbor. Their arms and backs rippled with strength, having spent years lifting and carrying. Could he achieve that in a shorter time?

"Wielding a weapon is difficult and requires might in the shoulder, chest, back, and legs," she said. She drew one of her own swords and held it out to her side.

"Slashing across the middle like this"—she swung the blade in an arc, attacking an imaginary foe—" engages the muscles in your torso."

"Slashing the other direction"—she reversed it, the blade returning to her side—"uses muscles in your back."

"Lunging forward and thrusting"—she jumped forward and impaled another imaginary combatant—"needs strong muscles in your legs, your chest, and your arms."

"When do I get to hold a sword?" Mykel asked.

"When you're strong!" she replied.

The rest of the day was spent doing push-ups, pull-ups, deep knee bends and holding the weighted saplings in different positions. Every time Mykel would lower a sapling in fatigue, Gwyn would bark at him. He would flare health, then resume the activity.

His strength grew quickly, and Gwyn challenged him every step of the way. By lunchtime, he was doing push-ups with her on his back and pull-ups from a tree branch while she pulled down on his feet.

The midday meal was fruit and gathered nuts and Mykel ate three times what he normally would have. By the end of the day, exhaustion had overcome him. He retired to his bedroll before the sun outside had even fallen below the horizon. Despite what Anne had promised at daybreak, he never once touched a weapon.

Bylo spent the day in front of the protection rune. He had never seen this pattern before, but after just a day using quill and normal ink, Bylo was confident that he would reproduce the design accurately. He was curious, however, as Anne had never told him exactly what it did. After lunch, she came by to check his progress.

"Doing well?" she asked.

"You're right," he said. "Definitely the hardest one I've seen, but I'm close."

"Easier when you have it right in front of you, eh? I can't imagine how you managed to find success scratching away with a faulty old book as your guide."

"What does it do?" he asked.

"It will protect him," she said.

"From what?"

"From Vorick's men. And from Vorick."

"Why would the minister want to hurt Mykel? I thought it was the church that posed the main threat."

"Ministers, kings, queens, and the church. They are much the same on these sorts of things, Bylo. Politics and religion are often intertwined, unfortunately."

"True," Bylo said. "Vorick is a blessed, no?"

"Yes."

"A cutter?"

"And a harvester too."

"Which does this rune defend against?"

"Both," she said.

What kind of gift would it be to withstand the magic of the most powerful man in the realm? Protection and health, an interesting combination. But without armor, and having no weapon skills, he would be vulnerable to Vorick's soldiers, wouldn't he?

"What does Mykel have that Vorick wants?"

"He has sent men to come for Nara. And they will find her."

A chill struck Bylo. He always suspected that the authorities would want Nara, but hearing it from Anne made the threat so much more real.

"Why?" Bylo asked.

Anne sat down on the stone bench next to him, providing comfort with her presence. "He collects valuable things. He collects power. Nara has power."

Was it that simple? "She's young, and she knows so little about her talents. None of us knows what power she possesses."

"Hear this," Anne turned to Bylo, looking into his two good eyes with her single, broken one, "Nara has more power than you could possibly imagine. Her potential is so vast that if she ever embraces her gifts, there are no limits to what she could accomplish. Or what she could destroy. Vorick may suspect this, and he will stop at nothing to own her. The man is hungry for power of every kind. Politics. Money. Magic. He wants it all, and nothing will deter him."

Bylo's heart raced with a growing fear brought on by Anne's words.

"Mykel is her protector. More than that, he is her inspiration and her encouragement. Make sure he is capable of doing his job. Practice this rune until you're sure. When you are, let me know." She walked away.

Bylo was not a leader, but he was an excellent follower. He thrived when given a meaningful task. He contemplated Anne's words, the threat presented by the minister, the need for Mykel to be able to protect her. Most of all, he considered the words about Nara.

More power than I can imagine?

Nara had always seemed gentle. Someone to be protected, not feared, and he wondered if he had misjudged the girl. Had he erred in discouraging the use of her talents, in keeping her hidden and ignorant? Perhaps she was a blessing from Dei that should have been trained to be a champion, to fight for goodness and justice in this dark world. Had he botched the only meaningful task he had been given? Had his fear ruined her? Put her in danger?

He sighed and moved back to his studies. As he returned to his work, he was further resolved to get this tattoo right. Everything he cared about depended on it.

26

KAVALIN

Kavalin

On the Kobac River

I t took less than a week for Vorick to muster five hundred men and travel to Kavalin, the town most recently lost to the barbarian rabble. The Kobac River's rapid downstream flow allowed for the quick deployment of the troops from Fairmont via barges; they would only have to march a dozen miles to Kavalin from the debarkation point.

Like many frontier settlements, Kavalin had been constructed near a natural resource. Some frontier ports were erected near wild runs of fish, huge herds of wild beasts, or dense timber forests. Fishermen, hunters, and loggers would earn their coins by practicing their trades and selling to merchants who would then carry the products to distant places.

Kavalin had a mine.

The ore extracted at Kavalin wasn't anything as valuable as gold or silver. Such treasures were heavily guarded by the queen's troops, and no barbarian would be so foolish as to attack them. Kavalin mined lead, a less-desirable mineral, but had recently discovered copper. The copper vein called for greater attention from royal resources, and plans had been laid to bolster the guard around the town as a result. But Vorick had been busy. He hadn't acted quickly enough to provide the necessary security, allowing the town and the mine to fall into enemy hands.

Upon arrival, Vorick and the army marched hastily to the plains south of Kavalin where they could see smoke rising from the captured town. From this distance, they couldn't see the invaders who had overcome it but had probably *been* seen by their enemies.

"Some scouts have certainly seen us, m'lord," a captain said. "We came too close, too quickly."

"That's fine," Vorick said, looking in the direction of the enemy from atop his horse. "Let them come. What's your name, soldier?"

"Captain Jahmai, sir."

"I didn't ask your rank. I asked your name."

"Yes sir," the man said, shifting nervously on his horse.

"Jahmai, worry not. You're about to see something that will find its way into the histories," he said. "That is if you obey me so that you can live long enough to witness it."

By the look on his face, Jahmai clearly thought Vorick insane. His concern was warranted. The minister had ordered no reconnaissance and stopped on a flat plain with no elevation advantage. The enemy knew of their presence. His men were tired and hungry, and Vorick hadn't ordered them to form battle lines. From the perspective of a simple soldier, this scenario carried the makings of a disaster.

"Where are the prisoners I ordered you to bring, Jahmai?"

"In the back, sir."

"March them forward."

Vorick dismounted and left his horse to wander. He walked alongside Triff, who guided a slow-moving wagon that was laden with a single large box. At Vorick's command, Jahmai and some soldiers pulled the box out of the wagon. One soldier groaned under the weight of it as they placed it upon the ground.

A horn sounded in the distance—probably the barbarians announcing their approach. Doubt spread among the soldiers and grumbling could be heard in the ranks as they grew eager to take defensive positions.

Jahmai and his men stepped back while Triff cracked open the crate and removed the lid to reveal the dark-red armor plates. Several men saw the coral and inhaled sharply with surprise. Word of the treasure spread through the soldiers and the grumblings stopped, silenced by wonder and curiosity.

As Vorick shed his outer clothing and put on the silk under-padding, the soldiers gazed upon his frame. He could guess what they were thinking—he didn't have the strength and size of a soldier. Yet, each of his small forearms bore a bracer, a cepp, a reminder of his power, invoking the fear all men held for his magic. He could kill them with a look, no matter how fragile he might appear.

He removed the bracers from his arms and placed them into the pockets of the silk undershirt. He then turned to see the wagon load of prisoners arrive. Eight men. All were dressed in the black garb of those sentenced to death.

"Bring me two to start," Vorick said.

It took a moment to unchain the prisoners and walk them over to Vorick. The irons around their ankles made for a slow, stuttering gait that drew out the moment with anticipation.

"Kneel," Vorick told them. They knelt, eyes wide. He wondered what they felt. Was there any relief that their deaths had finally come, or only fear?

It would have been proper to say something about justice for the Great Land's enemies, but his priorities remained set on the task ahead. Nothing of these men would be remembered, and they warranted no words. Reaching for the armor with his right hand, he tapped power in the armor plates, then gestured toward the two kneeling prisoners only a few feet beyond his grasp. He ventured inside their bodies with his mind, severing arteries with a thought. Blood spilled inside their chest cavities, pooling in their guts as panic struck their faces. The loss of blood pressure caused a slow loss of consciousness, and faces went slack as the men slumped, dying. He drew out their life energies, slowly at first, then more completely just as they died. Wounds appeared, and blackened blood oozed from fissures in the dry, hardened skin. The bodies shriveled, skin darkening and limbs contorting into odd positions.

The soldiers expressed horror at the display. All had heard of Vorick's power, but few had actually witnessed it. When the minister finished his task, that which remained of the two prisoners was not even recognizable as human.

Vorick sensed the armor's energy. It was enough to begin.

"Do it, Triff," he ordered the craftsman. "Jahmai, help him."

Once the armor had been assembled on Vorick, locked together with hinges and hooks and clasps, he cut an imposing figure.

"Still heavy," he said. "But I can move. Bring the others."

After draining the remaining six prisoners, the armor became light enough for Vorick to walk, though with some difficulty. He looked again to his soldiers and at the shocked expression upon their faces.

"You haven't seen anything yet," he said, grinning widely.

Triff retrieved Flay and handed it to his master. Vorick drew the blade, feeding energy from the armor into the ivory until it was fully charged. Swinging the blade back and forth, he relished the feel of it. Light as a feather. He then marched directly toward Kavalin. One man against an army.

"I'll be back soon," he called to his men. "Enjoy the show."

The enemy troops had assembled themselves in front of Vorick a short distance across the flat plain. At least three hundred men stood there, an impressive response in so short a time.

Vorick waited. Would the enemy charge, or would he be required to close the distance himself? Would the armor protect him as well as he had hoped? If they came all at once, he wouldn't be able to kill them fast enough to avoid being trampled and would never completely fill the plates. This was a gamble, but one worthy of taking. If he succeeded, the victory would be glorious and would pave his way to greatness.

He dropped the visor on his helmet, limiting his vision but providing protection against slings, arrows, or crossbow bolts; he had no idea what weapons these mutts had brought with them.

The weight of the armor was far less than when first assembled, but he still found it difficult to walk, stopping periodically to catch his breath. His heart pounded with anticipation as he sensed the energy coursing through the plates. Power from the lives of eight human beings flowed around him, yet the armor could hold so much more. The power from a single man would normally overwhelm his bracers, yet this armor had the capacity to hold oceans of energy. How would it feel after twenty? Forty?

A single spearman on the opposing line moved toward him. Of course. They thought this was a challenge to single combat. How fun! Since he held no concern for small projectiles at the moment, he lifted his visor; he would need vision to manage this challenge.

The man who approached was large, well over six feet in height. He wore a steel breastplate and carried a spear and round shield. Blond hair was pulled back in a long braid, and blue paint adorned his cheeks and forehead. A long, bushy beard grew on his face. He stopped a dozen paces in front of Vorick, spear pointed upward, its butt resting on the ground. A scowl was all that he offered.

"Show me," Vorick challenged, grinning. Was this beast of a man gifted, or was he just big, strong, and ugly? Vorick reached out his awareness, but his ability to sense a cepp on the barbarian was clouded by the overwhelming magic of his own armor.

The barbarian grunted, then took a few steps back. Vorick expected a charge. Barbarians with spears always charged, didn't they?

The man charged.

The spear impacted him directly in the chest and should have launched him back a dozen feet, but the energy in the armor must have dispelled the power of the attack—he felt only a solid push.

Still, it was enough to knock him over. He sprawled to the ground, resting on his back. The barbarian laughed and turned, walking away and allowing Vorick to crawl to his feet. The barbarian army cheered and Vorick felt a brief flash of shame come across him. For a moment, he was a child again, on the ground after being bullied by a bigger kid. But the feeling passed quickly. The fool standing before him had no idea what was coming. Vorick gestured for the man to try again.

The barbarian sprinted forward again, spear leveled for the kill. A few yards before contact, however, the man's charge was interrupted as Vorick severed the man's Achilles tendon with a thought, forcing the warrior to stumble and fall awkwardly into the tundra. It was now Vorick's turn to laugh, and he heard the cheers of his own men behind him. What must the champion be thinking now, cut down without even a weapon?

Vorick stepped closer, looking down at the man. "Get up," Vorick taunted. "Can you?" The warrior used the spear to brace himself and rose to one leg, his other foot flopping clumsily as he tried to plant it on the ground. The barbarian looked at his foot, his eyes squinting, and his face taut in obvious pain. He probably searched for blood on his boot, wondering what had hobbled him. Once on his feet again, he attempted to charge but was clumsy and slow. Without complete use of his leg, he was forced to rely on the spear as a makeshift crutch.

Even with the weight of the armor, Vorick easily moved out of the path of the clumsy charge. He swung Flay as the barbarian passed, and the blade impacted the man in the side. Skin, muscle, and bone separated under the magic weapon, and his opponent fell to the ground beneath, blood spilling onto the cool dirt.

Flay had done her dark work, and it was clear the man would not rise again. The single strike had torn through several ribs and a lung. Rasping sounds and bubbles of blood escaped the man's lips as he struggled to turn over and thrust his spear at his opponent without success. Vorick engaged his talent, tearing the warrior's heart to shreds, then siphoned the energy of his life force into the armor. It was easier than before, as if the power within the armor gave him greater control over his magics. Interesting. Did an abundance of power really give greater mastery of talents? Had he known this, he would have covered himself in cepps years ago!

He finished the task of draining the man, then left the blackened corpse at his feet, turning to face the awaiting army. Would they send another champion, or would they come en masse? He hoped they wouldn't run away, but that was a possibility. He suddenly regretted draining the warrior. If he had scared them away, how would he fill the armor with power?

All concern vanished as they charged, and Vorick smiled. It was commendable of them to continue in the face of the unknown as they did, and he wondered what sort of culture made for such fierce wills. He resolved to speak with one of these curs someday to learn what he could on the matter.

He dropped the visor on his helm as a few of the fastest arrived well ahead of the rest, small soldiers unencumbered by armor or heavy weapons. The first to be cut down was little taller than Vorick, wore nothing but furs, and carried a tiny sword. Vorick didn't have time to reach inside the man to do something as deft as severing an artery, so he simply decapitated the attacker from thirty feet away. Others that swarmed about received a similar fate, losing limbs or suffering the disintegration of organs as they approached their foe, falling into piles around him. As he could, Vorick reached out with both arms to his sides, draining the life essences of several foes into his armor at once. He reveled in the control he could exercise with this armor. Never before had he been able to drain more than two at a time.

They came at him, throwing spears and swinging swords as they fell. The attacks bounced harmlessly off the armor. He swung Flay, and she drank her fill of death. As the armor became lighter, he moved about more quickly, occasionally dodging the attacks of his injured opponents, playing with them, laughing as they fell. And they all fell. As he drained more and more, the armor filled with magic, and Vorick's powers became ever stronger. Soon he was able to kill and drain four at once, then six, then ten. More than a hundred fell before the horde broke away, running back to Kavalin, screaming and cursing the fate of their brothers under the crimson demon that had slain them today.

Nikolas Vorick had never found much value in religion and had never witnessed to his satisfaction convincing evidence of the divine. Until today.

Perhaps there is a god after all, he thought. *And I am He.*

After a time, practical matters overcame his delight, and he picked through the piles of bodies, draining the last of them for every ounce of power to fill the cepps that clothed him. He could sense the coral plates had not yet reached their limits and grew frustrated with himself for becoming caught up in the joy of the destruction and failing to completely drain all his victims. Some had lost their energy now, their power spilling out into nothingness as they died, and he cursed himself for his inattention. Still, he had turned at least eighty to dust and partially drained many of the others who had fallen. It was enough.

He hoped that the armor retained the magic as well as normal coral cepps did. He would not often have the chance to do this sort of thing. Perhaps he would need to create those opportunities. This had been fun.

He walked back to his army under a much lighter load than when he had left them. A slight rubbing of a coral plate in his back caused irritation, and he channeled power into the silk undergarment to strengthen it. He lifted the visor on his helm, then spoke to Jahmai, who stood in stunned silence along with the rest of the soldiers.

"You have five hundred men. They are down to two hundred," Vorick said. "Finish it. Rescue my town and my mine."

My town. *My* mine. He loved the sound of those words. Yes, they were his. Nothing would stand in his way now. Soon it would all be his.

The men were slow to move, having witnessed something that belonged in legend, or perhaps in scripture. Vorick noticed their inaction, yet didn't repeat himself. Instead, he raised his eyebrows and cocked his head to give Jahmai a look of impatient expectation. The captain snapped into action, shouting at the surrounding soldiers to carry out their minister's orders.

Vorick put Flay back in her scabbard, removed his gauntlets, then barked back at Jahmai. "And get me something to eat."

PART THREE

The Humble Guardian stood on the hill, surrounded by a thousand foes. His mighty men had fallen in the fight, and only he remained. Separated from his Oracle, he lamented his imminent death only because he would no longer be able to protect her. Squeezing his bare toes into the soft earth, he wondered how many of the enemy would fall before the soil would be wet with his own blood.

Oracle, Guardian, and King by Jehosephat Marque - 605PB

27

GUARDIAN

The Cavern
Twenty-Two Days after Announcement

Nara woke early, although morning could be hard to discern in the constant illumination of the cavern. She walked out through the tunnel to make sure that the sun had risen. She smiled as it greeted her, still low in the sky. She stood for a time, watching the breeze on the high branches of the trees, thinking of what would come next in their lives. They couldn't stay here forever, and an urgency was taking root in her. An urgency to find her sister. To learn more about magic. And to use it.

Anne had spoken of how some people were broken, and that was how magic leaked out. But the world was also broken. The rich preyed on the poor. Children were given gifts that were used in war. Used to kill. It was all wrong.

Dei seemed silent in all of this, but Nara didn't have to be. With Mykel by her side, could she change things? If she could find her sister, who might also have magic, they would be even stronger. They could make a difference. They could matter.

She walked back inside and found had Bylo already risen and was practicing the protection rune on the stone table. Anne stood next to him, watching.

Nara approached closely enough to hear, but remained behind the stone pillar, out of sight.

"Almost ready," Bylo said to Anne. "Soon."

"Okay," Anne said. "Soon it is."

"I'll need more ink," he said.

"And you'll have some," Anne said.

Mykel was going to get his tattoo. There was comfort in how Anne was guiding them, working for their protection, like a good friend. Or a mother. Nara wandered away from the pillar, crossing the cavern slowly to sit in the bed of fire weeds and wondering what it would have been like to have a mother. Or perhaps a grandmother. What would her life have been like if she had known a woman who made sacrifices for the benefit of those that she loved? Who cared for Nara like Bylo always had?

Her thoughts moved to the plants about her, how they gave up their seeds to power the light runes, and through the light, brought life to the entire chamber. Such a small creation, these weeds, but they gave so much life.

She gently touched a weed. The petals retracted slightly, and the action surprised her enough that she pulled away quickly, impacting another weed with the back of her hand. The weed she struck curled its petals rapidly in response, making a sound that was almost like a squeak. Pain? At the same time, several leaves on its stem stiffened and shot out to the sides, impacting neighboring weeds. Those weeds then contracted their own petals and shot out to the sides with the leaves on their stems, like the first, but to a lesser degree. It created a ripple effect among the bed of weeds, like the wave in a pond when a stone impacts the water.

Hurting one weed resulted in damage to so many others.

"I'm sorry, little weed," she said to the first one.

With the petals closed, she could no longer see the white fluffy seeds in the center of the blossom. They were locked away, as if the flower was protecting its treasures rather than sharing them with the world.

Nara swept her hand over a wide swath of the weeds. Many of them released white seeds, which were caught up in the air and drifted toward the ceiling, but the traumatized blossoms released none.

She blew air across the blossoms, and the undisturbed weeds let loose an even greater quantity of seeds than when she had swept her hand across them.

"Wow," she marveled aloud at the sight of the seeds floating upward.

She heard a sound and turned to see Anne approaching.

"They close up when you are harsh with them," Anne said, "but if you're gentle, they let go of their treasures."

"And if you blow on them," Nara said, "they release so much more." She blew on a blossom to demonstrate, and it loosed a plentiful puff of seeds. She turned back to the pained ones. "I wonder how long they need to recover from the shock."

"The same is true of people," Anne said. "When we are in pain, we bear little fruit. We often retreat into ourselves and are of little use to anyone."

"Or we spread the pain to others like this one did." She pointed to the weed that she had struck with her hand. Its petals remained tight, its leaves still stiff and out to the sides as if it was unforgiving, or perhaps, still afraid.

"Yes. But when they are ready, and shown love, even the wounded can forgive, forget, and bless others with their treasures." Anne said. "I'm going to teach Mykel. I could use your assistance."

Nara wondered what help she could provide in teaching someone how to fight. "You're going to hurt him, aren't you?"

"He'll be uncomfortable, yes. That's part of growth, isn't it?"

Nara said nothing.

"Your choice." Anne left her alone.

Seeing Mykel train, sharing the joy of his learning and the sense of victory he would have in acquiring new skills was appealing. He had wanted to learn these skills for a long time. Didn't every boy dream of becoming a soldier and fighting in battles?

But the pain.

Nara stood, finally resolving to be with him during this time. The walk across the cavern came with trepidation, however. The closer she was, the more she felt his pain. She felt it even more with Mykel than with other people, perhaps because of their friendship and the time they'd spent together.

Other people didn't experience sympathetic pain the way she did, but didn't they still feel it, in a sense? Didn't a parent suffer when a child was hurt? Didn't friends or lovers share each other's burdens—physical, emotional, or otherwise? She would try to endure it, for his sake.

When she came upon the training area, Nara found Mykel standing in a wide stance, arms held out in front of him, hands bladed, with fingers straight. Gwyn was next to him, a mirror image; both were following Anne's directions.

"Keep your hands high, but not in front of your eyes. You need to see what's coming your way," Anne said. "Keep your feet apart, providing a strong base. Shuffle them as you move, never cross them. Too easy to lose your balance. And don't wear shoes, Mykel. Not ever. Your bare feet give you a better grip of the earth, better balance, and a foundation for faster action."

Nara watched Mykel squeeze his feet against the stone floor, and she sat down. She took off her own shoes in solidarity with him, resting her soles against the cool surface of the stone, hoping to share in the experience.

Anne stepped closer to Mykel, one hand on her walking stick to support herself. "Time for some fisticuffs, young warrior."

Mykel grinned, and Nara could see his eagerness.

"Bend your knees more. Yes, that's the way. This deep stance is called earth stance. Solid, a great base for some actions, but slow to move or react. You can't lose your balance easily, but neither can you quickly attack. Now, you'll learn air stance."

Anne tapped his left foot with her stick. "Move this one back, bent, supporting most of your weight. Keep your arms out in front, bent at the elbows, hands bladed high and ready to react, palms forward."

Mykel followed her directions, and Gwyn mirrored Mykel's movements.

"Your front leg is bent as well, your heel is high, and some of your weight is borne on the ball of your foot. Light. Quick to react, to spring forward, to block, kick, or step aside. Light as air."

As Mykel moved his right foot, his hands relaxed.

"Hands up!" Anne said. "Always up! Ready to protect your face."

Anne gestured, and Gwyn moved to stand in front of Mykel.

"And no healing until you're told," Anne said. "Defend only; don't counter."

Gwyn punched him in the nose and Nara immediately put a hand to her own face, her eyes tearing up with the sympathetic pain. Slow to react, Mykel had taken the blow squarely, painfully.

"Air stance!" Anne yelled. "Hands up. Dodge the next one!"

He put his right foot forward, on its toes, left leg bent slightly in support, squaring his shoulders again, but getting the stance wrong. Anne moved his foot and adjusted his shoulders. Gwyn jabbed again, but this time Mykel stepped to the left with his support leg, dodging her attack, his left hand brushing against her fist to guide it away from its intended target.

"Good," Anne said. "Keep going."

For the better part of an hour, Gwyn punched Mykel. Sometimes in the face, sometimes in the gut. She tripped him and kicked him and elbowed him in the ribs. He tried to remain in air stance the whole time, and every once in a while he dodged or blocked the blows. Most of the time he just suffered.

At the end of the session, bloodied and broken, Mykel was permitted to take a break. He came over to Nara, his hair and brows wet with sweat, his shoulders slumped.

"I'm not feeling much like a warrior right now," Mykel said.

"I think you're doing great," Nara said. "But you should rest."

"I'm going to lie down in the grass for a while."

Nara smiled, grateful for the respite herself, as she didn't know how much longer she could endure Mykel's discomfort. Anne came over to sit next to Nara while Mykel walked toward the grass.

"How are you doing?"

"I'm okay," Nara said, but it was a lie. Feeling Mykel's pain was horrible, and she didn't see the point of all this training. Why did people fight? They should be building things, cooking, traveling, eating, and laughing. Not hurting one another.

"Want some help?"

"What do you mean?"

"Flare the earth rune, and at the same time reach to the ground below. But don't shape it. Just reach."

Nara did as she said, closing her eyes and flaring the symbol she had seen in Bylo's book, the symbol that had helped her command the earth. She reached out through the smooth, cool stone beneath her feet and sensed many of the things that the earth touched. Mykel's bare skin against the earth made him easy to detect, but she could also identify the roots of the trees, the grass, and, in the distance, the fire weeds. "I can feel his footfalls. And more."

"Yes," Anne said.

"Mykel. His feet walking across the stone. He's tired. I can tell that he's tired."

"Yes."

"How do you know all this, Anne?"

"Well," she said, chuckling. "You live a few centuries, you pick up a few things."

Nara smiled.

"When you reach through the earth, it should diffuse the pain for you. Make it more bearable, as if it is sharing the burden a bit. It won't take it all away, but it should help with the headaches as well."

"Thank you."

"You're welcome."

————————

A short time later, Nara joined Mykel on the grass near the fruit tree, lying down with care so as not to disturb him.

As her head reached the grass, Mykel stirred, looking over at her.

"I'm sorry," she said. "I didn't mean to wake you."

"I wasn't sleeping. Can't seem to calm down."

"Thinking about?"

"Dimmitt. Sammy. And how long we can stay here."

"I'm worried too," Nara said.

"When Bylo gives me the new tattoo—"

"We will go," Nara finished. "Yes. I want to find my sister, if I can."

"Okay," Mykel said. "Dimmit. Sam. Then your sister?"

"Yes. Hopefully, Bylo will be okay with it."

"Does it matter?" Mykel asked.

"Yes, it matters. I care what he thinks. But if he says no, I'll probably go anyway. Still coming?"

"Of course," Mykel answered. "I'll never leave you, Nara."

She reached over, and her fingers found his hand. She clasped it firmly, her head turning to look up at the cavern ceiling as she smiled. "I know you won't."

"What will you say to your sister if you find her?" he asked, still holding her hand as they now both stared up at the cavern ceiling.

"I really don't know."

————————

When the next training session began, Nara's bare feet were on the stone, reaching out to Mykel as he squared up against Gwyn. Nara felt him through the earth. Through her magic.

"Okay, now you know what happens if you're slow and let yourself get hit," Anne said. "This time, you'll learn counterattacks. Pull your punches. Gwyn can't heal like you can. And keep air stance light and tight; every time you get sloppy, you get hit."

Mykel nodded.

Anne taught that air stance was not merely a defensive posture, but allowed transition into offense once the attacker committed to closing the distance. With good balance and light feet, the posture allowed control over the engagement, giving Mykel his choice of several responses to his opponent. If his enemy came at him with a haymaker, he could stabilize his position with a deep bend of his knees, dodging the blow and pushing forward with his support leg to drive his elbow into the ribs of the unbalanced combatant. If the enemy led with a front kick, he might block the leg, crush the knee with his elbow, or simply push her off balance. If his opponent led with a roundhouse or wheel kick, Mykel could drop below the attack and take the attacker off her feet with a foot sweep, or use a low kick to break her shin.

But Gwyn was so fast that he rarely managed any of these things, and he got hit again and again. Due to her connection with the earth, Nara felt the pain lessen, but she knew it provided no salve for Mykel. Unless...

Eyes still open, she reached out to him, but instead of just sensing his movements and emotions, she sent her strength to him. He must have felt something because a look of surprise crossed his face, and Gwyn managed to land a front kick in his gut when he failed to react.

"Nara," he said, doubled over in pain, trying to stand back up.

"Sorry, Mykel."

Gwyn gave them an odd look, but Anne smiled.

"No, it's okay," Mykel said. "Do it again."

The second hour of training welcomed many more bruises and a few broken ribs, but Nara was able to keep the connection to him, lend him some of her strength, and mute the pain on her end at the same time. Even though she was standing more than twenty feet away, in a sense, she was fighting by his side. The pace of his movements picked up; her efforts were clearly empowering him.

Even though Anne had told him not to, Nara sensed Mykel flare health to repair a bruised thigh that had received one too many roundhouse kicks from Gwyn's lightning-fast feet. When Gwyn swung a kick for the injured thigh again, Mykel anticipated the attack and left air stance, interrupting her with a lunge forward. It closed the distance and placed him inside her guard to perform a double-punch to her gut and sternum. She flew back more than ten feet under the strength of his blow.

Anne clapped. "Well done. But you cheated."

Gwyn, breath knocked out of her, got to her feet.

"Sorry," he said, offering a hand and helping her up.

"It's okay. I deserved that," Gwyn said. "I was picking on you, but you are learning fast, Mykel. You were born to this."

"Thank you."

"I mean it," she said. "Even without your healing, you have a talent for this. I've never trained with anyone who learns so fast."

"I may have had a little help," he said, looking to Nara and smiling.

Nara gave a sly grin, and Gwyn returned a puzzled look. Then both Nara and Mykel laughed.

"Time for a break," Anne said. "Please get Bylo, then come find me."

Nara found Anne in the back of the sleeping alcove, staring at a darker section of the wall. There were no runes illuminating the area, yet Anne stared at the blank section of rock, motionless. Was she remembering something?

Mykel, Gwyn, and Bylo joined them just as Anne spoke. "Mykel," she said, pointing. "Please put your hand here."

He placed his hand over the rock as she directed. As he did so, surprise crossed his face.

"Feed it," she said. "You now touch the stone this rune is inscribed upon. As you do with your tattoo, when you're in contact with a rune, you can feed it with your magic."

Mykel closed his eyes, and Nara saw something inside the wall—no, on the other side of the wall—begin to glow. The sound of rushing water inside the wall came next, followed by a grinding sound, stone on stone. A door slid open in front of them, a well-lit chamber beyond. Sounds of trickling water emanated from within.

Mykel turned to Nara. "I just used magic! I opened a door!"

"Yes, you did," she answered. She smiled at the pride in his voice. The joy. A growing sense of self-worth that the years with his father had suppressed, but perhaps not destroyed.

The opening revealed a brightly lit room, perhaps thirty feet in diameter, with a high ceiling. Inscribed on the walls were numerous light runes. She wondered how the plants in the grooves accessed the seeds for food, until she saw the large holes in the upper part of the ceiling, obviously crafted to allow air and drifting seeds into the chamber.

A stream of water dripped down one wall, spilling into a pool below. Blue water.

"What's that?" asked Bylo, pointing to the stream.

"That," Anne said, "is your ink."

Bylo grinned. "Where does it come from?"

"Let me show you." She walked over to the wall, then reached up to one of the runes and pressed her fingers against the tiny plants therein. When she pulled her fingers away and showed them to Bylo, they were stained blue.

"The plants produce ink?" Mykel asked.

"Not so much from these little ones. The big ones high in the cavern—they produce more, and the ink drips down. This pool empties into the river that flows through the center of the larger cavern," she added. "It's one of the reasons the water is so invigorating. It's full of magic."

"It's full of life," Nara said. "Wow. I wonder what else that water could be used for. Treating sick people?" She looked at Anne.

"Maybe you should try it sometime," Anne said.

Mykel walked over to the pool. "It's blue," he said.

Nara came alongside Mykel. On the surface of the deep-blue water, she saw flashes of red, green, and orange. The fluid was opaque, and she couldn't discern what lay beneath. Mykel reached in, startling Nara with his boldness. He seemed to be grasping at something.

Wide-eyed, Nara threw a look of worry to Anne, whose calm visage betrayed no alarm.

"There's something in here," Mykel said. "Maybe more than one thing, I feel them bumping around in the ink."

Nara stepped back as he pulled out a long white stick. It was a staff, completely fashioned of ivory, and almost as tall as Mykel. It was bright white, almost shining, and bore ornately carved designs along the shaft. Two runes were inscribed on the head of the staff. Ink slid off the weapon, pooling onto the stone floor below.

"It's light." Mykel swung it about with apparent ease. "Like a feather. And I can sense magic within. Maybe a lot."

Gwyn took a step forward, eyes wide, as if she wanted to hold the staff herself. She then stepped back. Did she see something? Nara looked at the staff with her own vision and saw the warm, bright light of the weapon pulsing like a heartbeat.

"Mammoth ivory," Anne said. "Charged with power."

"Can't be," Bylo said. "Mammoths are extinct."

"Yes, they are," Anne said.

"It has to be walrus, then."

"Have you ever heard of a walrus with a tusk that long?"

"No," Bylo said. "Oh, my. If that is mammoth, it must be very old."

"More than a thousand years," Anne said.

Mykel didn't respond, his eyes transfixed upon the object in his hands.

"Still want a sword?" Nara asked, then chuckled.

"Not a chance," Mykel whispered with reverence. Gripping the shaft with both hands, he swung it about cautiously.

"He looks like one of the warriors of old with that thing," Gwyn said. "You know, those holy soldiers from eons ago with the white staves and bare feet?"

"Yes he does," Anne said.

"Nara, don't help him this time," Anne said as the next training session began. "Let Mykel do this alone. Use the earth to mute your own pain if you like, but don't interfere."

Nara nodded.

In this session, Gwyn used her sword, sharp and gleaming, without restraint. She thrust and slashed, low and high at him, fast and relentless. At first, Mykel was caught by her speed and ferocity and bled from multiple wounds. One slash cut across his forehead, down to the bone. Nara winced with each blow—not just because of the pain it brought her but also out of concern for her friend.

"Anne, please," Nara said. "Is this really necessary?"

"Bear it, girl. He'll be ok."

The blood flowed into his eyes, clearly obscuring his vision, but Anne would not let him heal or counterattack, only to block Gwyn's blows. If he could.

"Feel the staff in your grip. Let it be your hands, but also your eyes," Anne said. "Let it see for you in a new way."

The words seemed like nonsense to Nara as Mykel suffered under the attacks, the multiplying cuts across his body certainly contributing to a mass of confusion and discomfort. She longed to reach out and soothe his growing angst, but didn't want to rob him of the training he was so eager for.

"You are a living cepp, Mykel," Anne said. "A storehouse of energy. The staff is a weapon, but a cepp as well, having rested hundreds of years in a magical pool, absorbing magic. Learn from it. Flow with it like the magic that has been its home."

Flow with it? How did someone flow like magic? Anne had not taught Mykel how to strike with the weapon, nor how to block. Was he supposed to figure these things out when he could hardly see, bleeding and weak as he was? Nara didn't know how long she could withhold aid.

"Close your eyes!" Anne said. "Use the staff to see!"

He closed his eyes, and Nara closed her own. She reached out through the earth to feel Mykel, to sense his thoughts and his movements, but she did not send him her strength. Not yet.

Through the earth, through the magic, she could sense what he sensed. See what he saw. Runes. They were blurry, indistinct. The health rune from his hip was there, along with two new ones.

A new, hot pain sliced through his right shoulder, metal striking bone, and Nara reached for her own shoulder in reflex. She sensed fear rise in Mykel, then he pushed it back down and focused on the runes again. He focused on one of them, and she felt him feed it, then look around.

Awareness flooded Nara's vision through the shared link. Mykel could see the entire cavern at once—Gwyn moving in front of him, Anne standing a few feet away—and Nara could see herself through Mykel's eyes. No, not his eyes—through this new rune. He could even see the sword coming straight for his face.

Nara opened her eyes to see Mykel step back and to the side, catching Gwyn's right foot on her instep. She lost her footing and fell, narrowly avoiding an impact between the stone floor and her nose, lost the grip on her sword, and moved into an awkward, poorly executed somersault. She rolled to her feet and raced to retrieve her weapon.

Such speed and accuracy in that movement! How had Mykel done that?

"It will be hard for you now," Anne said to Gwyn, smirking. "He found it." Anne moved a step closer to Mykel and said, "Mykel, you can counterstrike now, but be gentle with her."

Gwyn retrieved her sword and engaged. Anne motioned for her to attack again, and although Mykel could now heal himself, his injuries must have sparked compassion in Gwyn. The blood on his face was now drying and caking in his eyes. He was utterly blind, and his red-stained tunic was slashed to pieces, hanging like rags about him. Fresh, gaping wounds were visible, caused by a dozen of her slashes and thrusts. He had lost a torrent of blood, and much of it was smeared on the stone floor, creating a slippery surface.

"Anne, this is too much," Gwyn said. "Let him heal."

Nara looked to Anne, hoping she would relent.

"No!" Anne said. "Attack! With everything you have!"

"I'm ok," Mykel said. "Don't stop."

Gwyn charged and came high with a thrust. Mykel used the staff to smack the back of her wrist as she jabbed with her blade, then he spun away as she passed him without connecting. She rubbed the back of her wrist as she turned back to face him. Despite being unable to use his eyes, Mykel had guessed her movements, her position, and where to attack. Perfectly.

She came at him again, faster this time, sweeping mid-waist then high. He stood there, bare feet unmoving in a gentle crouch, blocking the attacks with alternating ends of the staff. He spun in an odd motion and caught her in the back of her head with the bottom end of the staff as he completed his turn. The gentle smack could not have produced much pain. He was wielding it like a master teaching a student who had performed a maneuver incorrectly. Exactly what kind of magic did that staff carry?

Gwyn renewed her effort, sweeping toward his legs twice, then high with renewed resolve. She feinted and spun, yet he blocked or parried or dodged every time, hitting her softly in a dozen places, gentle taps to show his level of control, his complete mastery over the contest. Gwyn had no chance. None at all.

Mykel smiled, eyes still closed. "I see it all," he said. "Before it happens. Not long, just a moment, but the staff knows what you are going to do. *I* know it."

Nara looked over at Anne, who nodded, smiling. Gwyn put down her sword.

"Heal yourself, son," Anne said. "Then wash. You have suffered enough for today. Good job."

"How is he doing that?" Gwyn asked, her rapid breaths betraying her exhaustion.

"You're looking at someone the likes of whom the world hasn't seen in hundreds of years."

"What is he?" Nara asked.

Anne paused before answering, and when she finally spoke, Nara detected a nostalgic tone in her voice. "He's a Guardian. The first in a very long time."

28

CROWN

Fairmont
The Estate of Lord Vorick

The liberation of Kavalin had been accomplished without delay, and Vorick's return trip to Fairmont was pleasant. When he arrived at his estate, however, Kayna was nowhere to be found.

He thought for a moment how he might tell the girl about her twin. They would be together soon, providing for an interesting reunion. Kayna had never been the emotional type, but he wondered how she might react. Would she see her sister as a rival or ally? He hoped he could manage the chaos of it. Kayna was difficult enough to manage alone and having two of her might prove to be more than he could handle. Someday, they might lead his armies in a vast expansion of the Great Land. Or lead him to the discovery of new magics entirely, new powers to call his own. Regardless, they were *his* treasures, and he would let nobody else possess them.

Following a good night's sleep, he summoned a messenger and sent a dispatch to Holland, announcing that he would be coming by the chancery to discuss some changes. Triff arrived at the estate a short time later, then helped Vorick don his armor and sword.

"I'm off to claim what's mine, Triff," he said.

He walked out the front door of his home and down the middle of the street toward the chancery. It was a long walk, but the energy coursing through the armor produced a drug-like high and he enjoyed every minute of it. Fueled by the magic, he strode confidently in the suit of coral plates, presenting a spectacle that brought shock to all he passed. He smiled back at them, the visor of his helmet open. They should know who would be so bold.

Upon arrival at the chancery, Vorick scaled the steps and approached the large front doors. The tall columns and ornate carvings on the chancery exterior were magnificent but paled in comparison to the opulence that now walked into the building. Pages and politicians abounded, yet all stopped when they spied the man in the brightly colored coral. Once inside, he stepped to the center of the foyer. He stared at those who surrounded him. "What are you waiting for?" he said. "Bring me the chancellor!"

Several young pages scurried about in response, flustered by the show. One of them must have found Holland because the portly statesman hurried into the foyer holding a messy sheaf of papers in one hand and a pair of spectacles in the other.

"Hello, Archibald. How are you?" Vorick said.

"What in the name of all that is holy are you doing here, Vorick? And what is that upon you? Coral?"

Red-faced and angry, Holland practically stomped as he approached, but Vorick knew it wouldn't last long. After all, Holland was a watcher.

"Take a look at me. A *good* look."

In response to Vorick's invitation, Holland fell to his knees with a yelp of pain, covering his eyes in reflex. His spectacles fell, lenses cracking, and his papers scattered on the floor.

"Bright, aren't I?"

"What in hades is that?" Holland asked.

"This is a paradigm shift in the power of the Great Land, Archibald."

"What are you talking about?"

Vorick stepped toward the chancellor, who was still on his knees. Vorick's voice took on a menacing tone.

"You will call an emergency meeting of the council. You will hold it at the noon hour. Today." As he spoke, he placed his right hand on Holland's shoulder and squeezed. Holland winced as the sharp edges of the coral gauntlet bit into his skin. "I have some legislation for you to consider."

Vorick turned and walked out of the chancery, leaving Holland cowed. His next visit was to Archbishop Chayfus. It was a meeting without conflict. Chayfus had always favored Vorick and encouraged him to be ambitious. Vorick promised the greedy man a significant boost of wealth if the church would support his next moves. The treasure of coral that Vorick wore upon his person provided ample evidence of an ability to make good on the promise.

The cleric was quick to agree. Upon his departure, Vorick was confident that the archbishop had already begun to imagine how to spend his new wealth.

Vorick arrived late to the council chamber, which occupied its own hall inside the castle walls. It had been placed there to provide easy access for the royals in times past. Vorick wondered if some monarch, ages ago, envisioned a siege of Fairmont and the need for his advisors to be close. He likely never imagined that the power of kings and queens would fade, ceding authority to civilian council members.

Vorick aimed to change the course of such things.

As intended, Vorick's tardiness allowed the council ample opportunity to discuss his recent success in Kavalin, news of which had preceded his arrival in Fairmont. It also allowed them time to digest the news of his dramatic display at the chancery a few hours earlier.

When Vorick approached the large chamber, he stopped shortly after entering. The buzz of conversations hushed and all thirty sets of eyes turned to him. A dramatically slow pace took him down the long central aisle, after which he stepped up onto the dais and motioned the gathered men to take their seats.

Half a dozen remained standing, incensed and offering a silent rebuke for his audacity. Vorick looked at them all, bringing each of their names to mind. There were a few gifted in the mix but no watchers, aside from Holland. He glanced over at the chancellor, who sat in an abnormal silence. Several of the other ministers glanced back and forth between Vorick and Holland as if they expected the chancellor to do something. They would be disappointed.

"Good afternoon," Vorick stated. "You may take your seats."

Despite the second request, three remained standing. Vorick removed his helm and set it on the podium in front of him, visor closed and facing the crowd of men. The crimson color and menacing appearance encouraged two more to take their seats.

"Fellson Weis, I believe," Vorick said, stepping off the dais and approaching the sole protestor. "Minister of Transport, if I recall?"

"Correct. And I take personal offense to your manner today, Lord Minister," he said. "Congratulations on your success in Kavalin, but you're in Fairmont now, and I—"

"Sit down and shut up," Vorick said.

Weis stood slack-jawed, awestruck by the insult, but somehow found the will to protest. "I don't know who you think you are, and I don't care what sort of wealth you display here. I won't be intimidated."

The man never spoke another word. Vorick didn't even gesture in his direction. So full of energy was his armor that the command he held over his talents was absolute and no movement was necessary to focus his thoughts. He simply willed it and Weis ceased to exist, shriveling in place, then collapsing. He turned to dust in scarcely more than a heartbeat, the energy of his spirit sucked into the armor.

Stunned silence dominated the room.

"Are there any other concerns we need to address?" Vorick asked the other noblemen.

Dozens of mouths were agape. A few made nervous gestures,

and one man fainted. Vorick was thrilled with the apparent respect this crowd now held for him. No, it wasn't respect, although that might come later. This was pure fear.

"Excellent," Vorick said, stepping back onto the dais. "The first order of business for the day is a reinstatement of the crown's authority supreme."

A hushed rumble passed among the lips of many in the chamber, but it lasted only a moment.

"The royal abdication of 650 PB will be rescinded and the council's power abolished. Each of you will retain your positions as advisors only, with no vote on matters of state." He turned to one side and spoke to an elderly man in the front row. "Lord Minister of Administration."

"Yes, Lord." The man was visibly shaking.

"You will assemble the necessary paperwork?"

"Of course, Lord, but..." He paused. "Forgive me. There is a small matter if I may be so bold?"

"And what is that?" Vorick asked.

"Agreement must be unanimous on this matter. Such a move is unprecedented."

Vorick looked around the room at the faces before him, then chuckled.

"That won't be a problem."

A few hours later Vorick left the emasculated council carrying documents that bore the signatures of every member, including his own. His destination was the inner rooms of the castle residence.

Queen Mellice was doing what she often enjoyed at this hour: drinking tea and eating sweets in one of the many dining rooms. Her girth had grown unwieldy over the years as she found little occasion to leave the castle. Royalty had little need to venture about nowadays, for there had been ministers that attended to matters of state. A cadre of ladies dined with her, Kayna among them. Seated near the queen were two young men as well. Vorick was pleased to find that one of them was Prince Bertrand, sitting at Mellice's right. The other was a friend of the prince, the young and newly recognized Earl of Katch, who had taken the mantle of authority when his father passed away.

"Darin, is it?" Vorick intruded upon the gathering, carrying the resplendent helm under the crook of his left arm. "Sorry to hear about your daddy." His voice carried no sincerity. Darin fidgeted nervously with a piece of cutlery in response to the comment.

Kayna eyes grew wide with surprise. She had clearly seen the power in the armor.

The sitting room was modestly decorated compared to other royal dining areas. Several vents admitted cool air from the gardens below and the windows provided a beautiful view of the Twins. Vorick found the breeze refreshing. As comfortable as his armor was, it was quite warm.

"What is the meaning of this intrusion, Minister Vorick?" the queen stated indignantly. She struggled to rise to her feet, her ample girth spilling about her.

"I require an audience with you, Mellice."

His use of her first name, absent her title, was an obvious affront. She glared back angrily, clearly vexed at the insult offered in front of her guests.

"*I* summon *you*, Nikolas, not the other way around," she said.

Vorick drew Flay from her scabbard, holding the blade casually and flitting it about. He circled the table slowly. Bertrand stood and reached for the saber at his side, but it was ornamental, not meant for combat. Vorick thought back to the rapier he once bore for the same purpose and marveled for a moment at the scope of his own transformation.

"I wouldn't do that if I were you, Bertie," he said.

Bertrand hesitated. With no magic of his own, he had little ability to stand against the blessed lord. He sat back down.

Vorick moved between two of the queen's ladies, who were frozen to their chairs.

"The rest of you can go. Kayna, Bertrand, please remain."

He set the helm and scroll case on the table in front of the queen. The show had worked for the council; perhaps it would also work for her. He needed her obedience if his plans were to work.

The guests left without delay but muttered under their breath about rudeness and unfinished snacks.

"Marry me, Mellice," Vorick said. "Tonight."

Her head bobbed back as if she had been struck by a blow, her eyes widening in surprise. "How dare you? I'll... Well, I'll do no such thing."

The blade in Vorick's hand came down toward the prince, stopping inches above his head. It had moved with lightning speed, and the queen screeched.

"This bag of pomp you call your son holds no value to me," Vorick said, the blade now hovering menacingly near the prince's face. "You, on the other hand, hold some value. A marriage will provide a semblance of legitimacy, but I don't require it. If you refuse, I'll simply kill you both and take the throne by force."

"No, please," she said, her protests vanishing. "I'll do whatever you say."

"Of course you will."

A short time later, Archbishop Chayfus arrived at the castle and presided over a brief ceremony in the royal chapel. It was witnessed by Prince Bertrand, Kayna, and Chancellor Holland. The next day, a coronation was held in the Great Hall with a much larger audience. Spouses of royalty rarely received a coronation, but Vorick had insisted. At the beginning of the coronation, Mellice made an insincere statement to the assembled nobles and politicians about her devotion to Vorick and her faith in his leadership, then spent the rest of the rite standing beside her son.

Vorick was king.

29

PROTECTION

The Cavern

Gwyn stood watching as Bylo poured water from a canteen upon his stone table to clean the surface. He then set out several needles and a pot of ink. "Interested?" he asked.

"Fascinated, more like," she said. "Your magic is different from any I've ever heard of."

Bylo smiled, then called in the direction of the pool. "Mykel! I'm ready for you."

Mykel walked up, still dripping wet. "Where will you put it?"

"On your chest. Big. This will hurt."

"I can take it."

Gwyn chuckled at the interaction between the two, especially at Mykel's bravado.

Anne's approach interrupted her quiet admiration.

"He's near," Anne said quietly, more casually than the news warranted.

"Who is?" Gwyn asked, moving back from the table so the others wouldn't hear.

"Your general. At the Abbey in Eastway. Looking for you."

A coldness swept across Gwyn. Vorick sent Cross?

"What are you going to do?" Anne asked.

"What choice do I have?"

"You always have choices. And they define you."

Or get you killed, Gwyn thought.

"You know things, Anne. What happens next? Will Cross kill Mykel?"

"Would it change your mind if he did?"

"It might."

Anne remained silent.

"Will I see you again?" Gwyn asked.

Anne reached for Gwyn's shoulder and gave it a gentle squeeze. "Take care of yourself."

The intimacy shocked Gwyn, Anne's kindness standing in stark contrast to the treachery Gwyn intended. Confusion and anxiety swirled messily in Gwyn's mind, and she fought a desire to remain in the cavern. Awash in self-loathing, she stepped toward the tunnel, smothering her feelings with an iron resolve to fulfill her mission. This was by far the darkest task she had undertaken, and the consequences would be grave.

Nara sat in the dark cave, a dozen feet under the surface of the plateau, resting her head on a mound of soft dirt. Since finding the rune in Bylo's book, she could see the earth and feel its energy. Shaping now came with surprisingly little effort as she carved rock and dirt with her thoughts. Oh, if Bylo hadn't held her back, she would have learned this years ago! The symbols weren't power in themselves but they unlocked power—something she was just beginning to understand.

She thought of how the wind had moved the trees by the creek, and how the sunlight had warmed her face. She thought of the fire weeds, and of people. Dei's creations were beautiful, but so fragile. Sunlight waned, wind faded, weeds perished, and sometimes, people died.

She could hide from Him, and from everything else if she wished. She could close the large cavern door and lock herself inside for a long time. Away from people, and away from trouble. But she didn't want to hide. Not anymore. If she could learn to use her magic, perhaps she wouldn't have to.

Anne said Nara could become whatever she wished. Was that true? Earth was one of several elements, according to her schooling. Others were air, fire, and water. She thought of the ways her own talents had revealed themselves. Magic was primarily associated with livings things. She sensed the emotions of people and animals and how they might act. She could even influence those feelings. She had healed herself during the ambush by those terrible men and moved magic like a harvester. But until recently she had never commanded a prime element. Commanded. It wasn't the right word. *Coaxed* made more sense, as if it were a partnership and the earth needed convincing, not harsh orders.

Then there was the protection rune that Bylo practiced for Mykel. Could she summon that symbol as well? She pictured the design in her mind, remembering its complexity from the wall in the cavern. Despite several attempts, she manifested nothing, its shape eluding her. Although she wanted to try something else, she failed to remember what other runes Bylo had practiced over the years. Perhaps she would have to borrow his book again.

The sound of sniffing and a patter of little feet alerted her, and she looked up. Through the darkness, a small pair of glowing eyes stared back at her. A raccoon? Fox? Although too dark for normal sight, when she closed her eyes and engaged her vision, she found that a wolf pup had wandered into her cave.

"Come here, my friend," she said, holding her fingers out. The pup stepped back a few paces in surprise at her movement, then approached, sniffing. It barked. Such a tiny pup, its bark sounded more like a chirp or squeak. Then the animal charged her, leaping onto her lap with its soft paws, tongue licking wildly at her face. A few moments later, two more pups came down the sloped entry, followed by an adult female. The little ones joined in the play, but their mother approached apprehensively, growling.

Nara closed her eyes, reaching her thoughts toward the animal, sending peace and comfort to ease the fears. The wolf responded well, approaching Nara to lick her cheek, then sat on her haunches. Nara played with them for several minutes before a sound from above interrupted the fun. Was someone calling her? The animals bolted away, the little ones exiting at clumsy puppy speeds after their mother, leaving Nara alone again in the dark.

"Nara?" A worried voice called down the ramp. It was Gwyn. "Are you down there?"

"I'm here."

"Are you okay?"

"I'm fine. Come down and take a look."

"I saw wolves." Gwyn moved cautiously into the dark cave as she examined Nara's new creation.

"It was just a mother and her pups."

"What did you make?" Gwyn asked, her voice betraying amazement.

"A little hiding place," Nara said. "What do you think?"

"I think you could use a lamp," Gwyn said, running her fingers around the side of the smooth stone wall.

"It is dark, but if I plant fire weeds and carve light runes…"

"I am heading to the village outside the abbey," Gwyn said, still looking about. "For supplies. Just wanted to let you know."

"Thank you."

"And Bylo's doing the tattoo," Gwyn said. "Might take a while."

"I'm going to check on him," Nara said, and moved toward the exit. This tattoo was important, a big event for Mykel, and she didn't want to miss it.

"I'll be back before dark," Gwyn called after her as she ran up the ramp.

Nara returned to the large cavern, intending to check on Mykel's status, but when she saw him on the rock table under Bylo's needle, she stopped herself. Interrupting them would only invite errors, and Mykel might need the protection the rune would bring.

She returned to the bed of weeds where she had spoken with Anne earlier. Although most of the blossoms had returned to their normal state, the one pained blossom remained in place, petals tight and unyielding. She sat carefully to avoid disturbing it again, then hummed a happy tune she had heard at last summer's solstice party in Dimmitt. She recalled Amos Dak singing the song, half drunk, belly bouncing out of his shirt as he danced. She laughed at the memory, then smiled sadly at the loss of him, and for her part in it. Remembering Amos' lyrics, she sang the words to try to cheer up the flower, hoping the plant would recover from the earlier trauma. It remained unresponsive.

She stopped singing and blew gently upon the blossom, giving encouraging words, as if helping a fearful child to take her first steps. "Open up, dear thing. It's safe now." Her tender words and easy breath had an effect, the petals opening slightly to reveal the white seeds inside. "I'm sorry, little flower," she said. "Forgive me."

She blew again and whispered more encouragement. The petals unfurled slowly, and the seeds began to release—one, two, then five, and ten. Once they were airborne, she blew on them, encouraging them upward, then fought an urge to chase after and catch them again. She smiled at the childish impulse and turned back to the blossom. Although releasing fewer seeds than the other flowers, it had made progress, and she smiled.

It was odd to feel such encouragement at the flower's recovery. After all, it was just a flower. But its victory spoke to something deeper. Pain had a way of healing, over time. Fearful things might not stay that way if someone took the time to show them love and patience.

Despite her victory with the fire weed, a faint headache threatened her, and she dreaded allowing the pain to take deeper root. She lay down among the weeds to rest.

Several hours of careful work later, Bylo finished the inscription. It might be the only way he could contribute to Nara's safety, and he was pleased with the effort.

When Mykel returned from the pool, healed and clean, Anne invited him to sit next to her and Bylo at the rock table, the new tattoo vibrant on his muscled chest.

"I think I got it right," Bylo offered, looking back and forth between Mykel and the stone wall that bore the same image.

"You did well. Thank you," Anne said.

"Tell me what it does," Mykel said.

"Some people would use weapons against you, but there are others who have the power to tear your body apart," she said. "Like swords, magic can be used in destructive ways. This helps. Not fool-proof, but if you can flare protection, it will give you some resistance to both."

"To swords? Like a steel skin?" Bylo asked.

"Yes, like that. And to magical attacks, which carry a greater threat. The protection rune essentially protects the integrity of both your body and spirit, resisting malformation by magic, blade, or bludgeon. Much better than a steel skin."

Mykel beamed. "Wait till Sammy hears about this!"

"The problem is, the more symbols you have dancing about in your head, the harder it will be to find them."

Mykel grimaced. "Like the confusion when I first held the staff. The runes were blurry, not sharp and clear like the health tattoo."

"Not only do you have two runes on your body now," Anne said, "but when you hold the staff, you can be confused by even more."

Mykel retrieved his weapon from where he left it earlier—leaning against the large pillar. "I wanted to ask you about these," he said, pointing to one of the designs. "This one looks like the protection rune."

"Yes. Though it's slightly different, it protects the staff—not you."

"How do you mean?" Bylo asked.

"This staff is made of ivory, which is strong but much weaker than the steel used in other weapons. When the ivory is charged with energy, it becomes stronger, but like all cepps, the energy bleeds out. This variation of the protection rune helps keep it both resistant to impact and prevents the energy from bleeding out."

Mykel nodded. "When it gets low, do I put it back in the ink pool?"

"Yes. Or you could just fill the staff yourself. You have a store-house of energy in you, boy. Runes inscribed upon you give a conduit to channel your magic, but you can also fill cepps or runes inscribed on objects. That's how you opened that stone door."

"What about the other rune, the one that helped me fight when I was blinded?" Mykel asked.

"You speak of the staff's sight rune. Sight not only helps you know what is, but also what might be, at least in the next moment. Useful, but it only applies to combat. The sight is from the staff's perspective," she tapped the staff, "not your own. It sees what matters to *it*. You will not be able to use it to win at cards or dice."

"Is the staff alive?" Bylo asked.

"In a manner of speaking," she said. "The weapon doesn't have a mind if that's what you're after, but it is filled with life, wouldn't you say?"

Of course, Bylo thought. Magic is life, and life is magic.

"How many tattoos can I have?" Mykel asked.

Bylo smiled at Mykel's ambition.

"Oh, look at Mister High and Mighty," Anne teased with her deep, hearty chuckle. "Why don't you hold the staff and try to find the protection rune Bylo just gave you, then we'll talk about all the many powers you want."

Mykel stood, gripping the gleaming white staff with both hands, and closed his eyes.

"Keep them open. Good practice for you."

As Bylo watched him grip the staff, eyes open, the boy seemed to look out across the cavern, focusing on something that wasn't there. "I can seize the health rune right away, but I've practiced that."

"Look for the others," Bylo said, joining in the magic of the moment. "Can you seize the new one?"

"No," he said. "But there are several, very blurry. Maybe if I just pick one…"

Bylo looked at Mykel closely and saw his eyes glow for a moment, just as Nara's had when she first began to use her gifts, years ago.

"That's the staff's protection rune, Mykel," Anne said. "You can see it, but it belongs to the staff, not to you. Try again."

Mykel's eyes flashed again.

"That's the right one, but it will take time to get control of it. Keep practicing."

His eyes flashed again, but then Mykel frowned. "I can't grab the thing. It's blurry, and every time I try to feed it, the design dances out of view again."

"Now you understand what I am telling you. More tattoos mean more mental discipline, more practice, or you'll just confuse yourself and find none of them."

Bylo shared Mykel's frustration. So much for decorating the boy with gifts. Hopefully, practice would help him grab hold of the powers, and the addition of the latest tattoo wouldn't end up setting Mykel back.

Anne sighed, but Bylo couldn't tell if her frustration was from Mykel's failure, or because of some concern she had not yet communicated. "Let's grab a bite, then Nara has something to show you." Anne nodded toward the fire weeds. "Mykel, could you please wake her for dinner?"

After Mykel left, Bylo put away his needles and ink.

"Wait," Anne said. "Do you have a small vial?"

"Uh, yeah, I guess," he said. "Why?"

"Grab the vial and put some of the good stuff in there."

Bylo knew nothing would come from arguing with Anne and did as she asked, pouring the cavern ink from one of his larger containers into the small vial.

"And a couple of needles. Just throw them in the vial."

"I don't keep needles in vials, Anne," he protested. "I…"

"Please?"

He smiled and removed the stopper, dropped two needles inside, then capped the vial. "To the Oracle of Ankar, we all owe much. I'd be happy to throw needles into a tiny vial if such a small thing would please her."

Anne chuckled. "I'm no such person anymore—just a one-eyed old woman. Now tuck it in your sock," she said. "Deep down, but be careful not to step on it. You wouldn't want to break it."

"What is this for, Anne?"

"You never know when you might need a little magic ink, young man."

30

BETRAYAL

The Abbey at Eastway

I t was the oldest abbey in the Great Land. It was also the largest. The stone spires stood tall, visible to villagers and peasant farmers for miles around. Its opulence was a monument to the majesty of Dei, or perhaps instead a testament to the wealth of the church that had funded its construction centuries ago.

In an office deep within the giant structure, General Cross stood with his hand clenched around the neck of a certain man of the cloth.

"Nobody matching those descriptions has been here," the abbot said with difficulty. His voice was strained as he struggled against the fingers that encircled his throat. "I swear it. I swear to Dei."

Cross towered over the man, pulling him close and growling in his face. What had begun as a polite conversation had quickly become an interrogation. He had never killed a priest and preferred not to start today, but his patience was growing thin. He pulled a dagger from its sheath and inspected it menacingly as he retained a grip on the abbot with his other hand.

"Foolish man, I don't believe in gods," Cross said with disgust.

"And invoking their names will do nothing for you today. I serve another master."

He put the blade to the abbot's cheek and continued, articulating each word with deliberation and emphasis, wasting not a syllable. "And my master wants these people." The edge of the knife cut into the abbot's skin as the man stiffened with the pain.

"General." Almit entered the room, interrupting. "We may have something."

Almit pulled a young monk into the room by the sleeve. "Tell General Cross what you told me."

The young man shivered as he spoke, clearly overwhelmed by the circumstances. "Last night after dark, I was sweeping the south walkway." He turned and pointed out the window.

"I was distracted by a light on the top of Crone's Hill."

"Crone's Hill?" Cross asked.

"It's what we call the plateau, a few miles to the south," the monk said. "There's a cabin on the hill. Our groundskeeper lives there."

"Why should we care about that?" Cross asked.

"Well, we haven't seen the old woman in some weeks," the monk said, "although that's not unusual for her. But it wasn't just a lantern light. It was bright. So bright I had to shield my eyes from it. Then it was gone."

"It seemed to matter, sir," Almit added, shrugging.

"It's the girl," Cross said, releasing his hand from the abbot's throat and dropping the cleric to the floor. He moved for the exit, dagger still in hand. "We go."

———

Gwyn lingered in the cave after Nara's departure. Where did all the dirt go? Then she realized the answer to her question. The earth was right here but had been made into stone. The hard walls and ceiling were compressed earth, minerals re-purposed and made dense, providing strength and stability. Such an ability to shape earth, compacting it into stone in such a short time, spoke well of the girl's potential for military applications. A dozen men wouldn't complete this in a month, and they would require pillars and buttresses to keep the ceiling from falling down upon them. Fortifications, moats, bridges—this child could build anything with her talent.

Gwyn left the cave and set on her way toward the abbey. A well-traveled path made for a quick hike and despite her promises, she would not be returning with supplies. There was no choice. Vorick would not be defeated. Nara's value was apparent, and there would be no standing in his way. Gwyn justified her actions by promising herself to urge mercy for Nara and Mykel. Perhaps there would be some redemption in that. Anne said that choices were what defined one's value. If that was true, then Gwyn's value was quite unimpressive right now.

After a mile she stopped, unwilling to continue. She sat on a nearby log and closed her eyes. How long might Mykel last against trained killers? A minute? Two? Despite his ability to sense an opponent's actions and determine the best course for his own, she doubted he could defeat Cross. The man had slain hundreds, engaging in tournaments and battles in which he not only defeated his opponents, but struck so hard that he would crush spines, mangle legs, and bloody brains. He had developed, albeit without magic, an innate sense of how to strike and where to move, possessing a mastery of violence and death that had matured over decades. Mykel was out of his league, no matter what magic he wielded.

But what about Nara? Her ability to command the earth could trap Cross in his own grave if she so willed. But even if she chose to stand tall, Nara would be vulnerable to Vorick.

Hiding had been the smart choice, the only option for survival. The cavern would be revealed, raided and the children's freedom taken. Secrets about magic and runes would all be given to Vorick in the last chapter of a very sad story.

Doubts again invaded her calm, piercing the resolve she had used to cloak herself. Desire for self-preservation seemed small compared to the growing fear that harm would come to Nara, Mykel, Bylo, and

Anne. She bit her lip in frustration. Again, she tried to convince herself that the time for indecision had passed, that this path had already been decided, but she couldn't do it.

She rose from the log and turned toward the abbey, but couldn't take the first step. A lifetime of loneliness and self-interest had made the meager trust she had earned in the last few weeks seem precious. She was afraid to throw it away.

Neither could she stand against Cross and Vorick, but they weren't here. Not yet. If she could alert her friends in time, they could flee right now.

Had Anne known that she would eventually change her mind? Was that why the old woman had not warned them? Gwyn had wasted so much time coming to this decision, and her thoughts raced to what needed to be done now. She would run back to the plateau and grab Nara, then retreat to the cavern. They would lock themselves inside while she broke the news to the others. Perhaps she would say that she had discovered Cross when she went to retrieve the supplies. Anne would know she was lying, but perhaps she wouldn't tell. Gwyn would explain later when they had more time. Then they would run. Further east, perhaps, where the population was sparse and Vorick's reach would be weaker.

It was the best plan she could think of. She turned around and started back to the cavern, but before she took even a few steps, she heard movement on the path behind her. She spun to see two figures coming down the path. One was very large.

"Khoury," the big one said.

It was Cross. Her breath caught in her throat, and a shiver moved down her spine.

"We've been looking for you," he continued.

A snowflake landed on the back of her hand and melted on her skin. She looked down to see more flakes land upon it. It was the first snowfall since their arrival in Eastway, announcing the coming of winter. A fitting omen. Anne had misjudged her. Gwyn had come to her decision too late, and this story would end today.

"Hello, General," she said. "I've been waiting for you."

Nara woke to find Mykel sitting nearby. "Is it time to eat?" she asked, sleepily.

"Yes, but I couldn't bear to wake you."

"It's okay," she said. "I was dreaming."

"Good dreams?"

"Yes," she said. "About you, actually."

Mykel blushed and stuttered uncomfortably.

"Not like that." She blushed in return. "You were strong and proud, fighting on the plateau against evil men." She stood, helped by his offered hand. "Saving me."

He moved closer, still holding her hand. He was close, and she could feel his warm breath on her face as he spoke.

"I'll always protect you, Bitty."

"I know you will."

He squeezed her hand, and her heart leaped in response. So close to her, she longed for him to move even closer, to kiss her, but something seemed to stop him and he released her hand. Old habits of keeping his distance had apparently taken over.

"Anne says you have something to show us," he said. "But first we eat."

They joined the others for a dinner of fruit and venison from a deer that had been killed by Gwyn that morning. Nara explained that Gwyn had left to the abbey for supplies and joked with Mykel about needing a shirt to cover his gaudy tattoo.

Mykel seemed proud and confident, and his strength brought a feeling of security to Nara. The abundance of life in the cavern was also comforting, filling her with a sense of hope that had been largely absent in recent days. She thought of the wolf pups back in her little cave, and the joy of the earth magic as it moved under her fingers. Good things. Encouraging things.

Maybe she could find a future with this handsome young man after all. He loved her, despite how fragile she often felt. She could sense his feelings but he always held back, probably thinking that he would break her. Or that she would reject him. He shouldn't worry, she wouldn't reject him. And today, she was happy.

Anne walked behind the youths as they headed through the tunnel and outside the cavern, hand in hand. Young love was always beautiful to witness.

Bylo came up alongside Anne. "They look good together."

"Yes, they do," Anne said.

They stopped as they approached the tunnel exit, the sounds of the creek bubbling up from the ground near their feet. Bylo looked toward Nara and Mykel as they disappeared along the path that led to the plateau. "How long before they marry, do you think?"

Anne said nothing.

"Anne?" Bylo asked, turning to her.

"Yes?"

"Thank you," he said.

"For what?"

"Everything."

Bylo had no idea what was coming, and the strain of keeping it from him threatened to shatter Anne's resolve. Her voice cracked as she responded. "You're...welcome, Bylo." She longed to say something more, but feared it would be out of place and alert him.

"Go on ahead," she said. "I forgot something."

"Okay."

Anne walked back into the cavern and into the sleeping area, retrieving a cup from Bylo's pack. She then entered the chamber that held the pool of ink. She filled the cup and used an ink-stained finger to trace the water rune inside the chamber, then exited as the stone rumbled, the door sliding shut. Outside the cavern, she performed the same task at the tunnel exit, locking the cavern tight. It would sit vacant for now.

Tossing the ink into the stream outside, she ambled back to her cabin, the stained cup dangling on one finger. The weary cabin welcomed her home, a familiar but lonely abode. Her work was complete, for now. She had served her purpose. No, *His* purpose. There it was. The bitterness had returned. These last days had been rewarding but painful, and she was already reverting to the hard, crusty crone that had survived for so many years alone.

You did well.

He was back. She wanted to scream, to shout, to curse Him and wail, but she had nothing to give and settled for silence. She had prepared them well enough, but there would be pain to come, and she would not be there to guide them through it. Her efforts to stay strong in the face of this loss fell apart in a cascade of anger and sorrow. Then, in a lonely cabin on a cold night, the Oracle of Ankar set her head down on the old, weathered table and cried.

31

CAPTURE

Crone's Hill

Mykel was amazed by what Nara had crafted under the plateau. Even in the dim light, he could see the smooth stone—like that in the cavern—made with magic.

"It's incredible," he said. "*You're* incredible."

She beamed with pride, walking about the cave, brushing her hands against the stone. "The earth feels alive to me now. Really alive."

Bylo entered behind Mykel a moment later. "Wow," he said. "How did you do it?"

"I snuck a peek at your book when you weren't looking."

"The earth rune?" Bylo asked.

"Yes."

Mykel set his staff down and leaned against the wall, trying to feel the life Nara spoke of. It was just cold stone to him. "You're an earth shaper," he said. "Like the cavern makers."

"I am."

A strange voice then boomed down the ramp, interrupting the

moment. "You down there. Come out." The voice was deep and entirely unfriendly.

Mykel retrieved the staff and gripped it fiercely as he sprinted toward the ramp. Just before reaching it, he turned back. "Both of you, stay here. Nara, if you need to, close the entrance." Even in the near darkness, Mykel could see that Nara's face was full of fear. He hoped she could use her magic in such a state.

When he reached the top of the ramp, Mykel encountered two soldiers, each bearing a sword in their right hand. One of them was huge, even taller than Mykel, and twice as wide. Gwyn stood beyond the men.

"Gwyn, what is this?" Mykel asked, confused.

"Do as they say, Mykel."

He looked into Gwyn's face. Was she afraid of the men, or... their ally?

He couldn't fathom it. Gwyn was a friend. She had saved them from bandits, helped train him, eaten meals with them. The idea that she was capable of betrayal was as painful as any blow these men might deliver, and Mykel banished the idea immediately.

"We are here for the girl," the large man said.

All thoughts of cooperation disappeared when he heard the stranger's demand. Everything Bylo had worried about was coming true. They wanted Nara, and they had involved Gwyn in their evil plans. His mind raced for an explanation. Had they blackmailed her? Held her family hostage?

"You can't have her," Mykel said, moving into air stance and gripping the staff with both hands.

The large man stepped forward, tightening the grip on his sword. He gestured for Gwyn and the other man to stand back. Gwyn obeyed him, offering no protest.

"Gwyn, help us!" Mykel called in desperation, but she didn't move, and in a simple but telling act that confirmed his suspicions, she turned and walked away, leaving the plateau. Fury at her betrayal spurred Mykel to action. Realizing that he would battle the men alone, he tried to flare the staff's sight rune, but it danced away from him, blurry and indistinct. The large man's sword flashed, and Mykel brought up the staff, barely escaping injury as his parry diverted the blade from striking his face. This man was faster than he looked!

Mykel tried again to find the sight rune, but it wouldn't come. The man slashed high. Mykel moved the staff to block but realized the feint too late. The blade dropped, steel cutting into the top of his thigh. A supremely skilled attack; even Gwyn didn't move that fast. Mykel reached for health, gratefully finding the familiar design without closing his eyes. The gash on his thigh closed.

A flurry of attacks pushed Mykel down the ramp toward where Nara and Bylo stood, watching fearfully.

"Stay back," Mykel warned them.

Mykel summoned his resolve, blocking most of the attacks, but several made it through, shallow cuts on his upper arms. The man bore no shield but somehow used his off hand to counterbalance himself as he swung his weapon, feet moving perfectly as he advanced, expertly, delivering blows as if he had practiced each move a million times. He moved from stance to stance, and Mykel thought he saw air stance briefly, but there were others.

This giant must have mastered them all. I'm in big trouble.

Thrust. Parry. Slash. Feint. Riposte. New wounds appeared on Mykel's left shoulder, his cheek, and the top of his head. Blood flowed.

If Nara could wall off the cavern with her earth shaping, she and Bylo might be safe until they could plan an escape. "Nara, close the tunnel," Mykel shouted. "I can't hold him off."

He reached for the sight rune again, but with the confusion of the other runes dancing about, coupled with the chaos of the man's attack, he couldn't seize it. The protection rune wasn't protecting; it was creating confusion. If he had the staff's sight rune, he could win this fight, but he couldn't grasp it!

Below, Mykel heard footsteps and looked to see Nara moving up the ramp.

"Mykel!" she said fearfully, clearly recognizing the danger he was in.

"Block the entrance!" Mykel ordered, desperation in his voice. "Or attack him. Do something! I can't find the runes," Mykel said, angry and frustrated. "I can't find them!"

More blows. More wounds. More blood. Mykel stumbled to a knee.

"I don't wish to murder you, boy. I'm only here for her," the man said matter-of-factly. The voice was completely without passion, as if cutting men apart and kidnapping young women were everyday chores for him. "Give her up, and I'll leave."

"No!" Mykel bellowed, then stood and pushed forward.

Nara backed off at first, shocked by the sudden attack. She was torn between concern for Mykel, who was now bleeding from multiple wounds, and from a reluctance to close them all inside a tomb. She knew no way to attack the men; she could only build caves, talk to animals, or make her hands glow with light. None of that would stop men with swords, would it? But if she didn't act, Mykel might die, and the horror of it made her shudder. Where was Anne when Nara needed her? She thought of what she had learned about the earth, about it taking care of her. About how she had battled along Mykel's side during his training.

She kicked off her shoes and knelt to the ground, bare feet and palms touching the soft dirt of the ramp. She flared the earth rune in her mind and reached down with her magic to feel the warmth within the soil, coaxing it, waking it. The earth wanted to know what shape to become, and she had no idea what to say. All she could do was feed her energy into the soil. Mykel's bare feet were in direct contact with the earth. She sensed his pain and anger. Then Nara and her magic launched forward into him.

Mykel bled from a dozen cuts, despite having already healed several more serious ones. This man was more than a brute. He was a supremely skilled swordsman, and Mykel would meet his end right here if he didn't develop a better strategy. His concern for Nara's safety rose to a fevered pitch. Failure would bring Nara's suffering, and he could not allow that to happen.

Then something changed. It started in his feet. A tingle. A sensation of warmth coming up from the ground. Power. Strength. It flooded into him whenever his bare soles contacted the earth. He stopped moving and planted his feet like a tree, soaking in the magic. It was Nara. He could feel her strength and her personality, so familiar and oh so powerful!

He stole a look back and saw her kneeling on the ground at the bottom of the ramp, eyes closed and hands on the dirt. He closed his eyes to draw upon her strength, and the enemy's blade rammed straight through his gut, impaling him to the hilt. Pain lanced through his belly, threatening to drop him, but the magic came up from the earth, providing power enough to summon his runes. Four popped into view, clear, distinct, and within his grasp.

He felt the blade pull back, then he flared health, repairing his whole body. Every wound closed, including the otherwise fatal wound the man had just inflicted. Keeping his eyes shut, Mykel held all the runes in his vision at once, each begging to be fed. He chose the sight rune, and the contest abruptly changed.

As Mykel charged forward away from her, Nara sensed the growing distance and stood to walk up the ramp. She did not want him to move so far that she couldn't reach him with the magic. Now standing at the top, she continued to feed the energy to him but opened her eyes so that she could also see his efforts. Concern for his safety faded as she sensed Mykel heal his wounds and move forward, gaining ground on the man.

He attacked relentlessly, but not randomly. Each strike was

perfect as if he knew exactly where to aim. His dreams of being a warrior had come to fruition. He was amazing—at only sixteen, battling a man who was clearly a seasoned combatant. And Mykel was winning! Nara was proud of her friend, and wondered how he had grown to be so strong. To be so sure of himself. Was it the need to protect her that gave him this courage? Or the years of standing up to his father, of protecting Sammy?

The man blocked and countered but gave ground, retreating slowly as Mykel's staff whirled and swept and thrust, swinging perfectly. He predicted his opponent's every step and interrupted each of the man's attacks. Gleaming ivory impacted the giant's legs, arms, and belly, and then swept him off his feet.

The man rolled to his feet, eyes wide in shock. Nara reached out with her feelings to sense the distress in him. It wasn't fear, at least not yet, but instead a profound sense of surprise.

"Almit!" the man bellowed.

The smaller soldier joined in the fray, and Mykel paused, repositioning himself. A seeming reluctance in his steps made it clear that Mykel did not know what to do with multiple opponents. The two soldiers pressed forward in tandem, and Mykel moved back across the plateau in response, blocking blows as he retreated.

As he found his bearing and reacted to the attacks, Mykel seemed to gather confidence again. A deserved confidence, Nara surmised, as he barred every cut they attempted, every slash, every thrust, and he still had his eyes closed. Nara concentrated ever more on the magic that she sent to her friend, along with her hopes that he would defeat these men. She felt pain lance across her own skin as Mykel's arms were struck with the swords, then the pain abruptly faded as Mykel healed himself.

Suddenly, Mykel moved aggressively on them, overcoming the challenge of both at once. With the speed of lightning, he delivered a distracting blow to the larger man's rib cage, then charged the one called Almit, executing a spinning move that feinted a kick high but ended with the staff impacting the man's left thigh. A loud crack gave evidence of a crippling injury to the soldier's upper leg bone, and the man cried out in pain and shock.

"Get back," the larger man said to Almit. The large man then charged Mykel, who met the advance firmly, returning blows against the giant's torso and pummeling him again with the staff. Returning the aggression in kind, the man's blade cut muscle on Mykel's abdomen. Nara bent over with the pain that came to her, closing her eyes and reaching out to the earth to diffuse the discomfort.

The large man pressed again, but Mykel struck him several times in his legs and gut, ending with a strike that narrowly missed the man's head. With no helmet, a blow such as that would surely have ended the fight, and now that Mykel's victory was assured, Nara found herself curiously sympathetic toward the man, reaching out to sense his distress yet again. He expended a fierce amount of effort to hold his ground without taking a fatal blow, and the end of his endurance loomed close.

Nara sensed Mykel press again and expected that victory was imminent. As he battled the giant soldier, he guided a storm of confidence and fury, pushing the man back toward the birch trees, but she sensed Mykel's anger and frustration at the same time. Frustration at what, though?

Frustration at Gwyn. It was clear now. She had betrayed them. No, it couldn't be!

She opened her eyes to look for Gwyn, then was surprised to see that the smaller soldier was standing right in front of Nara, one arm supporting his injured leg. Nara's eyes opened wide as the man's blade moved quickly to impale her shoulder.

The pain was both sharp and dull at the same time. He had hit bone. She buckled to her knees, the agony breaking her connection to the earth and to Mykel. Nausea started in her belly and moved to her throat. Warm, stinging pain arced like lightning up through her neck, overwhelming her vision and causing her to stumble to the ground. As her head went fuzzy, she heard Bylo's shouts from behind her, screaming at her to get up.

Her head hit the dirt, Bylo's voice disappeared, and she became lost in the misery.

―――――――――

"Got her!"

The shout came from behind Mykel, and the strength coming from below his feet vanished, the warmth ceasing. He looked over at the center of the plateau, but the fallen soldier was gone. The man should have been incapacitated after the blow to his leg but had somehow found the strength to move.

I left her unguarded. I'm a fool!

He whirled to find the man standing over Nara's crumpled form at the top of the ramp, sword at her throat. Just a flick of his wrist and she would be dead. Mykel had been too absorbed in the contest and wandered away from her. His only purpose was to protect her, and he had failed. He had magic, and he had still failed!

"Move and he cuts her," the giant said.

Mykel fought back frustration, furious at himself for leaving Nara open to attack. She had counted on him, foolishly, and he had let her down. And yet, if she had defended herself, she could have beaten them all!

"If you hurt her, I'll..."

"You'll do what, little boy?"

Mykel just stood in place, agonizing over the fate of his friend, and his own failure.

"Drop the stick, or I give the order and she's done," the man said.

Mykel dropped the staff.

The giant's punch came with amazing speed. Mykel moved to block, but without the sight rune and the guidance it gave, his effort failed. The impact upon his temple dropped him into oblivion.

32

FAIRMONT

On the Road to Fairmont

The ropes around Bylo's wrists were tight, rubbing his flesh with each bump of the wagon as they ambled down the uneven road. It was nearly dawn, and he and Mykel were imprisoned in a cold, rolling cage of iron bars so small that they could not even stand. Mykel rested next to Bylo on the wagon floor, eyes closed and mouth silent, still unconscious. An ugly bruise was visible on the side of his head.

Bylo thought back to their capture, how the soldier had stumbled toward the ramp, sword in hand, and stabbed Nara in the shoulder. The larger man had followed thereafter, pushed Bylo aside then forced a vial of red liquid down Nara's throat.

"Don't kill them. They have value," Gwyn had told the giant. "The minister can use them."

The giant had grunted, clearly eager to finish them, but seemed to agree with the traitor. Bylo now felt foolish for allowing Gwyn to unravel their peace. And how could Anne have allowed that evil woman among them? Hadn't she seen this coming?

Just a few hours ago, Mykel and Nara had walked hand in hand through the cavern tunnel, leaving Bylo convinced they would live happily ever after. But now, disaster had fallen upon them.

Still, Bylo found himself oddly grateful to Gwyn that he and Mykel were still alive. Had she remained silent, the giant might have ended them both. But questions remained. What did the minister plan on doing with Nara? And was there anything Bylo could do about it?

The wagon continued through the darkness and the snow, over hills and across rivers that had started to freeze. The cold lay upon his old body, requiring him to frequently brush off the snowflakes that chilled his skin. Mykel remained shirtless and Bylo moved close to the boy to keep him warm, periodically checking the ugly bruise on the side of his head.

They arrived at an army encampment about mid-day. Among tents, fires, soldiers, and horses, they were transferred into a wagon with a larger steel cage. A short time later, Mykel stirred, then rose to his knees and frantically tugged on the bars.

"I already tried," Bylo said. "They are too strong."

Mykel tried anyway, even spending a few moments kicking at one fiercely. The bars held. Then, oddly, he sat back and closed his eyes, as if sleeping.

"Mykel," Bylo said.

"Leave me alone. Please."

After three days of travel, the chill brought a sore throat upon Bylo. On the fourth day, phlegm began to fill his lungs, and it was clear that an illness had come in a bad way. A soldier brought him a blanket that he tried to share with Mykel, but the youth refused it wordlessly and wouldn't speak. Sometimes he would open his eyes and look around, then resume his silence. At first, Bylo thought it was a profound depression at the circumstances, but when it lingered for several days, he began to wonder if the boy was also ill.

Bylo's own thoughts dwelled on Nara's safety. Wisdom dictated that her welfare was not as great a concern as their own. The wound she had endured at the end of the fight on the plateau was not life-threatening, and they would care for her, wouldn't they? The minister would surely not destroy such a rare treasure. Or would the villain use her for experiments, try to duplicate her power, or maybe siphon it for his own purposes? Bylo's fatherly heart ached as he pondered her fate and his own failure to protect her, but he resolved to dwell on the positive, trusting that she would be safe. Aside from his manufactured optimism, there could be found no warmth in the back of the wagon, and another coughing fit produced more phlegm, this time tinged with red.

Early on the fifth day, the wagon lurched upon a rock, jostling the prisoners, and Mykel sat up to look about. The youth had not yet eaten, and Bylo offered a bland biscuit he had saved for him. "Eat them yourself," Mykel said. "I'll be fine."

Bylo nibbled on the biscuits gratefully, knowing he would need all his strength to ward off the growing sickness.

"You're thinner already, Mykel. Please eat something."

"I'm good."

Perhaps he was being sustained by the health rune? Mykel's efforts to stave off the chill and survive without food might be possible with his magic, but there would be a price.

"They won't hurt her, son. She's too valuable."

"Maybe," he said.

Mykel tested the bars again. A shout from the soldier driving the wagon put an end to his efforts.

"You're alert," Bylo said. "I was worried."

"I'm fine," he said, a look of frustration on his face. "I'm thinking."

"About?"

He gave no response, but it was good to hear his voice, even if it was more curt than usual.

On the sixth day, they arrived in Fairmont near sundown, and the city seemed as busy as it had years ago when Bylo last visited. Shopkeepers swept their porches and sent disapproving looks as the prison wagon rolled by. Several times, children ran alongside to steal a glance at Bylo and Mykel.

"What did you do, old man?" one little girl said, climbing up on the side of the wagon and sticking her head between the bars before a soldier shooed her away.

Bylo's cough hadn't worsened today, but neither had it improved. The additional food had helped, as Mykel continued to give his rations to Bylo, accepting only water. The boy's form was ever thinner, but his spirit seemed strong. It was dark when they finally entered the palace gates and were released from the wagon.

They were led in chains through guarded passageways into a dark part of the grand structure before being thrown into separate cells. Iron bars divided them, but they could speak to each other. Enclosed by walls of damp stone, they were wet, cool, and uncomfortable, but Bylo was grateful that he had been allowed to keep his blanket. The meager light provided by a single lantern in the hallway chased few of the shadows away.

Escape would likely not be possible, for Bylo's illness made him weaker each day. Mykel could heal, but without his staff, he would see little success in a battle against armed men. Each day, he had been weakening, eating little and passing the food to Bylo to keep him strong. It was a kind gesture, but would ultimately be a futile one. They would both die here. Bylo was old and had played his part, but it would be a dark end to an otherwise promising young man.

Nara woke in a large room to find herself resting in a lavish canopy bed. Red and white lace draperies hung all around, obscuring the room beyond. How much time had passed? Days? Weeks? Where had they taken her? She reached to her shoulder where the blade had struck, only to find no wound and no bandages. Even unconscious, she must have healed herself. Since she had used the health rune previously, did it now work even when she slept?

She tried to shake herself awake, but a fog hung about her and she felt heavy. There was no headache to accompany the sluggishness, so this was something different. Had she been drugged? She pulled herself out from under the blankets and stepped into a sitting area with two chairs and a sofa arranged around a small coffee table. On the table sat a teapot and snacks. A young woman in long black hair sat in a chair, facing away from Nara and drinking from a teacup.

"You slept for a long time," the woman said. Her voice was young and strong.

"Who are you?" Nara asked. "And where am I?"

The visitor stood and turned to Nara, revealing a familiar face.

"You're home, Sister."

The sight of Nara's own face looking at her made her legs weak, and she nearly dropped to the floor. Delicate features, bright-green eyes. She gazed upon her twin. But black hair?

In the days since Bylo had shared the truth of her past, Nara had imagined this meeting many times. Thoughts of finding her twin were always associated with a joyful reunion, however. She imagined laughing, a meal shared with Bylo and Mykel, happy times. Not this.

There were so many questions Nara had wanted to ask in this moment, but they seemed to matter little now. Bylo and Mykel weren't here, and she had no idea where they were, or if they even still lived.

"Come eat," her sister said, then sat again.

Nara was hungry, but couldn't bring herself to indulge. Instead, she moved over to the couch to take in the sight of her sister. The girl was impeccably dressed, wearing a strapless black gown with ribbon and lace across her chest and waist. Five large teal jewels hung about her delicate neck, tiny diamonds circling each jewel in a beautiful setting. Rich, like a princess. The black hair spilled over her shoulders and down her back, clean and beautifully straight. Nara touched the mess on her own head, intimidated by the contrast.

"I dye it," the girl said.

"Oh." Nara fidgeted with a hole in the knee of her trousers. "Where are they?"

"Your friends? Safe."

"You won't tell me?"

"Why, so you can go to them?" Her sister ate grapes from the platter on the table, speaking between bites. "Papa forbids it. This is your home now. You'll stay here."

Papa?

The girl didn't smile, but she didn't frown either. Movements and expressions seemed mechanical, or forced, and her words were expressed in even tones, with little embellishment. Even so, her presence was oddly familiar, like a part of Nara long lost, and although there was little joy in this reunion, she experienced a strange peace in being near the young woman.

"I should do better, I'm sorry," her sister said. "I was hungry." She stood and took a step toward Nara, offering a hand and forcing a gentle smile on her face. "I'm Kayna."

Nara shook the offered hand, and Kayna sat down to continue eating.

"They've assigned a handmaiden who'll attend to you soon. Eat, dress, and then *His Majesty* will see you." Kayna rolled her eyes at the title. Who was she referring to? The prince? Was she in Fairmont Castle?

"His Majesty?" Nara's question came out softly, and she was frustrated at how she must sound. Weak. And the look of her—so disheveled. Her sister must think very little of her in such a state. Shame washed over her, reminiscent of the teasings of her youth, ridicule from Heidi Trinck or Fannie Taylor. She pulled her legs close, hugging them protectively like the pained blossom of a fire weed.

"Yes, I'm talking about Papa," she said. "Princess Nara, your father is the king."

More than an hour after meeting Kayna, two maids attended to Nara, explaining that she would be expected to present herself before the king. At first, she protested—she had no desire to meet him. She then realized that she would learn little about her circumstances and be unable to change them if she didn't play along.

It took hours to clean her dirty skin, brush the tangles out of her ratty hair, and find appropriate clothes. But the maids couldn't wash away the grief as her concerns remained on the welfare of those she loved.

When the maids were done attending to her, Nara gazed into a looking glass. Adorned with trails of ruffles, the stunning green gown matched her bright-green eyes. The fitting of it pinched at her waist and exposed her collarbones, but it was beautiful, nonetheless. A tiny green gem set on a pendant was draped around her neck on a silver chain. She didn't recognize this girl in the mirror. Not even a little.

A servant escorted her downstairs and across the large, cold palace, but so many days in bed had deprived her of strength and her legs ached with the effort. She walked in the odd shoes and bulky dress through the maze of stone corridors and knew that she would lose herself here if not guided. Beautiful paintings adorned the walls, accompanied by tapestries and silk window hangings. For all the grand nature of the place, it seemed lonely, dark, and without love.

The servant guided her into the foyer of the keep, but instead of continuing into the attached throne room as directed, she moved toward the front of the foyer. Two large, solid-wood doors stood open; an armored guard at each side carried a spear. When she approached, the guards closed the doors, then returned to their stoic poses. She would not be allowed to leave.

She turned around. The servant was beckoning with a wave of his hand, inviting her to enter the throne room. She took a step, then paused. The king awaited her upon a throne. The chair was ornate, inlaid with gold wire and adorned with plush purple cushions on the seat and arms. Its occupant wore a sleeved surcoat with an animal embroidered on its breast. A purple, hoodless silk cape was clasped about his neck. The crown on his head looked garish. Awkward—as if it had been poorly fitted to his head or simply didn't belong there. He was hawkish and small, and nothing like how she had imagined her father would be.

A grand table rested on the stone floor tiles in the middle of the room. Many important-looking men were seated there, speaking loudly and drinking from large cups. Each was dressed in finery—clothes that, if sold, could probably feed a family in Dimmitt for a year. Gwyn was among them, dressed elegantly as well in a fine linen pantsuit, swords still upon her back. Servants scurried back and forth with food and wine. Tapestries and the severed heads of dead animals were mounted on the walls. The room was big, cold, and loud.

"Come," the king said to her from across the expansive room. As he stood, the others grew quiet.

Nara feared the walk across the grand room alone, the focus of so many eyes. As she stepped forward, she sensed them drinking her in. The lust in some of their eyes was an assault upon her person and she squirmed inwardly, but she refused to let it show. After several pained moments, she arrived in front of the king, just as Kayna walked in from a side entrance to join her.

"Look at the two of you. Beautiful, I must say," the king said. "Treasures, for sure."

Nara thought about the mother she had never met, the mother who had surely died in childbirth. How might the woman have looked in this place, dressed as they were? Did she have red hair, like Nara? Was she beautiful?

In front of this man, despite her expectations, Nara now found that she had no desire to ask about her family. This place would never be her home. She sought escape from these people, not explanations.

"I've arranged for your tutors to come in a few days," the king said. "And clothes will be purchased so that you can wear more than the one dress, no matter how good it looks on you. Dinner will be later tonight, a feast to welcome your homecoming, and I expect you to present yourself well. If you need sleep before then, take it."

The man offered no hug for his supposedly long-lost daughter. No kisses. No tearful rememberings. Such coldness emanated from him and Kayna. What dark souls occupied these people?

Or was it that simple? If he were her father, and such a rich and powerful man, why had he left Nara in an orphanage and raised only her sister? He had then sent trained killers to capture her, to attack Mykel. His soldier had rammed a sword through his own daughter's shoulder. Where was the queen and why had she married this man? She knew from school that the Great Land had a queen, but had heard nothing of lost princesses or a king. None of it made sense, and she refused to accept this man in the role that he claimed.

And what about Mykel and Bylo? What had happened to them?

"That will be all for now," the king said, waving his hand in dismissal.

Nara moved to speak, but out of the corner of her eye, she saw Kayna put a finger to her lips, shushing her. Nara scowled at her twin, undeterred.

"Where are Mykel and Bylo?" Nara said to the king.

His eyebrows rose. "That is no concern of yours. You live *here*, now. And you won't see them again."

"Did you kill them?" She couldn't bear to think of it, but she had to know.

"No," he said. "They live. And will continue to live as long as you behave yourself and don't cause any trouble."

What a horrible man. Why would any father treat his child this way? She couldn't accept that he was any relation of hers, and she would not believe it for a moment. But she needed to play along if she wanted Mykel and Bylo to stay alive. Finding them would require cleverness so as not to alert this monster on the throne. Or her twin.

Nara sighed and dropped her head in a feigned display of defeat, then turned to leave the room using the side exit. She would remain captive for now. A beautifully dressed, pampered prisoner in a giant castle surrounded by soldiers. But she had magic if she could figure out how to use it. She would find a way to Mykel and Bylo. They would leave Fairmont.

And they would never return.

33

PAIN

Mykel awoke to find four strong men coming into the cell to grab him. Why they needed so many to handle his emaciated body was puzzling. They dragged him down a hallway into a small room where implements of steel hung on pegs hammered into the stone walls. Some tools were sharp, some were jagged, and others looked like clubs or hammers. A steel table sat prominently in the center. It was a torture room.

Dei, help me.

They tied him to the cold table using leather straps. When they left the room, he struggled against the straps, but they held fast.

A few moments later, a door that was out of view opened on creaky hinges, followed by the sound of shuffling footsteps. "Good morning," a voice said. High and raspy, the voice rankled Mykel, but he gave no response.

"I have an assignment. A research project, I suppose you could say. Would you be my assistant?" The sound of a metal implement scratching against a stone wall behind him grated on Mykel's nerves even further, raising a fearful curiosity. Terrified, yet eager to look at what was coming for him, he resolved to give no victory to his captor. He kept his eyes locked on the ceiling, hoping to preserve what remained of his dignity.

"Quiet, eh?" the man said. "We'll see how quiet you are in a few minutes."

Mykel succumbed to curiosity, shooting a look at the man as he came to the table. He wore a dark shirt and trousers, and although his balding head still bore some hair, it was thin, white, and grew only in a few patches. A pale-skinned face was pockmarked with red sores and he flashed a grin, revealing many missing teeth. To call him a man would have been generous; he looked more like a ghoul.

The sores led Mykel to believe him to be a victim of some sort of ailment, and he experienced a flash of pity for the creature. Mykel guessed him to be in his forties, and wondered if the pale skin and sores were the result of his time in the dungeon or instead a reason to be hiding here.

The ghoul lifted his hand into view, revealing a small, brilliant blade. Mykel shuddered. No matter what Anne had said about pain no longer being the same for him, she couldn't have expected him to endure this.

"This is one of my favorites. Razor sharp. I figured we would start small."

The man poked at Mykel's left shoulder with a thumb, as if testing a piece of fruit before purchasing it at the market. Then he drove the blade deep into the flesh. The pain lanced down Mykel's arm, and his entire body seized in response before he gritted his teeth and summoned the strength to quiet his groans.

"Muted response. Great pain tolerance. Impressive. But there is a nerve right here—"

Another stab, but far more intense, as the man shoved the blade under Mykel's left bicep, then moved the implement against the bone of his upper arm. Mykel uttered a loud cry, and tears came to his eyes.

"That's better," he said, licking his lips and clicking his tongue to make an odd sound. "At least I can be assured that you feel the pain, even if you can heal the wounds. And you seem to bleed normally."

The blood from his shoulder and his bicep began to pool on the cold table, and Mykel could feel the warm wetness spreading. He was tempted to heal but didn't want to give the man the satisfaction. But if he didn't, he might lose too much blood.

He closed his eyes and flared health, just a flash, hoping it would stop the bleeding but not completely repair the wounds. He didn't want to give the man a reason to inflict more damage.

"Well done! You can stop the bleeding at will. I severed the artery, and it might have been your demise had you waited. Good choice. This project is going to move along nicely."

The man clicked his tongue again as he shuffled away, and Mykel heard the scattered sounds of metal implements on the other side of the door from where he had first entered. Upon his return, the man began poking and prodding at Mykel's shoulder with something cold. It was less painful than before, but still uncomfortable.

"In case you're wondering, I'm just probing with a speculum. It spreads the flesh so that I can see inside the wound better. I want to know how much control you possess. You can stop the bleeding but —ah yes! You did it!"

Mykel raised his eyes in curiosity at his tormentor's examination.

"You healed the incision in the shoulder capsule. Soft tissue such as this is difficult to repair; it has so little blood supply. Yet you did it instantly. Wonderful talent."

Was this man a torturer or a physicar?

"Let's see what you can do with bone," he said. He grabbed what looked like a large hammer off the wall. A wicked grin crossed the ghoul's face, and he brought the implement down sharply on Mykel's left leg. The sound of bone crushing between hammer and steel table was accompanied a moment later by horrific pain, and Mykel cried out again.

"There you go; let it all out, son. It's okay to scream. I don't mind a bit."

Amid the excruciating pain, Mykel's hope drained out of him. His resolve to escape, to catch a soldier off guard, or find a weak bar in the cage seemed fruitless now. These men were professional murders. Mykel was just a simple villager. His ability to heal was of little value here. Moreover, their discovery of it had turned him into an experiment. He couldn't grasp the protection rune. He had no weapons, and he was getting thinner every day. Somehow, he must find a way to endure. He must escape, find Nara, and leave this terrible place. Oh, if they had just run east, long ago. To the Yukan and beyond, never to be found again. No training, no magic, no dungeons. Just freedom.

His thoughts were interrupted when the man brought the hammer down on his other leg, deforming it at an odd angle, bone poking through the skin. Mykel lost his resolve under the torture and flared the health rune fully. The wounds disappeared, his legs forcing themselves back into shape as the magic took effect, bone knitting, skin reforming.

"Excellent!" The man dropped the hammer on the stone floor and moved to each side of the table, inspecting Mykel's legs, one at a time as he clicked his tongue repeatedly. He poked Mykel's shoulder with his finger where the wound had been. "Bone, soft tissue, muscle —you can fix it all. You are truly amazing, Cross didn't exaggerate in the slightest. Thank you, thank you. We're going to have so much fun together!"

Bylo watched them take Mykel away every morning. There was no sunlight from which to judge the time of the sessions, but the sounds of birds outside suggested that it was early. Much closer, inside the walls, he would hear the screaming. When Mykel returned, he would bear new scars on his legs, his shoulders, and even his back. The scars were thin, but some were very long, and even in the half-light of the dungeon, Bylo could make out how serious those wounds must have been. Mykel said nothing afterwards—simply sitting with his back against the wall, staring at nothing.

One day, Mykel returned in a panicked state, fiercely gripping his left forearm with his other hand. Upon being thrown into his cell, he crawled to the bars between him and Bylo, reaching out to Bylo as if asking for help, but then passed out. When Mykel collapsed, he was close enough for Bylo to inspect the damage. A jagged scar, red and raw, encircled his arm halfway between wrist and elbow. Had they amputated it? While he was conscious? The horror of it overwhelmed Bylo, his revulsion mitigated only by the fact that they allowed his healing power to reattach the limb.

They clearly wanted to know how he healed and what his limits might be. It would only be a matter of time before they disrobed him and found the health rune—if they hadn't done so already.

After several more days of Mykel's torture, Bylo began to regret carrying the boy from the announcement ceremony in the first place. If he had abandoned Mykel in Dimmitt, he would have been given a quick, merciful death at the hands of the church–a far better fate than this. It wouldn't last much longer for either of them. Mykel couldn't endure endless torture, and Bylo's own condition was worsening as well.

It was a quiet evening in the dungeon, many hours after Mykel returned from a session, when he spoke to Bylo with promise in his voice.

"I have it." The words came loud and strong, disturbing Bylo from a fitful snooze.

"What?" Bylo asked.

"Protection," he said. "I can grab it every time now."

The rune! So that's what the boy was doing during all the silence. He was practicing. In his head! Bylo felt like a fool for ever doubting him. He should have had more faith in the young warrior's resolve.

A sense of hope arose in Bylo, dancing on the periphery of his consciousness. It nagged at him like a child in the back of a classroom raising her hand with eagerness to speak. Were there options here?

"If you have developed enough skill to use both your runes—" Bylo stopped himself, remembering something Anne said, then clumsily reached for his foot. The small vial remained tucked inside the cloth of his sock, forgotten. Anne had seen this coming and had already planted the seeds of their escape.

Joy surged in his breast, accompanied by gratitude. Under his breath, he whispered, "Anne, you come straight from Dei, you beautiful, grouchy angel."

Bylo looked at the guard, who watched them from his post at the end of the dungeon corridor. They would have to wait until tomorrow when they would be alone.

Mykel made a curious face at Bylo. It became even more perplexed as Bylo moved closer, reaching through the bars to squeeze the boy's shoulder.

"Young man, how would you like to become a bear?"

Late one evening, at least a week after arriving in Fairmont, Nara was standing on a high parapet atop an inner castle wall when Gwyn approached. Each using a vision most people did not possess, they looked down upon a courtyard devoid of activity.

Nara greeted her without turning to look. "Hello, Gwyn."

"Good evening."

"Why didn't you just kill us?"

"That wasn't my mission."

"You're a watcher, aren't you?"

"How did you guess?"

"I'm learning to see more clearly."

"Apparently," Gwyn said. "In more ways than one."

"And you're horrible."

There was a pause before Gwyn answered. "I know."

They gazed soundlessly upon the courtyard, eyes wandering to the windows in the keep. One such window opened, and a figure crawled out on the sill. It dropped from the opening, even though the rise was easily fifty feet, then became caught up on a gust of air. The figure lowered to the ground.

"She goes out often, doesn't she?" Nara asked.

"Yes."

"When she comes back, she glows brighter."

"And probably knows we watch, young lady."

"She kills people, doesn't she?"

Gwyn said nothing.

"Are you afraid of her, Gwyn?"

"I just met her recently. I've been away for a long time, and the king kept her talents hidden."

"You didn't answer my question."

"Yes, Nara, I'm afraid of her. You should be, too."

"Perhaps. But I think it's more that I'm angry with her. Disappointed."

"Your father kills too. You should fear them both."

"Yes. It's a family tradition," Nara said. "One that must end."

"Big words."

Nara swung around to face Gwyn and took a purposeful stride to close the gap between them. Gwyn's hand moved toward her weapon.

"What's it to you if I start acting like someone who can fight? Someone who can make a difference?" Nara let out a low, angry huff, but continued to stare accusingly at Gwyn, eyes locked. "Unlike you, I'm doing this for the people I love rather than people I'm afraid of. That's it, isn't it, Gwyn? You're scared. You hide behind kings and swords and pretend to be our friend only so you can bring us harm. Do you love *anyone*? Have you *ever*? Have you let anyone love *you*? Maybe someday you will, and you'll know what it's like to sacrifice for others, to give of yourself."

Nara turned slowly back to the empty courtyard. Quietly, she continued, "And to lose them."

Gwyn dropped her arm back to her side.

"You're a coward, Gwyn."

Gwyn said nothing.

"I am, too," Nara said quietly. "I could have saved them. I know I could have. But I was afraid. I'm often afraid. I'm like you. But this is unbearable. I miss them. *So much.* Maybe someday…" she paused for a moment before continuing, "…someday I'll stop hiding. I'll stand up for those I care about. I hope it won't be too late."

Then she walked away.

Nara's words sparked a change within Gwyn that she pondered as she left the high walkway and ventured back to her room. The change had been building for some time, starting with the first screams she had heard from Mykel. Yesterday, in a fit of disgust with herself, she had set out to find the young man's staff, perceiving its hearty glow even through the stone walls. The weapon rested in an armory on the second level above the dungeon, not far from the throne room. Two armed guards kept watch, and Gwyn feared she might not overcome them without help. If she was able to get the staff to Mykel, his escape might redeem Gwyn. It wouldn't help Nara, who would forever remain a prisoner, but the plan fell apart with one critical flaw.

Mykel would never leave her.

Still, she wondered if Nara's newfound resolve might turn the tide. Perhaps she could overcome fear more ably than Gwyn. Perhaps the young woman was stronger than she looked.

The shame of her own cowardice grew painfully in Gwyn's breast, a dark, lonesome thing. Gwyn would watch and wait, but if the opportunity came, she would act.

It was late and Nara couldn't sleep. She refused to be part of this family, these horrible people who loved to kill. Powerful, rich, but with cold souls. Nara had nothing in common with them.

Insomnia forced her out of bed and she returned to the parapet, watching Kayna as she returned, floating on the air and glowing more brightly than ever. Nara wondered what lives her sister had consumed in the dark outing, and her stomach turned at the thought of it.

"Yes, Gwyn, I'm afraid of her," she said, imagining the traitor still stood at her side. "But I will no longer stand idle in the presence of pain."

Still not ready to sleep, Nara stayed on the castle wall amid the darkness and silence, a cold breeze chilling her arms as she wondered what the king had really done with Mykel and Bylo. Had they been murdered? Imprisoned in an army camp? Could they be here, in this castle somewhere? She knew them to be alive, unable to accept that they would have died without her feeling it. Without her knowing.

She left the parapet to wander a corridor aimlessly, fingers dancing on the stone wall. Crude stone this was, fashioned with chisels and hammers. Placing her palm against the wall, she flared earth and reached out to it, a vain attempt to reach Mykel. What came back was nothing she had expected.

He was here, in the castle! Somewhere below, she sensed his presence through the rock. Of course. This whole edifice was made of stone and earth. She could reach him through it as she had through the earth on the plateau. She bit her lip in frustration for not trying it sooner.

As she maintained the connection, Nara could sense weakness in him caused by recent pain. His body was wasting from trauma and a lack of nourishment. He was no longer strong, and he slept fitfully, anxiety filling his mind. She tried to channel energy to him, to calm him so he could rest, but he was too far away for her to reach.

She bolted through the corridors to Gwyn's chambers and pounded on the door. After a long delay, she pounded again, confident Gwyn was within. The watcher finally appeared.

"Gwyn, they are here."

"I know."

"You know?" Nara's anger flared. "I don't trust you one whit, you evil woman, but I have no one else. You will help me, I swear, or I will—"

"Finally coming out of your shell? No need to threaten me, I have already begun to help." Gwyn looked up and down the hallway furtively. In a hushed tone, she said, "I know where they are keeping the staff."

34

ESCAPE

"We must wait until morning," Bylo whispered through the bars to Mykel. "This will take the better part of an hour, and after they hurt you, they eat. It is the only time they leave us alone."

Mykel agreed. Having grasped the protection rune now, he might armor his skin to prevent injury during an escape. The idea gave him hope for saving Nara, but the repeated sessions and frequent use of his health tattoo had drained his strength. He needed time to recover, but there was none to be had.

This session unfolded differently than expected. After they had strapped Mykel to the torturer's worktable, the guards and the sickly man left the room, leaving Mykel alone. When the door finally opened, a familiar face entered, accompanied by a new one. The first belonged to the huge man Mykel had battled on the plateau. Today, he wore black plate armor. A smaller man stood by the giant, dressed in a fine shirt, jewels, and wearing a crown.

"Good morning," said the smaller one. "You may call me 'Your Majesty.'"

A king? Mykel thought the Great Land had a queen, but he paid little attention to such things. Regardless, today might be very different than expected, and Mykel feared the change might change their plans. When he didn't respond to the king's words, the giant lunged forward, smashing a steel gauntlet into Mykel's gut. The pain was profound and he tried to bear it, but failed, convulsing as the waves of pain turned his stomach into knots.

The king cleared his throat before continuing. "You've already met General Cross. We share a curiosity about you. News from Dimmitt is that you're a cursed, and that you survived your announcement. Perhaps with a little help from your friend, I would guess?"

Mykel didn't respond, and feared another blow from the giant, but it didn't come.

"She's quite the treasure, that one. I haven't yet decided what to do with her. Do you have any suggestions?"

Again, Mykel said nothing. The king stepped forward and ran an index finger across Mykel's chest, partially tracing the outline of the protection rune.

"Who would have known that decorating a cursed with pretty scrawlings would produce such interesting results?" the king said. "You've opened up some possibilities for me, and I will know more."

He took a step back, then strummed his fingers against the top of Mykel's left thigh. Mykel grimaced as his skin sprouted a dozen narrow but deep cuts, each incision stretching deep into the muscle of his leg. Blood welled quickly to the surface, and the man looked at Mykel's face as if expecting something. Was he trying to make Mykel heal himself? To provide a demonstration?

With a look of disappointment, the king took a step closer and set his hand over Mykel's sternum. Pressing down, he spoke menacingly. "I could vaporize your heart with a thought, young warrior. Could you heal that?"

The man's proximity enraged Mykel and he pulled against the leather straps in defiance, but the words struck terror in his breast. Could he heal such a wound before dying? If not, what would happen to Nara? Would they kill her? Keep her imprisoned forever in this horrible place? Mykel's pulse quickened, and he felt his chest constrict. Was the king now engaging his talent? Should he flare protection or health? What would happen if they discovered that he held both an immunity to injuries and the ability to recover from them? He readied the health rune and closed his eyes, preparing for the fatal blow.

"Not now, I think," the king said, lifting his jeweled hand. "Sorry to disappoint you; I'm sure you wish for this all to be over. Besides, I am sure that the archbishop would love to have you when we are finished. It's not often that a cursed survives an announcement. He might enjoy putting on a public execution. I imagine that he would say words about defeating darkness and Kai's demons. Priests love that sort of thing. Gets everyone so fearful and obedient." He paced back and forth, a finger to his lips as if he was thinking of something.

"I've been doing some research of my own. This tattoo of yours—the one on your chest. It's not the only one, is it? It's not the one you're using to repair yourself."

He stepped back, then motioned with his arm. The cloth of Mykel's trousers fell apart on the left side, leaving his left hip partially exposed. "Ah, there is the culprit. A healing rune, I presume? I have never seen such a thing. Fascinating."

The secret was out. Now all would be lost.

"Has the magic been imprinted on you permanently, like the gifted, or must the pattern remain intact? I wonder, if we interrupt the design, would it work? Let's say I burned it, or simply cut it away, could you still heal?"

Mykel said nothing, but his heart thumped in his chest. Would the protection rune be enough to withstand the king's blessed-level magic? If so, how could he get out of the straps that held him fast? And how could he, without the staff, fight both the king and that armored monster?

"Stoic. Well done, boy. But you can't last forever. My guess would be that the old monk is responsible for this. Perhaps he has some things he can share with us. Cross, retrieve the other prisoner."

"No!" Mykel said.

"So he speaks after all," the king said.

"Bylo didn't do the tattoos," Mykel said, hoping they would believe the lie. "A monk in Eastway did."

"I doubt it," Cross said, his deep voice booming in the cramped room. "I questioned them and heard nothing about this boy."

"Cross, bring the old man here. Now."

As the general turned to leave, a steward leaned into the room from the dark corridor. "Your Majesty?"

"Not now," the king said. "I'm busy."

"But, ahem, Your Highness, there is a problem."

"What problem?"

"It's your daughter."

"Not again!" the king exclaimed, then sighed with disgust. "Who has she murdered now?"

The steward said nothing.

"We finish this later," the king stated. "There is no rush. Throw him back." He left the room, taking Cross with him.

Bylo was readying himself for the screams when Mykel was thrown into the cell by the guards far sooner than expected.

"We have no time," Mykel said. "You must do it now."

"What do you mean?" Bylo said.

"They know about the health rune. They know you inscribed it and are coming for you soon."

They both looked at the single guard, waiting and hoping that he would leave for his meal as he often did at this time. After a few minutes, the man stepped away and Bylo spurred himself to action, reaching to his sock and retrieving the vial. His weak fingers had difficulty grasping it, but once he pulled the vial out, its presence calmed his nerves and he found both strength and focus. He held it gingerly, reverently, knowing it to be more valuable than any object he had ever possessed. This vial didn't contain ink; it contained hope. Freedom. Life. Both Nara's and Mykel's.

"Can you put your leg through these bars?" Bylo asked.

Mykel squeezed his right leg between the cold pieces of iron, and Bylo squinted in the poor light to choose a canvas for his work. The most comfortable place for Bylo to reach was mid-thigh, which gave him ample room to make the design. Bylo pulled the stopper and reached inside to retrieve the needles. While doing so, some drops fell to the stone below, and Mykel's eyebrows rose. Precious ink wasted.

"It's okay," Bylo said. "We have enough."

Strength was the first tattoo he had ever inscribed, having experimented on himself long ago. While he had no scripture texts to guide him this time, he didn't need them—there were strength tattoos on his own thighs for reference. As he performed the task, Bylo looked at his marks several times to be sure. Success in this would require a hasty but accurate inscription.

A coughing fit interrupted the work, and more bloody phlegm decorated a stone tile nearby.

"Are you okay?" Mykel asked.

"I'm fine," Bylo said, continuing the important work. "But promise me something."

"Anything."

"Nara first."

"What?"

"When you leave here, go straight for her. Don't wait for me. I can't keep up. Save my little girl first. I'll find my own way."

"How will you escape?"

"Don't worry about it."

Almost an hour later, the tattoo was complete and Mykel closed his eyes.

"I see it," Mykel said. "The new rune is blurry, but I can reach it. Thank you."

"Don't *thank* me. *Save* her."

"I will."

With that, Mykel pulled himself to his feet and closed his eyes again. It seemed to take several tries, but once he accomplished it, the change was obvious. Mykel's stance deepened, he took a breath, then exhaled a long, comforting sigh. Bylo fell back against the stone, relieved. During the night, anxiety had robbed him of sleep over the possibility of failing this inscription, knowing he had only one chance to get it right. The most important inscription of his life.

"Tell her I love her."

Mykel smiled agreement with his eyes. "Stand back, Bylo."

Bylo moved away from the bars that separated them.

Mykel turned toward the outer stone wall. He looked for a moment at nothing, and Bylo wondered if he was pondering the birds they listened to each morning on the other side of the stone. This was to be the last moment of quiet for a time. Once Mykel began, chaos would break loose on the castle grounds.

Mykel drew back his fist and struck the wall. The blow produced a gargantuan concussion, shards of stone exploding as the ground shook. He struck again and the wall exploded outward with an even louder impact, rocking the ground below, as well as the fortifications above. Everyone in the castle must have heard it.

A man-sized hole in the stone wall outside allowed light to stream in and Mykel seemed to bathe in it for a moment. Then he moved toward the bars that separated Bylo from freedom and used his newfound strength to deform them easily.

In Bylo's mind, the memory of a single word came forth. A word told to him long ago by a friend he never saw again. Moving closer to Mykel, he put his hand on the boy's shoulder and whispered.

"Run."

Mykel ran.

After the boy left through the destroyed dungeon wall, Bylo pulled the stopper from the vial. There was little ink left, and he knew he would not be able to escape without help. He might have enough to inscribe a small tattoo, but didn't know which would be better: health or strength? Health would help him recover from his illness, but strength could make him useful in the conflict that had now begun. A coughing fit came over him again, spreading more blood than ever on the stone floor below.

There could be only one choice. He grabbed a needle between his shaking fingers and set to work.

35

CONFRONTATION

I t was early morning when Gwyn's plans were forced to change. Intending to retrieve Nara then make her way to the armory, she was interrupted by two loud concussions that shook the edifice, putting the entire castle on alert. Worries that siege equipment was bombarding the castle walls had sent the soldiers scurrying into defensive plans, and they moved to escort both princesses to safety.

Knowing Nara would be unable to help, Gwyn used the chaos to her advantage and sprinted to the armory. Upon arrival, she ordered the two guards to open the door and arm themselves with whatever they could find. One refused.

"But General Cross said…"

"The king is under attack!" she bellowed at him. "That puny sword will not repel any sizable force. Arm yourself with a real weapon!"

The command in her tone, or perhaps a fear of shirking their duty to protect the king moved them to action, and they removed the locks on the heavy door. They grabbed shields and spears and Gwyn ordered them to the courtyard to defend the keep, promising that she would lock the armory behind them. It left her plenty of time to grab a long piece of ivory from where it rested on a shelf inside the room.

Dirty, smelly, but weak no more, Mykel Aragos stepped into the light of day. Snow covered the ground outside and hung from the branches of a large spruce tree a dozen feet away. Looking around, he found himself outside the keep but still within the high castle walls. Armed soldiers moved about in a panic, and one stopped near him.

"You," the man said, pointing a spear at Mykel. "What did you...?" The man looked at the broken stones and then back at Mykel, obviously confused. "You're under arrest."

With strength flared, Mykel tensed his muscles and sprang toward the man, landing an open-handed strike to his midsection that knocked the soldier back twenty feet. He struck with far less force than he had just used on the wall and hoped the man would survive with only a painful story to tell. He then ran for the main keep entrance, intending to find those who held Nara.

The doors were guarded by six men, and without his own weapon, Mykel knew he could not take them all in hand-to-hand combat. They each bore a spear, and the giant oak doors behind them were closed—probably barred as well. In the chaos, they had not yet identified him as the cause of the disturbance. Surprise might be his ally.

Nearby, a horse cart absent its steed rested alone. Several sacks of grain in the back attested to having been parked recently, the alert likely interrupting those who had been unloading it. Exactly what he needed.

It must have come as a great surprise to those in the keep when a grain cart weighing a thousand pounds came flying into the foyer through the barred doors. The sound was deafening and soldiers were battered inward with the monstrous assault, crushed by the resultant debris. Grain was everywhere. At first, one might have thought the cart had been thrown by a catapult. When the dust cleared, however, the catapult walked into the foyer on two legs.

The general Mykel had seen this morning in the torture chamber stood inside the keep entrance accompanied by a dozen soldiers. Mykel wondered how he now looked to the powerful general. The weakened, tired, and tortured boy the man had pitied little more than an hour ago now stood before him, wielding the gifted strength of a bear. Filthy, and in tattered trousers, Mykel was a mess. Sweat and dried blood decorated his hair, torso, and limbs. Thin from days of torture without sustenance, it was a miracle that he could even walk. He was acutely aware that without the health and strength runes, he would not even be standing.

A rematch was in order, but Mykel resolved that this fight would go differently. He stepped past the shattered doors toward Cross with determination. Flanked on either side by a dozen soldiers, Cross motioned to the men, forbidding them to interfere.

Mykel did not have the staff, but he did have his runes. He squared off with the general while the soldiers moved into a circle to prevent his escape. This time, Cross wore plate armor and carried a monstrous sword, the likes of which Mykel had never seen. Good. Armor and big swords made warriors move slowly and Mykel needed every advantage to win this contest.

Cross charged first. Mykel flared protection, attempting to dodge, but failed. The giant's sword connected with the top of Mykel's shoulder, and he suffered a jarring blow that dropped him to his knees. It should have shorn him in two, but protection saved him, permitting the blade to leave no more than a painful bruise. Mykel spun out of the way, flared health, and both the pain of the blow and the bruise disappeared.

Despite the armor and the huge sword, this man was still fast. Flaring protection had drained much of his strength—several more blows like that and he would have no magic left.

Cross charged again and Mykel chose more wisely this time. He had no staff, but he thought back to the things it had taught him: counters, blocks, sidesteps, and moving inside the reach of a sword strike.

Although the knight tried to feint high with the sword, it was an obvious move—Gwyn had used this tactic many times. The sword would come low next, but the delay provided time to interrupt the transition. Mykel dropped protection and closed the distance quickly, getting inside the man's guard. He flared strength and punched Cross in the chest as hard as he could.

Somehow, the giant managed to turn, and the blow did not catch him squarely, instead impacting the man's left shoulder. The sound of metal deforming and bone shattering accompanied the sight of the general spinning through the air and smashing into the wall behind, taking two soldiers with him.

"Attack!" Cross ordered as he struggled to his feet, wincing in pain from the crushing blow. The surrounding soldiers collapsed on Mykel.

Spears and swords came at him, and he flared protection as the weapons met his skin. Whirling, he managed to seize a spear from a soldier. He closed his eyes and flared both strength and protection, then swept in a circle, killing two as the spear cleaved armor and flesh. He opened his eyes in time to dodge another attack, then grabbed a soldier by the leg, flaring strength to use the man as a maul. He crushed others with the body, then threw the bloody carcass across the entrance into a wall.

The battle raged, with spears bruising him but never puncturing the skin. Even so, the pain grew. Without Nara's strength, he could only grab one rune at a time unless he closed his eyes. He could not afford to drop protection and flare health after every injury, so the injuries began to build, slowing him. He alternated between protection, strength, and health, but without the staff's sight rune, he couldn't time his blocks and dodges properly against so many opponents.

A spear impaled his side while he tried to heal another wound.

The shock of it stunned him, then another pierced his calf, the shaft breaking, leaving the spearhead stuck in his leg.

"Fight me, coward!" Mykel screamed at the general as the swarm of spears continued to pummel and poke. He had defeated over a dozen, but more had joined them and at least nine soldiers remained. Mykel was awash with wounds, blood flowing onto the stone floor below. He had never trained to alternate between the strength, health, and protection runes, nor battled so many foes at once, and the effort was draining him.

He slipped on the bloody floor. A blow on his back from a soldier's cudgel dropped him to a vulnerable position on the ground, physically and mentally exhausted.

"You're done, young man," Cross said. "Too bad. There was much we could have learned from you. Had I been a blessed like you are, I would have been king. You failed, now you die."

The soldiers had stopped their attack when Cross began to speak, and he now admonished them for the delay. "What you are you doing, idiots? Finish him!"

Nara stood on the throne room floor next to Kayna and the king. Her plan to accompany Gwyn and rescue Mykel had fallen apart in the chaos. Gwyn was nowhere to be found. Following the loud concussions, the sisters had been brought to the room and now watched the king, who was livid as he stood in front of his throne. He screamed mindlessly at everyone, demanding to know who attacked him. They told Nara that this was the most protected part of the keep, but when another horribly loud crash sounded in the foyer, shaking the floor and walls violently, she questioned those assurances. In the chaos, she looked for a way to escape and rescue her loved ones.

A battle raged in the keep entrance, raging hot and loud but out of sight. People were hurting and dying, and although muted by the distance, she felt some of their pains. After a time, the sounds quieted.

Carefully, so as not to draw attention, Nara slipped out of her shoes and put her bare feet on the stone tile below, then closed her eyes. She flared earth and reached out with her awareness, finding Mykel immediately. He had escaped from confinement. He was close, but in so much pain! She felt the blows and punctures that he endured as if they were sustained by her own skin, and a panicked memory of the night on the plateau rushed back, accompanied by the resolve to prevent a similar outcome. She poured magic down through her feet, coaxing the earth to carry strength to her friend.

Face down on the stone floor, pierced by two spears, Mykel flared protection, his only option. If he suffered a single spear through his head or heart, he would never reach Nara. He gritted his teeth in anger and frustration, and though his spirit was not yet broken, his body was failing, and he held no idea how to survive this.

I will not die here. Dei help me.

With only protection flared, he climbed to his feet in the puddle of blood. His enemies stabbed and struck him, and he tried to block, but his footing was poor and his strength fading. He had no sight, no staff, and no hope.

Then a trickle of strength came up through the floor.

Nara.

The trickle soon became a river, then a flood. More strength than he felt during the battle on the plateau now flowed into him. Nara was giving much of herself, and he resolved not to waste it.

The increased power gave him command of all three runes, and he flared health, strength, and protection at once. He grabbed the broken spearhead that still impaled his calf and removed it, the wound closing immediately.

With it, he struck back, wielding the shortened spear like a dagger, dropping several soldiers before it slipped from his grip. He looked for another weapon, only to see Gwyn running toward the fray at full speed. At first, he thought she had come to fight, to finish what she had started. Then he saw what she carried.

In one hand she bore a blade, but in the other, she held something that was gleaming white.

36

AWAKENING

"**B**ring my armor!" Papa screamed, jarring Kayna with a strained, panicked voice. The man rarely yelled, his simple, quiet commands often carrying the necessary authority to make things happen.

Pandemonium reigned in the throne room as armed men scrambled in confusion between conflicting orders from their captains and their king. More soldiers trickled into the room from the side entrances to surround the royal family.

The armor was assembled around Papa in moments, the process having been rehearsed repeatedly since his return from Kavalin. A squire strapped Papa's sword to his belt. "At least something goes right around here," Papa barked, then turned to a captain. "Where is Cross?"

It didn't take long for Kayna to notice that Nara stood motionless nearby, eyes closed as she flooded the stones with power. The energy flowed across the stone to the foyer. Interesting. So, the girl was not as passive as Kayna had thought! Earth magic, something Kayna had not seen before. Fire and air, sure, but earth? What could Nara do with this? Confident that Papa would resolve things, she chose to remain uninvolved and enjoy the spectacle unfolding before her.

Mykel caught the staff in his right hand just as he dodged a thrown spear from behind him. More soldiers flowed in, but he felt little fear —he had the staff now. Closing his eyes, he flared every rune, relying on Nara's strength to help grab them all. She did not disappoint.

The power encompassed him, all the runes were his, and he kept his eyes closed. He healed completely, even the nicks and scratches. Strength returned, and his skin became like stone. But sight, oh sight, how he had missed that one! Welcoming the design into his thoughts once more, his confidence surged. This battle would not be lost after all.

His staff whirled and spun, executing strikes and sweeps, crushing the surrounding soldiers. As more men trickled in from the throne room and outside, he saw every move before it happened, dodged every thrust, and returned them in kind with a ferocious strength. Helmets deformed under the staff's blows, and bones were shattered by the power of Mykel's assault. Every enemy attack was thwarted, and bodies flew about. More than once, those bodies sailed in the direction of Cross, forcing him to move aside to avoid being crushed. Soon, three dozen men lay piled in the foyer, leaving nowhere to step without blood, bone, or discarded weapon underfoot.

Cross stood still, obviously petrified at the devastation before him. Then, General Cross, commander of the armies of the Great Land and the most powerful soldier in the realm, turned and ran away.

Mykel snatched a fallen spear from the floor with his left hand and leaped after his enemy. Power flooded his muscles as he pursued his quarry down the corridor, catching him just after he entered the large room.

Vorick stood in the throne room among Kayna, Nara, Gwyn, and his guards. They watched in awe as General Cross ran from a nearly naked, unarmored youth—It was the cursed boy from the dungeon. Even more shocking was that the youth rammed a spear into Cross' back as the terrified man labored in panicked retreat, the steel tip emerging from the plate armor where Cross' heart used to be. Vorick's general fell to the floor dead, and the room was stunned into silence.

The young warrior wielded a long white staff, his dirty black hair and tattooed chest striking a memory in the king. The tapestry from the hallway. The Humble Guardian. He should have made this connection before. A reborn legend now stood in the center of his throne room—one who meant him harm.

"Nara?" the warrior said.

"I'm okay, Mykel. Let's just go."

"You're going nowhere," Vorick said, stepping in front of Nara. "So the little man killed my big man." He paused as he stopped to within ten feet of the Guardian. "Perhaps you're not little after all. Skinny, though." Directing words to the whole room, Vorick lifted his arms and circled about, trying to lighten the mood with a mocking joke. "Don't we feed the good citizens in my dungeon?"

He dropped both his arms and the smile, then took a more serious tone.

"Drop the pretty stick and surrender."

"Free Nara," Mykel said, seemingly undeterred.

"Why?"

"Because I love her."

"And why should I care about your adolescent infatuation, you insolent wretch?"

"Free her or die," Mykel said.

Vorick narrowed his eyes. "I found her when she was a babe, boy. I saved her life. She owes me everything."

"You are a monster, she owes you nothing, and you die today," Mykel said.

With cruel, deliberate emphasis, teeth clenched and eyes hard, Vorick uttered the next words as a piercing attack at the intruder who dared challenge his sovereignty. "You have no claim, filthy dog. She. Is. Mine!"

Then he closed the visor on his helmet and drew Flay from her scabbard.

Mykel looked at Nara as he considered how to attack. The expression on her face revealed her doubt whether Mykel could defeat the king. She clearly wanted to leave, not to fight, because she was not feeding him energy at the moment. Perhaps the confrontation with the king had distracted her. Or maybe she didn't have any strength left.

Without her help, multiple runes were no option unless he closed his eyes, which only allowed him access to two at a time. He flared sight and dodged the king's first clumsy swing while he took in the view of his opponent.

The king's coral armor was big and bulky but didn't seem unwieldy. The man moved as if it wasn't even there. His weapon was crafted from ivory, with a bright red gem on the pommel. The blade moved through repeated attacks, quickly but poorly aimed.

After dodging a dozen such swings, Mykel felt confident this would be no great fight. He lunged with the staff, keeping his eyes open and dropping sight to flare strength and deliver a powerful blow to the center of the man's armor. The power in the blow should have crushed the armor and sent the man flying across the room, but although the impact made a thunderous, almost metallic sound, the force of the attack was largely absorbed. The king moved back less than a foot, barely stumbling before catching himself.

"Well now, that wasn't very impressive, was it?" the king said. "Care to try again?"

Mykel could hear the mocking tone in the monarch's voice, even if he couldn't see his face through the armored helm. He used sight to dodge a slash from the king, then lunged with the tip of the staff, again flaring strength with all the energy he could bring to bear. As with the first time, it produced little more than a loud noise. His eyes widened in surprise at the continued, ineffectual nature of his attacks. His confusion created a deadly delay and he spun away too slowly, failing to flare protection in time.

When the king's sword came down upon his back, it cut Mykel open from mid-back to hip. The agony ran to his core, dropping him to the floor and almost forcing the staff from his grip.

Stories he had heard about Minister Vorick flooded back to him from his memory. Stories of the man's blessed, legendary power. Mykel stumbled to his feet, fighting the shooting pain as the king came again. Mykel flared health and felt his flesh knit together, then flared sight to dodge the next series of thrusts and slashes.

It continued for a few more moments, then he felt Nara's strength come again. It was less powerful this time; she was weakening. Mykel flared strength and attacked with a dozen empowered strikes to legs, arms, and even the man's head. The ringing impacts from the blows seemed to have no significant effect, and Mykel imagined the king smiling under the helm, stepping one way or the other to keep his balance after a blow but taking the hits with no sign of injury. The armor didn't dent or deform. He heard no groans or cries of pain from his opponent. Mykel's hope began to fade.

Planning an attempt to sweep the monarch from his feet, or to find something heavy to pummel him with, Mykel circled around, but then the armored liege reached out with a gauntlet, pointing with a finger. It was then that Mykel felt his flesh pull apart from his bones.

Searing pain almost kept him from finding the protection rune, but Nara's strength helped, and he flared both health and protection with all his resolve. Nara's aid diminished further, weaker than ever, and he knew he must end the fight before they both expired.

But he couldn't. He didn't know how, and the pain from the king didn't stop—it only got worse. Mykel threw everything he had to flare protection, everything Nara gave him, still looking for a chink in the man's armor, a place to attack, a weakness, but the misery overcame him as his flesh struggled between the magic of his protection rune and the vast power of the evil man who was tearing his body apart.

Old doubts resurfaced in the midst of the paralyzing attack. He was fighting a blessed, the most powerful man in the realm, with nothing but an ivory stick and a few tattoos. Mykel didn't belong here, didn't deserve Nara, and could not protect her as he'd hoped. He was just a broken village boy with delusions of grandeur. A cursed. Destined for death. He was only pretending to be brave, pretending to be strong. He was out of his depth and about to die.

The disappointment crushed his spirit even as his enemy's magic crushed his body. Wounds opened upon his skin as the king began to siphon the essence out of him and he felt his personality, his will, his very *being* fracture under the strain. The man's magic was a cold death grip, like the ceppit but many times stronger, and it was tearing his soul apart.

Feelings of fear that he thought had been banished by his training flooded back into his mind. The unstoppable magic of this monarch had overcome his protection rune, outlasted his strength, and shredded his resolve.

His vision blurred as he lost focus on the enemy. He heard Nara screaming something, but he couldn't make out the words. His arms and legs stopped obeying, and in a cloud of unimaginable agony, arms and fingers contorting in pain, he lost his grip on the gleaming white staff. Through the fog of torment, he heard it hit the stone tiles and his thoughts moved to Nara.

I'm sorry, Bitty. I'm so sorry.

Nara focused her sight to look at the king in his audacious red armor. The power emanating from the plates stunned her. Regardless of the energy she was channeling to Mykel, the power the king commanded was unbelievable, and the life of her friend was under threat.

"Impressive, isn't he?" Kayna said.

In the middle of her growing panic, Nara had no response.

"Even with help, your lover won't ever handle that," Kayna commented, smirking. "Papa is a very big deal, sweet sister."

Nara wanted to attack Kayna right then, who seemed to be enjoying Mykel's suffering, but she was running out of strength and had nothing to spare. Mykel was unable to do any damage to the king despite the incredible blows he had delivered. Nara's weakness grew, and a wobble in her legs made it difficult for her to stand. She implored the earth to yield up its strength to her. Flaring the earth rune with greater passion, she reached below deeply, but although she sensed its presence, little of its energy came to her.

Without warning, a huge wave of pain overcame her—not like a headache but all over her body, on her flesh and deep in her bones. She was dizzy with the onslaught and lost her balance, falling to her knees, and panic rose as she realized it was coming from Mykel. The king was harvesting him!

She placed her hands on the cold stone floor for support, channeling her scant remaining strength to him, but it was not enough.

Holy Dei.

She prayed earnestly, with a desperation and panic she had never felt before. The prayer was less of a plea and more of a mandate to the Almighty, a demand to intervene in this horror to save them.

I have been looking for You my whole life. If You exist, help me now. I'm begging. I need You now. You must help me! PLEASE!

As if Heaven above ignored her, reveled in her suffering, or simply didn't exist, Mykel's skin came apart, and Nara shared in the agony of the attack. She screamed at the king to stop, to no avail. Like the announcement and the ambush, she now witnessed yet another attack on her friend. On her. This monster was killing Mykel *because* of Nara, to keep her, to own her like an object, a treasure to be hidden away. There would be no healing after this battle, and this was no dream from which she and her dear friend would awaken. There was no Dei, and no rescue. Mykel had seconds to live. There would be no intervention, no savior from this madness. Not Kayna, who watched the spectacle of Mykel's destruction like a soulless ghoul. Not Bylo. Not Anne. Not Gwyn.

There was only Nara.

Attempting to hold back the pain and despair, her eyelids wanted to close to block out the misery, but she forced them open. She engaged her sight to look for something she could do with what little strength remained inside her.

The blinding sun that was the king's armor stunned her again. There was so much power inside those plates. Unimaginable power. Power he now used to murder her friend. Then an idea came to her. Was he the only person who could use that energy, or could Nara touch it too?

She reached out with a hand, calling the armor's magic to herself.

The energy slammed into her with a devastating concussion, strong and hot. It was sudden, and it was joyful. Her headache and the sympathetic pains of Mykel's injuries disappeared in a cascade of pleasure like none she had ever felt.

And the power, so much power! Runes danced about her vision, even with her eyes wide open—all the designs she had seen on Bylo's writing desk and more. Earth was among them, but there were others. Sight, strength, health, fire, protection, and a dozen that she had never seen.

As she rose to her feet, each rune screamed its purpose, the power it unlocked, begging for attention, eager to be filled with the abundance of energy now at her command.

She went straight to her favorite, and the earth responded to her call. The stone tiles under her feet shattered as the earth rose with her upon it, a pillar of dirt and rocks that lifted her above the others in the room. She immediately called up a barrier, and an earthen wall rose between the king and Mykel, interrupting the attack.

She sensed the power of dozens of human lives coursing through her veins. Little more than their energy remained, but broken pieces of memory scattered about, and she nearly forgot herself in the maelstrom of power and emotion.

Her own nature evaporated in the swirling magic, uninhibited by any of her usual timidity or self-doubt. A new vision seemed to come over her, and she could almost see herself from afar, large and powerful compared to the small lights of the others in the room. Who was this girl she had now become, who seemed so proud and tall, her red hair blowing about in the magic and the madness? What did she want? Where was she going? This young woman who had been chased, captured, and then imprisoned in a place without love.

She saw the monster of a king who now sought to kill Mykel, the boy she adored. Yes, she saw it now, in this maelstrom of unrestrained emotion and strength: Nara loved Mykel with all her heart. But his thin, broken body now lay upon the stone tiles, bleeding, flesh falling off his bones, dying at the hands of the man who declared himself to be her father.

She channeled power into the earth, telling it to seek Mykel. It obeyed, but when it found his health tattoo, the magic stopped, refused by the symbol that belonged only to him. Nara siphoned more magic from the armor and pushed hard upon the health tattoo, overcoming its resistance, forcing it to submit. The symbol obeyed, knitting together his wounds, allowing Nara to turn back to her prey.

Towering over the king, she continued to tap the armor, his great weapon now having become a supreme liability. She felt the tug-of-war as he struggled to fight her for the strength within the coral plates, but in this, he was no match for her. She was not gifted. She was not cursed. She was not blessed. She was something entirely different, something for which a name had not yet been given. Her very nature allowed vast control of these energies, complete command of the magics he had intended to be his own.

Anne's words came back to her, *"... you could be dangerous if you wanted."*

Nara did want to be dangerous right now. She wanted to be very dangerous.

The king reached out with his talent, and her mind moved quickly, recognizing the attack. It was chaos, and it was powerful. Her skin began to tear apart with the energies he wielded, and she felt the pain, but somehow it brought no fear. This was *her* magic now, not his.

The protection rune from the cavern wall came to her memory easily, and she flared it. She drew ever more strength from the armor, deflecting the king's efforts and robbing him of fuel to power his assault. He lashed out again, weaker now, with less access to the energy he once thought his own. He was trying to siphon her spirit with his harvesting talent, but his efforts bounced off the shield of her protective rune. She flared health to repair the damage she had sustained from his chaos attack, knitting together flesh and skin, her strength and confidence surging.

It was her turn. She looked at the runes encircling her and chose another: motion. Holding it in her vision side by side with earth and protection, she flared it and looked at the king. Reaching out with an arm, she inflicted her will upon him, throwing him twenty feet into the wall that separated the throne room from the foyer. The impact produced a concussion that shook the room and shattered the stones where he hit.

The blow must have stunned him, for he lost his balance and fell to one knee, dropping his sword. The armor's protection against physical damage must have absorbed most of the energy, however, and he rose again, retrieving his sword as he took to his feet. He then began running at Nara, brandishing the weapon before him.

Nara turned toward Kayna, wondering if she would join in the fray. If Nara could tap the armor, then certainly her sister, who had practiced magic far more often, could use it as well. Nara didn't know whether it was the look in her own eyes or the apparent fury in her heart that cowed the dark twin, but Kayna took a step back, bowing her head as if to concede defeat or, perhaps, to invite mercy.

In her distraction, Nara had allowed the king to come too close. She directed the pillar of earth to carry her back to avoid several sweeping strokes with his sword. She commanded projections of earth from the ground to rise up toward the monarch, but he swept his blade through each of them, severing limbs of rock that fell, lifeless, to the ground.

She looked again at the runes that encircled her. This time, she chose fire.

Flames came out of her hands to engulf the king. Heat billowed about the armored monarch, waves striking off him and deflecting toward those who watched, forcing them to retreat. The few stray soldiers who had not been slaughtered by Mykel now fled the heat, and the room emptied of spectators. Vorick had survived the initial attack under the protection of his armor, but the energy within the plates was weakening, dimming profoundly in Nara's sight.

"Kayna!" the king said, fear apparent in his voice, his armor smoking. "Help me!"

As if in answer to her father's request, Kayna took a step back, her eyes wide, saying nothing. Nara detected no flare of energy coming from her sister, no help whatsoever for the doomed monarch.

Nara raised earth barriers, boxing the king in to prevent his escape. She attacked again, a flood of even hotter, more destructive energy. Her eyes grew hot, mirroring the holocaust she inflicted upon her foe. She was like something out of scripture, a goddess doing battle with evil, or having become one with the darkness herself. Powerful winds rose up, blowing the heated air about the chamber.

Vorick screamed in pain but she pressed on, not satisfied with mere victory, knowing the greedy man would never rest if allowed to live, never give her peace, never stop chasing her and those she loved. He screamed ever louder, holding his sword arm high in an attempt to shield himself, and again, he called to Kayna for help.

"You'll never hurt us again!" Nara yelled, her voice booming with augmented power, shaking the air with an unnatural bass. She burned and burned and burned him, screaming as she did so, her rage mirroring the horrible destruction she wielded.

The flood of hot magic continued long past the point when the king's screams abated. Nara vented all the available energy in the armor, then continued well beyond, powering the flames with her own energies. She continued to scream as she burned, rage and desperation fueling her mania until there was no magic left, nothing to give, no way to attack anymore, nothing but exhaustion remaining inside her.

Flames died, and the pillar of earth dropped toward to the floor with Nara still upon it. Smoke rose from the stone tiles, and gusts of hot air continued to buffet about the tumultuous chamber, filling the room with the stench of burnt flesh and charred earth. A moment later, Nara lay exhausted on the now inanimate pile of dirt. The tempest had passed, leaving only destruction in its wake.

She lifted her head to look for Mykel, hoping that he had completely recovered. He lay upon the stone tiles, still unconscious but breathing. She thought of Bylo. Mykel had escaped, but where was Bylo?

Kayna stepped forward tentatively to survey the scene. "Wow, Sister, very impressive."

Kayna observed the destruction with a smile on her face. The scene seemed to have had little impact on her, and what fear she may have expressed a few moments ago had now vanished. Perhaps she could sense that Nara was no longer a threat.

"I didn't think you had it in you," Kayna said. "Very creative with the earth magic, and toasting Papa like you did. It all happened so fast, I wasn't sure what to do."

Kayna went to Mykel. Nara could see that he had healed from the more serious wounds, skin, muscle, and bones intact once more. Nara's eyes were half-lidded with fatigue as Kayna used magic to lift Mykel into the air with a thought, suspending him before her as if he were her puppet.

Nara struggled to get to her feet but had no strength. Instead, she reached out, intending to summon earth to stop Kayna, but her sister motioned with a hand and Nara felt a powerful gust of air slam her backward onto the floor, the back of her head impacting the stone.

"Leave him alone!" Nara tried to shout, struggling to rise, but it came out as barely a whisper.

Kayna circled Mykel as she held him in the air before her, looking upon his weakened body and at the runes on his legs and chest.

"A cursed, then?" she asked, looking back at Nara. "He has the flavor of one. I saw an announcement recently where one died. They have a certain… taste to them." Kayna dismissed her magic, and Mykel fell crashing to the earth. Nara tried to crawl to him, but found nothing but weakness, collapsing upon herself in fatigue.

"I'll tell you what, Sister. He is pretty, but I'm going to let you keep him. I doubt he'd follow me anyway, as he seems quite smitten with you. Perhaps I'll find my own cursed and put some fancy patterns on him like you did."

As Nara struggled to prop herself up with one arm, Kayna moved over to the remains of the king. The blackened amalgam of charred coral, ivory, and flesh bore no resemblance to anything human. "My goodness," she added. "You do good work." She tried to pull a piece of hot coral away, but it fell to dust in her fingers, brittle and lifeless. She brushed the debris from her hands and turned back to her sister. "I have to admit, in the middle of all that, I worried that you would hurt me. Can you believe it? I was actually afraid! I don't think I've ever felt fear like that before. How delightful!"

She knelt in front of Nara, looking her in the eyes. "You are so vulnerable. You're afraid now too, aren't you?"

"I've done nothing to you," Nara whispered. "Please leave us alone."

Kayna reached out and stroked Nara's hair tenderly. "I could kill you right now. I kind of want to, I think." Kayna flared fire, and a bloom of heat appeared in her open palm, turning to dancing flames that she held in front of Nara's face. Nara shuddered and almost succumbed to the exhaustion, barely keeping her eyes open. There would be no defending against what came next. Nara had finally used her magic to fight. To save Mykel, to save herself, but now she would die at the hands of a sister who should have been a friend. Despair overcame her, but she was too tired to resist.

"Fire would be appropriate, since that is how you took Papa." Kayna stood, then walked around Nara, who remained on the floor.

Kayna was still for a moment, then stuck out her lower lip in a look of pity. "No, I don't think so. Not today. There is an odd comfort in having you near. I don't know what to make of that."

Nara's pounding heart slowed in relief as the flames in Kayna's palm diminished and winked out.

"Besides, you bring new things. Fear, for one. I hope to feel that again someday. And you present an interesting challenge, dear sister. I think there will be far too few of those for me in the future."

Kayna stopped for a moment, pondering out loud. "Mellice will present little trouble, and with Papa out of the way now, I must thank you for making me a queen. I really didn't know how I was going to get rid of him, but your efforts were both brilliant and unexpected."

Kayna turned and walked a few steps, then stopped, holding a finger up in the air as if she had forgotten something, still facing away from Nara. Nara hoped that she had not just changed her mind. If Kayna wanted to rule the Great Land, so be it. Nara just wanted to leave with Mykel and Bylo. To run far away.

"Oh yes, if you want to live, you might leave before some of those scared little soldiers find their way back in," Kayna said. "Or perhaps you should fear this one," she said, pointing to Gwyn, who stood near the throne with an eye upon Kayna and a dagger in her hand. "If she ever chooses which side she's on."

Then the new queen left the room.

Bylo cursed himself for the time he had lost. He had hoped to ink the rune more quickly, but a faulty inscription would have accomplished nothing, and he had been forced to take more time than he would have liked. A hot wind greeted him as he passed the destroyed doors and entered the throne room through the foyer. He surveyed the chamber, spying Mykel unconscious on the floor, Nara collapsed upon a pile of disturbed earth, and Gwyn, beyond Nara, standing near the throne. What had happened here?

He ran to his fallen daughter, who appeared too weak to stand.

Nara struggled to lift her arms as Bylo approached. He gathered her up and was about to leave, but she protested wordlessly, pointing at Mykel. She pushed at Bylo's chest, trying to extricate herself from his arms so that he could save her friend.

"No," Bylo said. "I can carry you both."

Nara squeezed his arm, tears in her eyes. She tried to speak, but words wouldn't come to her lips. Her grip was weak, her skin pale, and after a moment, her head collapsed against his shoulder.

Bylo carried her over to Mykel, who lay motionless, his staff nearby. Bylo lifted them both onto his shoulders and looked back at Gwyn, who stood near the throne, a dagger in her hand. Would she try to stop him? Their eyes locked for a moment and she re-sheathed the blade, then dropped her hand to one side. Bylo nodded his gratitude, then headed through the foyer and out the destroyed front doors of the keep, stepping between bodies and weapons as he carried his two treasures.

Looking at the position of the sun, he was determined to find his way east, to Anne. He ran to the edge of Fairmont, miles away from danger, the same urgency in his heart as when escaping Dimmitt. His new strength rune was small and weak, however, and wouldn't take them far. Perhaps it would be far enough.

37

REDEMPTION

S oldiers shuttled into the throne room past Gwyn, confusion on their faces, looking to her for guidance. She said nothing. They gazed upon the charred remains of Vorick and spoke in hushed voices as Gwyn took a deep breath, acrid smells persisting in the aftermath of the battle. She remained near the empty throne for a time, unmoving, not knowing what to do.

Vorick was dead. Cross was dead. Kayna had left the room. The young woman had declared her intention to be queen, and there was nothing stopping her. The Great Land would suffer under the rule of the dark sorceress, and Gwyn had no desire to stay. She was under no contract for a lord who could command or threaten her, and she was beholden to no one. Or was she?

Gwyn thought about Bylo. The man had served others his whole life and even now, in his old age, was working for the benefit of those he loved. His sacrifices were inspirational, and Gwyn felt like a villain by comparison, creating an emptiness that nagged at her. She had always served the needs of dark men but what did she have to show for it?

She walked across the room and knelt to pick the white staff off the stone floor. The cool ivory under her palm was comforting in the hot room. A priceless weapon, it could be sold in exchange for a lifetime of comfort. Or it could be returned to its owner, the young man who had wanted to be her friend.

She walked out of the room, through the foyer, and out to the streets of Fairmont. It took almost an hour, but she found a farmer who had just sold his wares at the market. It must have been an odd sight before him: a woman holding an ancient ivory staff in one hand and two pieces of gold in the other. It took only moments to convince him to turn over his horse, buckboard wagon, and traveling supplies.

Hoping to catch up to Bylo and the youths, she chose to go directly east, across farmland rather than on roads, pushing the single draft horse hard enough that it whinnied and protested her urgings. She found them by midday, pulling to a stop as she got closer.

"Bylo, wait." She launched herself out of the wagon seat and rushed to his side. The old monk plodded along through the thin layer of snow that covered the field, seemingly unaware of her, laboring under failing power. In her vision, the rune on his thigh was glowing weakly—flickering as the magic ran low. She reached out to him, putting her hand on the arm that held Nara securely upon his shoulder. "Bylo, it's Gwyn. I have a wagon."

Bylo stopped walking and turned toward Gwyn, his eyes glassy and carrying a faraway look. Blood stained his goatee and the front of his shirt. He coughed, producing more on his chin.

"You've carried them far enough," she said. "I'll take them from here."

Bylo dropped to his knees, and Gwyn helped him lower Mykel and Nara to the cool snow. Gwyn checked them; they were both breathing.

"They are okay, Bylo."

"I'm so tired," he whispered in a soft voice. "I need to sit."

He sat beside them and a moment later he lay down, putting his head in the snow. The coughing came again, and blood began to flow in earnest from his mouth.

"The strength rune," Gwyn said. "It's hurt you."

He didn't react. This was clearly not a surprise to him.

"Tell her that I'm sorry," he said. "I didn't know how else…" The coughing came again, stronger this time.

"You'll tell her yourself, Bylo. Stand and let me help you into the cart."

Gwyn grabbed his hand and shoulder, and Bylo lifted his head, struggling, then lay back again. Gwyn looked at the rune and saw that it was dark. The magic was gone.

"I can't," he said. He tried to lift his head again but failed, then his eyes seemed to wander again, losing focus. "I can't say goodbye to her."

"I'll tell her for you."

"Gwyn?" His eyes found her for a moment and he coughed again, deeper, his face grimacing.

"Yes?"

"Can we trust you now?"

"Yes," she said. "I'm so sorry, Bylo."

"Please take them to Anne."

"I will."

He tried to move his hand toward Nara but was unable. Gwyn helped his fingers find hers. Nara's hand was warm. Bylo's was very cold.

"You saved them," Gwyn said. "Again."

He smiled as he closed his eyes.

"And you saved me," she said.

But Bylo could no longer hear.

38

HOME

When Nara woke, she found herself lying in a wagon, bouncing along a road. It was daylight, it was snowing, and she was tired. Her head throbbed with a pain behind her eyes.

Mykel was also in the wagon, seated on her right. She sat up and he noticed her, turning to put his hand to her cheek, sadness on his face. His hair was matted with blood, and his skin was dirty and smelly. He shivered with the cold.

"What?" she asked.

"I'm so sorry."

Something was wrong. She thought back to what had happened. They had been in a big fight. The king. Kayna. Mykel was hurt. She remembered the power from the armor, so much power. Fire. Then Bylo carried her.

Bylo.

She wheeled her head around to see Gwyn on the wagon seat, reins in hand, but where was Bylo? She tried to get to her feet and tripped over a large bundle of cloth. Her right knee struck the hard boards of the wagon bed while her left knee fell upon the bundle.

It wasn't cloth.

Her hands found the seam even as the tears began to stream down her face.

Not Bylo. Please, Dei. Not him. Please please please.

Nara pulled back the cloth and uncovered his face. His eyes stared up, but didn't see her. Frozen blood stained his beard. She collapsed upon him, sobbing.

He was gone.

She was inconsolable for days. She refused to leave his side. Mykel and Gwyn tried to comfort her, to no avail. It was all too much. She spent the rest of the trip clinging to his wrapped form and wouldn't let them bury him; she knew where she wanted him to rest. They didn't argue.

Finally, they arrived at the plateau and made the climb up the snow-covered hill. Having recovered, Mykel was strong again and carried Bylo into Nara's cave. Anne met them and Nara ran to her, hugging the old woman for what seemed like hours.

Nara used earth magic to fashion a stone tomb. Anne held a lantern to chase away the shadows as Nara worked, then Mykel and Gwyn placed Bylo's body inside.

"He saved us," Nara said. "With his last act, he carried us to safety. Again. It cost him everything."

"He did much," Anne said. "A life of far more adventure than he would have planned, but also far more love." She looked at Nara. "You were his overwhelming joy, child. His greatest treasure."

"Did you know?" Nara said. "That I would lose him?"

"No," Anne said. "I only knew there would be pain. I can't see everything."

When they were done, they left the tomb and Nara sealed it over, covering even the ramp with earth. They walked down toward the cabin, snow crunching under their feet.

When they stepped up onto the cabin porch, Nara said, "You should have warned me."

"I'm sorry," Anne said.

"Not good enough," Nara said, gritting her teeth. "I trusted you." But Nara had no place in her heart for anger right now. Only pain. "I miss him, Anne," she said through tears. "So much."

"I am so sorry, dear."

"And Gwyn," Nara said, turning to their friend. "She helped us."

Anne nodded. "I thought she might eventually come around."

Nara moved to the side of the porch to take a seat upon one of the oak stools. Memories of their talk a few weeks ago came to Nara, although the snow and darkness cast a different mood than before. And a different concern.

"My sister is a monster," Nara said, "and now she's the queen."

Anne took a seat on the other stool. "The Great Land does indeed have a dark future with her on the throne."

"She kills for fun. Who could stop her, Anne?"

"I can think of only one person."

Nara grew quiet with that, looking out at nothing, thinking such a challenge might destroy her and still not put an end to the pain Kayna would bring. In the throne room, she could have used the armor's magic to kill Kayna. She could have ended it right there.

"I'm not sure why I held back. It's like she's a part of me, some-how. There was a strange comfort when she was near, something I had never felt before. Perhaps that's also why she spared me."

But she would have to find the strength to stop Kayna. Perhaps it would be possible with Mykel's help. She thought of a future with him, building a home, having children. With the challenges ahead of them, it was a life that might never happen.

"I prayed to Him, but He never came."

Anne said nothing.

"Dei never came," Nara said again, stronger this time, her rising voice fueled by indignation. "In the middle of it, when that evil man was trying to kill Mykel, I prayed as I'd never prayed before. There was nothing. He didn't help. I was *alone*!" Her voice cracked on the final word, overcome by abandonment and loss. It was an anger at being unprepared, with so much responsibility on her shoulders, and nobody to help.

"They need you, Nara," Anne said. "The people of Fairmont. Of the Great Land. They will be praying soon, as you did. For someone to save them. They will feel the same desperation that you felt. That same panic. Through the horror and the loneliness, they will look to Dei and pray."

Nara nodded. "And there is no god to save them."

"There is, oh, yes, there is. And He will answer those prayers…"

Nara turned to Anne in expectation, hungry for some indication that Dei existed. That He was real and would bring comfort to the people of the land. That He would bring comfort to her own heart.

"… by sending you," Anne finished.

Nara's expectation deflated as the words sank in. If Dei existed, His hand was invisible, at least to her. He would not help her directly. She may possess more power than any in the Great Land, save her sister, but she would receive no help from above. If Anne could be believed, Nara would *be* the help that He sends.

But the loneliness of it reached a deeper place within her. Dei's way seemed difficult, but maybe not senseless. The lack of His presence created a void that was drawing her into a role that must be filled. A part that would be played if the land were to survive the dark time that was coming. Recent events might not be an abandonment at all, but rather a calling. Could she embrace it?

Kayna would surely run roughshod over the land, taking what she would. Nara may have destroyed the king, but Kayna was every bit as powerful as the king was, probably more so, and would not be restrained by love or mercy. And now she was the sovereign, with wealth and armies at her command. Only Nara might have a chance to stop her, to rescue the land from the darkness to come. But how?

She wanted to ask Bylo, but he was gone. She looked over at Mykel, who stood quietly at the end of the porch. The task before her would be unbearable without him, but would he support her in this? Her eyes carried the question to him, and he needed no words to convey his answer. He nodded once, a gentle smile crossing his face.

It was enough. With him by her side, she might succeed. At very least, she would try.

"I'm willing," Nara said, "but I don't know how to start."

"I teach," Anne said. "You learn."

Nara looked out upon the dark, snowy landscape in the direction of the Twins, which were obscured by the night. Two lonely mountains, high above all, each defying the other.

"Then I am ready," Nara said. "Let's begin."

ABOUT THE AUTHOR

David A. Willson lives in the great land of Alaska with his wife and five children. His passions are faith, movies, books, traveling with his beautiful lady, and hanging out with his kids.

www.davidawillson.com

Lightning Source UK Ltd.
Milton Keynes UK
UKHW02f1305210818
327561UK00008B/308/P